THE WEIRD
TALES OF SILAS
FLINT

THE WEIRD TALES OF SILAS FLINT

KEVIN G. BECKMAN

KGB Books

This book is a work of fiction. Any references to historical events, real people, or real places are used fictitiously. Other names, characters, places, and events are products of the author's imagination, and any resemblance to actual events or places or persons, living or dead, is entirely coincidental.

© 2021 by Kevin Beckman

First Edition August 2021

Published by KGB Books, in the United States of America

ISBN 978-0-578-97088-2

The Weird Tales
Of
Silas Flint

Thou shalt not suffer a witch to live.

-Exodus 22:18

But there was a certain man, called Simon, which before-time in the same city used sorcery, and bewitched the people of Samaria, giving out that himself was some great one: To whom they all gave heed, from the least, to the greatest, saying, This man is the great power of God.

-Acts of the Apostles 8:9-10

The Ruin
Of
Witches

1

Two riders crested a hill. The sun was setting behind them, casting its reddish light into the valley where there sat a large city bisected by a river. Even from this distance, the riders could hear the faint echoes of music and the clamor of celebration. It was unlikely this isolated burg would have electricity, so the evening's revelries would go on by lantern-light or more arcane methods.

"Looks like they're getting an early start," chuckled one rider. He was a squat figure encased in thick leather body armor, an ancient rifle slung across his back, his chest criss-crossed with ammunition bandoliers, a pistol and tomahawk hanging from his belt.

"Indeed," the other rider replied. In contrast to his companion, he was tall, broad in the chest and shoulders, dressed from head to toe in black with a long coat and tall wide brimmed hat, two pistols and a sword on his belt. He stroked his horse's mane as he continued, "One would have hoped they'd spend such a momentous day in prayer and introspection, but I suppose these people need to indulge their appetites from time to time. I suspect that life can be difficult on the frontier."

"Aw, come on Silas," the first man replied. "It's VM Day for pity's sake. If this isn't the time to party hard, when is it?"

Silas sighed. "I take that to mean you wish to join in the debauchery? Very well Ricardo. I reckon you have earned a brief respite from the Lord's work. We shall make for the township. After we have secured our lodgings, you are free to immerse yourself in whatever drunken mischief you can discover. I expect you to be prepared for departure by first light tomorrow morning, regardless of how strong your hangover may be. Is that understood?"

"Yes sir, Captain Flint," Ricardo said, saluting.

Flint rolled his eyes. "Come along then Mr. Navarro. It won't do to be in the open come nightfall."

As they made their way toward the city, Flint observed his surroundings. Today marked 457 years since mankind won a hard-fought victory against the Great Magician. No one living remembered the world as it was before the appearance of Simon Magus, but relics of that bygone era were plentiful still. The road their horses trod upon was in better shape than most he had seen, with patches of asphalt still visible amidst the grass and dirt.

"Look at that Silas," Navarro said.

A wooden signpost proclaimed that they were entering the city limits of Canyon Cove. Further onward they encountered a rusting metal sign. The paint had faded but Flint could make out that the city was known as Ontario in the old world. He mused that the former Ontario appeared to have made a splendid recovery in the ensuing centuries. As dusk became night, the fluorescent glow emanating from Canyon Cove confirmed that they did indeed have electricity. It came as some relief to Flint. Lanterns cast longer shadows, and light generated by witchcraft made his skin crawl.

Flint and Navarro presently arrived at the gate of a great wall that surrounded the city. Two guards emerged from a shack beside the gateway. They wore leather armor similar to Navarro's, and each had bolt action rifles slung on their shoulders. One held up his hand and the two riders reined in their horses.

"Good evening," said the guard who had waved them to a halt.

"Good evening sir," Flint said.

"What is the purpose of your visit?"

"My companion and I seek room and board."

The guard raised an eyebrow. "Not here for the celebrations?"

"He isn't," Navarro said, nodding at Flint, "But me, you bet your ass I am."

Flint gave an exaggerated sigh as the guard chuckled. "Alright, you can head on in. There's several motels but I recommend the Sleep Inn. Best food and best beer in the city."

"I thank you for your help sir and I bid you good night," Flint said. The guard waved at his partner, who went back inside the shack. A few seconds later a buzz sounded, and the gateway doors swung open.

Flint and Navarro entered to a scene of pandemonium. Bands of drunken revelers staggered through the streets, occasionally doubling over to vomit or to urinate against buildings. Couples passionately kissed and ran their hands all over each other. Electronic music with pounding basslines poured from speakers affixed to streetlights and balconies, intense enough for Flint to feel the thudding in his chest. The air stank of beer, tobacco, marijuana, and deep-fried meat.

"This is degenerate beyond words!" Flint snarled.

"This is amazing!" Navarro shouted, a huge grin on his face.

Flint grumbled as he dismounted. "I shall proceed to this Sleep Inn and secure our rooms. Stable the horses. Once that is done, you are free to seek out whatever devilry that appeals to you. I meant what I said earlier. We leave at first light, regardless of what will no doubt be your debilitating hangover. Do not make me rouse you from your bed."

Navarro laughed. "Oh, don't worry about me sir, I know my limits."

"Yes, and you frequently ignore them. Off with you now."

Amidst the overwhelming sights, sounds, and smells of a city engulfed in rapturous joy, both men failed to notice a man in the alleyway next to the gate who had stood transfixed, staring them down with a mixture of rage and fear. After the witch hunter and his assistant parted ways, the man pulled a hood over its head and adjusted the scarf covering the lower half of his face. He scuttled up the side of the building like a spider, pulling himself up onto the roof. He sprinted, leaping from rooftop to rooftop. He had to inform his mistress that agents of the enemy were in town.

2

"So then the professor says, 'Supercollider? I barely know her!"

Mayor Julius Blackwood doubled over laughing at his own joke. His numerous hangers-on followed his example. Lilian Turner chuckled out of politeness. Her husband Timothy was the owner of Canyon Cove's wealthiest trading caravan, his wares finding their way onto shelves in cities from the United Mountain States and up into Cascadia. She enjoyed the luxuries his position afforded her, but it meant dealing with local politicians who were happy to look the other way when necessary so long as their campaign coffers received a generous donation.

Blackwood excused himself, shaking hands with Lilian. He approached another, lesser shipping magnate, and started telling the same joke all over again. Lilian maintained her perfect smile as laughter and music echoed throughout the grand ballroom, but on the inside she seethed. Victory over Magus Day was by far the most revolting celebration of all. It served as an annual reminder of how far she had fallen. Centuries ago, she was able to terrorize these lambs at will in her true appearance and the fullness of her power. Now she had to pose as the good socialite and blend in to survive. Still, it could have been much worse. Love was too strong a word to describe her feelings for Timothy, but she had grown fond of him. She sighed. The town gossips were already bringing attention to how Timothy was showing his age since they'd married twenty years ago, while Lilian seemed like she hadn't aged a day. She knew the time was fast approaching when she would have to find a new city and begin again. Fortunately, no one had yet made the connection between her showing up in Canyon Cove and the many disappearances that had followed. As much as she would have liked to get her claws on people like Blackwood, official investigations would have come. Better to prey on one of the many travelers, mercenaries, and vagrants that came through the city every day.

She smiled. That was one of the few silver linings of VM Day: more travelers than usual, and the constabulary would be stretched thin dealing with the widespread hooliganism. She'd sent Darien to stake out the west gate and be on the lookout for juicy targets that no one would miss. Once everyone had gone home and passed out, she could get to work...

Speak of the devil, she thought. There stood Darien at the top of the stairway in the foyer. He looked out of place in his boots, jeans, and black hoodie sweater at this white tie event, but Darien had a particular talent for remaining unseen even in front of someone's nose. Lilian made her way out of the ballroom, shaking hands and hugging people along the way, saying she had some business to see to but she would be ever so happy to return as soon as she could.

She climbed the stairs and stood beside Darien on the balcony, gazing at the endless throng of guests coming and going.

"I take it you found someone. Several someone's I hope."

Darien continued looking down at the foyer. "I think we should go somewhere more private."

"Oh? I've already taken the standard precautions. No one can see us or hear us up here."

"It's not the guests I'm worried about."

Lilian raised an eyebrow. She turned and walked down the hallway into the east wing. She let herself into her office and waited a second before turning around. Darien was there, as she knew he would be, silent and stealthy as ever. She locked the door and took a seat at her desk. Bookshelves lined the room, filled with heavy leatherbound tomes. She'd lived long enough to read them all, but only she and Darien knew that one of the shelves was a false doorway leading to her real office.

"There's a witch hunter here. In town," Darien said.

Lilian said nothing. She blinked. She rose from her seat, turned her back on Darien, hands held behind her back. Darien kept his mouth shut, waiting. Lilian's breathing grew heavier. Darien thought he could hear a growl. She turned around. The growl grew louder, her eyes glowing a dull red. The glow increased in intensity, now a bright blood red. With a snarl, Lilian brought her fists down on her oak desk and smashed it to splinters.

She closed her eyes and took a deep breath. Darien waited. She opened her eyes, now the light blue she normally maintained as part of her illusion. A brief flicker of disappointment crossed her face, and then a smirk. Explaining what happened to her desk was the least of her worries.

"Does he know?" she asked.

"I don't think so," Darien said. "From what I could overhear, it sounds like they're traveling elsewhere, and decided to spend the night here."

"You're certain?"

"As certain as I can be."

Lilian paced back and forth. Darien could be right. If the witch hunter knew about her, he'd have been at her mansion by now, no doubt leading an angry mob determined to exterminate the monster who had lived undetected among them for twenty years. Perhaps it was just a coincidence that he had happened upon her city. It did straddle both a major road and river. If she and Darien kept their heads down and maintained the masquerade, the witch hunter might move on in the morning, none the wiser about the kind of place he'd stumbled into.

On the other hand, this was a rare opportunity. Witch hunters could be formidable opponents, but they were only human. They could be caught unawares. They had to sleep. Killing one would give more of her people a greater chance of survival, plus it would give her the satisfaction of striking a blow against the enemy, however small. Just thinking about the witch hunter made the black ichor that flowed in her veins feel like it was boiling. These filthy cattle presumed to hunt down the children of the night, to raise their hands against their betters. It was a risk to be sure, but the more she brooded on it, the less she felt that she had a choice.

"What are you thinking?" Darien asked. He cocked his head. "You want to kill him."

"Yes."

"Are you sure that's wise? He doesn't know about us. A witch hunter dying in the city would draw attention from his order."

"Not if we go about this in a way that doesn't lead back to us."

Darien could see that the mistress's mind was made up. "What did you have in mind?"

Lilian favored Darien with a smile that didn't reach her eyes. She had taken a big risk turning him years ago, but Timothy's valet had proven himself a worthy servant to them both. She was taking another risk now, but she didn't anticipate the witch hunter to rise to the challenge.

"My dear Darien," she said. "Come into my office. You are in dire need of an upgrade."

3

Silas Flint marched through the city streets. It had taken a few tries before he found a reveler who was both brave and sober enough to give him directions to the Sleep Inn. Even frontier towns like these, where the Church's presence was thin, recognized the black garb and tall hats of the Knights Templar of the Order of Saint Benedict, patron against witchcraft. He was aware that people feared him, or rather what he could have done to them. As much as the wanton excess displayed on every street disgusted him, he didn't begrudge their jubilance. Victories against the forces of darkness were few and far between, and today's was worth remembering.

Ah, he thought. Across the street he spied a three story brick building with a flickering neon sign which read Sleep Inn and Vacancy. He pushed past a young man and woman in the throes of passion. They didn't even look up as he shoulder checked them out of his way. Music, laughter, and thick clouds of tobacco smoke wafted from the open windows.

Flint entered the Inn and the music and laughter stopped. The lobby had been converted into a bar. Every table was packed with townsfolk who all had large steins of beer and plates heaped with generous portions of greasy pub food. It smelled of smoke, alcohol, old wood, and sawdust. All eyes were upon Flint. A few nervously swallowed.

Flint gave them a grim smile.

"You needn't stop on my account," he said loud enough for everyone to hear. After a second, the music resumed, and conversation gradually came back. Flint headed toward the bar, serving girls going out of their way to avoid him as they made their rounds. Every stool at the bar was taken, but three men looked at Flint and excused themselves from their stools. Flint sat down on the middle stool. He took off his hat and placed it on the adjacent stool, adjusted his gun belt and the sword on his hip, and motioned for the bartender.

"Eh, yes sir. Can I help you?" the bartender asked.

"I should like to speak with the Innkeeper."

"That'd be me sir, John Dooley, at your service, sir."

"Mr. Dooley, I would like to rent two rooms, if you please."

Dooley swallowed and cleared his throat.

"Ah, well, you see sir, the thing is…"

"Well?" Flint said. "Spit it out man."

"We only have one room available. At the moment. And it only has one bed."

Flint stared at him.

"You know, what with so many folks being in town for today, and all…" Dooley said.

Flint said nothing.

"I… er… that is to say… ah…"

Flint continued staring. He didn't blink.

"Ah… yes, well… I suppose I could, er, stay at my son's house tonight, and you could have my room. I wouldn't want to put out a servant of the Church and all," Dooley said.

"Splendid," Flint said. He reached into one of his long coat's many pockets and withdrew a small pouch. It jingled as he dropped it onto the bar.

"I trust that should cover the cost of my and my companion's room and board. Plus something extra for your inconvenience."

Dooley loosened the pouch's strings. His eyes widened when he saw how much was silver was inside.

"Oh yes sir! That'll more than cover it! Jesus Christ, you two could stay here a week!" he said.

"That will not be necessary. And I'll thank you to mind the blasphemy."

"Oh, uh, right, sorry sir."

"Now," said Flint, putting his elbows onto the bar, "If you have a menu, I should like to see it. And I will take a glass of the best wine that you have."

After perusing the menu, Flint ordered the roast duck with oven roasted asparagus. Dooley gave a look that let on his cook didn't get that order often. He poured Flint a glass of wine. Flint swirled it around, sniffed, and took a sip.

"Ah," he said. "I believe this is the 2491?"

"Oh, uh, yes sir, it is," Dooley said. "You got quite a palate sir."

"Do I make you nervous Mr. Dooley?"

The bartender blinked a few times. "Uh, well, it's not you personally that's making me nervous sir. It's just that... well..."

"Yes?"

Dooley leaned over the bar and whispered in Flint's ear, "Are you here on official business sir?"

Flint raised an eyebrow as he said, "No. Should I be?"

"Eh, maybe. I don't know. It's weird."

Flint gave a wintry smile. "The weird and unexplained is my specialty."

Dooley nodded. He motioned for one of his serving girls to come over and had her take over bartending duty. Leaning over the bar toward Flint, he said, "Well, it's like this sir. For a long time, guests from the inns and motels and such have been going missing. Like in a weird way I mean."

"Go on."

"Like here, for instance. Once in a while a traveler will check in to a room. But he don't check out. I'll knock on the door and not get an answer. Door's always locked. I use my key to get in, and there's no trace of the guest. All of his personal belongings are still there, his room key is still there, but there's no trace of him. It's like he vanished from the face of the earth."

Flint steepled his fingers as he stared at Dooley. "I see. You said this has been happening at other inns as well?"

"Yes sir. It happens here every few months. I asked around, and the other innkeepers and motel managers have said the same thing's happened to them. We compared the dates and such, and someone disappears like that from one of our rooms every month, like clockwork, a different inn each month until they've gone through them all, then the cycle starts again."

"How long has this been going on?"

"Uh, well, let's see, it's been happening since I took over managing here. That was… fifteen years ago now. The previous owner said it started here about five years before that. So about twenty years altogether sounds like."

"Twenty years?! Has no one gone to the local police?"

"Oh yes sir, we have. Several times. They always come up empty. There's no body, so they can't call it murder. There's never any signs of a struggle. No fingerprints that don't belong to the guests. No hairs, no blood. They say all the physical evidence, and the lack of evidence, says they just up and left some time during the night."

"And yet their doors are locked from the inside, with their keys and all of their personal belongings left behind."

"Yes sir, that's about the size of it."

"Hmm. Interesting," Flint said.

"I figured that since you being here and being a witch hunter and all, somebody finally decided to report it to, uh, one of your offices, I suppose. Do you have offices?"

Flint smiled. "Yes. My superiors often suggest that I should spend more time in mine. But to my knowledge, we have never received reports of any unusual goings on in this city. You said this has been going on for twenty years?"

"Yes sir, I think so."

"Can you think of anything significant that happened twenty years ago? Anything at all unusual?"

"Uh... hmm... no, nothing unusual. Significant? Only thing I can think of is Timothy Turner got married."

"And who might that be?"

A serving girl brought Flint his meal. He gave it a careful appraisal before carving off a slice of meat and tasting it. He chewed, swallowed. Certainly not the best roast duck he'd ever had, but better than what he'd expected from an Inn that catered to the working classes.

"What do you think sir?" Dooley asked.

"Quite satisfactory," Flint said. "Now do go on."

"Right. Timothy Turner is the richest man in Canyon Cove. He runs the Snake River Trading Company. The Snake

River runs through the middle of the city, goes a long way through the country. He's got trading posts throughout the United Mountain States and Cascadia. I heard he's making plans to expand into Deseret. Anyway, twenty years ago he marries Lilian. It was a big to-do, hundreds of guests. I think every girl in Canyon Cove was heartbroken old Timothy was finally off the market."

Flint continued eating. "And that's when all of this began?"

"I think so sir."

"Have Mr. and Mrs. Turner lived here all of their lives?"

"Mr. Turner has. Mrs. Turner, no. Come to think of it, nobody really knows where she came from. Definitely not from around here. We're a decent sized city, but we're still small enough that everyone knows who has the big money. That's why it got everyone talking, this beautiful lady from out of town just comes in and marries our most eligible bachelor."

"I see. Anything else?"

"Mr. Turner is 50 and looks it. Mrs. Turner looks the same as on her wedding day Like literally the same. Some folks say it's downright unnatural."

"Hmm." Flint took another glass of wine and finished his meal.

"So what do you think sir?"

Flint gave Dooley an appraising look and asked, "What do you think Mr. Dooley?"

Dooley pursed his lips and thought for a few seconds.

"I don't know sir," he said. "I mean, the police are right. It looks like the guests just left on their own. But... I don't know, it just doesn't feel right, you know?"

Flint nodded. "Indeed. I agree that something unusual may be happening here Mr. Dooley. As it happens my assistant and I are on our way to our regional headquarters. When we arrive, I shall bring this matter to my superior's attention. God willing, he will dispatch a full-time investigator. For now, I shall retire to my room. I bid you good night. And happy Victory over Magus Day."

Flint donned his hat, took the key to Dooley's room, and rose from his stool. Again, conversation quieted. Serving girls were careful to stay out of his path as he walked toward the staircase. The innkeeper had given him much to ponder. If it were Flint's decision to make, he would have stayed to investigate the disappearances, but the Witch Hunter General of his chapter had insisted that Flint and Navarro return to their chapter house at all possible speed. He estimated they had another full day's ride ahead of them tomorrow.

He arrived at Dooley's room on the third floor and let himself in. The innkeeper lived modestly, with only loaded bookshelves, a recliner, and family photographs distinguishing it from an ordinary guest room. Flint removed his hat and gun belt, dropping them onto the bed, and he draped his long coat over the wooden chair in front of the steel desk. He unbuttoned the black waistcoat over his long-sleeved white shirt and sat down in the recliner. He drummed his fingers on the arm rest.

Witch hunters were given greater leeway in their duties than secular law enforcement. In theory he could compel testimony from anyone, but in practice, the rich and powerful could apply pressure on his superiors, which could make his investigations more difficult. The richer the community, the more they clung to the worst customs of the old world. And Canyon Cove appeared rich indeed.

He believed Dooley's account. It couldn't be a coincidence that guests began disappearing the same year that some mysterious woman no one knew married the city's most prominent citizen. At the same time, it wasn't much to go on. Unless...

Flint was a traveler and a witch hunter. If there was some mastermind behind these disappearances, a mastermind in league with the powers of Hell, then Flint himself would make for a tempting target. Indeed, the foul creatures could seldom resist an opportunity to do battle with their greatest enemies.

He got up and went to his long coat. He dug inside another pocket and took out a pouch full of blessed salt. He sprinkled it around the room, muttering prayers to St. Benedict, St. Julian, the Blessed Virgin, and finally asked the Holy Spirit to grant him vigilance this night against the infernal powers. He unbuttoned the top button of his dress shirt, and pulled out the crucifix and St. Benedict medals he wore around his neck so they were visible. Finally, he removed the sword from his gun belt and placed it on the bedside table, withdrawing the blade enough so a section of blessed steel was exposed.

Now he would wait. For what, he didn't know. Fortunately, Flint was a light sleeper.

4

Lilian and Darien stood inside her secret office in a hidden room that even Timothy didn't know about. A ball of witchfire illuminated the dank bricks and concrete floor. Shelves loaded with eldritch tomes and alchemical ingredients lined the room. Possession of any one of them would get their owner a ticket to the gallows or the stake. Lilian smiled. She had been an ordinary human woman when the great Simon Magus appeared to the world over four hundred years ago. He had offered humanity a new way of life, a new world. She had willingly pledged herself to him, but so many chose to resist, chose to reject the powers that could make humans into living gods.

She plucked a book from the shelf. Even she, with all of her terrible power, felt a shiver of fear go up her spine. The book was bound in cured human flesh, the text written in a language that did not originate from a human tongue. The slightest miscalculation could get her torn into bloody pieces and her spirit dragged into the fiery abyss.

"Are you sure you want to do this?" she asked Darien. "You have to be fully committed. Hesitation or fear will kill us both."

"I want to do this. I am prepared," Darien said.

"Very well."

Lilian took two jars from the shelf and mixed a compound of salt and powdered human skull. She poured it onto the floor in a circle. Darien set up candles to surround the circle. Lilian snapped her fingers, igniting the wicks all at once with a black flame that gave off a stench of sulfur. She took another jar off the shelf, this one filled with human blood, and used it to paint a pentagram and numerous arcane symbols within the circle.

Lilian opened the book and began to read aloud. Darien

winced. He could not understand the words, but they made his ears hurt and his eyes rattle. The hair on his arms stood up. He steeled himself for what was to come.

Lilian finished her incantation. A gust of cold air made them both shiver. Their breath became visible. A column of light rose from the circle. A silhouette coalesced inside the column. It appeared humanoid in that it had two arms, two legs, and a head but the proportions were off. Two great horns curled up from the head. Two balls of red fire appeared where the things eyes should be, and then another, greater fireball appeared in the center of its forehead.

"Who summons me?" it boomed. Its voice made their teeth vibrate.

"It is I who hath summoned thee, o great one," Lilian replied.

The demon laughed, a horrifying scratching noise that made Lilian want to cower, but she pushed the fear away. Fear would get her killed, or worse.

"I remember you," the demon said. "Have you finally decided to be with us? Break this circle and I shall bring you down to where you belong, your true home. Join us Lilith."

Only Lilian herself and the dark powers knew her true name. There were no secrets with demons.

"Perhaps some day, but not today. We require your assistance."

"Why should I grant you any boons? What have you to offer me?"

"I have two things to offer you, two things I believe you want very much."

"You have my interest."

"As we speak, there is a Knight Templar of the Order of Saint Benedict within this city. I would ask you to kill him for me."

The demon growled. Witch hunters had been crippling Hell's influence on the world of mortals for centuries. She knew it wouldn't say no to an opportunity to strike back.

"You know that I cannot fully enter the earth," it said.

"Oh but you can," Lilian said. "Darien is my thrall. He is offering you his body and his soul. Take him, and you can walk among men once again."

The demon made the horrible scratching sound that was its laughter.

"Indeed? Do you truly know what it is you are playing with, Darien?"

"I do," Darien said. "I want your power. I live to serve."

The demon regarded him. "Yes, I see that you desire the power, but do not lie to me, boy. You grow tired of being the servant. You seek to walk as a god among men. To make them cower before you."

"Yes."

The demon laughed again. "Take care, Lilith. This one may grow more powerful than you."

"I will take that chance."

"Then by all means, proceed."

Lilian faced Darien.

"Dost thou desire the power?" she asked.

"I do," Darien replied. Lilian turned toward the demon.

"Dost thou desire this soul?"

"I do."

"Then come forth, O dark powers! Blossom, O fallen seed!

I bid thee joined in spirit! Draw upon the princes and powers of Hell! These two are now one!"

The shadow of the demon left the circle and pounced on Darien's shadow. The man stood still, eyes shut, as the two shadows wrestled for control. They fought and

thrashed, a titanic struggle in shadow puppetry while Darien stood still and serene. Finally, the demon grabbed hold of Darien's shadow. It's jaws extended and it swallowed the man's shadow whole. Darien opened his eyes.

"Am I speaking to Darien?" Lilian asked.

"Yes and no," Darien replied. He appeared normal, but the shadow he cast had two great horns curling from its head. He smiled, revealing a mouth filled with too many needle-like teeth. His eyes were red. A third, bigger eye opened in the center of his forehead.

"I feel like I presided at a wedding," Lilian chuckled.

"In a way, you did," Darien said.

"How do you feel?"

"Like a new man."

"Then for your first birthday present, I offer you one witch hunter."

"Oh, you shouldn't have." Darien laughed, the sound a horrifying mix of his natural voice and the demon's squeal.

"One thing before you go," Lilian said. "What should I call your better half?"

"We are Robin. Robin Redcap."

She smirked. She doubted that it was the thing's true name, but on the other hand, they did have a penchant for giving themselves innocuous, even silly names.

"Well Robin, I suggest giving yourself a makeover before

you head out. We wouldn't want poor Darien to wind up in prison if anyone sees you having your fun."

Darien closed his eyes. Lilian watched as his skin seemed to melt. His bones stretched and contorted. When the thing had finished its foul reordering, the Darien she had known was a new man. He was six inches taller, his formerly lithe frame now bulging with muscle, his brown hair was now blond.

He opened his eyes, now blue, and favored her with a dazzling smile composed of perfect human teeth. The eye that had been in the center of his forehead was gone, as if it had never been.

"My goodness," she laughed. "Perhaps you should run for mayor when this is over!"

Darien smiled, bowed, and took his leave. Lilian waited a moment before leaving her inner sanctum. She secured the false bookcase, locked her office, and went back downstairs to the world of the living.

When she returned to the ballroom, she saw Timothy had made his entrance. He was a trim man with only a slightly receding hairline, tinged with the right touch of grey to give him an even more distinguished appearance in his white tie tuxedo. He was surrounded by Mayor Blackwood and his entourage.

"Ah, darling, there you are," Timothy said, giving her a peck on the cheek. "We were beginning to wonder if you'd gotten lost."

She laughed politely. "Oh, I'm sorry dear. I had some business to take care of and I lost track of time."

"Well, you're here now, and that's the important thing.

Say, have you seen Darien? I wanted to tell him he has the night off, but I can't find him anywhere."

"Oh, don't worry about him darling. I've already sent him on his way."

"Ah, splendid! He deserves some time off, especially tonight!"

"Yes, he does. I'm sure he's having a wonderful time."

5

Ricardo Navarro raised the stein to his mouth and began chugging beer alongside the other men at his table. The crowd chanted, "Chug! Chug! Chug!"

I can do this, I can do this... oh God, I can't do this, he thought. Navarro felt a tickle in this throat. He was going to choke, he just knew it. But then he felt the last of the beer enter his mouth and he slammed the stein onto the table. A second later, the other steins drummed a tattoo as they were slammed onto the table. The crowd cheered as he choked down the last mouthful, and promptly began coughing. Well wishers laughed, clapped him on the back, congratulated him on a job well done. He staggered back to his table on the bar patio, sitting next to the pretty young lady he had begun chatting up when he arrived. He'd met more than a few girls he wouldn't have minded getting to know better, but the nature of his work with Silas often interfered with a normal dating life.

"Very impressive," she said.

Navarro furrowed his brow for a second. This was Maria,

wasn't it? Or was her name Miranda? He hated it when this happened. Maria, that's it. Miranda was the redhead from the last bar.

"All in a day's work," Navarro said.

"What kind of work do you do again?" Maria asked.

"Uh, you want the short version or the long version?"

She laughed. God, she was beautiful when she smiled.

"I've never heard that one before," she said. "How about the short version first?"

"I assist in hunting witches and fighting monsters."

Maria's eyes widened. Her mouth hung open. Regaining her composure, she said, "Huh. Okay. I haven't heard that before either. So what's the long version?"

"Officially, I'm a Supernumerary of the Order of Saint Benedict."

"Oh!" she cried. "You're Catholic then!"

"Yes ma'am."

"Oh... so, uh, does that mean you're a priest? You know, like celibate and stuff?"

Navarro chuckled. "Oh hell no. If I couldn't enjoy good drinks and beautiful women after all the shit I have to deal with, I'd have quit a long time ago."

Maria smiled. "Hm. Well, I'm glad to hear that."

"Yeah?"

"Yeah. Now I won't feel bad about doing this." She leaned forward, her eyes half shut. Navarro moved in for the kiss when she broke away and gawked at the street. Navarro started, off balance on his stool.

"Now I appreciate a good tease, but come on, that's just cruel... what are you staring at?"

Now that he thought about it, all of the women on the patio… across the street too… were looking at someone with rapt attention, much to the other men's chagrin. Navarro saw a giant of a man, six and a half feet tall at least, his jeans and black hoodie barely containing his almost freakishly large muscles. He had a peculiar grin on his face that reminded Navarro of nothing so much as a cat stalking a mouse. He took no notice of all the female attention but strode down the middle of the street like a colossus who stood above the lustful thoughts of mere mortals.

"Maria?" Navarro asked. He snapped his fingers in front of her face but she didn't respond. Her face, and the faces of all the women present tracked the stranger as he moved past them.

Navarro had survived in his job for a long time because he learned early on to trust his gut. His gut told him there was something unnatural about the big guy.

"It's been a pleasure," he said, patting Maria's hand to no response. He excused himself from the table for a better view of the street. He should have known this place was too good to be true. He just knew he'd end up working tonight after all. Now he wished he hadn't drank so much.

He tailed the mysterious stranger down the street. Whoever he was, he didn't know or didn't care that Navarro was stalking him for he hadn't looked back once. Even at a distance, and with his back turned, there was something about the big guy that made Navarro feel on edge. Uncomfortable. Silas would probably use a word like uncanny. Navarro didn't always appreciate his boss's more flowery way of speaking – all part of witch hunter training – but yeah, uncanny was the word for how the big guy made him feel. The throngs of party goers avoided him, almost by instinct, even though he continued to draw lingering stares from women and a few men.

It was easy for Navarro to hide in the crowd, but something told him the big guy wouldn't care if he knew he was being followed. Then he stopped near a streetlight. Navarro leaned against the building, looking for all the world like a party goer catching his breath. Which he was, kind of. He really shouldn't have drunk so much. That's when Navarro saw it.

The man's shadow was elongated by the angle of the light, but there was no mistaking the twin horns curling up from its head. Navarro drew in a shuddering breath. This was not good.

Then it got even worse. The man turned around and locked eyes with Navarro. He maintained that predatory smile. Then the son of a bitch tapped the side of his nose with his index finger and winked.

Navarro stood transfixed for a second. Then he drew his pistol and aimed it at the big guy.

"Stop right there!" he shouted.

"Oh shit, he's got a gun!" someone yelled. It broke whatever spell the big guy had cast on the nearby women. Damn. This night kept getting worse.

"Is there a problem young man?" the big guy asked.

"By order of Holy Mother Church, and in the name of the Lord our God, I charge you with witchcraft, and consorting with demons. You are ordered to accompany me to my duly appointed superior where you will be put to the question."

Navarro shouted the words loud enough to break through the commotion that drawing his gun had caused. He hoped. Normally Silas took care of this part.

The big guy – or whatever he was – laughed. Navarro held his composure, but the celebrants winced, covered their ears, or began crying.

"Oh really Ricardo," the man said. "It's going to take more than a few silver bullets or that little axe of yours to stop me. As it happens, I was on my way to meet with our intrepid Captain Flint. I'd wanted to take my time and enjoy this new body, but now I suppose it's down to business. If you hurry, you might arrive in time to watch me devour his heart."

The big guy leaped, a great flying backflip, and he was on the roof of the building across the street. He saluted Navarro and leapt to the next rooftop. The crowd gasped, a few screamed.

"Shit," Navarro said. He doubted he could outrun this thing. He looked around, desperate. There – a bicycle rack. He drew his tomahawk and smashed the lock with one blow.

"Hey, what the fuck man, that's my bike!" yelled a man who had had even more to drink than Navarro.

"Did you see that guy just now?" Navarro snarled, waving his arm at the rooftops.

The drunkard blinked, swayed on his feet.

"Oh... uh... yeah, I did... yeah, uh, you take it man."

"I'll pay you back!" Navarro yelled as he pedaled after the monster. He weaved the bicycle between roving bands of party goers. He glanced at the rooftops, keeping track of his quarry, but the big guy was putting more distance between them. He had said that he was going after Silas. He'd said that he was going to get their rooms at the Sleep Inn. Navarro prayed that his boss was still there.

6

Silas Flint stood, hands behind his back, gazing out the window of his room. Sporadic fireworks lit up the night sky. He could hear the faint drumming of music from downstairs and the surrounding neighborhood. Flint suspected he wouldn't get any sleep until the rest of the city went to bed or passed out. Even then, he wasn't sure when or if he would finally nod off. He kept turning Dooley's story of mysterious disappearances over in his mind. What could account for them? The police said the evidence pointed to the guests leaving of their own accord. But then why would they leave their belongings behind? He could see one person disappearing, cutting ties, making a new life. But so many, and with such regularity?

He snorted in frustration. He needed more facts, but he didn't have time to launch a formal investigation. He'd bring the matter to the Witch Hunter General's attention. God willing it would be Flint himself dispatched to get to the truth of the matter. He hated leaving a mystery unsolved.

He saw light in his peripheral vision. Glancing toward the bedside table, he saw his sword emanating a faint glow. But that meant...

The window exploded, throwing Flint backward against the door, knocking the wind from him as he slid onto the floor. From the jagged hole where the window had been, an upside down face lowered into view. It wore a maniacal smile that displayed far too many needle-like teeth. The man - if man it be – had glowing red eyes with a third, larger eye in the center of its forehead.

"Hello Silas," it said. Then it giggled, a spine-tingling approximation of a child's laugh, if that child had been spawned from the bowels of Hell. It crawled in through the hole and up onto the ceiling, like some great gangling spider.

Silas rose to his feet, made a show of dusting himself off.

"I take it you are the responsible party for all of these mysterious disappearances," Flint said.

Darien giggled. "Found out about my handiwork did you? Yes, I've been the one plucking travelers from their beds."

Flint raised an eyebrow. "I see you have decided to forego the stealthy approach."

As if to emphasize his point, someone pounded on the door.

"Sir?!" came Dooley's muffled voice. "Sir, are you alright? What's going on in there?!"

"Piss off, we're busy!" Darien shouted in a voice loud enough to make Flint wince.

"Mr. Dooley, get yourself and your patrons out of here. Quickly now!" Flint called. He heard doors opening, guests screaming, a stampede down the stairwell.

Darien crawled back and forth along the ceiling, drooling a vile green saliva that hissed as it touched the floor.

"Tell me," Silas said. "What is your purpose in these kidnappings?"

Darien laughed. "You could come with me and find out. But I think I'll just kill you here."

He sprang off the ceiling to pounce, but Flint made a diving forward roll, just missing Darien's claws. Darien landed on all fours against the door and sprang again toward Flint, but the witch hunter had reached his gun belt. In one smooth motion he drew a pistol and fired. The crack deafened him but the bullet found its mark: Darien crumpled to the floor, a pool of malodorous black blood pooling beneath him. His hands sizzled and smoked when they touched the carpet. Darien cried out in pain. He scrabbled on all fours to the wall and crawled back onto the ceiling. He prowled back and forth, his three red eyes ablaze with demonic fury, growling like a tiger.

Keeping his eyes on Darien, Flint put his gun belt around his waist and donned his hat. He took his sword from the bedside table, drawing it the rest of the way from its scabbard. It glowed softly in the presence of the demonic and unholy magic.

"I took the liberty of scattering some blessed salt about the room before your arrival," Flint said. "Do you like my sword? It was blessed by the Holy Father himself, and it never fails to alert me to the presence of your vile kind."

"And silver tipped bullets," Darien rasped, clutching the bloody hole in his shoulder. "Very good witch hunter."

"Why don't you come down from there and tell me of your dark designs? If you cooperate, perhaps I shall behead you with one stroke instead of putting you to the torch!" Flint shouted.

Darien smiled. Flint stood his ground, but he knew that gazing into the things three eyes for too long was to court insanity.

"You know, this host of mine used to be an effective warlock in his own right," Darien said. "With only a minor exertion of his will, he was able to lure his victims out of their rooms and lead them to his mistress like lambs to the slaughter."

Flint said nothing.

"Darien here was an apt pupil. His mistress promised him even greater power if he would consent to joining with us. He's eager to give his new powers a try."

Darien's eyes flashed a bright light and Flint was paralyzed, unable to so much as blink. He could feel icy fingers probing inside his skull. Images appeared unbidden before his mind's eye. He was seventeen years old again, and he stood before the barn on his father's property. The sickly smell of death and rot permeated his nostrils. He knew that his brother waited for him inside the barn. Oh God... not again... please, not this again...

No! This isn't real! It's a memory! Flint thought. In his mind he focused on the cross, on his pledge to make amends, on his training, and his faith. The mental image of his family farm flickered, wavered, the invisible fingers inside his head relaxing their pressure a bit.

"Hmm... you have a strong will," Darien said. "But you are only human. It's only a matter of time before..."

A crash interrupted him and broke the spell over Flint. He was back in his hotel room. Someone had kicked in the door.

"Silas!" It was Navarro, rifle in hand. He aimed, fired, and the silver tipped bullet tore through Darien's side and out the other, spraying black gore and fragments of bone from the ragged exit wound. Darien roared, falling from the ceiling and down onto the floor where the blessed salt waited to be rubbed in his wounds. His corrupted flesh sizzled where it touched the floor, and the demon writhed in agony. Drawing on every ounce of its unholy willpower, Darien sprang up from the floor and out the hole in the wall that he had made. His wounds took their toll and he fell short of the adjacent rooftop, tumbling into the street below. The revelers screamed at this bloody apparition that had come crashing down into their midst.

"Rifle!" Flint shouted. Navarro worked the bolt, ejecting the spent casing, and tossed the rifle to Flint who caught it with one hand.

Darien was climbing to his feet. His legs had broken in the fall, but the demon drew upon its unholy willpower and sorcery to knit the bones at a preternatural speed. Flint dropped to the prone position, got his target in his sights, and pulled the trigger. The rifle cracked. Below, Darien's leg exploded in a shower of rancid gore. He fell to the ground again. He snapped his teeth, his red eyes rolled in every direction, he snarled and growled. Most onlookers fled in terror, but a few looked up at the hole in the building. Flint doffed his hat, waving at the people who were too stunned, too frightened, or too drunk to realize there was a demon in their midst.

Flint ejected the spent shell casing, handed the rifle back to his assistant.

"That was an incredible shot sir," Navarro said.

"Thank you, Ricardo," Flint said. "And I also thank you for appearing at just the right moment. I do not know if I could have resisted that fiend's dark illusions for much longer."

Flint sniffed. "Hmm. I am even more impressed you managed to find your way here after so much to drink."

"Should have known I'd end up working tonight," Navarro chuckled.

"Indeed, for the enemy never sleeps. Come, Mr. Navarro! Let us see if the monster is more willing to talk."

7

Flint and Navarro exited the building. Darien had tried to crawl away but hadn't gotten far before being accosted by townsfolk. They pelted him with beer bottles, garbage, and whatever debris was at hand. It made Flint's heart swell with pride that there were a few righteous men and women who recognized the devil's minions and did not quail in fear.

Darien's body rippled, quivered, and contorted. When he had entered Flint's room, he had been blond haired and blue eyed, about six and a half feet tall with massive muscles. Now the Darien-demon thing shrunk before everyone's eyes. Now they saw a brown haired man with a more slender figure. It rolled onto its back. The third eye and teeth were still there, but otherwise he was a new man.

Flint sneered and drove his sword down through Darien's chest, pinning him to the ground. Corrupted blood spattered onto Flint's clothes. Darien roared again, the sound a curious mixture of man and beast. The innkeeper, Dooley, shuffled forward for a closer look.

"Jesus Christ!" he said, and then winced as Flint looked over his shoulder at him with an offended look. "Uh, sorry sir."

"And I apologize for your room, Mr. Dooley," Flint replied. "Tell me, do you recognize this cur?"

"Yes sir, I do. That there is Darien Erhardt. He works for Timothy Turner!"

Darien writhed and whimpered. He wrapped his hands around the blade as if to push it away, but the holy steel only burned him. The stench of seared, rotten flesh caused onlookers to gag, and some to vomit.

"Darien is merely the host. I am interested in who came along for the ride," Flint said, twisting the blade.

Darien spat bloody phlegm onto Flint's shirt. Flint rolled his eyes.

"Mr. Navarro?" he said.

Navarro opened a pouch on his belt, taking out a silver crucifix. Darien's three eyes widened and he redoubled his twisting and thrashing. Navarro pressed the crucifix against Darien's ruined leg. A billow of putrid steam rose from the wound, and Darien howled like a wolf caught in a trap.

"Tell me your name," Flint shouted.

Darien screamed, twisted, his flesh bubbled and liquified as he struggled to shape shift, but Flint's sword and the crucifix held him in place.

"Tell me your name monster!" Flint shouted again.

"Robin Redcap!" Darien's shriek caused beer bottles and windows to break, spraying glass in all directions. A shard nicked Flint's cheek and he felt a trickle of blood run down his face, but he held his ground.

"How come you here, Robin Redcap? Speak!"

"The dark lady joined us with this man."

"Dark lady? Who is this witch?"

Darien tried to push himself away but the sword held firm.

"Her name, monster!"

"Lilith," Darien said. He gnashed and yowled, but the witch hunter and his assistant paid him no mind.

"Who's that?" Navarro asked.

Flint thought for a second. Then he took his own crucifix off from around his neck. He leaned in, holding it before Darien's face.

"In the name of our Lord Jesus Christ, I command you! Tell me, who is this Lilith? Does she reside here, in the city?"

"Yes," Darien growled, trailing off into more animal cries of misery.

"Does she use the name Lilian Turner?"

"Yes!" Darien bellowed.

Flint drew back. He looked at Navarro, and Navarro looked at him.

"I think we've heard all that we need to know, Ricardo."

"I think you're right boss."

"Shall we?"

"I thought you'd never ask."

Flint let go of his sword. He and Navarro stood side by side. They made the sign of the cross.

"In the name of the Father, and of the Son, and of the Holy Spirit," Flint began.

"Amen," Navarro answered.

"O Lord, hear our prayer."

"And let our cry come unto thee."

"The gates of Hell shall not prevail."

"Because Your Spirit is with me."

Darien arched his back, he pulled at the sword embedded in his chest, blood poured from his many wounds.

"This isn't over witch hunter!" Darien yelled, his voice now totally that of the demon. "We'll see you in Hell yet, Silas Flint!"

The two men continued their prayer, ignoring the monster.

"O Lord, stretch forth thy hand," Flint said.

"Protect your children from the night," Navarro replied.

"Banish this fallen angel..."

"And strike him with Your might!"

The two men strode forward, drawing their pistols. Together, they fired into Darien's third eye. The orb burst, showering them with viscous jelly and foul blood. In one swift motion, Flint drew his sword from Darien's chest and brought the blade down across his throat, severing Darien's head. A great gust of wind blew through the alleyway. Lights flickered. A black mist arose from the bloody stump of Darien's neck. Chilling laughter followed the mist as it rose and blew westward into the bowels of the city.

Flint and Navarro panted as if they had run a marathon. The sounds of celebration were distant, but here they were surrounded by silence. Then someone clapped. Dooley stepped forward from the alley where he had hidden. He was joined by other citizens who had remained hidden from the confrontation between light and dark. Soon Flint and Navarro were amid a small crowd who cheered, whooped, and clapped them on the back.

"That was incredible!"

"Amazing!"

"Wow!"

"Awesome!"

"Hear me," Flint said. "Hear me!"

The crowd fell silent. Waiting.

"You heard the demon," Flint said. "Our work here is not finished, for there is yet a great darkness befouling your fair city. From his own mouth, compelled by the Lord our God to speak true, he has testified that your own Lilian Turner is that most terrible fiend, the devilish mastermind behind tonight's dark happenings! Lilian Turner is a witch!"

The crowd murmured, shocked out of their jubilant mood.

"If any among you be God-fearing men and women, join my assistant and I! We cannot allow this devil in human form to linger in our world! God made this world for us, his children. We must root out this evil once and for all!"

The crowd was silent. Then the first shout came.

"Burn the witch!"

A second person took up the chant. Then a third. Then five more. Soon the street was thundering with dozens of voices shouting as one.

"Burn the witch! Burn the witch! Burn the witch!"

"The Holy Spirit is with us! We cannot fail! Forward!" Flint yelled. At the head of the crowd, he strode forth, an avenging angel sent to smite all the powers of darkness.

Navarro pulled Dooley aside. "Ah, maybe you could give us directions to her place?" he asked.

Lilian Turner stood back from the crowd in the grand ball room and sipped her champagne. It was good by post-war standards, but it was never quite the same as how she remembered it from the old world, from before the Great Magician had changed everything. She had been twenty-nine years old then, when she learned of the spells and elixirs that could preserve her youth and her life indefinitely. She didn't expect Darien to return after dispatching the witch hunter. Robin Redcap was right. She had seen Darien's hunger to strike out on his own from the moment she had finished teaching him the spells to mesmerize victims, luring them out of their hotel rooms, locking and unlocking doors with a gesture, and bringing them to her.

Now with a lesser demon magnifying his powers tenfold, Darien would no doubt seek to stretch his legs and experiment. Newborns always did. If he began openly terrorizing the lambs, more witch hunters would come, and it would be a simple matter to pin all of the disappearances on Darien if they figured out that travelers had been going missing for twenty years. Still, she expected that, one way or another, the time was fast approaching when she would have to pull up stakes and set herself up in a new city. She had enough of her elixir stockpiled that she wouldn't need another victim for a few months. Perhaps she would set herself up in Deseret. The Church and the Deseret leadership had a prickly relationship in the best of times and...

"Everyone! Your attention please!" called Mayor Blackwood, tapping his champaign glass with a fork. He stood on a raised dais at the head of the ballroom, surrounded by other elected officials, with Timothy at his right hand.

"I want to thank you all for joining us this evening. And I want to extend my sincerest gratitude for our host, Mr. Timothy Turner for his gracious..."

Lilian tuned him out. It would a typical droning speech thanking God for humanity's victory over Simon Magus, talking about the challenges of a new world, patting themselves on the back for all that they'd accomplished, and so on, and so forth. She'd had to listen to similar speeches hundreds of times over the last few centuries. You hear one, you hear them all.

The temperature in the room fell and Lilian perked up. It was too subtle for ordinary human beings to detect in their packed surroundings, but Lilian knew what it meant. She glanced at her champaign glass and saw a shadow flicker over it.

She finished what little alcohol was left and excused herself. Her dress and high heels made running a delicate business, but she hurried upstairs and into her office, letting herself into her inner sanctum. The column of light from earlier in the night was back, rising from the circle she had drawn, the silhouette of Robin Redcap inside, its three eyes burning brightly.

Lilian closed her eyes and sighed.

"Darien is dead," she said.

"Yes," the demon said. "He's with us now. Would you like a word?"

"No."

The demon laughed. "This is no ordinary witch hunter Lilith. My masters have had their eyes on him for some time. He is Silas Flint."

"Is that name supposed to mean something to me?"

"He interfered with a plan of ours that had been years in the making. Not many humans would have had the strength of character to do what he did. And now he's coming for you."

"What?!" Lilian cried. "How?! How does he know of me?"

"Oh Lilith," the demon chuckled. "You of all people should know that even with a demon inside them, the human body can only take so much punishment. I tried to stop him, but that small part of Darien that still existed gave you away. I decided to give you a warning because even we are curious to see how you will extricate yourself this time."

"Begone!" Lilian snapped. The light disappeared, taking Robin Redcap with it, his mocking laughter echoing in her ears. She drove her fist into the wall, shattering the brick. She swept the alchemical ingredients off of the work table, growling and spitting like a caged animal.

Lilian grabbed a vial of her elixir from a shelf, pulled out the cork with her teeth, and drank the contents in one swallow. She didn't need to take it for another few weeks, but she needed as much vigor as she could muster for the next step. The victims Darien brought her provided the cerebrospinal fluid that was a key ingredient in her life extension formula, and their flesh and organs were useful in her other experiments. Right now, it was their bones that she needed.

She levitated as she drew upon every reserve of magic that coursed in her veins. Lilian was surrounded by a nimbus of blue flame that did not burn her, her eyes glowing with unholy fire. She stretched out with her will and sensed the scattered bones along the bed of the Snake River. Incantations flowed from her lips in a language never meant for human tongues. As the victims had served her in life, so too would they serve her in death. In her mind's eye, she could see the river bubble and steam. Moldering bones swirled, reassembled, formed themselves into complete skeletons. Their empty eye sockets burned with witch fire.

Lilian saw all of this in her mind and smiled. Twelve victims a year over twenty years meant she had a formidable fighting force at her command. She had hoped to make a discreet exit when the time came. She still could. A small army of undead rampaging in the streets would occupy everyone's attention. But no. She wouldn't leave just yet. Something about this Silas Flint intrigued her. He'd managed to not only survive, but kill a demonically enhanced warlock like Darien, who had been no minor conjurer even as a mere human being. What's more, the powers below seemed to have a particular grudge against him. A man like that had to be formidable indeed.

Not that he stood a chance against her. She could strike him dead with a word and a gesture. But where was the fun in that? No, if this witch hunter thought to drive her from her life here at a time that was not of her choosing, if this worm really thought he could put her to the torch, she would craft an even greater challenge for him. Let us see what this Silas Flint is really made of.

Lilian had kept the skin and flesh of her victims carefully preserved around Timothy's property, enchantments placed around their hiding places to prevent any stench from escaping or any insects from settling. There was no evidence connecting an army of skeleton warriors emerging from the

Snake River to her, but this, this would let the cat out of the bag so to speak.

She sighed. Timothy would surely turn on her over this. She hoped that he had the sense to take cover and stay out of the way until it was all over. A hundred years ago, she wouldn't have cared one way or the other. She might have killed him herself. But as far as she was able to appreciate such things anymore, she thought of Timothy as a good man. Her original plan had been to disappear, leaving a Dear John letter in her wake. Lilian snorted. She must be getting soft in her chronological old age.

Well, she thought, enough of the sentimentality. There was a great ritual that needed doing. She took deep breaths. Levitating again, the baleful fire engulfed her body and she began the incantations.

9

"And now, I'd like to turn things over to our host, and a very dear, close, personal, long time friend: Mr. Timothy Turner!"

Mayor Blackwood stepped away from the lectern and motioned for Turner to take his place. Turner smiled and waved at the hundreds of guests crammed into the ballroom, shaking the chandeliers with the thunder of their applause. He felt uncomfortable with such public displays of emotion, especially when they were directed at him, but he learned to accept them with stoic good grace. He knew he was a popular man, even though few could say they really knew him. His trading company had brought hundreds of good jobs to communities throughout this section of North America. Turner always drove a hard bargain with his competitors, but he'd found that paying his employees a decent wage for an honest day's work did wonders to cement him in the people's hearts.

The woman whose heart he cared about the most was nowhere to be seen in the crowd. It disappointed him. Lilian often disappeared like this, saying she had "business to take care of," though she never elaborated on what that business was. In the early years of their marriage, he'd wondered if she was going off to some clandestine rendezvous with a lover, but after confronting her about it one day, she'd admitted that she just needed to get away from people sometimes. Turner sympathized. There were many times he wished he could do the same, like now for instance.

"Thank you. Thank you. Thank you all. Thank you," Turner said to the guests. They finally settled down enough for him to give his prepared remarks. He shuffled his index cards.

"Mayor Blackwood, distinguished dignitaries, honored guests, friends," Turner began. "We gather here tonight in order to remember the great sacrifices made by the entire world four hundred and fifty seven years ago. On this day, the Great Magician was vanquished by..."

"Look!"

The crowd murmured in confusion. One of the guests was pointing and staring out a window, his mouth agape in shock and horror. More people crowded around him. A woman let loose a shrill scream. Others backed away from the window in terror.

"What the hell's going on..." Mayor Blackwood muttered.

He rose from his seat and Turner joined him as they looked out a window. Blackwood gasped, dropping his drink, the glass shattering on the floor. Turner's mouth fell open and he only made a strangled squeak.

Pairs of tiny blue fireballs looked like they were floating in the distance, moving closer, closer to his property. When they reached the floodlights surrounding his manicured lawn, he saw that these fireballs burned inside the eye sockets of skeletons. Skeletons that were walking.

More screams echoed in the ballroom. Guests who had seen the oncoming mob of undead turned and ran. Their panic was infectious, other guests began scrambling for exits. Turner swore. These people were going to trample each other to death before the monsters could reach them.

"Come on," he growled, tugging on Blackwood's sleeve. They faced the crowd, waving their arms, yelling to be heard.

"Everyone please! Calm down! Calm down!" Turner shouted.

"You need to exit in an orderly fashion!" Blackwood shouted.

It was no use. The guests pushed, shoved, and dashed for the exits.

"Plumley!" Blackwood yelled.

Joseph Plumley, the Canyon Cove Chief of Police pushed against the flow of guests, making his way to the dais where the mayor stood.

"Sir!" Plumley called out.

"Plumley, gather as many officers as you can. Organize a defense, get these people to safety!"

"Yes sir! You should come with me!"

Turner barely heard the commotion around him. He had remembered who was missing.

Lilian.

"Come on Tim, we need to get out of here!" Blackwood said, grabbing Turner by his sleeve.

"I have to find Lilian!" he said. "Go on without me, we'll catch up. I'm not leaving without her!"

Turner was getting up in years, but he still had enough strength to push his way through the crowd and into the foyer where guests poured out of the front doors in a mad flood. He frantically looked about, frozen in place for a moment before remembering that Lilian often took refuge in the office she had requested made for her. God, please grant that she's still there.

He sprinted up the steps, taking them two at a time. When he reached the top, some doors in the hallway crashed open. He froze in place. What new madness could this be? Christ, why hadn't he brought his gun with him to the party?

A gust of icy wind made him shiver. Blue light emanated from the doorways. Then they came out. Turner wasn't sure what he was seeing, but they appeared to be long strips. They moved toward him. He cowered, falling backward onto his ass. He held up his arms to shield his face, but the floating strips moved past him and down into the foyer. He dared to open his eyes and saw that now there were balls and patches in addition to the strips. He sniffed. Blood?

Oh God… skin! This was human skin and flesh!

He felt his stomach lurch, and he vomited onto the carpet. His instincts were screaming at him to flee. He staggered to his feet. No. He couldn't abandon Lilian. He put his hands on the wall to support himself as he pushed himself down the hallway to the door of Lilian's office.

He entered and found it empty. But one of the bookcases had swung away from the wall on hinges. He swallowed, the sour taste of vomit still in his mouth. He shook but he urged himself onward. He carefully stepped into the hidden passage. He had no idea this had been here. How long? Did Lilian have this built? At the end of the passageway he could see the same blue light that he'd witnessed in the hallway.

He reached the end. Lilian was floating a few feet off the ground, her arms outstretched, her body engulfed in blue flame that did not consume her. Then the flame dissipated, and Lilian alighted upon the floor which was cluttered with books, beakers, and a circle of powder with what looked like human blood used to draw evil symbols within.

"Lilian?" Turner whispered.

She turned to face him, a weak smile on her face.

"Hello Timothy," she said. "How's the party?"

10

Ricardo Navarro struggled to keep up with his boss. Flint marched down the middle of the street at the head of a mob. They had started out with the people who had witnessed Darien's death, keeping up the steady chant of "Burn the witch." The closer they came to their quarry, the more of them peeled off, to be replaced by other townsfolk who either wanted to perform their Christian duty, or who thought hunting down a sorceress sounded like a good time, and some who were simply drunk and decided to follow the crowd.

Some had pistols, rifles, or shotguns. Others picked up whatever sharp or blunt instrument they could find along the way. Navarro estimated their followers numbered in the dozens, pushing one hundred.

He'd been with Flint for five years and had already seen enough horrors to last a lifetime. He had a bad feeling about this mission. It took a tremendous amount of power to merge a human being with a lesser demon, like what had happened to Darien. A simple possession could be solved by an exorcism, though Navarro didn't think there were any Catholic priests in this city. When the demon gets far enough into someone's soul that the bodily mutations began, there was no other choice than to put them down.

"Rico!" A woman's voice called Navarro's name. He looked around the street, the avenues still packed with party goers.

"Rico!" There. A woman was waving at him. She pushed her way onto the street.

"Maria!" Navarro hadn't thought he'd ever see her again.

"Hey! What happened earlier? Where'd you go?" she asked. "Where are you going now?"

"Do you remember seeing a big blond man?"

"Uh... yeah, yeah I do. We were talking and we were about to... uh... well, you know. Then I got this weird feeling. I saw him and then it's just kind of blank. When I came to, you were gone."

"Oh, well, he was a demon."

Maria's eyes widened. "What?!"

"Yeah. He'd merged with a demon. Guess he went out for a stroll, wanted to check out his new powers."

"Holy shit..."

"Yeah."

"What happened to him?"

"Me and Silas, we shot him, then Silas cut off his head."

"Oh..." Maria said. She silently kept pace with Navarro. Flint turned and faced his followers.

"The Holy Spirit guides us! Together we shall erase the vile stain of witchcraft from this land! Deus Vult! Follow me!" He drew his sword and pointed the way. Cheers erupted from the crowd, and more people left their revelry behind to join them.

"That's Silas?" Maria asked.

"Witch Hunter Captain Silas Albert Flint, in the flesh."

"What's he talking about?"

"We're off to go pay Lilian Turner a visit. Before it died, the demon said she was the one who summoned him."

"Lilian Turner?! Oh shit..."

"You know her?"

"I've never met her, but everyone knows about her... she's a witch? Her?"

"That's what we're going to find out. We're on our way to the Turner mansion."

Maria fell silent again but continued walking with Navarro. The churn continued as well, with followers leaving and others taking their place.

"Can I come with you?" she asked.

Navarro glanced at her. He said, "We don't know exactly what we'll be up against. It'll be dangerous."

"I understand."

"We can't guarantee your safety."

"I understand."

Now Navarro was silent.

"Are you really sure about this?" he asked.

"Yes, I'm sure."

"You got a gun? Any kind of weapon?"

Maria smiled. She lifted her shirt from the small of her back and drew a compact 9mm handgun. Navarro gave it an appraising look. He raised an eyebrow.

"An autoloader huh? You didn't tell me you were a rich girl."

She laughed. "I'm not. My older brother gave it to me when I turned 18."

Navarro smiled. "Hell of a first date, isn't it?"

"Oh? We're on a date?"

"We're in each other's company, we're about to go on a group activity, we're sharing personal info... I'd call this a date."

"Hmm... I guess you're right. It is a hell of a first date."

They heard screams up ahead. Panicked townsfolk streamed past them, running for their lives.

"You there! Stop!" Flint called out to one who was passing nearby, but the woman paid him no heed. Their mob had come to a halt. Uncertain murmurs rippled. Party goers on the sidelines looked bewildered, not knowing whether to run or join the safety of Flint's company or whether this was a part of tonight's entertainment. Navarro unslung his rifle and reloaded it to full capacity.

"What's happening?" Maria asked.

"Don't know," Navarro said. "But if you have to use your gun, aim for the head."

Flint wrestled a panic stricken runner to the ground. The

man was gibbering and crying. Flint gave him a backhanded slap.

"Pull yourself together man! What devilry has unmanned you so?!"

Maria looked like she couldn't decide whether to be confused or appalled. She whispered to Navarro, "Uh... does he always talk like that?"

Navarro chuckled, "Yeah. All witch hunters talk real formal, but I think Silas overcorrected for how he grew up."

Focusing their attention on Flint again, they saw him lean down closer to the man he held on the ground. It looked like the poor guy was whispering. Flint released him. The man scrambled to his feet and took off at a sprint.

Flint faced his followers and cried, "Hear me! The witch knows that her final hour draws nigh. In her desperation, she has summoned a horde of undead that rampage through the streets as we speak!"

A collective gasp rose from the crowd. The music on their block had ceased. All eyes were on Flint. The faint rattle of gunfire could be heard in the distance.

"Canyon Cove's finest have organized the defense of your city, but they are too few to face this menace! If we stay together, if we watch out for one another, if we have faith in our hearts and songs of praise and glory on our lips, we shall annihilate these unholy monsters and return them to death's cold embrace where they belong!"

The crowd whispered. A few faces looked panic stricken.

"These are your homes! Your families! Your friends!" Flint bellowed. "You shall never be safe so long as the vile witch draws breath! I have devoted my life to doing battle with the powers below! So long as there is life in my body I shall never give in! I will never surrender!"

Navarro heard a few scattered shouts of, "Yeah," and, "You tell them." He smiled. As long as he'd been at this job, he still enjoyed hearing Flint get wound up.

"This is your city! This is our world! Today is Victory over Magus Day, the day when all mankind cried out with one voice that they would not surrender to the night, they would not surrender to sorcery, they would not surrender to evil!"

"Woo!"

"Yeah!"

"That's right!"

"Our ancestors buried the most powerful sorcerer in human history! He thought to destroy our world, to enslave God's children, and remake the heavens in his own blasphemous image! Now he is dead, and we are still here!"

Flint raised his sword to the sky. The crowd screamed, cheered, stamped their feet, clapped their hands, a few fired shots into the sky with their weapons. Navarro and Maria cheered along with them.

"I shall lead the way! God walks with us! Forward!"

Flint ran toward the sound of gunfire. The crowd roared its defiance of the night and followed him.

11

"Lilian… what… what are…" Turner stammered.

Lilian sighed. "I'm sorry you had to find out this way Timothy. But yes. Your eyes do not deceive you. I am a sorceress, an enchantress, a necromancer… a witch."

Turner backed away until he collided with the wall. He slid down until he was sitting on the floor, mouth agape. He buried his face in his hands.

"Oh God..." he whispered.

"Let's not bring Him into this," Lilian said. "Now's not the best time to talk Timothy, but I promise I will tell you the truth about myself once I've finished my work here. Please believe me when I say I mean you no harm. I'll explain everything. You deserve that much."

Turner said nothing, but made no move to flee.

Lilian gave him a sympathetic look. Come to think of it... was that sympathy she actually felt? Whatever it was, she couldn't recall the last time she had felt this way about anyone. Interesting.

She would worry about it later. There was still the great ritual to finish. Mankind wasn't as fearful of the night as it used to be. When her master, the Great Magician, had appeared in the mid 21st century, one skeleton warrior would have had entire nations screaming in terror. Here, now, in the 26th century, she expected the populace of Canyon Cove would organize an impromptu defense to make short work of her skeleton army. She shook her head. It was amazing what humans could grow used to.

Lilian left Timothy behind in her inner sanctum and went to the head of the stairs in the foyer. The strips and patches of skin and flesh that she had summoned from their hiding places were hovering downstairs, circling the center of the room like the planets orbiting the sun. It had been many years since she tried this spell. She wasn't sure it would work this time, but it was of no great concern. If the summoning failed, she would simply kill the witch hunter herself.

Why didn't she simply kill him now, and have done with it? She wasn't sure. Partly it was her curiosity about how this Flint character, who had gained the attention of Hell, accounted for himself. Then she realized it: she was reluctant to leave. Lilian had no attachment to Canyon Cove itself. She had relocated to new cities hundreds of times in her life. She cared nothing for how many people would die here, whether at the bony hands of her undead army or at this new creation she planned to make. Her twenty years with Timothy had made her feel... she didn't know the right word for it. Domestic? It had been the first time in centuries she had played the part of a simple housewife. It wasn't as bad or as boring as she had thought it would be. Lilian laughed aloud. Oh, if only she could tell her 21st century self how she would feel later in life!

A plan formed in Lilian's mind. She would finish her work here, then she would go back to Timothy and explain the truth about herself. Then she would make him an offer. If he refused, she would leave him in peace and disappear from Canyon Cove forever. She hoped that he would accept.

Now, to business, she thought. She extended her hands, now alight with blue witch fire. The orbiting human flesh began to coalesce at the center of the foyer. She exerted her will and the flesh responded. She waved and scooped and pulled and pushed with her hands, sculpting the flesh like a potter sculpts clay. Slowly, her creation took shape. It stretched and contorted. At this rate it would burst through the roof. Oh well, Timothy could afford to repair it.

She was right. It bumped against the ceiling. Lilian made a crushing gesture with one hand and the roof caved in, showering the foyer with wood and plaster, allowing her creature to rise to its full height. There. That should do it.

Before her stood a humanoid giant. Its skin, made up from over two hundred donors was blotchy with different shades scattered about its misshapen body. The head had two empty eye sockets, two slits for a nose, two holes where the ears would be, and a mouth that stretched too far.

"Hmm, I knew I forgot something," Lilian said. She whispered a spell, and the flesh monstrosity grew a set of jagged fangs.

"Now we just need that special spark," she said. She conjured two balls of blue witch fire in hands and tossed one, then the other. They floated up, up toward the giant's face, and settled in its eye sockets. A faint blue glow emanated from beneath its skin. Then the thing howled, an almost human cry. It looked down at Lilian.

"Kill Silas Flint," she said. "Kill anyone who gets in your way."

The giant cried again. It moved forward, smashing through the wall of Timothy's house, leaving the front half exposed to the night sky. The monstrosity's blood chilling howls continued as it made its way down the dirt road leading into the city proper.

Lilian smiled. Not too bad if she did say so herself. She made her way back down the hallway, into her office and her inner sanctum. Timothy was still seated where she had left him. She didn't think he had even looked up.

"Timothy?" she asked. "It's done. We can talk now."

"Just go away," Timothy said, not looking at her. "Just leave me alone."

She sighed. "Well, in that case, you can just listen."

12

Police Chief Joseph Plumley was having a bad night. Normally, the force only dealt with petty thievery and drunken brawls. The city was wealthy, but not wealthy enough to provide the force with enough automobiles or radios for every officer. He had no idea where these skeleton things were going but they seemed to be sticking together, and not dispersing throughout the city. They still attacked anyone unlucky enough to be in their path. For not having muscles, they were unnaturally strong. He'd seen one punch through a police officer's chest, the poor man's still beating heart plopping onto the pavement. Shots aimed at center mass either passed through their ribs or broke a few bones, but didn't put them down. They'd learned that shattering their skulls with gunfire or blunt force trauma extinguished the fires burning in their eye sockets, which did the trick. Headshots on moving targets from shooters that were panicked or terrified out of their minds was easier said than done though.

Plumley stood behind a makeshift barricade in Canyon Plaza. The skeletons were making a beeline west. Assuming they maintained their course, they'd come through the Plaza. Sporadic radio transmissions, word of mouth, and the flow of fleeing civilians had brought a significant force of cops toward Plumley's position. He checked his revolver, spun the cylinder and flicked it back into place. He knew it was loaded. He knew it would work. But he always became obsessive-compulsive about checking his weapon when he knew a shootout was coming.

"Sir?" said a young officer. He pointed down the street. "Here they come."

Plumley heard them before he saw them, the clattering and clicking of thousands of bones. Neon signs for storefronts buzzed and flickered. There. Dozens of pairs of witch fire seeming to hover in the distance. As they came closer, Plumley could make out the skeleton army. Some had picked up boards, pipes, and whatever other makeshift weapons they could find.

"Alright, listen up," Plumley said. The officers gathered around. "I'm not going to lie to you: we're outnumbered. But they're walking right through a bottleneck into the Plaza here. I don't know when more ammo is coming, or if it's coming at all, so make every shot count. Headshots only. If it comes to it, go hand to hand. The people are counting on us. Let's do this."

The officers took their positions. A few had shotguns, but most were armed with revolvers. Sweat trickled on their brows. They prayed that word of mouth would reach officers stationed elsewhere in the city in time about their stand in Canyon Plaza.

Plumley thumbed the hammer of his pistol. There. The first skeleton appeared, a vanguard for his undead comrades. Plumley aimed and fired. The skeleton's skull exploded into a cloud of bone fragment and dust, the body clattering to the ground in a pile of bones.

Another came, and an officer shot it down. Then three more. Then five.

"Fire at will!" Plumley shouted.

The Plaza erupted with the cracks and rattles of gunfire. The skeletons kept coming, pushing through the rapidly accumulating pile of bones from their fallen comrades. Officers called out when they needed to reload. Every time they did, the gunfire slackened, giving the skeletons more time to funnel into the plaza.

Plumley fired six times, dropping a skeleton with each shot. They were getting closer.

"Reloading!" he screamed. His fellow officers gave him what cover they could, but they too needed to drop down to reload. The skeletons grew closer, silent as the grave but for the clicking of their joints. If he survived this, Plumley planned to have a long talk with the mayor about purchasing more autoloading pistols for the police force.

A rookie officer fumbled his ammunition trying to reload his revolver. A skeleton grabbed his wrist. The kid screamed. Plumley winced. He could hear the kid's wrist bones cracking. The skeleton flung the officer into the advancing horde. Other skeletons set upon the boy and ripped him into bloody chunks, his screams degenerating into wet gargles before falling silent.

"Shit," Plumley said. He finished reloading, thumbed the hammer back. The skeletons were on top of them now. One officer managed to blow two of them back into hell with his shotgun. His weapon now empty, the cop swung it like a club, shattering more skulls, but the numbers told, and he too disappeared in a mass of rending claws, clicking bones, and bloody spray.

"Chief!" cried another officer. Plumley looked around. The surviving officers were walking backwards, making a fighting withdrawal.

"Fall back!" Plumley called. They'd made a significant dent in the oncoming tide of bloodthirsty undead, but still they kept coming. Plumley tried to think. There had to be other bottlenecks where they could set up more ambushes.

"Begone, foul monsters! Your judgment is at hand!"

Every cop simultaneously turned to stare at the source of that archaic language. On the opposite side of the plaza they saw a tall man dressed in black, made even taller by his wide brimmed hat. His face was all sharp angles, his icy blue eyes ablaze with hatred.

In one hand he held a sword that glowed with white light. In the other, a small autoloading pistol. The man strode forth into the Plaza.

"Stand fast!" he yelled to the officers. "God is with us!" The cops stood frozen in indecision.

Plumley was just about to ask just who in the hell this guy thought he was, when a Hispanic man with a bolt action rifle and a Hispanic woman with an autoloader came sprinting after the man in black, bellowing inarticulate battle cries.

Then the flood came. More cries, yelling, shouting, a stampede of townsfolk, some with guns, others with two by fours, more with empty bottles, all eager to do their part against the forces of darkness.

"Show no mercy to these unholy wretches!" the man in black yelled. "Smash their skulls to splinters! Charge!" He broke into a run, leading the makeshift army toward the on-coming horde of undead, waving his sword in circles about his head.

"Chief?"

Plumley looked at his officers. He pursed his lips.

"You heard the man!" he called. "Charge!"

Plumley and what was left of his police force fell in with the advancing tide of humanity.

13

Lilian paced back and forth. Timothy still hadn't risen from the floor, or even looked at her. Where to begin? May as well start at the beginning.

"I'm much older than I look Timothy," Lilian said. "I was born Lilith Harkmoore in the year 2030, in a city called Washington, D.C. It doesn't exist anymore, but it was located in what's now the country of Columbia. I was there, Timothy. I was there when Simon Magus appeared before the world."

Timothy said nothing.

Lilian pressed on. "Oh, it was incredible. Even now, centuries later, I can still remember how it was that day. You and everyone else here grew up in a world where you take magic and monsters and all manner of otherworldly things for granted. When I was a child, things like sorcerers, vampires, ghosts, and all the rest were works of fiction. Myths. Folklore. They didn't exist! And one day, one glorious day, the Great Magician proved beyond a reasonable doubt that they were with us the whole time. I was 25 when Simon Magus revealed himself. I was a medical student, if you can believe it."

Timothy said nothing.

"The churches would all tell you that he was a monster who sought only to destroy God's creation and remake the cosmos in his own image. But they're wrong Timothy! That wasn't his goal at all. Simon Magus came to teach us, to help us relearn that which God took from us, to return us to our true home."

Timothy looked up. His eyes were red and puffy from his quiet weeping.

"What are you talking about?" he asked.

Lilian felt something close to joy. She got down on her knees to be level with her husband, to look him in the eyes.

"Magic, Timothy!" she said. "God forbade us to know and to use magic because He was jealous of us! He made us in His own image and likeness, the churches say. God knew that we could be like Him in glory and power. We could gain the power of creation! We could bend the laws of reality with our wills!"

"You said our true home?"

Lilian scoffed. "The holy men say Heaven is our true home, that Magus wanted to conquer it and take God's place. But no, my master didn't aspire quite that high. God banished our parents from Eden. And for what? Because Adam and Eve wanted knowledge? Because they weren't content to live in ignorance? Because they dared to aspire to something greater, God banished them. And with that banishment came labor. Toil. Sickness. Death."

Timothy said nothing.

"'Original Sin' the holy men call it. I ask you, where is the justice in condemning us for something we didn't do? For a choice that was made before any of us were even born?"

Timothy said nothing.

"God exists, but He is an absentee landlord. They say He loves us. But how can He love us and allow us to live in a world like this, with pain, and misery, and suffering? I saw, Timothy. When I studied medicine, I saw children wither away from cancer. I saw parents pray for a miracle, and their prayers go unanswered. And they expect us to worship such a God? No. If He were to appear before us right now, I would spit in His face."

Timothy's jaw dropped.

"My master is gone, but he himself taught me my craft. It was he who taught me the power of life and death."

"How are you... still alive?" Timothy stammered.

Lilian giggled. "How indeed? I gave serious thought to becoming a vampire, you know. They're superior to us in many ways. But I decided against it. I couldn't bear the thought of never seeing another sunrise, nor giving up the taste of good food and good drink. We wouldn't have been able to have our lovely wedding in broad daylight, would we?"

Lilian smiled but Timothy remained silent.

"My master taught us the recipe to a special elixir. One that can extend one's life indefinitely. I only wish I'd learned it sooner. I'm forever 29 now."

"This elixir..."

"I have some right here," she said, pointing at a rack of vials on a shelf. "Darien helped me acquire the ingredients over the years."

"Darien...?"

"He's gone, alas," Lilian said. "But he brought me mercenaries, bounty hunters, outlaws, and other vermin who contributed to the great work."

"What are you...?"

"Human cerebrospinal fluid is a necessary ingredient," Lilian said. "The extraction is always fatal, but they died for a good cause."

"Darien... you... killed...?"

Lilian waved off Timothy's question. "No one will miss them. I doubt anyone ever learned that they were gone. They were useless in life, but they serve a greater purpose in death."

Timothy swallowed. "What is this... work, this purpose?"

"Simon Magus is gone, but we his students remain. We continue his work. One day we shall reclaim our birthright. We shall live in Eden once more. Pain and sickness and death will be no more."

"But... you're killing people."

Lilian frowned and shook her head. "Too many still cling to the old ways. Too many still believe that if they obey the laws of a cruel and absent God, He'll reward them with an eternity in Heaven. Bah! I would sooner go down into Hell then spend one second with that heartless God. It is regrettable that so many choose to remain blind, but if they are not with us, they are against us. If they choose to live as cattle, then that is how we shall treat them, as fit only for the slaughter."

Timothy looked at her. "Is that how you see me? As cattle?"

A flicker of hurt passed over Lilian's face. "Oh Timothy,"

she said. "I've kept so much from you, but my feelings for you are real. Please believe me."

"Your feelings," Timothy said. "Do you love me? Did you ever love me?"

Lilian sighed. "Please understand Timothy... I'm not sure if I'm capable of the kind of love you're thinking of. I... I think you're a good man. I've come to trust you, admire you, even. I want to love you the way you want to be loved. I just... I'm not sure I can really do it."

"Why am I still alive then?"

Lilian paced again. She wasn't accustomed to feeling... was it anxiety? She said, "I've lived a long time, but I haven't had as many husbands as you might think. You are the first man I've consented to wed, to live with, in centuries. And I've grown... attached to this life. To you. I want to offer you something."

Timothy said nothing.

"I took Darien on as a student, but he could never have been my equal. I see that you could be. Timothy... I'd like you to come with me. I can't live here anymore, not after what I've done tonight. But I... leaving you is... the thought is difficult."

"Come with you?"

She faced him, a smile lighting up her face. "Yes! I've lived alone for much of my life. But you have potential Timothy! I've made enough elixir to last me long enough to settle elsewhere. But I hope that you would settle with me. I can teach you what my master taught me. We can live forever, we can continue his great work! We can enter Eden together!"

Timothy rose to his feet, swaying, unsteady. He leaned against the wall.

"This is..." he said. "This is so much to take in."

Lilian rushed forward and embraced him, nuzzling her head against his chest.

"Oh darling, I know it is. I know it is."

"What happens if I...?

Lilian's eyes snapped open. She growled low in her throat.

"Lilian?"

"Timothy dear," she said, "You don't have to make a decision right now, but you should decide quickly. My children have found my enemy."

14

Silas Flint cleaved a skull in two. With his off hand, he fired his pistol at point blank range, exploding the skeletal face into dust and fragments. He dodged, whirled, sliced, and shot his way through the wall of bone, opening up a wedge in the undead forces for the townsfolk and police officers to plow through the undead warriors.

The pistol slide locked open. He clubbed a skeleton with the empty gun and called to Navarro, "Reload!"

Navarro tossed Flint a new magazine. Flint slammed it home, thumbed the slide release, and shot down another skeleton. Navarro fired his rifle, worked the bolt, fired again, the high powered rifle rounds tearing through several skeletons at once. He had apparently made a lady friend on their way here, for Flint saw an attractive young woman close by Navarro's side, a crowbar in one hand, a pistol in the other.

"Press on!" Flint yelled. "These dusty bone walkers shall not stand in our path! Praise Jesus!"

Flint didn't believe these automatons were capable of human feelings, but otherwise he would have sworn that the ferocity of the townsfolks' counterattack had caught them by surprise. These creatures had preternatural strength despite their frail appearance. The corpses of police officers littered the ground. Occasionally the skeletons would bring a citizen down to the ground and tear him to bloody shreds. Others would tear hearts from their living opponents, or rip their heads from their shoulders.

A few civilians decided that discretion was the better part of valor and fled upon seeing their neighbors die in such gruesome ways. But to Flint's grim satisfaction more stayed in the fight. New civilians, hearing that a great battle was underway, made their way to the sound of gunfire. They brought whatever weapons they could find, whether ancient firearms that had been passed down for generations, or empty alcohol bottles, or any blunt instrument to send these abominations back to hell.

Navarro's rifle was empty. A skeleton was nearly upon him. He slung it and drew the tomahawk and pistol that hung from his belt. He brought the tomahawk down hard on the skull, shattering it, extinguishing the unholy fires in its eye sockets. He fired two shots, bringing down more of their undead opponents.

"Reload your rifle, Ricardo!" Flint yelled over the din. "I shall cover you!"

Navarro holstered his sidearms, and with the speed that came from long practice, he loaded five rounds into his rifle and slammed the bolt home.

"Much obliged sir!" he shouted.

They stood back to back, shooting, slashing, swinging, and smashing skeletons to bits.

"I see that you have made a new acquaintance," Flint shouted.

"Yes sir! That's Maria! I met her at the bar, before I joined you at the Inn!" Maria was fighting alongside a police officer and the innkeeper, John Dooley. She had apparently run out of ammunition for her 9mm for she was now firing a police-issued revolver. "We were saying on our way here that this is one hell of a first date!"

Flint slashed with his sword, cutting the heads off two skeletons who were nearly on top of him. "I am glad that you are changing your ways Ricardo. When this is over, I shall make the arrangements for a priest to properly marry you two."

Navarro jammed the butt of his rifle into a skeletal face, knocking it from its shoulders. "I don't know about that sir, we just met!"

Flint shot a skeleton down. "Nonsense, marriage would do you good Mr. Navarro, it would be better for your soul than your fornicating ways! Reload!"

Without looking, Navarro reached into a pouch on his belt and handed off a fresh magazine to Flint. "Besides sir," he shouted, "We're leaving town once this is over!"

Flint sliced the top of a skull from its body, the bones clattering to the ground. "I suspect we may be here a while yet Mr. Navarro!"

Together, the witch hunter and his assistant continued to strike their enemies down. Occasionally a civilian fell, but the tide of undead was slowing to a trickle. A police officer smashed the butt of his revolver into a skull, the skeleton collapsing. The clatter of bones stopped. The Plaza fell quiet but for the distant echoes of music. Flint was about to wonder aloud at these people's commitment to celebration even in the midst of a crisis when it occurred to him that the humans were alone. The skeletons had all been put down. It was over.

Everyone looked at their handiwork in quiet awe. Then the cheers began. Civilians embraced police officers, they clapped, and laughed, and some even showboated, dancing in the Plaza, kicking bones out of their way. Flint kept quiet. Yes, they had won, but tonight's work was far from over.

A police officer in full dress blues made his way toward Flint. He extended his hand.

"Joseph Plumley, chief of the Canyon Cove Police Department."

Flint shook the proffered hand. "Captain Silas Flint, Knight Templar of the Order of Saint Benedict."

"I don't know what brought you to our city, Captain, but I've never been so happy to see a witch hunter. You saved all of our asses."

"Give thanks and glory to God alone," Flint said.

"Right. You have any idea what's going on?"

"I was about to ask you the same thing, Chief Plumley. Judging by your dress, I would surmise that you were attending a formal function."

"Yeah," Plumley said. "The Mayor and I were attending a party at the Turner mansion when…"

Flint grabbed him by the shoulders. "The Turner mansion you say?! What happened there?!"

Plumley shrugged out of Flint's grip. "Mr. Turner was just

about to give his big speech for today when one of the guests noticed this... this mob of, uh, skeletons. The guests panicked and ran. Last I saw, the Mayor was trying to get Turner to follow us, but he said he had to find his wife Lilian first."

"Lilian Turner," Flint said through gritted teeth, his fists balled at his side.

"You got a problem with her?" Plumley asked.

"I daresay she is the problem, Chief. My assistant and I were accosted by one Darien Erhardt earlier tonight. He had been possessed by a demon, who admitted under questioning that he pursued us on Lilian Turner's orders."

"What?!"

"Further, she is responsible for a series of disappearances that have plagued the inns of your city for the last twenty years, though I know not her reasons just yet."

"Disappearances?" Plumley asked. "What are you... wait." He wracked his memory. "You mean to tell me Turner was kidnapping them this whole time?"

"I do not know the details, but I plan to question her most thoroughly."

"But... how? I remember that some inn keepers and motel managers came to us claiming guests disappeared, but there was never any evidence of foul play."

"As for the how of it," Flint said, "It's simple. Lilian Turner is a witch."

Plumley's mouth dropped. "Jesus Christ," he said.

Flint glared at him.

"Oh, uh, sorry. But if she's a witch... suddenly a lot of shit makes more sense. I always felt like there was something off about her."

"In any case, witchcraft and crimes against God fall under the jurisdiction of myself and my order. Rest assured, I plan to solve these mysteries and bring her to…"

"Uh, Silas?" Navarro said, tapping Flint on the shoulder.

"What is it, Ricardo?"

"Listen."

Flint heard nothing. Wait… there. It was faint at first, but now he felt it too. A rhythmic booming, like a giant drum. The ground shook. Flint's makeshift militia noticed it too. They looked around, bewildered. Flint thought he heard screaming the distance as well.

A gargling howl split the night sky. It sounded almost human, but no human vocal cords could project such volume. Now Flint heard the screams more clearly. They were born of terror, of sheer unthinking panic. Then he saw the source of their terror.

It was a man, or at least it had the shape of a man, that was at least three stories tall. And it was moving toward them. Its steps caused the shaking to grow worse. Townsfolk unlucky enough to be caught in its path were crushed underfoot, their cries cut off in a nauseating squelch. Some brave souls fired at it with whatever guns they could find, but the creature grabbed them from the rooftops and devoured them, its long fangs chewing them into a bloody pulp. The creature cried out again. Like the skeletons, its eye sockets were empty but for balls of witch fire. It had two slits where a nose would be, and two holes where a man would have ears.

The citizens and police in the Plaza stared, struck dumb with fright. Chief Plumley only squeaked. Maria backed up until she had found Navarro and held his hand.

"Boss?" Navarro whispered.

For one of the few times in his life, Flint was at a loss for words. The creature's progress was slow, frequently stopping to smash buildings or devour civilians, but there was no mistaking that it was headed in their direction. The creature screamed and brought both fists down upon the roof of a building, smashing it into rubble down to its foundations.

"Oh shit," said Navarro.

"Oh dear," said Flint.

The giant didn't have eyes, but Flint felt that it made eye contact with him when it rose from its latest fit of destruction. It picked up its pace, great loping strides that caused the earth to tremble and windows to rattle.

"Boss... what do we do?" Navarro asked.

"Run!" Flint cried.

15

Lilian Turner smiled. She had sensed that her skeleton warriors had all been wiped out, but she could see with her own eyes that her flesh golem was wreaking havoc throughout the city. She and Timothy stood atop the staircase in what was left of the foyer, the giant having torn through the façade of the Turner mansion in its birth pangs.

Timothy silently gazed at what his wife had wrought. Lilian couldn't sense his thoughts or feelings. That was one of the things that had impressed her about Timothy: the man was extraordinarily disciplined in all areas of life.

"You made that thing?" he asked.

"Yes," Lilian replied. "It's a simple creature, crafted from the skins of hundreds of men and women over the years. I shaped and molded its body, and then I gave it the spark of life."

"Why? Why are you doing this?"

Lilian scowled. "There is a witch hunter on his way here. Or rather, he was on his way here," she laughed.

"How did he...?"

"It doesn't matter anymore. What matters is that if he finds me, he will arrest me. I'll be tortured, put on trial in some kangaroo court, and burned at the stake."

Timothy said nothing.

"That is a fact of life if you choose to join me, Timothy. Constantly hunted by lesser beings with primitive minds too dull to use the great gifts bestowed on humanity by the Great Magician."

"But all of those innocent people! That thing is killing them!"

"Anyone who dies, it is their own fault. I gave my golem a simple command: kill the witch hunter and anyone who tries to stop it. If the people stay out of its way, it won't follow them."

Timothy said nothing. Normally she admired his discipline, but right now it bothered her that she could not sense his emotions or his thoughts.

"As soon as the creature kills the witch hunter, the spell giving it life and purpose will dissipate, and it will collapse from its own weight," Lilian said. "When you think about it, what happens now is the witch hunter's fault. If he'd just be a good boy and die, fewer people would get hurt."

Timothy said nothing. He looked at his wife. Then he

walked down the hallway, back toward her office and inner sanctum. Lilian followed.

"I know it sounds harsh darling," Lilian said. "But it's a mercy, really. These people choose to live lives of meaningless toil, barely earning enough to feed their families. Whatever money is left over, they spend it on cheap alcohol to temporarily dull the pain of knowing that their lives are bereft of all meaning and purpose."

Timothy stopped. "Who are you to judge meaning or purpose?"

"Who am I? I'm a goddess among mortals. I work for the greatest purpose of all. I work to spread the teachings of my master. I work to take back the home God unjustly took from us. Back then, during the war, my colleagues numbered in the millions. All of us, able to shape reality according to our wills! I survived the war because my life has meaning, has purpose."

Timothy said nothing.

"Don't get me wrong Timothy. You've built up a powerful business empire from nothing. I was here, in Canyon Cove, when you left home as just a boy, determined to make something better of yourself. And you succeeded with nothing more than your wits, your determination, your strength of character!"

Lilian approached him and put her hands on his shoulders. "You are precisely the kind of man Simon Magus sought out. You are the kind of man he would have taken as an apprentice. I'm not as good a teacher as he was, but there is still so much I can show you. So much we can do together."

Timothy faced her. "At what cost though?"

Lilian shrugged. "I admit that magic and the elixir of life

have... side effects. But they are small prices to pay for eternal life. I would endure them a thousand times all over again for the power I've gained. The power to chart my own destiny. That's what I'm offering you husband. Together, we can see Magus's project through to the end. People will die along the way, but what are their lives compared to humanity's return to Eden?"

Timothy walked a few steps, hands held behind his back. Lilian hung in anticipation. She couldn't sense his thoughts, but she did sense that they had reached the tipping point, one way or another.

Timothy took a deep breath. Exhaled. He turned to face her. She could see that determined look he sometimes had, that made her black heart feel almost warm again.

"What must I do?" he asked.

16

Silas Flint sprinted through streets and alleys, Navarro, Maria, and Plumley close on his heels. His militia had scattered in every direction, fleeing for their lives. The creature was in no great hurry it seemed, for they managed to put a good distance between them. They took shelter inside a bar. The place was deserted. The party was finally over.

"What... what... what is that thing?" Maria panted, out of breath.

"It's... a golem," Flint replied. "It's a simple-minded creature with hell-fire flowing in its veins."

"How do we stop it?" Plumley asked.

"I do not suppose your police force has heavy artillery?" Flint said.

"No. We can't even afford to give everyone radios."

"Hey," Navarro said. "Chief, does the force have automobiles? I haven't seen any since Silas and I got here."

"We have a few," Plumley said. "Gasoline is so expensive and hard to come by out here, we only use them for emergencies."

Maria laughed. "I'd say this qualifies as an emergency."

Plumley looked at them. "I'm sorry, you two are...?"

"I'm Ricardo Navarro, Captain Flint's assistant."

"Maria Lopez."

Plumley nodded. "Like I said, we only have a few gas operated vehicles in the city, some squad cars, a firetruck, and a few ambulances. Everything else is bicycles, horses, and carriages."

"Do you have a radio on your person, Chief?" Flint asked.

"Yes."

"Do the autos all have radios?" Navarro said.

"Yes... what are you two getting at?"

Maria's eyes widened. "No."

Navarro grinned. "Yes."

"Would one of you please explain what's going on here?"

"Chief," Flint said. "My assistant and I make our living exterminating the forces of darkness wherever they show their unholy faces. I tell you plainly, we do not currently have the means to fight this golem. Small arms are of no avail. We have a chance to bring down the monster, but we will require the aid of the city."

Plumley nodded. "Just tell me what you need."

"We shall need every automobile that you can find, your entire reserve supply of gasoline... and as many bottles of liquor as we can carry."

"What are you... oh."

"Indeed," said Flint.

17

Navarro drove a police cruiser through the city streets, with Flint riding shotgun. The golem was a few blocks away, slamming into buildings, sounding its mournful cries that made the flesh crawl.

"I never thought I'd get to pilot an automobile ever again," Navarro said.

"As I recall you were fortunate to have survived your last encounter," Silas said. "There really ought to be laws against driving while intoxicated. However, I will admit that these vehicles are most useful, as far as pre-war technology goes. I've read that they were once so commonplace that every family in North America owned one."

"And now we're taking away the few that this city has."

"It is regrettable, Mr. Navarro, but I fear it is the only way to stop this rampaging monster."

"And if it don't, sir?"

"It will work. There is an old saying among the Knights Templar: 'when all else fails, kill it with fire.'"

The two companions fell silent. The police cruiser hummed along, the radio crackling with transmissions, officers asking each other if they were ready. Plumley had had every gasoline vehicle in the city converge on the bar where

Flint's party had taken refuge. Now it was a matter of luring the creature into their trap. Flint suspected that the witch had summoned it to kill him specifically with no regard to civilians caught in its path. If that was the case, then Flint himself would make irresistible bait for the golem. If not... well, God would provide.

Navarro's new lady friend had requested to ride along with them. An automobile trip was a rare luxury on most of the continent. But no, that wasn't the whole of it. Flint could see that she liked Navarro. He gave a grim smile. Shared hardship was by far the most efficient way to create an emotional bond.

"Something on your mind, sir?" Navarro asked.

"No, it is nothing," Flint said. "Stop here."

The cruiser stopped. Navarro put it in park and left the engine running. They got out. The flesh golem was a few blocks down the street. Citizens fled from its path, a stream of humanity flowing around the two men.

"Are you ready, Mr. Navarro?"

"As ready as I'll ever be sir." He unslung his rifle from his shoulder. "Sir, if this don't work, it's been an honor."

"It will work Ricardo. But I feel the same. You may fire when ready."

Navarro shouldered his rifle. He centered the creature's head in the iron sights. Flint could hear him controlling his breath. He pulled the trigger. The rifle cracked. He worked the bolt, expelling the shell casing.

The flesh golem froze. Flint couldn't tell if Navarro had hit his mark, but that was not as important as gaining the monster's attention. It craned its head in their direction. It sniffed with those two horrible slits that served as its nose. The witch fire in its eye sockets locked onto their position. The monster made that hideous ululating cry. It stepped toward them once. Then again. It gained speed.

"Excellent shot, Mr. Navarro. Now get us out of here, if you please," Flint said, opening the passenger door of the police car and taking his seat. Navarro scrambled into the driver's seat, balancing his rifle on the center console. The flesh golem was moving at greater speed now, having sighted its quarry.

The tires squealed and smoked as Navarro twisted the wheel into a U turn and sped away from the giant. The ground shook with its monstrous tread. Navarro kept his arms tight on the wheel. The car swerved and bounced. The giant was now in a full run. A creature of that size should have shaken itself to pieces at that speed, but the dark magic fueling its life held it together. Flint glanced at the passenger side mirror. Faded lettering read, "Objects in mirror may be closer than they appear." Flint barked a laugh. The golem must have been close indeed.

Navarro rounded a corner. Several blocks ahead lay their trap. Every gasoline powered vehicle that Plumley could command or commandeer was parked there, blocking the street. He pressed down on the accelerator to put more distance between them and the oncoming giant.

"Remember Ricardo, tuck and roll," Flint said.

"God…" Navarro whispered.

"He shall protect us."

The creature increased its pace to keep up with the police

cruiser, but the automobile was pulling away. The wall of cars was growing larger.

"Steady," Flint said.

The giant howled in fury, determined to catch its prey.

"Steady," Flint said. Navarro squinted through the sweat dripping into his eyes.

The golem was nearly on top of them. The roadblock was coming up fast.

"Now!"

Flint and Navarro opened the doors and flung themselves away from the vehicle. Flint grunted as he hit the pavement. He felt the burning and tearing of the asphalt through his long coat. He kept his head tucked toward his chest and rolled with the impact as best he could. Flint crashed into garbage cans in an alleyway, knocking the wind from him. Dazed, he pushed himself up into a seated position. Citizens who had been watching from indoors rushed out to check on him, pulling him to his feet. Flint staggered. He touched the back of his neck and felt wetness, the raw skin bleeding. Looking across the street he saw that Navarro was also being pulled to his feet. Flint smiled. He didn't think Navarro could do it, but the man had saved his rifle. Flint's hat, however, got lost somewhere in the tumbling.

The now driverless police cruiser kept going, losing speed but still fast enough to stay out of reach of the creature. Flint didn't know if it had seen them bail out, but he didn't think it would matter. It was a magical construct born from the fires of hell, but even it was still subject to the laws of physics. It would not be able to shift momentum in time.

The police car crashed into the roadblock, its hood crumpling. Onward came the flesh golem, screaming in fury, howling for blood. It made a beeline toward the assembled vehicles, so focused on its prey that it failed to notice it was splashing through puddles of gasoline and alcohol. Flint held his breath, ignoring the welts, cuts, and bruises on his battered body. The creature was nearly upon the pile up of vehicles. It was out of his hands.

Flint saw Maria hiding in the alley across from the roadblock. He prayed that she made it through the next step.

She held a glass bottle filled with gasoline. Stuffed inside was an alcohol soaked rag. When the monster got close enough, she lit the rag which caught fire immediately. She hurled it at the monster.

The bottle shattered. Flames ignited at the golem's feet. It howled again, this time in pain. Flint winced. The sound made him feel unclean. Maria threw another bottle of alcohol. Plumley and several police officers followed her example, throwing more flaming bottles toward the monster. They shattered, ignited, fed the flames ever higher.

Ah, there it is. Flint picked up his hat from the ground. Navarro made his way across the street, his face sporting cuts and bruises.

"Are you alright sir?" he asked.

"I am a little worse for wear, but otherwise unharmed. That was excellent driving Mr. Navarro."

"Thank you sir."

"It would have been safer to have left your rifle in the back seat, you know."

"To hell with that sir, I've been through a lot with this thing."

Flint smiled. "Indeed, you have."

"Can I offer you a bottle of whiskey?" Navarro proffered the open bottle, along with a rag.

Flint took them. "Remind me to recommend you for a raise when we reach Fort Marsing."

The two advanced toward the shrieking golem, whose legs were now engulfed in flames up to its knees. The stench of its burning, corrupted flesh caused their eyes to water. Maria, Plumley, and the other police officers came running in the opposite direction. She embraced Navarro, laughing, and kissed him. Navarro froze at first, but then returned the embrace and kissed her back.

"I can't believe that worked!" Maria said.

"It is not over yet, Miss Lopez. A lighter, if you please," said Flint. Maria handed him a lighter. Flint stuffed the rag into the bottle of whiskey, ignited it, and threw the bottle. It shattered in a pool of gasoline at end of the block, cutting off the flesh golem's avenue of retreat. Surrounded by flames, the monster staggered back and forth, its burning legs making it roar, and howl, and whimper.

The creature lost its balance and fell backwards onto the lined up automobiles. The crumple of metal, the shattering of glass, the frantic cries of the beast, the stench of gasoline and burning flesh... Flint wondered if this is what Hell was like. The creature thrashed, and in its agony, its arms swept out and destroyed the surrounding buildings, razing them to their foundations. It tried to rise, but the fuel tanks of the destroyed automobiles ignited with a loud whoomph.

The flesh golem was now ablaze from head to toe. Acrid smoke made them all cough. A few onlookers vomited from the stench. Flint kept his eyes on the creature. It attempted to rise, but the flames had eaten away at its legs. It crashed to the ground. Its howls of agony tampered down to a whimper. Its thrashing slowed. The ground shook with its death throes. At last, the monster lay still and quiet. All was silent but for the crackling of putrid burning flesh.

Plumley came to Flint's side. He shielded his eyes from the glare of the towering inferno, coughed into his fist. His eyes watered.

"Is it dead?" he asked.

Flint squinted at the burning carcass, scanning for any signs of life. Seeing none, he said to the Chief, "Yes. I believe we have put the monster down."

Plumley exhaled. A crowd of gawkers soon formed behind Flint's party. There were no cheers this time, no clapping, no exuberance. Everyone gazed in horror at the destruction wrought by the beast. Most of a city block in rubble or in flames. The few automobiles owned by the city gone up in flames. Several tons worth of charred, gooey flesh.

Maria held on to Navarro. "God," she said. "What a way to go."

"You feel sorry for it?" he asked.

"No, no… I just don't like seeing anything suffer."

"Suffer," said Flint. "Suffer? Yes, the creature suffered. And there is much more suffering to come." His fists were balled.

He turned to the crowd. Raising his voice, he yelled, "You see the wages of evil. The witch crafted this golem from human flesh and let it loose upon your city. She let it loose this night! Victory against Magus Day! The day of humanity's greatest triumph, soiled by her foul sorcery!"

The crowd was silent.

"These outrages against the laws of God and nature will never stop so long as that witch draws breath!" He paced back and forth. "Many of you accompanied me into battle with her skeleton army. You have gone above and beyond the call of Christian duty! I cannot ask more of you. My assistant and I must now make haste to the Turner mansion. The golem's fate awaits Mrs. Turner. For the crime of witchcraft, for the crime of murder, I swear before Almighty God and all of the angels and saints that Lilian Turner will burn!"

Flint marched. The crowd parted, making way for the grim witch hunter. He heard Navarro's footsteps rushing to catch up, as he knew he would. Eyes straight ahead, Flint pressed on. Mr. Dooley had given them directions. Their mad dash away from the golem had taken them far afield, but Flint's sense of direction was true. He knew the way to tonight's final confrontation.

"Sir?" Navarro said.

"What is it?"

"Look behind us."

Without breaking his stride, Flint looked over his shoulder. Plumley and Maria were several paces behind them, following. They were accompanied by uniformed police officers, and countless townsfolk. Flint's energy had infected them in the fight against the skeletons. Now, however, their features were as set as the witch hunter's. Lilian Turner had unleashed hell on their city, on their homes. Friends and neighbors had died at the hands of her creations. Flint and

Navarro were professionals. These people went forth on a burning personal grudge.

Flint set his face forward again. He'd never met Lilian Turner, but he too held a grudge against her and all of her kind. Flint knew that his was the kind of grudge that could never be settled in this life. But he'd pledged his life to do all within his power to put down the threat of magic, that power that had caused so much death and destruction over the last four and a half centuries. In his mind, he recited prayers, asked the Holy Spirit to guide him and Saint Benedict to protect him. By sunrise, either he would be dead, or Turner would be. Flint wasn't afraid to die, but he intended to make sure that it was Turner who left the mortal coil.

18

Lilian whispered a spell and a bolt of energy shot from her fingertip to her rolling suitcase. It glowed for a second and was still.

"What was that?" Timothy asked.

Lilian laughed. "Oh, just a little something I like to use when I'm in a hurry. Watch."

She unzipped it, revealing a black hole within. She grabbed books from a shelf inside her secret chamber and dropped them into the suitcase. The books disappeared, falling into the hole and out of sight.

Timothy gaped. "Where did they go?"

"Inside a pocket dimension of my own design. I could fit an entire household's worth of goods in here."

"But how do you find them again?"

"It just takes the right spell and sufficient willpower. I can show you how later."

Timothy smiled weakly. "I'm, ah, going to get some air. I guess the foyer is the front porch now, huh?"

"Of course, dear. I shouldn't be long."

Earlier Lilian had sensed that her flesh golem was gone. The magic holding it together dissipated, meaning it had fulfilled its purpose. The witch hunter Silas Flint was dead. She did sense, however, that a crowd was moving toward the ruins of Timothy's mansion. The damned witch hunter must have spread the word that she was responsible for tonight's happenings.

It would have been easy enough to frighten them off or kill them all, but she had Timothy to think about. He had tentatively agreed to go with her, but she could tell that he didn't have the stomach for wanton slaughter just yet. That was fine. She would play along for now. The citizenry would arrive, find the front of the mansion destroyed, herself and Timothy nowhere to be found. She doubted any of them had the stomach to follow them into the wilderness. There were countless abandoned structures in the Deadlands to the far east. She would lead Timothy there. That cursed place was rife with magical energy, with plenty of the walking dead to practice on. She could give Timothy the proper tutelage he needed, not rushed and furtive like the lessons she'd given Darien.

Lilian smiled. She hadn't felt this hopeful about the future in a long time. Timothy deserved to be a living god. Together, they would make the lambs pay for their crimes against progress. Together, they could build a haven for magic users on this continent. Eventually, they would have the power to bring the gates to Eden back onto this plane of existence. They would annihilate the angel who guarded that gate, and humanity would reenter paradise.

She dropped her stockpile of elixir into the suitcase. She was going to miss living in luxury. Perhaps some time in the wilderness would do her good. One needed to keep one's senses sharp. It was easy to fall into lethargy after centuries of life.

The candles surrounding the circle she had made earlier that night flickered to life. Lilian felt a gust of icy wind. The familiar column of light rose from the circle again. Robin Redcap had returned.

"Leaving so soon?" he purred.

"Yes. My work here is finished. There's nothing more to do but take Timothy and go."

"So sweet," the demon hissed. "Lilith has found true love." It laughed. "Surely you don't believe you can turn him? What would he say if he knew you were consorting with my kind?"

Lilian glared at the three eyed demon. "He will learn to accept it in time. He's agreed to come with me, you know."

"Has he? Perhaps one day I can have him too."

"You will not touch him!" Lilian shrieked. A bolt of lightning shot from her fingertip, striking Robin Redcap in its chest. The demon grunted.

"A sensitive topic, I see. Good," it said.

"Why have you returned? I have no further need of you tonight."

"Oh, but you're wrong Lilith. Your little flesh golem has fallen."

"Yes, I know."

"But you don't know why. Silas Flint lives. It was he who destroyed it."

Lilian stopped. Sighed. Of course he destroyed it.

"I begin to understand why the powers below have taken an interest in him," she said.

Redcap chuckled. "That is why I have returned."

"I do not consent for you to enter my soul. You will not have Timothy."

"Yes, yes, I know my fun in the mortal world is over for tonight. There is another way that I can assist you though. Are you not the least bit curious why we hate him so, what distinguishes him from other members of his pitiful little Order?"

"You mentioned earlier that he had foiled some scheme of yours."

"Yes. And in so doing, he demonstrated an uncommon strength of character. But he damaged himself too. Oh yes, he scarred himself forever. Silas Flint is strong, but he is also brittle. His hatred of us is powerful. With the right twist of the knife, that hatred can be directed inward, toward himself. If you hope to defeat him, you must break his spirit first."

Lilian scoffed. "I hardly think one witch hunter is capable of beating me by himself. I could call down lightning from the heavens and burn him to cinders."

The demon laughed. "Try it then. See what happens."

Lilian frowned. What was the demon's game here?

"The enemy has plans for Silas Flint," Redcap said. "We do not know what they are, but it would seem Heaven is playing favorites. If you attack him head on, you will surely fail, and find yourself tied to a stake by sunrise. I'm offering you a way to catch him unawares, to penetrate that shield of faith, to break him before you kill him."

"What's in it for you? You're not offering me your help out of the goodness of your heart."

"If he dies in despair, we can drag his soul into hell where he can pay for what he's done."

Lilian thought for a few moments. She looked into Redcap's three burning eyes. "Very well. Tell me about Silas Flint."

19

Word spread. All of Canyon Cove now knew the truth: Lilian Turner, wife to the city's wealthiest citizen, was a witch. Some chose to remain indoors and pray for the best. More came pouring out of their homes, their businesses, carrying whatever weapons they could find. It wasn't difficult to find the ever-growing army that silently marched after Silas Flint and Ricardo Navarro.

Flint said nothing. He was battered and bruised and wanted nothing more than to fall into a warm bed, but his resolve pushed him ever onward. It occurred to him that he was leading a proverbial torch bearing mob. He was both pleased and worried for them. Lilian Turner had to be a woman of singular power for her to raise so many undead, and craft that hideous golem out of human skin and flesh. He couldn't guarantee these people's safety if she chose to resist, which she surely would. Flint prayed that he could subdue his opponent with minimal casualties.

"We're getting close, sir," said Navarro from his place at Flint's side.

The trading barons lived in a neighborhood the locals called Young's Hill. Flint supposed they needn't have bothered with directions, for the golem had cut a swath of destruction through the city. The air was rank with dust, ozone, and smoke from the buildings it had leveled. Mangled bodies littered the streets, along with smears of blood. Flint scowled. Yes, it would be most satisfying to put this murderous wench to the torch.

Plumley and Maria jogged to catch up to the head of the crowd, falling into step with Flint and Navarro.

"What happens when we arrive?" Plumley asked. His dress blues were soaked with sweat.

"I shall exhort the witch to surrender into my custody," Flint said.

"Think she'll do it?"

"Certainly not."

"Then why bother?"

Flint smiled. "The proper forms and rituals must be observed, Chief, even when her guilt has already been established beyond a reasonable doubt. I should think a police officer of all people would appreciate that fact."

Navarro chuckled. "Admit it sir, you enjoy letting them have it."

"I admit that it can be most cathartic."

Maria smiled and shook her head.

"Do you find something amusing, Miss Lopez?" Flint asked.

"I've just never heard anyone talk like you before. Like... where are you even from?"

"I myself hail from the city of Mount Angel far to the west of here. Now, as much as I would like to share more with you Miss Lopez, we have a more pressing engagement ahead of us."

"Speaking of which," Plumley said, "I've never been a part of something like this before, but if you need me or my officers to do anything for you, just give us the word."

"Thank you Chief. I confess that I do not know what awaits us so I cannot give you advice beyond the platitude of be prepared for anything."

They pressed on. The militia reached the wall that surrounded Young's Hill, separating it from the rest of the city. The gates had been torn off their hinges and the surrounding masonry reduced to rubble.

"It's up ahead, down this street," Plumley said.

The neighborhood appeared deserted. Some houses had been demolished by the golem on its way into the city proper. Flint drew his sword and one of his pistols. The sword gave off a faint glow.

"What's that mean?" Maria asked, pointing at Flint's sword.

"It means there's trouble nearby," said Navarro.

Presently, they arrived at their destination. The townsfolk gathered behind Flint. Before them stood the remains of the Turner mansion. The façade has been smashed, leaving much of the interior exposed to the night sky. There was no sign of the Turners. Flint's eyes narrowed. He sniffed. His senses told him nothing, but somehow, he knew that Lilian Turner was nearby.

"Lilian Turner!" he shouted. His voice echoed. Nothing. But he knew she was listening somewhere, somehow. Plumley and several police officers drew their service revolvers and fanned out among the crowd. Navarro held his rifle at the ready. Maria had found another magazine somewhere along the way for she now held her 9mm pistol by her side, close to Navarro.

"Lilian Turner!" Flint shouted again. Still nothing.

A ball of blue fire appeared at the top of a stairway in what was once the foyer. It expanded. The townsfolk gasped, almost as one, backing up a few steps.

A woman's laughter split the air. There was no warmth or joy to it. It was the laughter of a fiend who relished cruelty for its own sake.

A silhouette now coalesced inside the witch fire. The fire dissipated, revealing the villain who had plagued Flint since his arrival. She was no wizened hag, this witch. Her hair was black as midnight, her porcelain skin flawless. Her eyes though... this woman appeared no older than thirty, but something about her eyes spoke to several lifetimes worth of dark sorcery, of madness. She was dressed as for a formal occasion, an elegant dress and high heels, no doubt for the party her husband had been hosting.

Flint and Navarro stepped forward, away from the townsfolk who looked on in quiet awe at this terrible creature who had lived undetected among them for two decades.

"Good evening everyone," she said. "Hello Captain Flint."

"Lilian Turner!" he yelled. "You are charged with the

crimes of witchcraft, of consorting with demons, of the murder of two hundred and forty persons, and the deaths of countless citizens on this very night!"

Lilian smiled.

"It's over!" Flint shouted. "Surrender and face public execution! Or resist and face summary execution by my hand! Either way, I promise you that you shall burn for what you have done!"

"Burn?" she said. "Hmm. Yes. Fire does have a certain purity to it, doesn't it? Your kind is always so eager to dish it out. I wonder if you can take it?"

She extended her hand. A stream of fire shot from her palm toward Flint. The townsfolk screamed. Flint held up his sword, its glow now a radiant white. The fire was drawn to it. The blade absorbed the fire, but the sword remained pristine and cool to the touch.

Flint gave it a flick, as if to remove some disgusting slime.

Lilian snickered. "Well, well. Redcap was telling the truth after all."

"Been speaking with that unholy wretch, have you?" Flint said. "Then you surely know we dispatched your creature, Darien, and sent the foul demon back to Hell. So shall it be with you monster!"

Lilian laughed harder. "Oh, I really have to thank you Captain Flint. It's been too long since I've been able to cut loose. That little sword of yours absorbed my spell... I wonder if the others have ones like them?"

She raised both hands and conjured an enormous ball of fire. Flint felt his stomach drop. She was going to hurl it at the townsfolk!

Navarro raised his rifle and fired. A small hole appeared in Lilian's chest and her back exploded, showering the wall with black ichor. The fireball dissipated and her body collapsed face down in a boneless heap. Navarro worked the bolt and loaded a fresh round. He and Flint crept forward, their weapons aimed at Lilian's body. All was still and silent, the townsfolk stunned at the sudden reversal.

Lilian rose, levitating from the floor. Flint pursed his lips, scowling as the holes in the witch's body closed, healed. She opened her eyes, now ablaze with unholy fire. The townsfolk gasped and drew back. Flint and Navarro opened fire. Lilian held up one hand and the bullets froze in midair. She held them still. The two men ceased fire. Lilian let the bullets fall to the ground.

"That was rude," she said. She pointed at Navarro. "You may go now."

An invisible force slammed into both men. Navarro was flung backwards like a ragdoll. He sailed toward the assembled townsfolk. A few attempted to catch him, but his momentum knocked them down like bowling pins. Flint had raised his sword in time. He too was pushed backward, the soles of his boots smoking, but remained on his feet.

Lilian raised her hands and a wall of earth erupted from the ground, separating the mansion and Flint from everyone and everything else.

"This is between you and me, Captain," Lilian said. "But don't worry. I have friends who are looking forward to entertaining your little band."

She moved her arms in a circle, chanting in a language that made Flint's ears hurt. Her hands left a trail of witch fire, leaving a burning ring in the air. From the ring came a blackness that swallowed all light. Winged demons emerged from the blackness, grey creatures of horns, fangs, and claws, slavering and laughing as they flew over the wall and into the city. Flint could hear gasps, screams, crying, on the other side of the earthen wall. Then Navarro's and Plumley's voices calling out orders, and the sound of gunfire.

"Catch me if you can, Silas," Lilian said. Laughing, she fled into the bowels of the mansion.

Flint took off after her. If he could slay the witch, the dark magic sustaining the portal she had opened would die with her, closing it. He prayed that Navarro and the others could hold out for that long.

20

"Get out of the open! Take cover!" Navarro yelled. The cops and the civilians who had firearms shot at the winged demons as they divebombed into the crowd. Their claws rendered flesh, piles of guts spilling from split abdomens, and sent decapitated heads flying. Navarro aimed and fired, the bullet tearing through the wing of one of the fiends. Crippled, it came crashing down to earth. It was soon surrounded by civilians who emptied the magazines and cylinders of their handguns into the creature's head which disintegrated into a disgusting gray mush.

"They can bleed! We can kill them!" Plumley shouted. He swung open the cylinder of his revolver, dumped the empty shells, and loaded new rounds one at a time.

"Look out!"

One of the winged demons landed behind Plumley. Before he could turn around, it rammed its claws into his back, erupting through his chest. Plumley's eyes bulged, he gave a strangled moan, and blood poured from his mouth. The creature flung the corpse away and into the melee. Before it could take off, Navarro sprinted to the creature and cracked the butt of his rifle across its jaw. Stunned, the demon shook its head to regain its senses, but Navarro had already shouldered his rifle and fired into its face. The back of the demon's head exploded, and it crumpled to the ground. Whispering a short prayer for Plumley's soul, Navarro began to reload his rifle.

"Rico!" Maria shouted.

"Get out of here! Find cover! Get inside one of those houses!" Navarro yelled at her.

Maria took off for one of the abandoned mansions, a stream of civilians following her. Now it was just Navarro, the remaining cops, and the townsfolk who had guns versus demons spawned from the depths of Hell.

"Let's go! We need to take cover!" Navarro shouted. The militia gave each other covering fire as they leap frogged their way to the house where the other civilians had taken refuge. Navarro swore. They were burning through ammunition. At this rate he would be the last one with a working rifle, and his bandoliers wouldn't last forever.

The last cop entered the mansion. Navarro took a final shot, destroying the wing of another one of the creatures before he too ducked into the house, slamming and bolting the door behind him.

Everyone panted. Some were crying. Navarro estimated that dozens of their number had fallen in the mad dash to safety, but the house was still packed with refugees from the chaos outside. He touched his bandoliers. He had enough rounds left to go down fighting, but there weren't nearly enough to put down every monster outside.

Maria came running and embraced Navarro. He held her tight. He wanted to whisper that everything would be okay, but he knew he couldn't make it sound convincing.

"What happens now?" she asked.

"Now we pray that Silas can kill Lilian before we run out of ammo," he said.

21

Flint pursued his quarry. The mansion rippled and wavered around him as though he were underwater. Eyes appeared on the walls, following his progress. A suit of plate armor inside a display case, holding a sword point down, tracked him as well, the empty helmet turning. Lilian's giggle echoed in the hallways.

"Do you like what I've done with the place?" her disembodied voice asked.

Flint said nothing, stalking the hallway, gun and sword held at the ready.

"It occurred to me that I should have taken Darien's advice. When he saw you arrive in the city, he suggested we keep our heads down until you were gone. But here we are. No sense in crying over spilt milk, as they used to say."

"And so here we are," Flint said. "Your hubris was your downfall, witch, and I shall be the one to deliver the coup de grace."

"Yes, you're good at that aren't you?"

"Good enough to put you down, witch." Flint kicked in a door. A guest room. Empty.

"Good enough to put down your family."

Flint scowled and continued on his way. His breath fogged with every exhale.

"Robin Redcap told me something of your history. Your little trip down memory lane was interrupted, but your assistant isn't here to save you this time Silas."

Everything went black. Flint's sword continued to glow, but it wasn't enough to see his own hand in front of his face. When the light returned, Flint was on a country farm. Fields of corn and potatoes stretched as far as his eyes could see. A dirt road led to a familiar cottage. To his left was a barn. Standing in front of the barn doors was himself, seventeen years old. His younger self's hair was an unruly black mop, his physique toned from a childhood spent working in the outdoors.

"Let's try this again, shall we?" Lilian's voice echoed. The younger Flint took no notice of either his older self or the witch's voice.

"Charles?" the young Flint called. "Charles, are you in there? Where have mother and father gone?"

The older Flint closed his eyes and shuddered.

"Stay with me Silas," Lilian said. "We're getting to the best part."

Teenaged Flint nudged open the barn door. "Charles?"

"Hello brother," said another voice.

Old Flint opened his eyes and now he was inside the barn

looking over his younger self's shoulder. Before them stood Charles Julian Flint, his younger brother.

"Mother and father are right here," Charles said.

Two creatures emerged from the stalls. The first was a pale naked humanoid with vicious talons and dripping fangs, stringy black hair fringing its skull. The second was a similar monster but smaller and with blonde hair.

"What... what have you done?" young Silas asked.

Charles smiled. "I've made some improvements to our parents. Oh Silas, if only you could see what I see. If only you could experience this kind of power. I know you all never approved of magic, but now mother and father obey my every command. As will you."

A tear streamed down the older Flint's face.

"The Flint family," Lilian said. "Your ancestors have been on this continent for over seven hundred years. Even to me, that is quite impressive. Faithful servants of God, all of you... except for dear Charles, no?"

"This is an illusion," Flint said. "This is not real. Robin Redcap failed, and so shall you."

"We're not finished here," Lilian said. "Let's speed things up shall we?"

The scene shifted again. Charles was gone. Young Silas was on his knees, weeping, a hunting rifle by his side. The ghouls that had been his parents were sprawled on the ground in pools of blood, but they dragged themselves closer to the boy. The thing that had been his father reached out with a clawed hand and grabbed onto the rifle. It held the barrel against its forehead. Young Silas looked into the creature's eyes. Before there had been nothing but animal blood-lust. Now they were watery with tears that would not fall.

"Sssonnnn…" it said. "Pleeeaasseee…"

The younger Flint broke down in heaving sobs. The ghouls waited in silence. The creature that had been his mother reached out to him, but its body was too shattered to move any further. The younger Flint's hand reached for the trigger.

The old Flint closed his eyes. There was a sound of thunder. A few seconds later, a second crack of the rifle.

He opened his eyes, now bleary with tears. He was back in the Turner mansion, inside an empty guest room.

"Those were good kills," said Lilian's voice. "Young Charles managed to escape, and he left you to clean up his mess."

"Silence," said Flint. He resumed the hunt. The eyes in the walls continued to follow him. Portraits of previous generations of the Turner family ran along the walls, but as Flint passed them, their skin seemed to melt, leaving portraits of rotting corpses in his wake.

"Charles is still out there, you know. He would be, what, 31 or 32 now?"

"Silence I say!"

"You failed Silas. You killed your parents, and your own brother came over to the winning side. You're all alone now."

Flint shook his head. He had to remain vigilant lest…

A bolt of energy struck him in the back. Flint was flung to the ground. Arcs of electricity crackled over his long coat. He rolled onto his back and scrabbled into a seated position. There was Lilian. Waves of darkness emanated from her person, snuffing out the light from the lamp fixtures. All was plunged into shadow.

"You're all alone Silas," she said. "Where is your God now? Why doesn't He strike me down? Your parents raised you to love Him and serve Him. And yet your own brother turned his back on Him, and your parents, faithful to the end, died by your hand. Why do you persist?"

Flint raised his pistol, but it flew from his grasp and into Lilian's hand. She dropped the magazine and field stripped it in fluid motions, dropping the now useless weapon to the floor.

"You're alone Silas," she said, advancing on him. A nimbus of sorcerous fire surrounded her. "And now you will die alone."

Flint gave her a grim smile.

"If a man keeps the faith," he said, "He is never alone." His eyes focused on a spot behind her.

Lilian's lip curled. She made to raise her hands when a blade pierced her back and punched through her chest, spattering ichor over the floor. She made a deep, guttural roar, arms waving to grab hold of the ceremonial sword that had been rammed through her body. Behind her was an older man in a white tie tuxedo, his eyes ablaze with rage and hatred.

Lilian staggered, turned toward her attacker. When she saw him, her face dropped in an expression of shock and pitiful hurt.

"T... Timothy?" she wheezed.

Timothy Turner drew a pistol from his waistband and fired into her gut. She shuddered and fell back against the wall. The lights flickered back on. Turner kept his gun trained on her.

"You..." he said. He fired into her chest.

"The very idea... that you think... I'd come with you..." He fired twice. Lilian twisted and writhed.

"It sickens me... you sicken me!" Timothy shrieked. He fired again and again, Lilian's blood spattering everywhere.

"Murdering bitch! Bloody whore!" The crack of gunfire kept coming.

"Go back to hell!" he bellowed. He shot her in the forehead. The pistol's slide locked open, empty. He stood there trembling with fear and loathing. He looked at Flint.

"Burn the witch," he said through gritted teeth.

Lilian shot to her feet, grabbed Timothy by his lapels.

"I offered you eternal life," she growled. "I trusted you. I could have loved you. But if this is what you want, then you can die with him!"

Flint got to his feet, drew his spare handgun, but it was too late for Timothy. Electricity poured from Lilian's hands and Timothy convulsed, smoked, his flesh burning. His eyes melted in their sockets and his mouth fell open in a silent scream.

Flint aimed and fired. The bullet entered through Lilian's temple and she dropped Timothy's smoking corpse. The magic in her body attempted to heal her many wounds, but the sword from the armor display case was still stuck in her back. She reached to pull it out but Flint was on her now. He slashed with his sword, cutting a deep gash across her face. He kicked her in the gut, making her stagger down the hallway. He knew now that taking her into custody was not an option. It was kill or be killed. A desperate plan formed in Flint's mind. If this was going to work, he had to remain on top of her, keep the attacks coming, not give her a chance to heal her injuries.

Lilian raised her hands but before she could cast a spell, Flint headbutted her in the nose, shattering it, spraying ichor everywhere. He spun her around and grabbed the hilt of the sword Timothy had run through her. He gave it a twist and Lilian screamed as he pushed her forward. He put his pistol to the back of her head and fired, the blessed silver tipped bullet coming out of her forehead, making her face even more of a ravaged, bloody ruin. The wounds twisted and malformed and tried to close, her power struggling to keep up with the sheer volume and severity of blows that would have killed an ordinary human being a dozen times over. All the while he shoved, punched, slashed, kicked, and guided her to the foyer under the flurry of violence. She twisted, snarled, wild bolts of lightning and balls of fire flew from her fingertips, missing Flint but scorching the walls. Sweat streamed from his brow.

There. He could see the portal she had opened earlier, the ring of fire that opened into an endless void. Almost there. Flint's body was ready to give out under the strain it had endured this night, but he drove on. His life, every life in this city, depended on it.

He made to pistol whip Lilian, but she caught him by the wrist, intercepting his blow. He rammed his sword into her gut. She doubled over, coughing corrupted blood onto his hand. He withdrew the blade, more blood pouring from her fresh wounds. Lilian fought on, but she was weakening, the spells flickering out on her fingertips. Even when fueled by magic, the human body could only take so much punishment. They were getting closer.

Lilian's breathing was ragged as her magic was strained to the breaking point trying to both heal her and strike out at Flint. She tried to laugh, but only coughed instead, spitting blood onto the floor.

"Look at you go... a man of your size... beating a defenseless woman. Did I strike a nerve back there?" she rasped.

"You were wrong, witch," Silas wheezed. He advanced on her. She was in position. "Neither of us shall die alone this night." He cut a deep gash across her sternum with his sword.

"You will die in front of an audience," Flint said. He shot her two times in the chest. Now.

"Suffer not a witch to live," Flint said. He gave her one last kick and she flew backwards toward the portal. She grabbed on to the flames that marked its boundaries and screamed. Her hands sizzled and burned. Her legs kicked in the emptiness that awaited her.

"Flint!" she screamed.

22

Navarro, Maria, and several police officers held their ground. The demons had finally broken down the front door and advanced on the civilians. They gibbered and laughed, eager for the feast of blood that would begin momentarily.

"Rico," Maria said. "I'm scared."

"Me too," he said.

He aimed his rifle at the nearest demon. He was scared,

but damned if he was going to quit. Maria took a deep breath and aimed her pistol. The cops did likewise.

"Take down as many as you can," Navarro said.

The demons stopped. They cocked their heads, as if listening to a voice only they could hear. They filed out of the mansion and took to the sky with the flapping of their great wings.

The civilians were stunned. They'd been delivered at the last moment from certain death.

"Silas," Navarro said. He sprinted out the door, toward the wall of earth that still surrounded the Turner mansion. First Maria, and then the police soon followed. The townsfolk whispered, wondering at this turn of events. Finally, they too began to leave their refuge, curious if it was finally over or if there was more to come.

23

Lilian had both hands on the edge of the portal now. She pulled herself forward with all her might. Flint aimed and fired. The bullet entered her shoulder and she let go with that hand.

"You can't win, Flint! You will never stop us!" she shrieked.

"Your war against God is over Turner!" he yelled at her. "Your master is dead! Fall into the void that awaits you!"

"I'll... never... surrender!" A ball of fire formed in her free hand. Flint shot at her, missed. Her body was being whipped around by unseen winds within the darkness that awaited her. Her grin was manic. She would burn the witch hunter if it was the last thing she did.

Demonic howls split the night sky. Flint directed his gaze upward. The flying demons she had summoned earlier were returning. Perhaps the powers below had turned on the witch who had presumed to command them.

The first demon entered the portal from whence it had come, plowing into Lilian, tearing her hand away from the edge of the portal, her body slung over its shoulder.

"This isn't over Flint! I'll get out of here! And when I do..." her voice faded into nothingness, and she disappeared from sight. The demons continued to fly through the portal and into whatever realm they had come from. When the last one passed from this world, there was a great tearing sound as the portal closed in on itself.

The ground rumbled and Flint staggered on his feet. The wall surrounding the Turner estate shook and crumbled, a cascade of soil and rocks crashing to the ground. Breathing hard, Flint leaned on the banister at the top of the staircase. He sagged to the floor and sat at the head of the stairs.

He didn't know how long he'd been there when he noticed a light on the horizon. The sun was rising. Then he noticed people coming toward the ruined mansion. At the forefront was Navarro.

"Silas?" he called.

Flint rose to his feet, dusted himself off, hitched up his gun belt, straightened his long coat.

"Ah, Mr. Navarro," he said. "I knew that you would live through the night."

Navarro said nothing, stared at his boss with a mixture of confusion and awe.

"Is something amiss?" Flint asked.

"Oh, uh… you lost your hat. Sir."

Flint rubbed a hand through his close cropped hair. "So I did. Be a good assistant and fetch it for me, would you? It should be somewhere inside. I believe you will find the parts to my other pistol as well. Oh… I should like to amend my orders from yesterday evening: you may sleep in as long as you like."

Navarro shook his head and laughed. The townsfolk cheered, clapped, high fived, embraced each other, and danced.

24

Mayor Blackwood organized an impromptu ceremony to honor Knight Templar Captain Silas Flint and Supernumerary Ricardo Navarro. Most of the city turned out to get a glimpse of their saviors, and to honor the fallen.

"This city owes you two a debt that can never be repaid," Blackwood said, concluding his remarks.

The crowd cheered. The mayor gestured for Flint to take the lectern. Presently, Flint stood before the assembled citizenry who had gathered before City Hall. Flint cleared his throat.

"Thank you for your kind words, Mr. Mayor," Flint said. "I wish to thank all of you as well. I have traveled the length and breadth of this continent, and seldom have I encountered a city whose citizens are so willing to assist in the Lord's work. The witch, Lilian Turner, resided among you for twenty years, as crafty as the Serpent, so cunning that not even her own husband was aware of her true nature. Timothy Turner gave his life in the battle against Lilian, and I daresay that were it not for his intervention, I might not be standing before you this afternoon. Let us bow our heads and pray for his soul."

Flint bowed his head, the crowd following suit. They remained silent for a few moments.

Resuming, Flint said, "With faith in God, and the love of God in your hearts, I am certain that Canyon Cove shall be reborn, with renewed vigilance against the forces of darkness. Mr. Navarro and I must be on our way, but rest assured, this city, and all of you, shall forever hold a place in our hearts. I thank you, and may Almighty God bless you."

The crowd applauded and Flint acknowledged them with a wave of his hat. The ceremony ended, and Flint prepared to head to the stables for their horses. Looking around for Navarro, he found him holding hands with Maria Lopez. Flint stood a respectful distance from them as they exchanged parting words.

"Do you have to go?" Maria asked.

"Yeah, I do," Navarro said.

"I figured." She sighed.

"Hey. I promise I'll write. And the road's even a little safer now for the mailman."

She smiled. "Yes, I suppose it is."

They embraced and kissed. They gave each other's hands a final squeeze, and Navarro joined Flint. They began their walk to the stables.

"A fine young woman," Flint said.

"Yeah, she is."

"I admire your commitment to the Lord's work."

"Well, somebody's got to watch your back, and save your ass when it needs saving."

"Ha!"

They arrived at the stables, mounted up, and resumed their journey, waving goodbye to the townsfolk who had followed to see them off. Navarro looked at Flint, who was scowling.

"What's on your mind boss?" Navarro asked.

"Lilian Turner."

"What about her?"

"I swore an oath that she would burn."

"I imagine kicking her straight to hell is the next best thing."

"Hmm. Perhaps. But I never trust that our enemies are truly dead unless I put them to the torch myself. I fear we have not seen the last of that witch, but rest assured, if we encounter her again, I shall be her final ruin."

They continued in silence. They would arrive at their Chapterhouse later than Flint had anticipated, but he expected the Witch Hunter General would understand their tardiness. They lived in dangerous times.

The Witch's
Repentance

1

Captain Silas Flint took his seat in the Great Hall of Fort Marsing, Chapter House for the Knights Templar of the Order of Saint Benedict for the Eastern Division of the Empire of Cascadia. The morning air was crisp as it seeped through the cracks of the stone walls. A firepit in the center of the chamber warded off the worst of the chill, but Flint nonetheless pulled his long coat tighter around himself. Murmured conversations rippled throughout the Hall as his fellow Witch Hunters filed in. Flint's assistant, Ricardo Navarro, was sleeping off a night of prodigious drinking. For once, Flint sympathized with Navarro's hard partying ways. After their adventure in Canyon Cove on the way here, Flint had been sorely tempted to drink himself into a stupor as well.

"All rise."

The assembled Witch Hunters rose from their seats. Witch Hunter General John Abernathy entered the Hall. He was a trim man in his late fifties, though the strain from a lifetime of service to the Order made him appear twenty years older. Gold epaulettes on the shoulders of his long coat were the only marks of office which distinguished him from the men and women under his command. He took his place behind the lectern on a raised dais facing the other Witch Hunters.

"Let us pray," he said. Everyone bowed their heads.

"In the name of the Father, and of the Son, and of the Holy Spirit," Abernathy said as he made the sign of the Cross.

"Amen," his audience responded in unison.

"Almighty God, we give thee thanks and praise for guiding these men and women in their work, for protecting them in their journeys, and strengthening them in their struggle against the powers below. We beseech thee to grant us faith and courage in whatever trials thou sees fit to set before us. We ask this in the name of thy son Jesus Christ, amen."

"Amen."

"Saint Benedict."

"Pray for us."

"Please be seated," Abernathy said. He waited until the rustle of clothes and the creaks of wooden chairs ceased before continuing. "Thank you all for making the journey here. Believe me, I know how it is in the field, stalking your prey, about to put someone in manacles, when a courier from the Chapter House arrives with a letter, and you wonder, 'How in God's name are they always able to find me?'" The assembled Witch Hunters chuckled. Abernathy had risen through the ranks, starting out as a Supernumerary – a Hunter's assistant – before becoming a Knight Templar in his own right and later appointed General of his chapter.

"I'll get right to the point," Abernathy went on. "The government of Deseret has requested our assistance. They've detected a wave of undead headed west, from out of the Dead Lands. They've managed to hold off the zombies, but they believe a necromancer is guiding them."

"An invasion?" someone asked.

"They think so," Abernathy said. He looked out at the audience. "Hummel, Van Graf, Crocker," he said, pointing to each Witch Hunter in turn, "I want you three and your assistants to head out there. Make haste. If there is a necromancer at the heart of this, you're authorized to summarily execute him. Or her."

Abernathy went on, describing reports of supernatural activity throughout the Chapter House's territory, assigning Witch Hunters to various tasks. Flint waited. He drummed his fingers. Abernathy ticked off names one by one, but he still hadn't assigned anything to Flint. It happened occasionally, a Witch Hunter not receiving an assignment. Most took it as a relief and an opportunity to relax. Flint never knew what to do with himself when it fell to him.

"Finally," Abernathy said, "We have a bit of a mystery on our hands. I recently received a telegram from the city of Jordan, about sixty miles south of here. A woman claiming to be a witch turned herself in to the local police the other day. She's refusing to talk to them. She said she'll only speak with one of us."

Confused whispers rippled through the Hall. Flint leaned forward, Abernathy holding his complete attention. It was a rare occasion indeed when a witch willingly offered herself to the Order. What could this mean?

"Flint," Abernathy said. "I want you and your assistant to head down there. See what this woman has to say."

The meeting concluded with another prayer, and the assembled Witch Hunters dispersed to their assignments. Abernathy beckoned for Flint to join him on the dais. The

Witch Hunter General waited for the hall to empty before addressing Flint.

"How are you, Silas?" he asked.

"I am eager to resume the Lord's work, sir."

Abernathy smiled. "That's what you always say when I ask."

"Because it is always the truth, sir."

A raised eyebrow. "Is it?"

"I am afraid I do not understand."

The Witch Hunter General held his hands behind his back and paced. "You remind me of myself when I was your age. Always champing at the bit to get back into the field and make the world a better place for humanity."

Flint said nothing.

Abernathy stopped. Facing Flint again he said, "You and Ricardo were nearly killed on your way back from your last assignment."

"A chance encounter that led to a minor inconvenience, sir."

Abernathy smiled and shook his head. "I suppose what I'm trying to say is that it's okay to take time off if you need it. You haven't taken a vacation once since you were sworn in. That was, what, fifteen years ago now?"

"...No sir, I have not."

"Take it from me, Silas: this work takes its toll in ways you may not yet realize."

"I understand, sir. Will that be all?"

Abernathy regarded him for a moment. "Have you any questions regarding your current assignment?"

Relieved, Flint asked, "How would you prefer us to handle it?"

"I'm not sure, to be frank. According to the Jordan police, she walked into their headquarters, confessed to being a witch, asked – demanded, really – to be put in a cell, and has since refused to utter a word except to say she will only speak to one of us."

"Most curious," Flint said.

"Curious indeed. Speak to her. I leave it to you to determine if she's worth bringing back here for further interrogation or trial."

"And if it proves to be some sort of trap?"

"Lethal force is authorized, of course. However, if you place her under arrest, I would prefer it if you brought her here alive. I've noticed that a great many of your shackles die before making it to trial."

"I shall make every effort to do so, sir."

"Oh, and one more thing. Jordan has its own train station, so I suggest you head to the Cascadia Express station southwest of here. You and Navarro can at least take a small break from being on horseback."

"I am sure it will be most restful."

"Go then. God be with you."

Flint strode from the Great Hall. His fellow Witch Hunters nodded to him as he passed, but he scarcely took notice. It felt good to have an assignment again. He knew not what awaited him Jordan, but he was confident that with the Lord on his side, he could face any challenge. He pondered Abernathy's words. The man had a point: many of Flint's arrests wound up dead before they could be put to the question at Fort Marsing. But Divine Providence had seen fit to lead Flint into many dangerous encounters where arrest was not always an option.

Exiting the West Wing of the fortress, Flint marched across the courtyard to the Supernumerary barracks. It was 10 a.m. Plenty of time for Navarro to have slept. Flint dared to hope that he'd find his assistant awake and eager to resume the work to which they'd sworn an oath.

Flint made a beeline toward Navarro's room. He heard the snoring in the hallway, from the other side of the door. Flint sighed. He pounded on the door.

"Mr. Navarro!" he called. The snoring stopped. He pounded on the door again. "Mr. Navarro! Wake up, I say!"

The door opened. Navarro's eyes were bloodshot, his hair an unruly mop.

"Silas…" he mumbled. "What time is it?"

"It's time to get dressed and prepare for the road!"

Navarro groaned. "The creatures of the night don't come out until night!"

"All the more reason to get started during the light of day! Now come! We must away!"

Navarro bathed, brushed his teeth, and got dressed while Flint tapped his foot in the hallway. Navarro strapped on his ammunition bandoliers, slung his rifle, and put on his gun belt which was loaded with pouches in addition to his tomahawk and pistol.

"Where to now sir?" he asked, falling into step with Flint who was already on his way.

"We are on our way to an interview with a witch."

"Huh. That's a change of pace."

"Indeed. And I have good news: we shall be making most of our journey via locomotive."

"Ah, thank God. I can sleep on the way."

2

Sheriff's Deputy Vanessa Gellar checked her pocket watch. As the minute hand reached 12, she heard the train's whistle blow and its wheels screech as it pulled into the station. Right on time, as always. Sheriff Darius Arnett had received a telegram from the Witch Hunter Chapter House up north that they were sending someone to interview their unusual guest who had been sitting in a jail cell for the last few days. Gellar had been the lucky deputy sent to escort the Witch Hunter and his assistant.

Gellar was in her late twenties and wore her long brunette hair tied back in a ponytail, a revolver and a baton on her gun belt. She shielded her eyes from the afternoon glare, trying to spot her guests among the disembarking crowd. Jordan was a sleepy community nestled along the point where the Jordan creek branched off into the Baxter River. She never imagined she would have occasion to deal with the men in black.

There they are. Hard to miss, she thought. The first man was tall, broad in the chest and shoulders. He wore a long black coat over a white dress shirt and black waistcoat with black trousers. He carried two guns and a sword on his belt. His face was severe, like he'd nursed on lemons as a boy, his icy blue eyes scanning the crowd. If nothing else, his tall wide brimmed black hat denoted his office as a Witch Hunter. The second man, his assistant no doubt, was a shorter Hispanic man in leather armor, with two ammunition bandoliers criss-crossed over his chest. He had a bolt action rifle slung across his back, with a gun and a tomahawk on his belt. He carried a large black leather suitcase.

Gellar went out to meet them. She preferred criminals to be of the mundane variety. The sooner these two got their mysterious prisoner out of there the better.

"Excuse me," she called, waving. "You're the Witch Hunter?"

"I am. Captain Silas Flint, Knight Templar of the Order of Saint Benedict, at your service, Deputy," said the man in black. He indicated his companion. "This is my assistant, Supernumerary Ricardo Navarro."

"Pleased to meet you ma'am," Navarro said, giving Gellar a nod.

"Deputy Vanessa Gellar," she said, extending her hand. Flint gave it a brief shake. "If you two will follow me?"

She led her charges away from the platform and onto the main boulevard that ran through the city. Horse drawn carriages passed them along the way, their hooves clip-clopping on the cobblestone street. The city was surrounded by marshy grasslands, the buzzing of flies a constant background noise. Houses and businesses all had clapboard siding.

"Charming city," Flint said. Gellar wasn't sure if that was sarcasm or not. "Tell us more about this supposed witch."

Gellar thought for a few seconds before speaking. "She's young. Early twenties, I'd guess. Couple days ago she just shows up at the station, says, 'I confess to witchcraft, lock me up.' So we give her a cell. We asked her where she's from, what she wants, and so on, but all she says is, 'I want to speak to a Knight Templar.' So the Sheriff contacted your boss."

"Hmm," Flint said. "Has she attempted to practice her blasphemous art?"

"Nope. We bring her three squares a day. Gave her some books to read. Other than that, she just paces her cell."

"What do you think sir?" Navarro asked.

"Most curious."

Presently they arrived at the Sheriff's office which doubled as the town's jail. Gellar opened the door and motioned for the two men to enter. Sheriff Arnett rose from his desk to greet them.

"Sheriff Darius Arnett," he said, shaking hands with Flint and Navarro. Arnett was a black man in his early 40s with a muscular physique that had just begun its turn to middle age fat.

"A pleasure sir," Flint said. "I understand that you have a witch in custody."

"Yes sir. At least she claims to be one. Honestly, I'm starting to wonder if she's just here for three hots and a cot."

"We shall soon get to the truth of the matter," Flint said.

"Do you want us to, uh, wait outside or anything?" Gellar asked.

"That will not be necessary I should think. If she meant you harm, I daresay she would have done so by now. Come along Mr. Navarro."

Flint and Navarro followed Arnett toward the back of the building where there were four jail cells. Three of them were empty. The fourth had a small pile of books stacked near the gate. Stretched out on one of the cots, gazing at the ceiling, was a young woman with long black hair. She wore an ankle length dress that had seen better days, covered in patches and dark stains. Arnett used his baton to tap on the bars.

"Zelda! You have a visitor," he said.

The woman – Zelda – sat up and turned to face them. Her face lit up when her eyes met Flint.

"Thank God," she said.

Flint raised an eyebrow. This was the first time in his career that a self-professed witch was happy to see him.

"Sheriff, would you mind excusing us?" she asked.

Arnett looked to Flint, who nodded. Arnett and Gellar left the cell area and went to their desks out front.

The woman extended her hand through the bars. "I'm Zelda, Zelda Fletcher," she said. Flint and Navarro stared her down.

She withdrew her hand and began pacing her cell. "I suppose you're wondering why I've called you here today," she said, then chuckled. "I've always wanted to say that."

Flint and Navarro said nothing.

She cleared her throat. "Right. Well, I confess. I'm a witch. I've practiced the dark arts. You got me. I confess, and I want to repent and amend my life."

The two men remained silent. Flint crossed his arms.

"I'd like you to take me into custody and take me to... wherever it is you take prisoners."

Still, they said nothing.

"Look, what more do you want?!" she cried. "I'm guilty. I confessed. Take me away from here! Please." She was close to tears.

Flint and Navarro looked at each other.

"What do you think Mr. Navarro?"

"I don't buy it."

"Nor do I," Flint said.

Turning to face Fletcher, he said, "Young lady, you appear to be operating under a misapprehension."

A look of confusion passed over her face. "Say what now?" she asked.

"I said that you appear to…"

"No, I meant did you seriously just say 'appear to be' and 'misapprehension?'"

Sighing, Flint continued. "My dear, the Knights Templar of the Order of Saint Benedict do not simply take people from their homes whenever we choose. We gather evidence. We hear testimony. We do not pass sentence without a careful evaluation of the relevant facts."

"I confessed. I said I want to make amends. What more do you need?"

"Sheriff Arnett suspects you are simply seeking room and board. My Chapter House is not a hostel for vagrants."

Fletcher scoffed. "Please. No offense to my hosts, but I could find better than this."

"Why's it so important that we take you away?" Navarro asked.

Fletcher said nothing.

"She's hiding something."

"I concur Mr. Navarro," Flint said. "Miss Fletcher, in my experience, witches seldom feel true repentance for their crimes. The dark arts are as addictive as they are malevolent. I am willing to accept your confession and your desire to change your ways. But if you wish us to return you to our

Chapter House, then I must insist you tell us the whole truth. Or you may remain in this cell for as long as Sheriff Arnett decides to hold you. The choice is yours."

Fletcher closed her eyes and sighed. She paced, gathered her thoughts. Flint and Navarro waited. A minute passed. Finally, she stopped and sighed again.

"Okay," she said. "The truth."

Navarro opened his suitcase and took out a pen and notepad.

"I promise you, I'm a witch. I can sense magic all around us. I can feel it, tap into it, use it to conjure stuff, make people more... suggestable. My ex taught me how to do it all. For the past few days I've been using everything I've got to... well, to suppress my talent."

"And why might that be?" Flint asked. Navarro was scribbling away, taking notes.

"He and I had a... a falling out. We broke up," Fletcher said. "He didn't take it well. So I ran away from him. I ran and I ran until I made it here. The problem is he can sense it whenever I use my power. It's like shooting a flare into the sky. I'm worried that if I start casting spells again, he or his gang might come after me."

"A gang, you say?"

"Yeah." Fletcher ran her hands through her hair. "He was running a gang. All of them had some talent for magic, a whole gang of warlocks and witches. We started out with petty stuff, you know? Levitating people's wallets out of their pockets, that sort of thing. Then we moved on to robbing stagecoaches, mugging travelers on the road. Normally, we'd scare them with a fireball or a bolt of lightning, something like that, they'd give us their valuables and then we'd let them go. But that wasn't enough for Francisco. He started getting into other stuff. Dark stuff."

Navarro's pen flowed over his notepad. Flint stepped closer to the cell. "Please go on," he said.

3

ELEVEN DAYS AGO:

Zelda Fletcher led a dozen of her friends into the tavern. It was a busy night, every table packed with customers, the air thick with tobacco smoke and the sound of conversation and laughter. An ancient jukebox in the corner played some lively bit of old world music. Those machines only ever seemed to play 20th and 21st century songs, reminders of a civilization that no longer existed. Fletcher was in no mood to dwell on the past. Tonight was for dreaming of the future.

One of the girls in her party shouted to be heard over the noise, "Should we go somewhere else? It's pretty crowded in here."

Fletcher snickered. "Why should we do that?"

She whispered a spell and a ball of light materialized over the palm of her hand. She moved her hands in circles, drawing in more magical energy, making the ball of light grow. The noise in the bar gradually tapered off, the patrons staring open mouthed at this display of witchcraft. Fletcher raised her hands and the ball of light floated to the ceiling. It exploded in a dazzling display of fireworks that sparkled in a rainbow of colors before everyone's eyes.

"I think you've had enough," she said, addressing everyone. "It's time to go home."

"It's time to go home," the patrons repeated in unison. As one, they rose from their seats and shuffled outside in a single file. They would return to their homes and go straight to bed, waking up in the morning with no memory of what had transpired. Fletcher smiled. Get a little alcohol in their system and influencing other people's wills was almost effortless.

"Not you," she said, pointing to the bartender. He stopped in his tracks. She pointed at the wall of liquor and the bartender went back to his position. He stopped, waiting for further orders.

"The first round is on the house," Fletcher said. She snapped her fingers.

The bartender blinked, looked confused. He saw Fletcher and her companions and smiled, holding his arms wide like he was greeting his closest friends.

"Hey, Zelda!" he cried. "Long time no see! Come in, come in, take a seat! First round is on me!"

"Oh my gosh, thank you so much!" Fletcher said, favoring him with a winning smile. Her friends pushed tables together, some using their hands and others their minds. After everyone was seated, Zelda took her place at the front. The bartender brought everyone their drinks, acting for all the world like he was the happiest man on earth. Fletcher had no compunction about mesmerizing others to obey her will, but she saw no need to be cruel about it. Plus, it wasn't good business to shit where you eat. If any of her compatriots wanted a second round, they could pay for it themselves. After all, they were flush after that last job.

"Everyone!" she called, raising her wine glass. "A toast! To Francisco Cortez and a job well done!"

"Hear hear!"

Everyone downed their favored beverage. The bartender snapped out of his trance and looked around, bewildered.

"What... what happened? Where did everyone else go?"

"Don't worry about it," Fletcher said. She tossed him a sack of silver coins. "Be a dear and open a tab for us, would you?"

"Uh... yeah... sure..."

Fletcher took a moment to wallow in self-congratulation. She and her fellow witches and warlocks had just returned from robbing a locomotive owned by the Bank of Cascadia, taking all the silver that they could carry. An illusion here, a hypnotic suggestion there, and the locomotive personnel would arrive at their destination with no memory of being robbed.

"Where's our fearless leader?" one of the men asked.

"He couldn't be here tonight, but he wanted me to tell you that this night is to celebrate all of you, and your hard work!" They all ordered another round of drinks. Fletcher raised a shot glass. "Here's to our future success!" Everyone cheered and drank.

Fletcher made her rounds, conversing, reminiscing, joking, and laughing with these men and women who had made Francisco's dreams a reality. Fletcher had been twenty years old, a homeless girl making ends meet through pickpocketing and the occasional prostitution, when she met Francisco. He offered her a way out of that life, and that way turned out to be magic. Fletcher had been an apt pupil, discovering that she had a talent for influencing the minds of others. She and Francisco progressed quickly from a student-teacher relationship, to friendship, and then to love.

From there, they built up a respectable empire. They used their magical powers to steal from the city's wealthier citizens, leaving them baffled at how anyone could have penetrated their vaults. They recruited more students, eager to enrich themselves at their enemies' expense... after promising to give Francisco his cut, of course.

Speaking of, Fletcher thought, I should check in. He'd grown more withdrawn over the last few weeks, seldom participating in any of his meticulous plans. He used to live for the thrill of a big heist. Now he stayed locked away in his library, pouring over eldritch tomes he'd found, purchased, or stolen over the last year.

"Hey everyone," she called. All eyes turned to her. "I'm going to excuse myself and go see Francisco, but don't stop the party on my account. Have fun! That's an order!" Everyone laughed and waved their goodbyes. Technically she had no authority over them, but as Francisco's girlfriend, her words were often taken to be his words.

Fletcher walked toward Francisco's house. Some townsfolk waved at her, and she waved back. As far as they knew, she was simply Zelda Fletcher, the nice girl who worked as a library clerk. They had no idea that she was the better half of a magical crime lord.

Arriving at Francisco's house, she let herself in with her key. Francisco's day job was teaching mathematics at the high school in town. He could afford a much larger house than his two bedroom one bath cottage, but he chose to remain in a home that was more in accord with a teacher's salary.

"Hey babe," she called. No answer.

Something was wrong. The night was warm but the chill inside the house was unnatural. Fletcher's breath was visible, and she shivered. She stood in the entryway, listening. The electric lights were off. Candlelight flickered from the spare bedroom Francisco had converted into his library and office. All was quiet but for the ticking of the grandfather clock in the living room.

Fletcher rubbed her arms, her breath smoking in front of her. She could sense it when others used magic – they all could – but this was unlike anything she'd felt before. It felt uncanny. It felt evil.

A floorboard creaked, and she jumped. That wasn't the house settling. She'd been here enough times to know that was a footstep, but Francisco was nowhere to be seen.

"Francisco?" Nothing. She flicked a light switch, but nothing happened. Had he lost power? Every other house on the block had lights on. She swallowed and crept toward the office. The candlelight was casting odd shadows. Wait... oh God.

A silhouette on the wall was shaped like a man, except for the two curling horns extending from its head. Fletcher froze, afraid to breathe. The shadow looked like it was shaking, its shoulders rising and falling. Was it laughing? Whatever it was, it stopped. The shadow raised one arm and made a come-hither sign with its index finger.

Fletcher was shaking, and it wasn't just from the cold. She wanted to run, but her concern for Francisco drove her onward. The shadow reached the doorway to the office and disappeared. Fletcher summoned magical energy through her will. Electricity arced between her fingertips. If that thing had hurt Francisco, she was prepared to blast it straight to Hell. She hoped. Taking a deep breath, she rounded the corner and into the office.

Francisco was levitating over a pentagram he had painted on the hardwood floor, his back to Fletcher. No, that wasn't paint. The coppery tang in the air told her it was blood. The pentagram was surrounded by black candles. A woman's body laid on top of Francisco's desk. Her chest was a ragged bloody ruin, the incision reaching from her throat to her belly button, her ribcage pried open.

The electricity on Fletcher's fingertips flickered out. Her mouth was agape. She tried to scream but it came out as a squeak.

Francisco turned at the sound, still hovering two feet from the ground. His eyes were shut. He was whispering too faintly for Fletcher to hear, but his lips were forming words in a language she didn't recognize.

"Francisco?" she whispered.

He opened his eyes. Normally a deep brown, they were now a burning yellow. He smiled, but it wasn't the smile she had fallen in love with. This was predatory.

"Hey babe," he said. Even his voice sounded different. Deeper. More guttural.

"Francisco... what have you done?"

He alighted upon the floor, hands held behind his back.

"I'm so glad you're here Zelda," he said. "We need to talk. I've had a revelation over these last few weeks."

Fletcher said nothing. She took a step back. Then another.

Francisco reached out with his hand and squeezed. Fletcher felt her arms pin to her sides. Her body rose, feet dangling in midair. Francisco brought his hand back, Fletcher levitating closer to him as though he had her on a leash.

"Please, stay," he said. "I insist."

Fletcher struggled against the invisible grip that held her.

"Babe, please… you're hurting me…" she said. She felt panic rise in her gorge. Whatever power Francisco had tapped in to was far beyond anything the gang had ever practiced before.

Francisco inhaled deeply, shuddering with… pleasure?

"I'm sorry Zelda," he said. "But oh, if only you could feel what I feel. The taste of human fear… it's intoxicating."

Fletcher struggled to control her breathing before she hyperventilated.

"We've had a good ride together, haven't we?" he said. He took a step closer, ran the back of his hand up and down her cheek. Fletcher wanted to look away but found she couldn't even manage that. The invisible grip was merciless.

"We've built up considerable wealth," he said. "We've shown others how to use the power God presumes to forbid. Yes, we've become the most powerful criminal element in the land." He laughed, cold and cruel. "I've since realized that our pursuit of money is ultimately meaningless."

Fletcher said nothing.

"I've devoted these last few weeks to research. I came across a book that has proven most enlightening. Would you care to hear what I've learned? Hmm? Just like old times?"

Fletcher said nothing.

Francisco reached out with his hand, a book flying from a shelf and into his grip. "This book is called the *In Realis Magicae*. It was written by Abdul Hakim Nazari, a powerful wizard who lived over four hundred years ago. He learned his craft from Simon Magus himself!"

Fletcher closed her eyes. A tear rolled down her cheek.

Francisco went on. "Nazari conquered many nations in the old world. He recorded everything here: the Great Magician's lessons, the spells he learned from him, how he ruled in his name, and he wrote of the true nature of magic."

He laughed. "Oh Zelda, we've been like children splashing around at the shallow end. The true nature of magic isn't about accumulating money and shiny trinkets. We have the potential to be like God Himself, bending the cosmos to our will."

"What…" she croaked.

"Hmm?"

"What did you do to her?" She nodded toward the dead woman on his desk. The invisible grip had weakened.

"She was a simple prostitute. No one will miss her. Communicating with my benefactors, receiving a sample of their power, requires a price to be paid."

"Your benefactors?"

"The ones who came before us. They too were banished from paradise, just as our parents were banished from Eden. They know what it means to be struck down, cast out, and abandoned by a vengeful God."

"Francisco…"

"I see it all clearly now Zelda," he said, his burning yellow eyes shining with a manic gleam. "This city, this world, is not where we belong. These people, they're nothing! We have the power, we have the talent! It is our birthright to rule! It is our destiny to take back what God took from us!"

"Babe," Fletcher said. "Francisco… please. Put me down."

He started, as if waking from a trance. He nodded, and Fletcher touched down on the floor, the invisible grip releasing her.

"Er, sorry. It's easy to get carried away with this new power," he said.

She rubbed her wrists.

"You've always been my favorite," Francisco said. "We started this together, and we'll see it through to the end. Together!"

Fletcher approached him. She smiled and opened her arms. Francisco went to meet her, embraced her.

"Oh Zelda, there's so much I want to teach you."

"There's one problem babe," she said.

"Hmm?"

She whispered in his ear, "I'm not really here."

"What?!" Fletcher was gone. Vanished. Francisco looked around, confused.

She was behind his desk. Fletcher didn't know how long her hypnotic suggestion would last, but for now Francisco could neither see nor hear her. The knife he had used to butcher the woman was stuck into his desk.

Fletcher stood frozen with indecision. This was not her Francisco. She lied, she cheated, she stole, but she didn't sign up for cold-blooded murder or consorting with… with whoever or whatever he was talking about.

She could run. She could slip past him while her spell was still in effect. But where? And how many people would she be condemning to death if Francisco continued down this path? No. I may be a criminal, but I won't be a monster, she thought. It had to end here and now, before more people died to feed Francisco's ambitions.

If she used magic, Francisco would detect it, breaking her spell. She would have to do this the old-fashioned way. She picked up the knife and advanced on Francisco.

She waited until his back was turned. She grabbed onto his chin with her off hand and pulled back, exposing this throat while ramming the knife into his kidney, twisting the blade. Francisco grunted. She pulled the knife out to slit his throat, but he grabbed her wrist, squatted, and threw her over his shoulder. Fletcher hit the floor, the wind knocked from her. Francisco, still holding on to her left wrist, pulled her arm out to full extension and broke her elbow with a palm strike. The bones made a sickening crack, and Fletcher screamed her throat raw.

"I'd forgotten how fun it could be to do this with your bare hands," Francisco laughed. He stood, kicked her in the ribs. Fletcher's scream was cut short in a fit of gasping and coughing.

How? She wondered. A kidney shot like that should have left the victim paralyzed in shock. Francisco looked down at her, a manic grin on his face.

"Very good Zelda," he said. "An ordinary man would be dead. But as you can see, I'm not an ordinary man anymore." He lifted his shirt and Fletcher saw that the puncture wound was healing at a preternatural speed. "I really should thank you as well. You showed me I'm still vulnerable to your little mind tricks. I won't make that mistake again."

Fletcher tried to focus. She too could heal her injuries with magic, but her mind was clouded with fear and pain. She couldn't heal herself and attack Francisco at the same time. She made her decision.

She willed electricity to form on her uninjured hand, drawing additional power from the house's electrical wiring. A bolt of lightning shot from her fingers, striking Francisco square in the chest. The smell of ozone and burnt flesh assaulted her nostrils as he was flung against his bookcases with a crash. The shelves splintered, books falling to the floor and on top of Francisco's body. She doubted that her assault had killed him. She refocused her energies onto her injured arm. The bones reset, knitting at an unnatural pace. Fletcher struggled to her feet. She had to get out of that house. She had to get out of town. She had to run.

Fletcher had just left Francisco's house when she heard a demonic roar. The windows of every house on the block rattled, then shattered, deadly shards exploding from every pane. Dogs barked, cats hissed, lights turned on. Men emerged from other houses on the block, husbands, fathers, ordinary civilians, armed with everything from baseball bats to kitchen knives, to shotguns. Fletcher ran.

She heard the crack of gunfire. Then screaming. She ran. Police officers on horseback and bicycles sped past her toward the sound of carnage. She kept running. The gunshots and screams were growing fainter, but still she ran. Fletcher arrived at a stable near the edge of town, panting.

"What's the hurry young lady?" the wizened stablemaster asked her.

She locked eyes with him. "I need your fastest horse. I paid you well for it."

The stablemaster's face went slack. "Fastest horse is down there, third stall on the left," he said, pointing. "Thank you for your business."

Fletcher threw on a saddle, pulled herself up, and urged the horse into a gallop. She didn't know where she was going but figured east was as good a direction as any as long as it was away from here.

4

"I pushed the horse until it died. Then I kept going on foot for about a week. Jordan was the first city I found with living people in it, and now here we are."

Navarro finished writing. Flint stroked his chin.

"You abandoned your neighbors and your compatriots to that fiend," Flint said.

"I'm not proud of it, but… yes, I did."

"And you have not practiced the dark arts since you fled."

"No. Like I said, if I do, Francisco will sense it. I'm pretty sure he's still alive, and he was never the forgiving type."

"Do you renounce the power of magic? Do you forswear the works of Satan and all of his empty promises?"

Fletcher hesitated.

"That's how repentance works, Zelda," Navarro said.

"I…" she began. "I… I'll try."

"You must steel your will and swear to it with a firm purpose of amendment," Flint said.

"I said I'll try, alright?!" she snapped. She rubbed her forehead. "I'm sorry, it's just… you were right. It is addictive. I feel like a junkie trying to get clean."

"An apt analogy," Flint said.

"So what happens now?" Fletcher asked.

"Sheriff Arnett!" Flint called.

The sheriff stepped toward the cells. "Yes sir?"

"When is the next train leaving for the north?"

"Not until tomorrow morning at 8 am."

Turning to Navarro, Flint said, "Have the sheriff take you to the telegram office, if you please. Wire Fort Marsing that we are returning with a prisoner some time tomorrow."

"Yes sir," Navarro said. He and Arnett took their leave.

Fletcher smiled with relief. "Thank God," she said.

"You have a long road ahead of you if you seek to repair your relationship with God, Miss Fletcher," Flint said. "But you have made an auspicious first step."

Deputy Gellar entered the holding area and approached Flint. "Out of curiosity…" she said.

"Yes?" Flint asked.

"Well, I overheard some of her story. She confessed to a shitload of crimes like assault and grand theft. How are you going to handle that?"

"Miss Fletcher, your criminal activities all took place in the environs of New Rome, correct?"

"Yeah," Fletcher said.

"Deputy Gellar, I suggest you follow the sheriff and my assistant to the telegram office. Contact the New Rome authorities and notify them that Miss Fletcher is in my custody. My Chapter House shall make the necessary arrangements for extradition if they so choose."

"What the fuck?!" Fletcher yelled. "I thought I was going with you? I told you I repent!"

"True repentance requires penance, Miss Fletcher," Flint replied. "Were you guilty of witchcraft alone, the Order could absolve you and send you on your way. You used your powers to commit crimes against the laws of man, however, in addition to the laws of God. God will forgive you, but that does not excuse you from the consequences of your criminal activities in this world."

Fletcher swore and kicked the pile of books in her cell, scattering them. Flint's face softened.

"It sounds harsh my dear, but it is for the best," he said.

"Captain Flint, I just have some papers for you to sign," Gellar said.

"Of course. Lead on."

5

After they had left Fletcher, she paced in her cell, muttering and cursing to herself.

That son of a bitch, she thought. She didn't know what to expect when she asked for a Witch Hunter, but she never dreamed that she'd be sent back to New Rome. Jesus Christ, if they knew everything she'd done, she was looking at 20 to 30 years in prison. It wasn't fair!

Her mind raced. *You can do this Zelda,* she thought. *You've gotten out of tougher situations than this.* If only there was…

She had it.

"Hey! Captain Flint!" she yelled. "Are you still here? I need to talk to you!"

After a moment, Flint returned to the cell area. Fletcher had seen a lot of rough characters in her time, but she had to admit that the grim looking Witch Hunter was an intimidating presence. Not that she'd ever give him the satisfaction of admitting it.

"What is it, Miss Fletcher?" he asked.

"I was thinking, maybe we could make a deal, yeah?"

Flint frowned. "We have already made a deal: you repent of your heresy, and we do not put you to the torch."

"Yeah, I get that, but I meant a deal about the other stuff, the robbery and assault and all that."

Flint raised an eyebrow. "I do not have the authority to make such a deal."

"Sure you do!" She beckoned for him to come closer.

Flint folded his arms. "I will not get close enough for you to exercise your mesmerism skills, thank you."

"Fine, whatever. But Witch Hunters have universal jurisdiction for witchcraft, right?"

"That is correct."

"Suppose I help you take down Francisco?"

Flint stroked his chin. "You have my interest."

"Yeah, I thought I would. Like I said, Francisco was getting into some dark stuff, consorting with demons and all that. But what if I told you where you could find him?"

"I already know that your gang operates from New Rome. You told me yourself in your account."

"Yeah, but who knows if it's still standing anymore? I know all of our old hideouts, I know where we ambush travelers, which rail lines we stake out, I know names, places... everything!"

"Withholding information in the hopes of leniency? I could have you placed on the rack at Fort Marsing to loosen that tongue."

Fletcher was on the verge of tears. God damn this stubborn bastard!

"Hmm," Flint stroked his chin. "You have given me an idea, however. I agree that Mister Cortez must be stopped. I know of that book in his possession. Anything written by a hand-picked disciple of the Great Magician is too dangerous to be left in the wrong hands. I should like to make a counterproposal."

Fletcher held in her sigh of relief. Anything was better than rotting in a jail cell for decades.

"I will ask the Witch Hunter General of my chapter to declare you a ward of the Order. The records of your previous life will be sealed, your criminal record expunged."

Fletcher felt her stomach drop. She knew the price she'd have to pay for that kind of fresh start would be steep.

"I will do this if, and only if, you stand by our side when we engage Mister Cortez."

Fletcher's mouth dropped.

"I take it all back," she said. "I'll take my chances in prison."

"As you wish." Flint tipped his hat and started to leave the prison area.

"Wait!"

He stopped.

"Alright," she said. "Alright, goddamn it, I'll do it."

"Splendid. And I'll thank you to mind the blasphemy."

"Whatever."

"Now if you will excuse me Miss Fletcher, I have telegrams to write."

6

The telegram office was bustling with traffic. Jordan was a small city, but it served as a communication hub for eastern Cascadia. Merchants, politicians, and police officers came and went every day, coordinating interregional trade, arranging extraditions of criminals, and forging new trade deals.

The crowd inside the office parted to let Flint through to the telegram machine. Navarro was waiting for him.

"What's going on boss?" he asked.

"There has been a change of plans. Please send another telegram to the Chapter House. I shall dictate."

Navarro took his seat, his hand resting on the machine, prepared to tap out Flint's message.

"Subject wishes to make a deal, stop," Flint said. "Subject will lead us to coven, stop. Leader possesses copy of *In Realis Magicae*. Please advise, stop."

The response came a minute later. The machine spat out tape. Navarro pulled it off to read.

"Deal is acceptable," he read. "Book must be captured or

destroyed at all costs. Proceed with caution. God be with you."

Navarro chuckled. "I should have known this job wouldn't be that easy."

"Truly God has smiled upon us," Flint said.

"He's done something upon us all right. What now sir?"

"The hour grows late. We shall rest, for now. We have a long journey ahead of us. New Rome is some distance from here. We shall have to acquire horses before our departure."

"I'll take care of it."

"Thank you. Secure lodgings for the night as well."

"Ah... you want me to get a room for our prisoner too, seeing as how she's agreed to help us and all?"

"Whatever for? She already has one."

7

Deputy Vanessa Gellar made her rounds in the city. The Witch Hunter had said that he and his assistant would be taking the prisoner west to New Rome instead of up north as they had originally planned. That suited her fine. Gellar had overheard most of Fletcher's story. It made her shiver to recall the details. God, how could human beings subject themselves to that? History wasn't Gellar's strong suit, but it was impossible to not know how magic and the Occult Wars had destroyed the world almost five hundred years ago. Centuries later, human beings were still screwing around with powers they were never meant to touch. Madness.

Thinking back on Fletcher's story, Gellar had worried that Francisco had destroyed the city in a fit of rage, but the New

Rome police responded to her telegram, said all was well, and that they'd make arrangements with the Witch Hunters to extradite Fletcher. That was that.

"Hey Vanessa!" a girl cried out, waving. Gellar smiled and waved back. This is how law enforcement should be, she thought. A nice small town where everyone knew each other and nobody got into any serious trouble, like selling their souls to demons.

A figure approached her. It was swathed in shadow, but it moved with a shuffling limp. It stepped out into the light of a lamp post, revealing a man in a police uniform. His face was a battered, bloody ruin, his belt tightened around his thigh which was dripping a trail of blood. Gellar rushed to him, wrapping him in her arms.

"Hey! Sir! What happened? Are you alright?!" she yelled.

"You're... human..." he whispered.

"Yes! Yes, I'm human!"

He sagged and she gently lowered him to the ground. Gawkers had gathered round, wondering at this bloody apparition that had come to their town.

"You!" Gellar said, pointing at a man who had come to stare. "Go tell the doc. Hurry!" He took off at a sprint.

The police officer tried to speak, but Gellar shushed him.

"It's going to be alright. Don't talk. Save your strength," she said. She laid his head on the ground and held his hand. He closed his eyes. Gellar thought he had died, but his chest still rose and fell. The patch on his shoulder caught her eye. It read NRPD.

Her brow furrowed. New Rome Police Department? What on earth was he doing so far from home? Gellar stayed with the officer until the hospital carriage arrived. Together with the driver, she hoisted the officer inside.

"You know this guy?" the driver asked.

"No."

"Shit... well, get in anyway. Talk to him. Keep him steady until we get to the doc!"

Gellar climbed inside the carriage and knelt beside the patient. The carriage bumped and rattled on the cobblestone street as the driver urged the horses onward. She whispered a quick prayer that the wounded officer would make it to the doc in time.

8

Zelda Fletcher lay stretched out on her cot, staring at the ceiling. She thought about Flint's words and the events that had led her here. Fletcher never stole from anyone who couldn't afford it. She enjoyed the feeling of power that magic gave her. She could bend the minds of others to her will, but, looking back on it, she'd never intentionally caused anyone physical harm. She used her mesmerism mainly to erase a target's memory of her, or for the occasional practical joke.

No, she thought, *I never had any interest in seriously hurting anyone.* What Francisco had done – what he was still doing for all she knew – was pure evil. The Witch Hunter had said that magic was as addictive as it was malevolent. She didn't know about the second part, but the first was definitely true. It saddened her that she wouldn't be able to use magic anymore, but if that was a condition for avoiding the gallows or the stake, well, there really wasn't a choice to be made, was there?

And then there was her deal. She'd proposed it in the heat of the moment, but now, upon reflection, she wondered if she'd made the right decision. Sure, she'd stay out of jail if Flint and his Order went to bat for her. But she'd be putting herself in harm's way. And what exactly did Flint expect her to do? She doubted that he'd allow her to use magic, but she wasn't exactly built for physical combat. Oh well. She'd figure it out. She always figured out a way to come out ahead.

Hmm, that's weird, she thought. She could sense a familiar presence in town. She'd learn to tune out the mental noise she overheard from everyone around her, but this one, she knew him. Not a member of Francisco's gang, no. Wait... that was it, he was a cop from New Rome. Shit, what was an NRPD officer doing here? There was no possible way they could have gotten here a few hours after that Gellar chick telegrammed them. No trains ran between the two cities. She sensed that he was gravely injured. Dying. Why would...?

Francisco. She'd hoped that the combined forces of angry civilians and the NRPD had put him down. Witches and warlocks had their limit. But if Francisco had wiped them all out, she was in even bigger trouble than she'd thought.

Fletcher rose from her cot. She grabbed her tin cup and began rattling it against the bars.

"Hello? Hello?! Is anyone there? I need help!"

A deputy she didn't recognize came to her cell.

"What's wrong?" he asked.

"There's a police officer who just came into town. He's injured and he needs help!"

The deputy's brow furrowed. "I haven't heard anything about that," he said.

"Trust me, he's here. Uh, could you get the Witch Hunter for me? Or let the sheriff or that one deputy, Gellar, know about it?"

The deputy gave her a skeptical look and left the prison.

An idea formed in Fletcher's mind. Francisco may have leveled New Rome in his rage. If that was the case, then surviving police officers and citizens would have scattered in every direction, including here. If Francisco and his gang decided to pursue them, then she and the Witch Hunter might be working together sooner than either of them had expected.

The minutes ticked by. Fletcher paced her cell. Had the deputy done as she'd asked? Imprisonment was driving her mad. After another agonizing few minutes, she heard the door open, and the rhythmic tapping of boots. Silas Flint had arrived.

He approached her cell. "You asked to see me, Miss Fletcher?"

"I think there's trouble."

"Oh?"

"I, ah, sensed someone arriving in town. A police officer. From New Rome."

Flint's eyes narrowed. "I believe I made it clear that a condition of your pardon is forswearing the dark arts."

"Look, I can't help it, alright? I hear things, I sense people... that's probably not ever going to go away."

Flint crossed his arms. "Go on."

"He's injured. Dying."

Flint said nothing.

"Look, if you don't believe me, go ask one of the other deputies. He's still alive but fading. If they've got a hospital or a doctor here, he's probably there by now."

Without a word, Flint turned and left the cells.

9

After getting directions from the deputy on duty at the sheriff's office, Flint arrived at Jordan's hospital, or what passed for one. The city's doctor had added on wings to his personal residence to accommodate extra beds for patients who needed them. It reminded Flint of his hometown out west, so he banished the thoughts from his mind as soon as they arose.

The door was open, so Flint let himself in and found Deputy Gellar waiting in the front parlor.

"Captain Flint," she said. "What are you doing here?"

"I was about to ask that very question of you, Deputy Gellar," he said.

"I was patrolling on foot when an injured man came to me, so I rushed him here to the doc."

"Was he an officer with the New Rome Police Department by any chance?"

"Wha... yes, he is. How did you know that?"

"Miss Fletcher informed me." Flint filed that way for later. It spoke well of Fletcher's desire for repentance, and if he had the opportunity, he would put in a good word for her during the upcoming legal proceedings.

"Was he able to speak?" Flint asked.

"Not much. He'd lost a lot of blood. He was happy to find human beings, but that's about all I got from him before he passed out."

"You telegrammed the NRPD earlier today, did you not?"

"Yes."

"And they did not mention any unusual happenings in their city."

"No, they didn't. They said, and I quote, all is well. I told them we had a prisoner who had confessed to a series of robberies and assaults in their jurisdiction. They said they'd contact your Chapter House and make arrangements for extradition."

Flint perked up. "In your telegram, did you mention that she had confessed to witchcraft?

Gellar's brow furrowed. "No... I didn't."

"Where is the patient now?"

"He's down that hallway, third door on your right, but the doctor said..."

Flint strode toward the patient's room, letting himself in. The doctor was adjusting an intravenous drip for a man who lay in bed. The man's face was a battered ruin, his skin held a grey pallor that spoke to his tremendous blood loss.

"Excuse me," the doctor said, glaring at Flint. "This man is in no condition to be answering any..."

Flint ignored the doctor and approached the wounded police officer. He leaned down to study his face. Blunt force trauma to be sure. Cuts and abrasions on his torso. A deep stab wound to the right leg. And a peculiar smell. It wasn't offensive but it was familiar. Flint sniffed deeply. Ozone.

Flint said, "I beg your pardon, Doctor...?"

"Mitchell."

"Doctor Mitchell, this man is the victim of sorcerous assault. You will note the smell of ozone about his person. I daresay he suffered a murderous flow of magical lightning. Have you noticed calcification to his bone structure?"

"Right now, I'm trying to get this man more fluids, I'll worry about his bones la..."

The patient's eyes opened. He gasped and pushed himself up in bed. The doctor rushed forward and held his arm.

"Easy, easy! It's okay. You're safe now."

Deputy Gellar entered the room and stood at Flint's side.

"What..." the police officer said. "What happened? Where am I?"

"You're in my house, in Jordan," Mitchell said. "It's okay. I'm a doctor. Deputy Gellar here brought you to me. You've lost a lot of blood, but I've got you on an IV right now."

The police officer groaned and leaned back into his pillows.

"Are you able to speak?" Flint asked. Mitchell glared at him. "Can you tell us who you are?"

"I'm... Officer Russell Connolly... New Rome PD."

"What happened?" Gellar asked. "What happened to you? Why are you all the way out here?"

Connolly closed his eyes. He took deep breaths.

"Take your time, Officer," Flint said.

Connolly winced. "A week and a half ago, there was... an incident. A monster... showed up... from out of nowhere."

"A monster you say?" Flint asked.

"Yes... it was... Christ..."

Flint scowled but said nothing.

Connolly went on. "It was... tentacles and eyes... everywhere. We tried to stop it. Probably dumped hundreds of mags into it... just kept coming. But that's not even the worst part."

He stopped to catch his breath, while Doctor Mitchell took his vitals and adjusted the IV.

"Please go on Officer," Flint said.

"Witches showed up. Men and women."

Flint and Gellar looked at each other.

"At first we thought we were in even deeper shit... but then they started attacking the monster too."

"Indeed?" Flint said.

"Yeah..." Connolly said. "They were throwing lightning bolts, fireballs, throwing shit with their minds. Never thought I'd be happy to see human beings messing around with the dark arts."

Flint scowled. "Were you successful in bringing down the unholy fiend?"

Connolly closed his eyes, bowed his head. "No. It killed so many of us... we had to keep falling back. Eventually, it just became every man for himself."

"And you ran," Flint said.

"You don't understand," Connolly said. "That thing... it killed everyone. There was no one left to defend." His eyes watered with tears.

"Do not despair, Officer," Flint said, patting his shoulder.

"You did everything that you could, above and beyond the call of Christian duty."

Connolly leaned back into his pillows, closing his eyes with a deep sigh. He was fast asleep within moments.

"You two should let him rest," Mitchell said. "I'll take it from here."

Flint and Gellar returned to the front parlor. Flint gazed out the front window, hands held behind his back. Gellar rubbed her temples, her face a mixture of fear and bewilderment.

"If what he says is true," she said, "Then who answered my telegram?"

"Who indeed," Flint said. There were any number of possibilities to account for this, and none of them boded well. Whoever had answered knew that Zelda Fletcher was incarcerated here. He doubted that the mysterious correspondent would contact his Chapter House. In any case, it sounded as though Francisco Cortez had succeeded in summoning some sort of demonic entity. The creature would have to be put down. If it had slain most of the police force, then Flint and Navarro would be on their own. They'd need reinforcements.

Flint straightened his long coat, adjusted his wide brimmed hat.

"Deputy Gellar," he said, "I suggest you locate Sheriff Arnett and inform him of what has transpired. Whoever you spoke to knows that Miss Fletcher is here. It is possible that someone may come for her."

Gellar nodded. "Or something."

"I shall proceed to the telegram office and notify my Chapter House as well. If anything comes for Miss Fletcher, we must be prepared to give them a warm welcome."

10

Flint picked up Navarro from the hotel bar, much to the latter's annoyance, and once again headed to the telegram office. Navarro took a seat in front of the telegraph.

"Ready when you are sir," he said.

"New Rome destroyed, stop. Hostile entities may be headed toward Jordan, stop. Request reinforcements, stop. End message."

Navarro leaned back in his chair. "You really think someone will come for Zelda?"

"I do not know," Flint said. "If the hellspawn destroyed New Rome as Officer Connolly said, then it is either intelligent enough to operate a telegraph... or there are citizens who are in league with it."

Navarro shuddered. "Why do they do it boss? What's in it for them, working for a googly eyed tentacle monster?"

"Miss Fletcher claims to have talent for manipulating the minds of others. Perhaps the creature does as well. Or perhaps it gained disciples through promising power. In any case, this creature will prove no match for dedicated warriors of God."

The telegram jumped to life. Flint heard a series of beeps and taps as it received an incoming message. Navarro pulled off the tape to read.

"Let's see," he said. "Acknowledged. Sending reinforcements by carriage. Will push on through night. Should arrive in several hours. God be with you." He sighed. "Looks like we're on our own for now, sir."

Flint nodded. It was unfortunate, but not unexpected. The train between Jordan and the train station near Fort Marsing would not resume its schedule until the next morning. Better for them to ride hard for Jordan now, than wait until sunrise.

"We shall make do with what we have," Flint said.

"Maybe we'll get lucky. Maybe nothing will come for Zelda. Maybe whatever's coming for her won't get here for a few days."

Flint raised an eyebrow.

Navarro sighed. "Yeah, you're right sir. I'll expect the worst, as usual, and probably still get scared shitless anyway."

Flint gave him a wintry smile. "If it is any consolation, Mr. Navarro, true courage is doing one's duty even when one is frightened out of his wits."

Navarro scoffed. "Well, that's easy for you to say sir, no offense. I've never seen you scared of anything in all the time we've worked together."

"You have not seen my fear, but I assure you that it exists," Flint said.

11

Flint and Navarro returned to the sheriff's office and Fletcher's cell. She was on her feet, pacing as usual. She perked up when she saw the two men arrive.

"Was I right?" she asked Flint.

"You were correct," he replied. "Are you familiar with an Officer Russell Connolly?"

"I know of him, never spoken to him. He's the one who's hurt?"

"Yes."

Fletcher sighed. "What happened?"

Flint summarized Connolly's account of the demonic entity that had laid waste to New Rome. Fletcher took it all in, looking more and more depressed as she heard the story.

"Francisco," she said. "Damn him."

"You said you heard something roar when you were running away from his house, right?" Navarro asked.

"Yeah, that's right."

"Do you believe Mr. Cortez summoned the creature?" Flint asked.

"I don't know. Maybe? None of us had ever tried conjuring demons before, but who knows what Francisco got from that damned book?"

"We have reason to believe that someone or something will be coming for you here," Flint said.

"Yeah, I figured," Fletcher said. "Guess we'll be working together sooner rather than later, huh?"

"Yes, it appears so." Flint got closer to her cell. "I will make the details of our arrangement clear, Miss Fletcher. I have summoned reinforcements from Fort Marsing and they will arrive here in Jordan within several hours. You will be released from this cell, and you will fight by our side. If you attempt to rejoin your comrades, you will be summarily executed. If you disobey our orders, summary execution. If you attempt to escape, or work mesmerism upon us, or otherwise hinder us in any way..."

"Yeah, I get it, I'm dead," she said. "Is this your idea of a pep talk? Because your presentation needs a lot of work."

"He has his moments," Navarro chuckled.

Flint turned to Navarro. "Please notify one of the deputies that we will be releasing Miss Fletcher once our brothers and sisters arrive." Navarro nodded and went on his way.

"Uh, Captain Flint?" Fletcher asked.

"What is it?"

"What exactly do you expect me to do? I mean I'm guessing I'm not allowed to use magic, right? So either give me a gun or something, or leave me in this cell. I'm not going out there unarmed."

Flint frowned. "Have you ever worked with firearms before?"

"Ah... no, not really. Don't really need to when you can throw fire and lightning, you know?"

Flint rolled his eyes. "I shall decide what to do with you later. However, know that your willingness to help is noticed and appreciated." With that, Flint took his leave and joined Navarro.

"What are you thinking you'll have her do, sir?" he asked.

"I do not know," Flint said. "If she has no experience with firearms, she may prove more hindrance than help."

"Do you trust her?"

Flint considered. "She is an insolent heretic. However... I believe her desire for redemption is sincere. She informed me of Officer Connolly's plight, which she did not have to do."

"Well, there's one other possibility. I mean besides giving her a gun or leaving her in jail."

"I already know what you are going to suggest Ricardo. It is out of the question."

"I'm just saying, sir. She's got the power. She could use it to do some good for a change."

"That is how it starts, Mr. Navarro," Flint said. "Those who possess the talent for magic seldom set out to become devilish fiends. First, they use their power to lend unnatural aid to their family. Then their friends. Then they begin to wonder why they should not use it for their own benefit. It is not long before they see the enslavement of others as being to their benefit. Magic is altogether evil. Miss Fletcher has expressed her desire to give it up. I would not ask her to return to her former ways, like a dog to its vomit."

"I suppose you're right sir."

"However, she said something to me earlier that may prove useful."

"What's that sir?"

"She has the ability to sense the presence of others. She claims to have no control over it, but we may be able to adapt it to our purposes."

12

Hours later, Flint and Navarro waited at the outskirts of town. It was nearly three in the morning. The skies were clear, and the full moon lit up the grassy marshes surrounding Jordan. Sheriff Arnett had little to go on beyond a vague warning of possible coming trouble, but he said he would deputize every citizen with a gun if necessary.

Navarro laughed.

"Does something amuse you, Mr. Navarro?" Flint asked.

"I was just thinking, sir. A witch wanting to repent is causing us as much trouble as one who don't."

"The thought had crossed my mind as well."

They continued their vigil. Navarro scanned the horizon with an ancient pair of binoculars. He tapped Flint on the shoulder.

"Sir," he said, handing off the binoculars.

Flint raised them to his eyes. He could see a faint light on the horizon. A lantern. Then a second one. Then a third. Then a long line of them. The Witch Hunters' carriages were making good headway, their teams of horses a frothy mess from maintaining the pace. Flint prayed the horses weren't completely blown and would be able to remain in service. Human beings chose their fates. The poor animals did not know any better.

Flint was just about to praise God for their fortuitous arrival when Deputy Gellar came running to their side.

"Captain Flint!" she cried. She doubled over, panting.

"What is it Deputy?"

"We've got trouble."

"What sort of trouble?"

"The hell-spawn kind."

Flint turned and faced the opposite direction, binoculars held to his eyes. The night was dark, but darker still was the mass on the horizon. Flint strained his vision. The mass was moving closer, but that wasn't all. The mass was writhing, quivering all over. It had a gelatinous oblong body with squirming tentacles and baleful eyes everywhere. A vicious beak, like that of a giant octopus or squid, gnashed in fury.

Flint couldn't hear it at this distance, but he was certain the beast was making blood curdling howls as it approached fresh prey.

"What do we do, Captain?" Gellar asked.

Flint pressed his lips together. The monster and his fellow Witch Hunters were rapidly converging on Jordan.

"Deputy, you will accompany Mr. Navarro and I to the prison. We will collect Miss Fletcher, and then we shall join your fellow deputies on the far side of town."

"But…"

"No buts woman! My fellow Templars will be joining us! Until they arrive, it is our duty to face this monster with faith in our hearts and songs of praise and glory on our lips!"

Flint took off at a sprint. Gellar stood still, mouth agape.

"Uh…" she said.

"You heard him," Navarro said, charging after the Witch Hunter. Gellar got ahold of herself and followed.

13

Presently, the trio arrived at Fletcher's cell. Navarro and Gellar were breathing hard, but Flint wasn't even sweating.

"Miss Fletcher!" he called.

Fletcher had been asleep, but she rolled out of her cot, rubbing her eyes.

"What time is it?" she mumbled.

"It is time to stand fast against the forces of darkness!"

Fletcher snapped fully awake. "What?!"

"Deputy Gellar, release the prisoner, if you please."

Gellar hesitated. Navarro prodded her. She stepped forward, inserted the key into the lock, turned, She pulled the gate open.

Fletcher stood fast, stunned at this turn of events.

"Is… is something here?"

"Yep," Navarro said. "It's all tentacles and eyeballs."

"Oh Christ," Fletcher said.

"Mind the blasphemy," Flint snapped. "You said earlier that you possess certain mental abilities that you cannot control."

"Uh… yeah…"

"Tell me, what can you sense of our approaching nemesis?"

Fletcher closed her eyes. Her eyelids fluttered. A few moments passed.

"It's… it's familiar… somehow…" she said.

The trio waited.

"How… I don't… oh shit…" Fletcher said. "God… that's Francisco!"

"Say what now?" Navarro asked.

"I… can hear him…" Fletcher said.

"And?" Flint asked.

"I don't know… it's like… it's him but it's not him. Like the man's an echo of something else."

"That something else being a bug eyed tentacle monster," Navarro said.

"What… what happened to him?" Fletcher asked, horrified.

"We can worry about that later," Flint said. "For now our task is clear: this unholy fiend must be destroyed at any cost!"

Fletcher shrank back. "Uh, Captain Flint… you remember what we talked about earlier?"

Flint stared her down. Finally, he drew one of his pistols and handed it to her, butt-first.

"This weapon is loaded with blessed silver tipped bullets. If you need another magazine, speak to me or to Mr. Navarro. I would ask you to remember another subject we discussed."

"Yeah, I remember, if I look at you wrong, summary execution, right?"

"That is correct. Deputy Gellar, if the prisoner attempts to escape or to attack us, you have my permission to put her down."

"Ah… yes sir," Gellar said.

"Onward!" Flint yelled, drawing his sword. "We must hold this beast off long enough for my brothers in arms to join us! The Holy Spirit is with us!"

Fletcher and Gellar looked at each other, then at Navarro.

"I told you he has his moments," he said, before following his boss out of the jail.

14

The foursome joined Sheriff Arnett, the other deputies, and gun owning citizens whom Arnett had deputized. They gathered in Jordan's central plaza. Flint thought the only things missing were the pitchforks and torches, but those were from a bygone age in a better world.

"Hear me!" Flint cried. All eyes focused on him. He paced back and forth. "A foul darkness approaches your fair city! It has laid waste to the city of New Rome, and now it means to do the same to your homes, your families!"

A ripple of murmurs passed through the crowd.

"Fear not! As we speak, my fellow Knight Templars ride hard! Together, all of us, the children of God, the brothers and sisters of Christ, shall be guided by the Holy Spirit, and we will banish this fiend into the darkest circles of Hell from whence it came!"

The crowd stood still, their faces set.

"Everyone on me! Forward!" Flint pointed the way with his sword. He, Navarro, Sheriff Arnett, Deputy Gellar, and Fletcher led the crowd toward the western outskirts of Jordan.

"Captain Flint?" Arnett said.

"Yes?"

"Do we have a plan of attack?"

"Mr. Navarro?"

"Hmm," Navarro said. "Well, from what I saw, it's a big blob of jelly with eyes and tentacles. I'd say shoot out as many of its eyes as you can."

"Oh Jesus, oh God," Fletcher said, breathing hard.

"Steady Miss Fletcher," Flint said. "The way you carry yourself tonight may well determine your future."

"Right now, I'm not sure if I even have a future."

"Nonsense! Never despair, for if God is with us, who can stand against us?"

"A fucking giant tentacle monster?"

Flint shook his head. Changing the subject, he asked, "Can you tell us anything new about our adversary?"

Fletcher concentrated. "It's like I'm hearing several minds at once. Francisco's is one of them."

"And?"

"He's… he's all over the place. Angry, terrified, lost… I can feel one mind that's overpowering all the others. It's not human, whatever it is. It's old. Very old. And… I want to say evil, but I don't know. It's like evil isn't strong enough for it."

Flint scowled. Whatever it was, it would prove no match for dedicated servants of God, of that he was certain. He had been telling the truth to Navarro earlier, when he said that Navarro had never seen his fear. Flint did fear one thing: failing in his solemn duty to God and man. The deputies, the citizens, even Fletcher, needed him to lead with courage and faith, and he swore to Almighty God that he would not fail.

A blood curdling roar echoed in the night. The townsfolk gasped and drew back a few steps. Flint swore to himself. The courage of his militia was balanced on a knife's edge.

Without breaking his stride or looking back, Flint called out, "Steady! Trust in God! It is He who guides us!" He pushed on, eventually hearing the shuffle of hundreds of feet behind him. He silently gave thanks to Jesus Christ for shoring up their courage.

As the crowd approached the edge of town, they could hear a slithering sound, along with a horrifying moan that was like dozens of voices crying out at once.

Fletcher fell to her knees, clutching her head, screaming in pain. Flint and Navarro rushed to her side.

"Zelda!" Navarro shouted.

"Get out… get out of my mind… Francisco…" Fletcher growled through gritted teeth.

Flint reached into his shirt and pulled out the crucifix and St. Benedict medals he always wore around his neck. Clutching the chains in his fist, he dangled them in front of Fletcher's face.

"Begone foul demon!" Flint snarled. "The power of Christ compels you! It is not I, but He who commands you to depart from this child of God!"

Fletcher laughed in a raspy, guttural voice that was not her own. She looked up, her eyes a blazing yellow.

"This one is ours, Witch Hunter," the demon said through Fletcher's body.

"Not so long as I draw breath," Flint said. He pressed the crucifix and the medal into Fletcher's forehead. Her flesh sizzled and the demon screamed in pain. Fletcher collapsed.

"Zelda! Are you alright?" Navarro yelled. He gave her face a few gentle slaps.

She awoke with a sputter, and then winced at the pain on her forehead.

"What…" she began, then touched the burn marks. "What the fuck just happened?"

"You were temporarily possessed by our enemy," Flint said. "Stay close to me. I shall protect you." He offered her a hand. She took it and he pulled her to her feet.

"Now! Let us put down this monster!" Flint yelled.

Fletcher continued to rub the burn marks on her forehead. She turned to Navarro and said, "Maybe I had him figured wrong."

Navarro chuckled. "Most people do."

The posse reached the edge of town and beheld the approaching demon. Flint and Navarro had seen it from a great distance, but up close it was even more horrifying: an enormous gelatinous mass with suckered tentacles writhing and twisting in every direction, pulling its great bulk along the ground with a slither. Worse were the many rolling eyes, all a sickly yellow, embedded in its body. Human faces pressed against its skin from inside its body, locked in permanent screams, pushing to get out but trapped forever in that fleshy hell. Its squid-like beak gnashed at the air, hungry for more human flesh.

Some townsfolk screamed. Others took off running. Flint knew he would have to take charge or he and Navarro would be alone.

"Mr. Navarro."

Navarro got out in front of the crowd, his bolt action rifle at the ready. He aimed at one of the demon's eyes and fired. The eyeball exploded in a cloud of black ichor and viscous jelly. The beast screeched in pain and drew back a few inches.

"The monster can bleed! If it bleeds, then we can destroy it!" Flint shouted. The townsfolk and sheriff's deputies advanced a few steps. Flint had stemmed the tide of desertions. Now it was time to put them to the ultimate test.

"On me! Kill this devil! Charge!" His sword swinging above his head, the blessed steel on fire with holy power, Flint advanced on the creature, firing his pistol with his off hand. The small caliber bullets didn't cause as much damage as Navarro's high powered rifle rounds, but they were still good for taking out the monster's many eyes.

The crowd roared in defiance and charged the beast. Tentacles whipped out in every direction. Flint parried them with his sword, severing some altogether, his blessed sword cauterizing the putrid flesh as it sliced through them like butter. The deputies and townsfolk put down a wall of lead from rifles, shotguns, and handguns, tearing into the creature, causing its corrupted blood to spray and leak everywhere.

15

The creature was large enough that Fletcher was able to shoot it, but her aim wasn't good enough to destroy its eyes. Her pistol locked open. Empty. Flint and Navarro were both at the forefront of the crowd, shooting and slashing the beast like men possessed.

Zelda, a familiar voice echoed in her mind. *Zelda, it's me. Are you going to let them kill me, Zelda? After everything I've done for you?*

She dropped the pistol and clutched her head in pain.

Francisco, what happened to you?

I've merged, Zelda. I am one with the demon Ichthil.

Why?!

Blood and souls Zelda. They are the true power. Come. Join me and I will show you.

With a scream, Fletcher pushed the demonic presence from her mind. The burn marks on her forehead hurt more, but she gritted her teeth against the pain. Picking up the spent pistol, she made her way to the forefront to join Flint and Navarro, who were still fighting hard.

"Do you require another magazine?" Flint said between gunshots and slashes.

"Actually sir, I'm here to give this back to you," she said, holding out the pistol.

"Whatever for?"

"I don't need it anymore."

She dropped the weapon at Flint's feet. She focused on all of the rage, the fear, the remorse, the self-loathing, and the hatred she had felt over the days since she had turned on Francisco. A low growl escaped her throat. A nimbus of blue fire crackled about her. Electricity formed on her fingertips. She'd had enough of this, and Francisco was going to find out that the student had surpassed her teacher.

Screaming an inarticulate roar, Fletcher channeled as much magical energy as she could handle into one mighty blast of fire.

16

Flint shielded himself with his long coat as flames streamed from Fletcher's hands into the demon's flank. His sword was remained cool to the touch, but thanks to its proximity to so much magical energy, its brightness stung his eyes. He pursed his lips and looked down his nose at Fletcher. She took no notice of his disapproval, pouring fire and lightning into the shrieking monster. The acrid stench of burning flesh permeated the air.

"What do you think sir?" Navarro yelled, firing and working the bolt of his rifle with the skill of years' worth of practice.

"We shall deal with her when our mission is complete! Do not relent!"

One of the demon's tentacles whipped out, slamming into a crowd of townsfolk, crushing them against a storefront, and out the back of the building which exploded into a cloud of dust, wood, and blood. Another tentacle snaked around the waists of several sheriff's deputies. It yanked the screaming men and women into its gnashing beak, crushing their bones and swallowing the bloody pulp.

Its meal lent new vigor to the monstrosity as eyes that had been shot out regenerated, bullet wounds healed. Flint observed and noticed that the monster's hide expelled the lead slugs, but the silver tipped rounds from his and Navarro's guns remained inside. Further, the burns caused by Fletcher's magical assault were healing more slowly.

Flint saw a tentacle moving toward Fletcher, who failed to notice it, so focused was she on pouring out witch fire upon the accursed beast.

"Look out!" Flint yelled. He sprinted toward Fletcher, knocking her down with a shoulder check. He brought his sword down upon the tentacle, slicing it off in one stroke. The stench of the putrid, cauterized flesh made his eyes water. He noticed then that the monster was not regenerating wounds caused by his blessed sword.

Fletcher climbed to her feet. Her mouth hung open in shock.

"You are quite welcome," Flint said, taking aim and shooting out another of the demon's eyes. He could feel its roars of pain and rage deep in his chest.

"I'm sorry," Fletcher yelled, "But I'm better at this than I am with a gun!" A bolt of lightning shot from her palm, striking the beast in its side, electricity crackling over its body.

"Less talking and more killing!" Flint shouted back. Between them, Flint, Navarro, and Fletcher were holding the demon at bay while the townsfolk and sheriff's deputies poured on the gunfire. The monster's bulk was shaking the outlying buildings of Jordan to pieces. Sweat dripped into Flint's eyes.

"Begone foul demon! Your judgment is at hand!" yelled a familiar voice. Flint looked over his shoulder. The townsfolk had parted like the Red Sea. Standing before them was Witch Hunter General John Abernathy. His face was twisted with righteous anger, the sword in his right hand was ablaze with holy light, his left held a pistol of the same make as Flint's.

Even the monster paused its assault.

"Your hellish kind do not belong in this world!" Abernathy bellowed. "I swear before Almighty God and all of the angels and saints, we shall send you back to the fiery abyss! Charge!"

Abernathy ran to the front line. Behind him came a throng of men in black with their signature wide brimmed hats, all armed with swords and pistols. They were accompanied by their assistants, armed with rifles, shotguns, and grenades.

Flint rushed the monster while it stood still. Screaming an inarticulate battle cry, he slashed a deep cut into its side, the black ichor sizzling and evaporating on contact with the blessed steel. Fletcher screamed in rage and conjured an enormous fireball which slammed into the monster's face, just above its fearsome beak. The demon screeched and pulled back. Navarro fired his rifle, worked the bolt, fired again.

Abernathy rushed toward Flint's side. They sliced off tentacles that reached for them, they fired their pistols into the creature's eyes, they spun, and cut, and shot.

"I did not think you would come here yourself sir!" Flint yelled over the din.

"It's been too long since I've been in the field!" Abernathy shouted back. The dozens of other Witch Hunters closed the distance and began a relentless assault on the towering demon. Their swords and silver tipped bullets caused an ocean of black ichor to spill upon the ground. In the back of his mind, Flint pitied the people of Jordan, for their land would be poisoned for years.

Their courage strengthened by the arrival of reinforcements, the townsfolk and deputies cheered and renewed their own assault. Their mundane weapons may not be able to kill the beast, Flint thought, but they can hurt it, and that may be enough.

A tentacle whipped out and wrapped around a Witch Hunter, pinning his arms to his sides. Flint rushed to him and cut the tentacle off. The beast withdrew the stump, the remaining length loosening enough for the Witch Hunter to shrug out of it.

"Thank you, brother!" he cried, returning to the fray. Fletcher continued to hurl fireballs and lightning bolts into the demon, which shrank back from the magical onslaught.

"I take it she is the one who wanted to confess?" Abernathy yelled to Flint.

"That is correct sir!"

A tentacle whipped out, fast as lightning, and pulled a screaming citizen of Jordan into the demon's beak, cutting off the man's cries with a sickening crunch.

"Do not relent!" Abernathy yelled. "Show no mercy!"

17

Fletcher was nearly spent. She'd never used this much magical energy before, and it was taking its toll on her body. Her hands smoked, the flesh raw from handling so much power.

You cannot win this, Zelda, Francisco's voice whispered in her mind. *I was always better than you.*

We'll see about that, she thought. But as much as she hated to admit it, he might be right. They weren't causing enough damage to outpace the demon Ichthil's ability to regenerate wounds. They needed something bigger. She glanced over her shoulder. The Witch Hunters' assistants, clad in leather armor like Navarro, were standing back, firing their rifles at the beast. She spied Flint's assistant in the firing line and rushed to his side.

"You alright?" Navarro shouted to her.

"We're not hurting it enough!" she said. "We need more power!"

"I think you've had enough!" he replied, nodding toward her scarred hands.

Desperate, Fletcher looked around. Then she saw it: some of the Supernumeraries had grenades dangling from their belts. A wicked smile crossed her face.

"I have a crazy idea!" she said.

"Those are my favorite kind!" Navarro replied.

"I need grenades!"

18

Flint cut his way through a sea of tentacles. For every one he sliced off, it seemed like two more took its place like a hydra. The creature screeched, the human faces on its sides twisted and writhed. The fight appeared hopeless, even with the reinforcements from the Chapter House.

Fletcher came running to him, two orbs in her hands.

"Captain Flint!" she cried. "I have an idea!"

"I am open to any suggestions!"

"We have to get onto its back!"

"Just how the devil do you propose to do that?!"

"Take these!" she yelled, handing off the orbs, which Flint now saw were grenades.

"What do..." he began, but Fletcher wrapped him in a tight embrace. He saw her mouth move but could not hear the words over the sound of gunfire. They were launched into the air. Flint's stomach lurched with the sudden change in pressure. The witch had made them levitate!

"What foul sorcery is..." Before he could finish the sentence, they dropped on top of the monster. The spongy flesh sank beneath their feet.

"We need a hole!" Fletcher screamed. Flint then realized what she planned to do. He stuffed the grenades into his pockets and drove his sword down into the monster's back. It roared and bucked, nearly throwing them, but the Witch Hunters on the ground pushed on, distracting it with their frontal assault.

Flint carved a circle into the monster's hide and used

leverage to pry out a chunk of flesh. Fletcher, surrounded by blue fire, levitated toward the wound, above it, and unleashed a stream of fire straight down. It burned its way further into the monster, deepening the hole that Flint had started. She alighted upon its back, made her way to Flint, and wrapped her arms around him again.

"Now!" she screamed. Flint drew the grenades from his pocket. He pulled the pin from one, dropped it in, and did likewise with the second. They splashed into the creature's disgusting ichor. Fletcher whispered her spell, and she and Flint were airborne again.

"Take cover!" Flint yelled as they passed over the crowd. The Witch Hunters dove away from the monster, covering their heads as they hit the ground flat.

A deafening explosion thundered as the monster's face exploded in a shower of gore and burnt flesh. Its body sagged and was still.

The Witch Hunters rose to their feet and carefully approached the carcass. Flint, Fletcher, and Navarro joined them. All were silent, on the lookout for any signs of life.

"Oh, you've got to be shitting me," Fletcher growled.

"What is it Miss Fletcher?" Flint asked.

"It's still alive."

Abernathy, overhearing her, pointed his sword at the smoking pile of demonflesh.

"Burn this disgusting creature!"

19

Fletcher stood back from the Witch Hunters and Supernumeraries as they hunted down any scraps of demonflesh that so much as twitched.

This isn't over Zelda, she heard in her mind.

Looks pretty over to me.

Devilish laughter. *If you had stayed with me, I could have shown you that death is only the beginning.*

No thanks.

20

The crowd – Witch Hunters and assistants, and townsfolk – gathered around the great pyre that had once been the colossal demon. Flint, Navarro, Fletcher, and Abernathy stood at the forefront.

"When in doubt…" Abernathy said.

"Kill it with fire," Flint said.

Abernathy turned to Fletcher. "So, you're the one who turned herself in."

Fletcher straightened her posture, smoothed her dress. "Uh, yes, that's me sir."

"Captain Flint, your report?"

"She is impudent, disrespectful, shows no regard to proper authority, she is a petty criminal, and blatantly used witch-craft after I made clear to her what the penalty would be."

Abernathy raised an eyebrow. Fletcher shot Flint a venomous look of outrage.

"However," Flint said, "I daresay she saved all of our lives with her quick thinking and… creative use of her powers."

Abernathy nodded and addressed Fletcher. "How long were you in prison before Captain Flint arrived?"

"Four days. Sir."

"In that case, I sentence you to time served."

Fletcher blinked. Her mouth dropped. Recovering, she sputtered, "Uh, yes, I understand. Thank you sir."

Before Flint could react, she rushed forward and embraced him. Flint started, unsure how to react, but made no move to back away from Fletcher. She let him go.

"You're not such a bad guy. You know, for someone who burns witches and all."

"Hmph," Flint snorted. "Do not misunderstand the General's generosity, Miss Fletcher. If you use your talents to harm the children of God…"

"I know, I know, summary execution." She looked a Navarro as she pointed a thumb at Flint. "Do these guys ever relax?"

"Not as I've noticed."

"Our work isn't finished," Abernathy said. "We still need to secure that book."

Flint nodded. "I suspect Mister Cortez used *In Realis Magicae* in some devilish ritual that bound his soul with the creature."

"New Rome was destroyed though," Navarro said.

"Nevertheless, it's too dangerous to ignore," Abernathy said. "We have to check it out, comb the ruins. If the book survived, we must secure it and destroy it."

"Mister Navarro and I will proceed to New Rome," Flint said.

"What the fuck," Navarro said.

Flint sighed. "That is we shall go once he has had time to drink and rest."

"That's more like it," Navarro said. Fletcher laughed.

21

Far to the west, the ruins of New Rome still smoldered. The once thriving city was razed to its foundations. Francisco, possessed and mutated by the demon Ichthil, had laid waste to everything in sight, devouring the townsfolk to fuel his growing power with blood and souls.

A lone figure strolled through the ruins. He was tall, broad in the chest and shoulders, with a shock of brown hair and shining blue eyes. He had heard rumors that someone in this city had acquired a certain book which contained an ancient and evil power, written in the elder days when Simon Magus walked the earth. The man had come prepared to slaughter every living soul in the city if that was what it took to acquire his prize, but it looked like someone had beat him to it. He hoped the book was still here, but if not, no matter. He would pursue its owner to the ends of the earth if he had to.

The man stretched out his senses. There. It shone like a beacon in the murk of residual magical energies that still hung about the town in a haze. He took no notice of the rotting corpses that Francisco hadn't devoured. That's what they get for resisting their betters.

He turned onto what was once a residential street. The houses were piles of rubble, with wooden beams stretching up into the sky like skeletal fingers. He sensed that he was drawing closer to the power.

It was buried beneath the rubble of what had once been a modest cottage. The man gestured with his hands, and the broken wood parted for him. He continued weaving magical energy, the stones and debris flying off to the side. Finally, he spied his prize. He called it to him and it flew into his grip.

In his hands was *In Realis Magicae*. The man smiled. The author, Abdul Hakim Nazari, had been one of Simon Magus's handpicked apostles. His thoughts, his account of meeting the Great Magician alone were worth more than gold. More importantly, the man hoped to learn the spells and harness the power that Magus had personally bestowed upon his children. He was going to need all the power that he could muster if he hoped to make his vision a reality.

Charles Julian Flint snickered as he tucked the book under his arm.

"I'm looking forward to our reunion, dear brother Silas," he said to himself.

Evil Never Rests

1

Witch Hunter Captain Silas Flint and Supernumerary Ricardo Navarro reined in their horses. They had arrived on the outskirts of the city of New Rome, or rather where it used to be. They beheld a scene of absolute devastation. Scorch marks and human bones littered the ground. The streets were strewn with splintered wood, shattered glass, and broken stonework. Chimneys and wooden beams stretched toward the sky like skeletal fingers. The sun beat down on them from a cloudless sky where vultures and other carrion birds circled overhead. A raven was perched atop the remains of the wall that had formerly enclosed the city. It cawed at them as though to scold them for disturbing the meal of its brethren.

"Guess we can't be asking for directions sir," Navarro said.

"No, it appears we cannot," Flint replied. "Nevertheless, we must begin the search. We have the address. Perhaps God saw fit to spare the street signs from destruction."

Several days earlier, a source had informed the Witch Hunter and his assistant that a coven of warlocks and witches had been operating from the city. More importantly, their leader possessed a copy of the accursed tome, *In Realis Magicae*, written by Abdul Hakim Nazari, a handpicked disciple of Simon Magus himself. Their mission was to destroy or secure the book at any cost.

Flint took a swallow from his canteen. "Come along Mr. Navarro. Evil never rests, and neither can servants of the Lord."

They urged their horses forward, hooves clip clopping on

the cobblestone streets. A murder of crows took to flight, screeching as they left a moldering skeleton behind them. The two riders weaved around piles of rubble.

"This place gives me the creeps," Navarro said.

"I concur that it is rather morbid," Flint said. He spat upon the street. "It infuriates me that so many innocent souls perished because one man chose to dabble in powers men were never meant to wield."

"Sir?" Navarro pointed at a bent metal street sign that read Harley Boulevard.

"Ah, splendid," Flint said. He reached into one of his long coat's many pockets and withdrew a scrap of paper, reading it. "We turn right, proceed three blocks, and then left. The house should be the third one on the right."

"Assuming it's still standing, sir."

"Even if it is not, we must comb the ruins. I doubt that such a wicked work of sorcery as that book is so easily destroyed."

They proceeded on their way. But for the cawing of birds and their flapping wings, the city was as silent as the grave. Flint suppressed a shudder. The source of the city's destruction was long gone, but he could still feel the evil radiating from the ruins. He mentally recited the Pater Noster and the Ave Maria and pushed on.

Presently they arrived on the street where their destination could be found. It looked like a residential neighborhood, but not one house remained standing. Everything was broken wood and shattered bricks. They found a bent mailbox sitting on the curb which read 239.

"This is the spot," Flint said as he dismounted. He adjusted his hat and his gun belt, which held his two pistols and sword.

"What's left of it anyway," Navarro said.

They stood before the shell of a ruined house. To Flint's eyes, it appeared that something had burst out from within. The side of the house facing the street was torn open.

"I see no need to knock," Flint said.

Navarro chuckled. "You should joke more often sir. You got the deadpan delivery perfect."

"I was not joking."

"I know."

They made their way to the threshold where the front door used to be. Peering inside, Flint saw broken furniture, a smashed grandfather clock, broken dishes, scattered cutlery, and other detritus. There was a hallway branching off to the right from the living room.

"God has smiled upon us. The interior is largely intact. Come," Flint said.

"Watch your head sir. The roof might come crashing in," Navarro said.

They crept inside. Flint thanked God for their arrival during daylight hours, for only He knew what fresh horrors may have taken up residence in the ruined city. The forces of darkness were drawn to locales that had seen much bloodshed. He sniffed. The stench of decay filled his nostrils. Behind him, Navarro pinched his nose and made a disgusted sound.

Flint and Navarro arrived at the end of the hallway. To the right was a bedroom, the queen-sized bed disheveled and covered with dust and plaster. On their left was what looked like a library or office. The floor was strewn with rubble and broken bookshelves, but Flint could make out a faded penta-gram on the floor. The dark rust color told him it had been painted in blood. In the center was a large oaken desk. On top of it lay the mummified corpse of a woman. It had been slit open from throat to groin, the rib cage pried open like a gate.

"Shit," Navarro said, making the sign of the cross.

Flint silently offered a prayer for yet another soul lost to the designs of a madman.

"Let us search this room," he said. "We can afford this poor girl a proper burial once we are finished."

"Uh... do you know what this book looks like sir?" Navarro asked.

"Every known copy of *In Realis Magicae* is bound by cured human flesh. The author, Nazari, believed that the strongest magic always comes at the cost of flesh, blood, and souls. The cover will look and feel like stiff leather."

The two men dug through the rubble, studiously ignoring the corpse and other signs of the evil which had taken place in this room. The day was warm, but Flint felt a chill in the air. The stench of decay was ever present, but there was some-thing else, faint, but distinct. He sniffed again. Ozone. That was it. There had been no recent lightning storms in this area. The city's electricity had died days ago. The only other explanation was sorcery. Strange that its telltale odor would linger for so long.

"I'm not having any luck sir," Navarro said. He was on his hands and knees, peering at the scattered books on his half of the room. Some were burnt beyond recognition.

"Nor am I," Flint said. "We must search the surrounding neighborhood if necessary."

"Maybe the owner took it with him."

"I strongly doubt that..." Flint stopped. Something caught his eye in his peripheral vision.

"You find something?" Navarro asked.

"Perhaps." Flint squatted. It was some sort of jewel. Leaning closer, Flint supposed it could be a sapphire with its blue hue and brilliant cut.

Navarro came to his side. He let out a low whistle.

"That's quite a rock. How much you think it's worth boss?"

"It doesn't belong to us, Mr. Navarro."

"Well, it's not like the owner needs it anymore."

2

Flint reached to pick up the jewel. The moment his hand touched it, a column of light shot from it up to the ceiling. Flint backed away, drawing his sword and one of his pistols, Navarro unslinging the bolt action rifle from his back and aiming it at the column. Flint's sword, blessed by the Pope himself, gave off a soft white glow, as it always did in the presence of dark magic.

"What demented devilry is this?!" Flint shouted. Within the column of light, a shimmering translucent figure appeared. It was a man, broad in the chest and shoulders, hands behind his back. His hair was an unruly mop. His mouth was twisted in a cruel smile. His eyes spoke of madness and unspeakable evil. Flint squinted at the apparition. The man was familiar somehow. He couldn't put his finger on it, but he'd swear to it that he'd seen him before.

"Ave Frater," the man said. Flint's mouth fell open. He felt his stomach drop. His mind went back sixteen years to a farm on the outskirts of Mount Angel far to the west. He recalled the vain, cruel, stupid boy who had mutated their parents into hideous monstrosities thanks to his experiments with magic. He remembered the twisted things that had been their mother and father begging him, with their last scraps of humanity, to put them out of their misery. He remembered pulling the trigger twice, twice hearing thunder. And the tears. He remembered the tears that he thought would never end. Flint hadn't seen his younger brother once since that day. He would be 32 now. Flint could see it clearly. This man, it was exactly what he would look like today.

"Charles?" Flint whispered.

"I'm sure you have many questions, but I'm afraid I can't answer them for you. You see, I'm not really here. I've probably been gone for days," said Charles Flint. "This spell allows me to leave messages that can only be activated by their intended recipient. Think of it as... a video recording. That's the mundane term, I think. In any case, I thought you might be coming here for this." He took out a book from behind his back. Even accounting for its translucence, there was no mistaking the cover which appeared to be cured leather.

"You should have taken my advice back at home Silas," Charles said. "You should have pursued the magical arts as I did. Then you might have gotten here first." He snickered. "I've been following your career you know. You, born on the first day of the year, a devoted servant of God, always seeking out new dragons to slay. And me, born on the last day of the year, a magician who will one day surpass even Simon Magus himself. It's almost poetic, don't you think?"

Flint said nothing.

"Be that as it may, *In Realis Magicae* deserves to be in the possession of one who will make proper use of it. I trust you and your Order want to destroy it? Such a waste. And you, Silas, your whole life is a waste. Do you really think you can burn every witch and warlock on earth? In North America? In Cascadia?"

Flint scowled.

Charles laughed. "Oh, but I know you dear brother. You would try. If you could live a thousand lifetimes, you might even succeed at it. But you'll die, and the world will go on, never taking any notice of a single spark that flickered briefly in a tide of darkness. Me though, I plan to live forever. Not in your Heaven, but here, on earth."

Flint closed his eyes.

"I look forward to seeing you in person again someday. And I will. I'd hate for our reunion to be spoiled with bloodshed but make no mistake. If you interfere with my plans, you'll beg for death, but I won't kill you as you did our parents."

Flint balled his fists.

"Farewell, Frater," Charles said. "There's always a place for you by my side. I may be the younger brother, but we both know I am your superior in everything else." Charles's figure shimmered and disappeared, the column of light returning to the jewel.

Flint stood still, his head bowed in silence. After a few moments, Navarro approached him, put a hand on his shoulder.

"Sir?" he asked.

Flint said nothing.

"Silas?"

Flint looked up.

"Are you alright sir?" Navarro asked.

"Yes. I'm fine."

Navarro raised an eyebrow. "You just used a contraction sir. I'm pretty sure you're not fine."

"I do not wish to talk about it."

"Okay, okay, fair enough." Navarro backed away. "But... well, you know, if, if you ever need to..."

"Come. Let us bury this girl and be on our way. There's nothing more for us here in this dead city."

3

After the two men buried the desiccated corpse from the library, they mounted their horses and departed eastward from New Rome, toward their Chapter House at Fort Marsing. They rode in silence through the grassy plains of eastern Cascadia along a well-traveled dirt road that had once been paved with asphalt centuries ago. Presently Flint did not feel like speaking, and Navarro, to his credit, didn't press the matter.

The sun dipped below the horizon, casting the landscape in an orange and purple glow. The Occult War ended nearly five hundred years ago, but the immense magical energies of that long ago era still lingered, playing tricks with the light and shadows even to the present. He reined in his horse, signaling Navarro to stop.

"Let us make camp here for the night," Flint said.

"Sure thing boss."

The two men dismounted and began unpacking their horses' saddlebags. Flint erected their tents and unrolled their sleeping bags. Navarro gathered rocks and kindling to make a fire for the evening. They worked in silence, but Flint's mind was elsewhere. Charles. The boy had fled from their farm while Flint did battle with his mutated parents. Flint had dared to hope that Charles may have repented of his ways in the ensuing years, but he knew now there could only be two possible outcomes: either he would kill Charles, or Charles would kill him.

Navarro got the fire going, and the two men sat down on large rocks. They dined on a meal of hard bread, dried beef jerky, and water. Afterward, they stared into the fire together in silence. Flint took off his hat, ran a hand through his close cropped black hair.

"What do you remember of my account?" Flint asked.

Navarro stirred. "You mean what happened between you and your brother?"

"Yes."

Navarro thought for a few moments. Flint had told Navarro something of his background when they were paired together by the Order, but that had been five years ago. "Well, he never liked going to Mass. When he got older, he fell in with a bad crowd. Warlocks. He got into magic, experimented on your parents."

Flint nodded. "Yes. I was ruminating on his words. He is correct, it is almost Shakespearean, the two of us."

"You mean about your birthdays?"

"I was born on January 1, 2500. Charles was born on December 31, 2500. I have never given serious thought to the significance of our dates of birth, but there may be something to it after all. I was born at the dawn of a new year, he at its dusk. I am a servant of the light, and he of the darkness."

Navarro said nothing.

Flint went on. "After what happened to my mother and father, Charles fled from the scene. I briefly considered hunting him and putting him down like the rabid dog he has become, but when you pursue vengeance, you must dig two graves, as they say."

"You forgave him?" Navarro asked, incredulous.

"I forgave him in the technical sense that I would not actively seek revenge against him. Vengeance is mine, sayeth the Lord. The hatred I harbor for him is a daily struggle. He is partly responsible for my choosing this vocation. He proved to me that magic is altogether evil, and it must be purged from the earth."

"Well, I hate to say it boss, but he kind of had a point. You can't possibly burn every witch on earth."

"No," Flint said, shaking his head. "But I can do my duty and make a small corner of it safer for God's children."

"Damned shame he got to the book before we could," Navarro said.

"Indeed. God only knows what diabolical sorcery he will discover within the accursed tome. We must make our way back to the city of Jordan and telegram Fort Marsing about this development. Apprehending Charles must become a priority."

"He's in the wind though, sir."

"Yes. However, I suspect he will eventually seek us out. His fiendish pride was never able to tolerate my own achievements."

Flint and Navarro passed the rest of the evening in companionable silence. Flint checked his pocket watch. It was nine p.m.

"You shall take the first watch," Flint said. "Awaken me in four hours. Good night Ricardo."

"Good night sir."

Flint removed his long coat and gun belt, placing them, along with his hat, on the floor of his tent, making sure to leave one pistol and his sword within easy reach. He zipped open his sleeping bag and climbed in, rolling onto his side, using a saddle bag as a pillow. He doubted that he would get much rest, if any. Charles had given him much to think about. Nevertheless, he soon fell into an uneasy sleep.

4

"Sir? Silas, wake up."

Flint's eyes snapped open, and he bolted upright. Navarro was squatting by his side. Flint looked around.

"Is it one a.m. already?" he asked, fumbling for his pocket watch. He felt like he had just nodded off.

"No sir, it's only eleven," Navarro said. "There's someone coming. On horseback."

Flint rolled out of sleeping bag. He shrugged back into

his long coat, put the gun belt back on, and adjusted his hat. Navarro pointed east. This part of Cascadia was officially listed as pacified in Flint's travel book, The Witch Hunter's Guide to North America, but that didn't necessarily mean safe. He joined Navarro at his side. The skies were clear, and the moon illuminated the grassy plains in its pale light. Sure enough, there was a rider approaching them, no doubt drawn by the fire.

"What can you make of him Mr. Navarro?" Flint asked.

"Hard to tell in the dark sir. How you want to play it?"

"Let us wait for now. He could simply be a passing traveler."

"Have we ever been that lucky?"

The two men took seats around the fire, Navarro resting his rifle across his lap. The rider was making a beeline for them at an easy pace. Presently, he reached the light of the fire. He was dressed in leather armor like Navarro's, with an identical bolt action rifle slung across his back, his chest crisscrossed with ammunition bandoliers. Flint and Navarro exhaled, neither realizing they'd been holding their breaths. Their guest was a Supernumerary of the Knights Templar of the Order of Saint Benedict, just like Navarro.

Dismounting, the rider called, "Captain Silas Flint?"

Flint rose from his rock. "I am."

The visitor extended his hand and Flint shook it. "Sam Breckenridge. I'm a courier with the Order."

"Ha!" Flint barked.

Breckenridge cocked his head. "Sir?"

"Forgive me Mr. Breckenridge. General Abernathy recently commented that you couriers have a preternatural talent for finding us in the field."

Breckenridge grinned. "'Neither snow nor rain nor heat nor gloom of night stays these couriers from the swift completion of their appointed rounds,'" he recited.

Flint nodded. "Herodotus."

"Huh?" Breckenridge and Navarro said, almost in unison.

"Your motto. It comes from the Greek historian, Herodotus."

"Really?" Breckenridge asked. "I always thought it was from the old United States Postal Service. Huh."

"I presume you have a letter for me."

"What? Oh! Right." Breckenridge opened a pouch on his belt, removing a sealed letter and handed it to Flint. Flint opened the envelope and began to read.

> *Captain Flint,*
>
> *If my calculations are correct, you and your assistant are presently traveling east on Highway 95. General Abernathy directs you to continue your present course until you reach Dry Creek and then head due south to the city of Oglethorpe. We have received reports of several violent murders in the area. General Oglethorpe believes that a werewolf may be responsible. You and your assistant will investigate and deliver the appropriate judgment. God be with you.*
>
> *Signed,*
>
> *Andrew Archer, KTOSB*

Flint considered this new mission. The city of Oglethorpe was named for Abernathy's predecessor, Witch Hunter General Matthew Oglethorpe, one of the few Witch Hunters who had lived long enough to not only retire but marry and father children. Oglethorpe had to be in his mid-70s by now. It was unfortunate that his retirement was being spoiled by some new devilry. But as Flint had said earlier, the forces of darkness never rest.

"What's the good news boss?" Navarro asked.

"We have been directed south, toward Oglethorpe. Apparently, some mass murdering beast is terrorizing the townsfolk."

"General Oglethorpe still lives there, doesn't he?"

"Yes, as far as I know."

"Maybe we can get his opinion."

"An excellent idea. He retired shortly after I took my oath with the Order. He and I never had the opportunity for a personal introduction. I should be most interested in meeting the man face to face."

Breckenridge nodded. "If that will be all, sir?"

"Not yet," Flint said. "I require a pen and paper, if you please."

Breckenridge went to a saddle bag and returned with the items, along with a clipboard. Flint wrote a quick note, informing Abernathy of what had happened in New Rome and the threat posed by Charles. Flint folded the note and handed it to Breckenridge.

"Please return that to General Abernathy at your earliest convenience."

"Yes sir." Breckenridge put the note in his pouch and climbed up onto his horse.

"Hey," Navarro called. "Before you go…"

Breckenridge cocked his head.

"I don't suppose you have, uh, some of your allowance left? I could really use a drink."

Breckenridge laughed. He reached down into a saddlebag, removed a flask, and tossed it to Navarro.

"Keep it," he said. "You look like you need it more than I do."

"Thank God," Navarro said, catching the flask. He unscrewed the cap and took a gulp. He swallowed and gave a contented sigh. "Man, couriers always get the best stuff."

Flint rolled his eyes. At least one of them would sleep well tonight.

5

Matthew Oglethorpe sat in his wheelchair, hands folded on top the blanket that rested over his lap, as his son George pushed him down the main boulevard of the city that had been named in his honor. The morning sun promised a warm day ahead, but Oglethorpe still felt a chill that never seemed to leave him. George said that he was losing his padding, which Oglethorpe took to be a polite way of saying he was getting older. He loved George and his daughter Julia with all his heart, but he was sometimes sorry that he had become a father at an age when his contemporaries were grandfathers. Both his children were in their early twenties, too young to be caring for an elderly parent.

"Good morning General!" a passerby called out, waving.

Oglethorpe's hand was halfway to his head before he remembered that he no longer wore the trademark hat of a Witch Hunter. He waved back.

"Old habits die hard, huh dad?" George asked.

Oglethorpe grunted. "The funny thing is I don't miss the hats. Too damned easy to lose them whenever things got exciting in the field."

"Which was every day, right?"

Oglethorpe chuckled. "That's my story and I'm sticking to it." He had to admit one thing though: the black hats and black coats of his Order lent a certain authority to a man's pronouncements, regardless of the man's personal qualities. When a Witch Hunter started barking orders, people listened and most of them obeyed. That would have certainly made this morning's errand easier. He was the city's most prominent citizen, but he held no official power to command anyone. He could only persuade, cajole, or berate, and he'd done plenty of all three over the last few weeks. This morning he expected to be on the receiving end.

George stopped. Before them stood City Hall, built in the Greco-Roman style with graceful columns and a great dome. Oglethorpe smiled. Speaking of old habits dying hard, the United States was long gone but government officials at every level, in nations throughout the continent, still favored the ancient architectural style as a symbol of authority.

"Here we are," George said.

"Yes."

"Are you sure you want to do this again?"

Oglethorpe pursed his lips. "No. I should have only had to do it once. But she left me no choice. Let's go."

George wheeled his father up the ramp that adjoined the staircase leading to the entrance. Oglethorpe had only begun needing a wheelchair two years ago, but the townsfolk, God bless them, had all added ramps wherever he frequented. He wished that he hadn't needed to frequent City Hall over the last few weeks. A police officer standing guard nodded to Oglethorpe and opened the door for George.

In the central rotunda was a life-sized marble statue of Oglethorpe in his prime, wearing his long coat and tall, wide brimmed hat, holding his blessed sword aloft as if calling down the Heavenly Host. It was meant to commemorate his slaying of the necromancer Arturo Vasquez who had terrorized Eastern Cascadia 40 years ago. Oglethorpe didn't recall striking that pose back then, but then sculptors often had a flair for the dramatic. George pushed his father's wheelchair around the statue and toward the hallway that led to the mayor's office.

Along their way, civil servants and bureaucrats waved and tipped their hats to the elderly Witch Hunter. Oglethorpe waved back or acknowledged them with a nod of his head. It was no great secret that he and Mayor Lisa Burns were at odds, but no matter the chilly relations between their boss and their hero, they wouldn't be denied the chance to pay their respects. Speaking of...

"Hey George!" cried a lovely young woman from an open office door. Sara Burns had her mother Lisa's eyes and none of her sour disposition. She rose from her desk and went out to meet the two men.

"Hey Sara," George said. Oglethorpe couldn't see his son's face, but he could imagine the fierce blush that was surely blooming.

"General Oglethorpe," Sara said, making a small curtsey.

"Good morning Sara. And please. You may call me Matthew."

"Are you here to see mother again?" she asked.

"Yes. Hopefully for the last time. No offense intended."

"None taken. Even I'll admit she can be a little... difficult sometimes."

Oglethorpe chuckled. "You'll make a fine diplomat some-day, my dear."

She smiled and turned her attention to George. "George, I was wondering... do you... have any plans tonight?"

The young man cleared his throat. "Me? Well, um... Julia and I are going to drop by my parents' house for dinner..."

"Oh..."

Oglethorpe smiled. "You're welcome to join us, Sara."

"Oh! I don't want to impose..." she said.

"Uh... you... that is..." George said.

Oglethorpe laughed. "You wouldn't be imposing at all. Come. I insist."

"Oh... well, in that case, sure! I'd love to!"

"Great!" George blurted out.

"Dinner begins at seven," Oglethorpe said. "But both of you feel free to drop by earlier."

Sara excused herself and went back to her office. Oglethorpe couldn't remember what it was she did, exactly, only that Mayor Burns had given jobs to both of her daugh-ters when she won the election three years ago. Oglethorpe supposed it was nepotism, but then he might have done the same thing for his children if he had any interest in running for office. To the victor go the spoils.

"Thanks for the save, dad," George whispered as he resumed wheeling his father.

"You've nothing to be nervous about, son. She's a fine young woman who clearly has good taste in men. God willing, I may live to be a grandfather yet."

"Dad, geez, come on."

"I'll thank you to mind the blasphemy, young man."

Presently, they arrived outside the oak double doors leading to the mayor's inner sanctum. Since the founding of the city twenty years ago, there was an unspoken rule that Oglethorpe was always welcome to visit the mayor's office unannounced. He suspected he was pushing the rule to the breaking point. George pulled the doors open, and Oglethorpe wheeled himself inside.

A red carpet lay in the middle of the room leading up to the mayor's desk. Above the fireplace on Oglethorpe's right, a large oil painting depicted the battle between Simon Magus and the Archangel Uriel outside the gates of Eden almost five hundred years ago. Behind Uriel, who wielded a giant flaming sword, a gateway lay open with a pastoral grove visible on the other side. The artist took some liberties, portraying Magus as a devil in human form, with horns and pointed ears, his hands crackling with sorcerous energy, and an army of witches, warlocks, and undead at his back. Oglethorpe thanked God he had not lived during such a terrifying time in human history.

Mayor Lisa Burns was seated at her desk. Her husband

Paul was on her right, her other daughter, Sonya, on her left. They were engaged in a discussion about something when Lisa looked up and took notice of Oglethorpe wheeling himself toward her. The discussion stopped. Lisa rose from her desk and went to meet Oglethorpe.

"General Oglethorpe," she said, extending her hand.

"Mayor Burns," he replied, giving her hand a brief shake.

"To what do I owe this honor?" she asked, even though they both already knew.

"There was another murder last night."

Lisa sighed. "Yes, I know. The police investigation is ongoing."

"They're not the ones who should be investigating."

"Not this again," Lisa grumbled. "General. I have every confidence in the Oglethorpe Police Department. Frankly, you should too. I assure you, there is no evidence of witchcraft, or sorcery in this city."

"Don't you find it interesting that these murders always happen on the night of a full moon?"

For several months, townsfolk who lived outside the walls had been murdered on the full moon, their bodies torn to bloody shreds, leaving barely enough to bury. Oglethorpe thought the explanation was obvious but for reasons unknown to him, Mayor Burns was stubbornly refusing to acknowledge what should have been plain to anyone.

Lisa took a deep breath. "General Oglethorpe. My heart goes out to the families who have lost loved ones in these tragedies. But it's understood that living outside the walls of the city proper carries a certain risk. We're doing everything in our power to get to the bottom of these gruesome deaths. I've dispatched several squads of police to comb the local woods. Personally, I believe it's a rabid wolf or possibly a bear. How else can one explain the... nature of these deaths?"

Oglethorpe scoffed. "A wolf or a bear, that breaks into people's houses once a month under a full moon and drags them from their beds? You're half right, madame, but it's no ordinary animal. Clearly it's a were..."

"Not another word!" Lisa snapped. Oglethorpe blinked. Even Paul and Sonya looked shocked that Lisa would take such a tone with the celebrated Witch Hunter. Paul came forward, put his hand on his wife's shoulder, reached out toward Oglethorpe.

"Lisa, Matthew," he said. "Surely we can have a civilized discussion about this?"

"I'm sorry, General," Lisa said, bowing her head. "But I have to think about the scandal that would come from this. Supernatural monsters, witches, running loose in Oglethorpe? It would cause a panic. I'm currently involved in negotiations with the Snake River Trading Company about their new field office and I can't..."

"Damn it, woman!" Oglethorpe shouted, bringing his fist down on his wheelchair's armrest. "People's lives are at stake! We need an active duty Templar!"

Lisa shook her head. "I'm sorry, but for now my answer is still no."

Oglethorpe scowled. "Fortunately, it's out of your hands now."

"What is that supposed to mean?"

"I've taken the liberty of contacting my Chapter House at

Fort Marsing. An investigator should arrive within several days."

Lisa's mouth fell open. Paul backed away a few steps. Sonya looked as though she was about to explode.

"You had no right..." Lisa whispered.

"You son of a bitch! You'll ruin everything!" Sonya yelled.

"Silence your unruly child, Mr. Burns," Oglethorpe said to Paul.

"Mother, an active duty Witch Hunter in the city will scare off the investors! The SRTC will bail out for sure! Think of all the jobs we'll lose!" Sonya shouted.

"Enough!" Lisa bellowed. The office fell silent. Lisa closed her eyes and gave a deep sigh. Facing Oglethorpe, she said, "This city may be named for you, but I am the mayor. The people put me in charge, not you. You had no right to go over my head like this."

"Lisa, we both know the police are getting nowhere. If I'm right, they don't have the tools to stop... the one responsible for these murders. I appreciate that you're making a sales pitch to people who could bring new prosperity to the city, but it won't do us any good if there's no one left alive to enjoy it."

"I hardly think..." Sonya said.

"That's enough," Lisa and Oglethorpe said to her, almost in unison. She scowled, but kept her mouth shut.

"I also appreciate your desire to keep things in-house, so to speak," Oglethorpe went on, "But I'm too old to be doing field work anymore. We both want what's best for the city. We need fresh eyes to investigate what's happening and put a stop to this killer. The Trading Company will find out about the murders eventually, if they haven't already. They'll want to know we're doing everything we can to stop them. Including inviting a Knight Templar."

Lisa said nothing.

"You can tell them it was your idea. I won't say anything. All I've ever wanted was a quiet retirement and to watch my children grow up in a safe environment."

Lisa put her hands behind her back and gazed at the painting above the fireplace. After a few moments, she smiled and shook her head.

"Hard to believe there was once a time when people didn't have to worry about magic and monsters," she said.

"They were always with us. Magus just broke the masquerade," Oglethorpe said.

Another few moments passed in silence. Paul maintained his distance. Sonya quietly fumed.

"Fine," Lisa said.

"Mother!" Sonya blurted. Lisa silenced her with a wave of her hand.

"But I want a few things understood," Lisa said, pointing at Oglethorpe. "I want this Templar to check with this office before he begins throwing around accusations or putting people to the question. Under no circumstances is he to execute anyone without my explicit authorization."

Oglethorpe raised an eyebrow. "Things happen in the field."

"If he keeps his investigations quiet, I'll put the police at his disposal. But if he makes a scene or otherwise fails to stop the murderer, then he will no longer be welcome in my city. Do I make myself abundantly clear?"

"Crystal."

"Good day to you, General."

"God be with you." Oglethorpe turned himself around and wheeled himself out of the mayor's office, giving the painting another glance before taking his leave. He knocked on the double doors. George opened them for his father and took his place behind the wheelchair to take him home.

"How did it go?" he asked.

"It could have gone worse," Oglethorpe said.

6

Flint and Navarro sat before their campfire. They had spent the last two days following the course of Dry Creek, making their way south toward Oglethorpe. Flint estimated that if they set out at dawn, they should reach their destination by the early afternoon.

Navarro moved a cleaning rod back and forth through the barrel of his rifle, while Flint studied his travel book.

"Curious…" Flint muttered.

"What's that sir?"

"According to the guide, there should not be any were creatures in this part of North America. They tend to favor the temperate climate and forests of Western Cascadia, not the semi-arid plains of the East."

"First time for everything I suppose."

"Hmm… perhaps…"

Flint didn't like it. Lycanthropy not only affected the body, but it gradually seeped into the soul as well. Those who were afflicted with the disease often went feral, allowing the beast within to take complete control. If a werewolf was responsible for the murders as General Oglethorpe feared, then the lycanthrope would eventually go mad and begin a killing spree of unimaginable savagery. The silver-tipped bullets every Knight Templar and Supernumerary carried could pierce the beast's hide but shot placement would be vital. Easier said than done when 800 pounds of fur and muscle were bearing down on you.

Navarro perked up. Flint noticed in his peripheral vision and locked eyes with his assistant. Navarro nodded toward a spot over Flint's right shoulder. Someone, or something, was coming. With a speed that came from long practice, Navarro reassembled his rifle, inserted a five round stripper clip, and moved the bolt home as quietly as he could. Flint put his book down and grabbed his sword and one of his pistols from the tree stump by his side. He gently drew the blade partway from its scabbard. Its white glow was visible by the light of the fire. Nearby, their horses were uneasy, snorting and pulling at their ropes.

In one swift motion, Flint rose from his seat, drew his sword, aimed it and a pistol toward the spot Navarro had indicated. A woman stood before him in an ankle length white dress, her hands behind her back. Her face was young, but her hair was long and white as snow. Her blue eyes glowed in the darkness.

"Sir?" Navarro said.

Out of the corner of his eye, Flint detected movement. Another woman was on his left. She wore a dress identical to that of the first white haired woman. Her face looked identical to the first woman's as well, but her hair was black. There.

Movement on his right. A third woman appeared, identical to the other two but for her red hair.

Flint took several steps backward toward Navarro so that all three women were within his field of vision. The glow of his sword was brighter now, which could only mean one thing: these three were all witches.

"Good evening Hunter," the white haired woman said. "I am Mallory."

"I am Monica," the woman with black hair said.

"I am Madeline," the red headed woman said.

"I suppose you three are supposed to be the Weird Sisters?" Flint asked.

In unison, they cocked their heads.

"We are sisters," said Mallory.

"We are not weird," said Monica.

"At least we do not think so," said Madeline.

"Nevertheless, you are witches," Flint said.

"We practice the mystic arts," the sisters said simultaneously.

"Call it what you like," Flint said. "That does not change the truth of your vile natures."

"Poor Silas," said Mallory.

"He has good reason to hate our kind," said Monica.

"But we come bearing a gift," said Madeline.

"I warn you, heretics," Flint said. "Make any sudden moves, and we shall strike you down."

The three sisters slowly spread their arms. From behind Mallory's back came a sheathed dagger. It levitated toward Flint, stopping at arm's length from him, the blade pointed down.

"What is the meaning of this?" Flint asked.

Navarro had his rifle aimed at Mallory, but Flint knew his assistant was quick enough to put down all three of them before they could cast any major spells.

"A gift, Witch Hunter," said Mallory.

"You will need to make use of it soon," said Monica.

"The wolf's master knows that you are coming," said Madeline.

"We have no need of your unholy assistance," Flint said.

"I'll trust my rifle over your letter opener, thanks," Navarro said.

The sisters giggled. "Keep it as a memento then. Or sell it at the market. Whatever you do with it, it will say much about you," they said together.

There was a flash of light. Where the three women once stood, there were now three ravens. The birds took flight and moved south. Toward Oglethorpe. The dagger fell to the ground.

Flint's sword stopped glowing. The witches were gone. The dagger they had left behind apparently had no magical properties. Flint sheathed his sword and holstered his pistol.

Navarro lowered his rifle. "What the hell was that all about?" he asked.

Flint scowled. "God only knows what blasphemous devilry those three are up to."

"You want to take a look at that blade?"

"I am of a mind to toss it into the creek. But I suppose we ought to secure it should it prove bewitched or cursed."

The two men advanced toward where the dagger had fallen. Flint squatted, put his hand on the hilt. Nothing happened. He rose and drew the blade from its sheathe. Navarro whistled. The blade appeared to be shaped from pure silver.

Flint traced a finger along the flat of the blade. It seemed like a normal dagger, but there was no telling what trickery the witches were playing at here.

"What do you think boss?" Navarro asked.

"I detect nothing unusual about it. Yet."

"Is that real silver?"

"Yes."

Navarro stroked his chin. "Huh. That could come in handy if we have to go up against a werewolf."

Flint said nothing.

"I don't get why they'd want to help us though."

"I strongly doubt that they gave it to us out of a sense of Christian charity," Flint said. "I suspect we shall be seeing more of them in the days to come."

"Fine by me," Navarro said. "All three of them are pretty easy on the eyes. I'm kind of surprised you haven't commented on their outfits. Man, I haven't seen that much skin since I went to this beach…"

"I beg your pardon?"

"Tank tops, shorts short enough they barely cover…"

"What the devil are you talking about? All three of them were in rather modest dresses."

"Huh? Okay, now I'm confused," Navarro said. "You didn't see three Mexican girls dressed for the beach?"

"No. They appeared to me as three young Caucasian maidens, all with different hair pigmentation."

Navarro's mouth fell open. "Shit," he said. "You were right sir, those are some weird sisters."

Flint gave a wintry smile. It was a pity that Shakespeare was so little known these days.

"You want me to hang on to that dagger?" Navarro asked.

"Not yet. I shall keep it on my person for now," he said, putting it into one of his long coat's inner pockets. "I suggest we get what sleep that we can. We must press on to Oglethorpe at all possible speed."

7

Flint checked his pocket watch. 10 a.m. They'd made even better time than he'd anticipated. The walls surrounding the city of Oglethorpe were in sight.

Beside him, Navarro stifled a yawn. Their horses knickered and tapped their hooves on the grassy plain.

"Eyes open, Mr. Navarro. We have arrived at our destination."

"Easy for you to say sir. Sometimes I think you don't even need sleep."

They pressed on, urging their horses forward. The countryside was dotted with farms and clusters of modest cottages with the occasional grand mansion. Each of the mansions had a tower that reached high enough to allow their owners a bird's eye view of the surrounding landscape and the city. It was just such a mansion that caught Flint's eye. It was surrounded with yellow police tape, with more blocking off the front door. He saw uniformed officers loitering outside, with several going in or coming out at regular intervals.

"Come Mr. Navarro," Flint said, directing his horse toward the crime scene. They arrived several minutes later.

They dismounted and tied the horses to a hitching post. Even from this vantage point, Flint saw deep gouge marks in the front door frame.

"Looks like claw marks," Navarro said.

"Indeed. Let us see if Oglethorpe's finest can offer any input."

They made their way to the mansion. Police officers looked up from their work and followed Flint with their eyes. By the time they arrived at the front porch, a man in a rumpled suit came down to meet them.

"Captain Silas Flint, Knight Templar of the Order of Saint Benedict, at your service sir," Flint said. "May I present my assistant, Supernumerary Ricardo Navarro."

"Uh, also at your service, sir," Navarro said.

"Thank God," the man said, extending his hand. Flint gave it a firm shake. "I'm Detective Mark Barnes, OPD. As you can see, we've got a hell of a mess here."

"Judging by these gouges on the door frame," Flint said, nodding toward them, "I daresay you're having trouble with a lycanthrope."

"Uh…"

"A werewolf," Navarro said.

"Well… that's what me and a lot of the boys think," Barnes said. "To be honest, we were hoping a Witch Hunter would show up. We're not equipped to deal with that kind of monster."

"May we enter?" Flint asked.

"Please," Barnes said, gesturing with his arm for them to proceed.

Flint and Navarro entered the mansion. Although the

door frame had deep claw marks, the front door itself was intact. Looking around the foyer, Flint saw a trail of blood along the floor, leading from the doorway, across the central floor, and up the stairs. Additional claw marks were etched into the tiled floor. Interesting. He got down on his hands and knees and sniffed deeply of the bloodstains.

"This is the monster's blood," Flint said. "I presume there are signs of a struggle somewhere upstairs?"

"Yes," Barnes said. "That's where we found the victim's body. Or what was left of it."

Flint thought of the silver dagger he'd put in one of his inside coat pockets. "Who was the victim?" he asked.

"The victim was Roger Child. He was the president and founder of Child's Dry Goods. Basically, it's our local grocery retailer. Oh, and he was a member of our city council. Represented the lower east side of town. Lot of traders and merchants there."

"What was the time of death?" Navarro asked.

"We estimate it was between twelve to thirteen hours ago."

Flint and Navarro looked at each other.

"The thing is," Barnes said, "This doesn't fit the pattern."

"How do you mean, Detective?" Flint asked.

"Like I said, me and the boys thought it was a werewolf responsible for these killings. You've seen the claw marks. There's been a series of killings just like this one, usually on the full moon. But the full moon was a few nights ago."

"I may be able to explain the discrepancy," Flint said. "We know of two ways that human beings can acquire the affliction of lycanthropy. The first is to be bitten by one of the monsters. Once that has transpired, transformation into the beast will occur only on the full moon."

Barnes nodded, then raised an eyebrow. "And the other?"

"Some witches have the power to bestow lycanthropy directly through their foul sorcery. Those who receive the curse in that manner are considered to be of higher status within the were creature hierarchy, such as it exists. Men and women who contract the disease through witchcraft are able to transform at will."

Barnes's eyes widened. "They don't have to wait for the full moon? Shit."

"Kind of," Navarro said. "They can transform any time they want to, except on the full moon."

"Yes, quite," Flint said. "When the full moon rises, their transformation is involuntary, much like that of the lesser lycanthrope. Then they give themselves over fully to the beast, and woe to any living creature that is in their path. On other nights, they retain some semblance of their human memories when they wear the form of the wolf."

"This is even worse than I thought," Barnes said.

"I should like to go upstairs, if you please," Flint said. Barnes led Flint and Navarro up the stairs to the second floor and down a hallway on their left. Bloody handprints, too large to be human, were spaced at regular intervals along the wall. Paintings and photographs had been knocked to the floor, the glass shards crackling beneath their boots. A faint odor lingered in the air, which Flint likened to that of a wet dog. The third door on their right was ajar, a pool of blood extending past the doorway.

Barnes led them into an office. Flint thought it would

have had a rustic charm to it if not for the spatters of blood everywhere. Torn flesh and splintered bone were scattered among the debris from the smashed desk and broken bookshelves. Papers were strewn about. Near the broken desk was the bloody carcass of a man who looked to be in his mid-fifties, with a fringe of grey hair circling his skull. His face was frozen in a rictus of pain and terror.

"Roger Child," Barnes said.

Flint approached the body, noticing something clutched in its right hand. He squatted for a closer look. It was a knife. Leaning closer, he saw that the blade was pure silver. It had a thin film of blood along the blade.

"Our victim managed to wound the beast," Flint said.

"So we should be looking for anyone who got treated for a stab wound recently," Navarro said.

"Yes. Assuming they went to a doctor. And assuming they live within the city," Flint murmured. He rose to his feet and turned to face Barnes. "The other killings... they all took place on the full moon?"

"Yes... well, most of them."

Flint raised an eyebrow. "Most of them?"

"The first one that we know of was four months ago. It was a farmer, the farmer's wife, and their son. All of them torn to pieces on the night of a full moon. There was another killing a week and a half after that. Same M.O.: bodies looked like they'd been torn apart by giant claws and gnawed on. That was Jennifer McCool and her husband."

"I take it she too was a prominent citizen?" Flint said.

"Yes," Barnes said. "She was another member of the city

council actually. She represented the textile district. Damned shame. My wife loved her dresses."

"Hmm..." Flint said.

"After the McCool murder, the killer struck on the next full moon, the one after that, the full moon this month, and now this one from last night."

"The other victims?" Flint asked.

"No pattern we can see, other than the full moon. There was another farmer, an accountant, and a writer for our city newsletter."

"All outside the city walls?" Navarro asked.

"Yes."

"Tell me Detective," Flint said, "Did anything strike you as unusual in this particular crime scene?"

"You mean besides the whole fucking thing?" Barnes thought for a moment. "Well, I think it's strange that the upstairs is completely trashed, but not the downstairs. I mean there's claw marks on the front door frame, but the door isn't smashed. Like why would a werewolf be so delicate downstairs but..." His face lit up.

"Are you saying...?" Barnes asked.

"Yes," Flint said. "I daresay our victim knew his killer. The lycanthrope came to visit Mr. Child some time last night." He knelt upon the floor and picked up a handful of coarse black hairs. He sniffed, and then handed them to Barnes. "You will note the scent of those hairs."

Barnes gave them a sniff. "Smells like a wet dog."

"Indeed," Flint said. "I believe Mr. Child's guest transformed in this very room. Mr. Child had the foresight to keep a blade of pure silver either on his person or somewhere in this room. The struggle ensued, and Mr. Child managed to wound the beast." Flint walked out of the office, Navarro and Barnes following. Flint pointed at the bloody handprints along the wall.

"The werewolf's injuries were such that it leaned on the wall for support as it made its escape," he said. He pointed at a trail of blood along the floor. "The creature made its way back to the stairwell, leaving this trail."

They proceeded downstairs, following the droplets of corrupted blood. Arriving at the door frame, Flint pointed at the claw marks.

"By this point, the wounds were taking their toll. Judging by the angle and depth of these gouges, it leaned against the door frame with its full body weight."

"How come he didn't smash his way out?" Navarro asked.

"I suspect it was either too weak to batter down the door," Flint said. "Or... it transformed back into its human self and let itself out. Detective Barnes?"

"Yes?"

"Did your men discover a trail of blood outside? Any footprints?"

"No. There were hoofprints and carriage tracks, but no blood, no footprints."

"Hmm..."

"If he was a rich man on the city council, I guess he's got a lot of people he knows, huh?" Navarro asked.

"Yeah... but that does narrow it down some," Barnes said.

"Tell me Detective, why do people choose to live outside the protection of the city walls?" Flint asked.

"It's cheaper," Barnes said. "Property taxes are higher

within the city proper, so out here you'll find the poor, the working classes, and rich folks who want to save some coin, or who just want to get away from the crowd."

"And the police presence is accordingly thinner," Flint said.

"That's about the size of it, yeah. We have patrols out here, but not as many as within the city walls."

"Did Child live alone?" Navarro asked.

"No. His wife was visiting her mother within the city. Mrs. Child was the one who discovered the body this morning."

Flint stroked his chin.

"What do you think, Captain?" Barnes asked.

"That a lycanthrope is preying on your citizens is beyond doubt," Flint said. "However, I believe there is a larger game being played here."

"Like what boss?" Navarro asked.

"I do not believe all of these killings are at random."

Barnes blinked. "You want to walk me through that?"

"Consider," Flint said. "We have established that there is a werewolf in your midst. Accordingly, it has killed on every full moon, when it is little more than a rabid animal."

Barnes and Navarro nodded.

"However, there are two killings that break the pattern of being under a full moon. They were performed with the same modus operandi: violent dismemberment. Is that correct, Detective?"

"Yeah, both of them torn limb from limb."

"You are certain that an ordinary human being could not have killed them in such a grotesque manner?"

"No. No way a human being could rip and tear like that."

"In that case, Detective, I have reached two preliminary conclusions." Flint held up his index finger. "One: our suspect is a greater lycanthrope who is able to transform at will. And two: greater lycanthropes receive their curse through witchcraft. Which means…"

"It's… possible that there's a witch here too…" Barnes said.

"Yes," Flint said.

"So, Child and McCool weren't random murders," Navarro said.

"I believe they may have been targeted assassinations," Flint said.

"Shit," Barnes said.

"They have any enemies? Like the kind that would want them dead?" Navarro said to Barnes.

"They were both in business and in politics… you don't get to where they were without making enemies."

"Indeed," Flint said. "We shall have to gather more evidence. Detective, I suggest you pursue the line of inquiry Mr. Navarro devised: search for suspects who knew the victims and may have carried a grudge. Focus on those who have suffered a stab wound recently. Mr. Navarro and I shall do likewise."

"You got it. The mayor said to give you any help you need."

"In that case, I should like directions, if you please."

8

Flint and Navarro made their way through the city streets.

All around them townsfolk waved, called out greetings, and a few even asked for autographs.

"I feel like a celebrity," Navarro said, as he signed an autograph book for a young lady. Flint thought he saw him adding his contact information but couldn't be sure.

"As do I," Flint said. "I admit that my feelings are ambivalent."

Navarro laughed. "You like it better when you intimidate people?"

"It does have its advantages."

Following Barnes's directions, they arrived at a house within one of the city's more isolated neighborhoods. The house was constructed in the old Gothic style with creepers of ivy making their way up the sides. The lawn was immaculately groomed. Flint noticed a ramp leading up to the front door in addition to the stairs.

"Come Mr. Navarro, let us pay our respects."

Before they could reach the entrance, the front door opened. A middle aged woman guided an elderly man seated in a wheelchair. The woman's hair had streaks of grey, but otherwise Flint thought she looked remarkably comely for her age. The man he recognized instantly from his portrait at Fort Marsing. General Oglethorpe was in a well-tailored suit, his hands folded on top of the plaid blanket laid across his lap. His face was more wrinkled, his hair whiter, but General Oglethorpe looked the picture of vigorous old age.

Flint marched to the foot of the stairs and doffed his hat.

"General Oglethorpe," he said. "I am Knight Templar Captain Si..."

"Silas Flint," Oglethorpe said.

Flint blinked and put his hat back on. "You know me, sir?"

"Not half as well as I should like," Oglethorpe said with a smile. "Please, come in."

Flint and Navarro followed the woman as she turned Oglethorpe around and led them into the front parlor. Flint scanned the walls, noticing paintings and photographs of Oglethorpe at various points in his career. There he was shaking hands with the Emperor of Cascadia. There he was with his sword planted in the earth before the ruins of the necromancer Vasquez's fortress. And there was a photograph of him in his dress uniform leading a woman in a wedding dress underneath the raised swords of a phalanx of Witch Hunters standing on either side of a red carpeted pathway. Flint realized the middle aged woman must be his wife.

Awaiting them in the parlor was a young man and a young woman. Flint noted the resemblance to Oglethorpe and his wife. She got Oglethorpe settled near a couch and two chairs.

"Captain Flint, may I present my wife Jane, my son George, and my daughter Julia." As he named them off, the women made curtseys. George stepped forward to shake Flint's hand.

"And may I present my assistant, Supernumerary Ricardo Navarro," Flint said.

"It's a pleasure, sir," Navarro said, stepping forward to shake Oglethorpe's hand. He locked eyes with Julia. She looked away, blushing.

"It's a pleasure to meet you, sir," she said.

Navarro smiled. "My friends call me Rico."

"Welcome to our home," Jane said. "Would you two care to join us for lunch?"

Before Flint could say a word, Navarro said, "Yes, please, thank you. I'm starved."

Oglethorpe laughed. "Getting sick of hard bread and beef jerky I take it?"

"Yes sir."

"Mr. Navarro, why not assist our hosts in preparing our meal? I should like a word with the General."

The other four excused themselves. Oglethorpe indicated one of the guest chairs. Flint took off his hat and long coat and seated himself.

"I wish that my visit was under better circumstances," Flint said.

Oglethorpe nodded. "As do I."

"May I ask how it is that you know me sir?"

"I remember you of course. From your swearing in."

Flint remembered standing in the Great Hall of Fort Marsing with dozens of other young men. Oglethorpe had been at the front, standing atop a raised dais. They all raised their hands and took the oath of the Knights Templar together.

"That was fifteen years ago," Flint said.

"And? We never had the opportunity to speak one on one, but I never forget a face. And I may have heard through the grapevine about your recent adventure up north in Canyon Cove."

"It was a near run thing," Flint said.

"Either you're quoting the Duke of Wellington, or you have a gift for understatement," Oglethorpe laughed.

Flint smiled.

"Did you just arrive today?" Oglethorpe asked.

"Yes sir."

"Have you had an opportunity to hear what has been happening?"

"Yes, as a matter of fact." Flint summarized their findings at the most recent murder site and his working theory about the killer.

Oglethorpe pursed his lips. "A greater lycanthrope... if he can change at will, that would explain the killings that don't fit the full moon pattern."

"You have lived in this city since its founding," Flint said. "I was hoping you could lend new insights into this matter."

"I'll help in any way I can."

Flint thought for a few moments. "The two victims who were killed outside of the full moon were both members of the city council. I should like to know how your system of self-government works."

"Well, it's based loosely the old United States Constitution," Oglethorpe said. "The mayor is the chief executive. He or she oversees the police and the permanent bureaucracy. Then you have the city council. Each member represents a different district of the city. They're the ones who propose new laws or ordinances, and they serve the interests of their home districts. In theory, anyway."

"The two council members who were killed... what can you tell me about them?"

"I only knew them by reputation. I got enough of politics to last a lifetime running the Chapter House. Let's see... Mr. Child was the grocery magnate, and Mrs. McCool was the textile heiress... both fabulously wealthy. From everything I ever heard about them, they were pillars of their communities. Took care of their employees. Fought hard for their constituents."

"You said they were wealthy," Flint said. "What will happen to their fortunes and their businesses?"

"As far as I know, those will be staying in the family. The mayor appointed McCool's replacement. He'll serve until the next election cycle, probably run for election in his own right. Mayor Burns will have to appoint a replacement for Child as well."

"I see," Flint said. "I take it these appointments will be obedient to their benefactor."

"Most probably, yes."

Flint drummed his fingers on the armrest of his chair. "Were Child and McCool noted opponents of the mayor?"

"No, not really," Oglethorpe said. "But now that you mention it... the mayor has proposed inviting the Snake River Trading Company to open a new office and shipping hub here in the city."

"Go on."

"It's caused some controversy. Some see it as bringing new jobs and more wealth. Others see it as inviting a major corporation to crush family owned businesses."

"Family owned businesses... like those of Mr. Child and Mrs. McCool?"

"Exactly," Oglethorpe said. "If it had come to a vote when they were still with us, they were firmly in the nay camp." His eyes widened. "By God..." he whispered, "Why didn't I see it before?"

"The devilish fiends seek to conceal their plot in an ocean of blood," Flint said. "With the police focused on the full moon killings, they would be less likely to deduce that our werewolf is waging a campaign of targeted assassinations." Flint rose from his chair and paced around the front parlor.

"How many council members are there?" he asked.

"Nine. Eight until Mayor Burns names Child's replacement," Oglethorpe replied.

"How do you believe the vote would go?"

"Let's see... if they voted right now... three would definitely vote yes. There are three firm nays, and two who haven't expressed a strong opinion one way or another and could go either way. I assume the ayes will increase to four once the new appointee takes his seat."

"I presume the business of the government proceeds even if the council is down one member."

"Yes. The council only needs a quorum of five."

"What happens in the event of a tied vote?"

"In that case, the Chief Secretary for Legislative Affairs casts the tie breaking vote. That would be the mayor's husband, Paul Burns. He'd definitely be with the ayes."

Flint calculated the probabilities. Five potential votes against inviting the Snake River Trading Company to set up shop within the city of Oglethorpe meant there were five possible targets for the werewolf killer's next assault. Detective Barnes had said the mayor ordered the police to assist Flint. There was not yet enough evidence to suggest who the lycanthrope could be, only that they had a compelling interest in seeing the SRTC come to Oglethorpe. The potential suspects were still too many. In any case, his next destination was clear.

"I apologize General Oglethorpe," Flint said, "But I…"

"Think nothing of it my boy. Duty calls. I know," he said. "Before you go though, I have something that may be of use." He reached into his breast pocket and withdrew a small plastic bag which contained a greenish powder and several dried sprigs. He held it out for Flint, who took it.

"Be careful, it's quite deadly," Oglethorpe said.

"Aconitum, I presume."

"Wolf's Bane, yes. I suggest you put it in your shirt pocket and open the bag a bit. If you encounter the lycanthrope…"

"They will react most violently, even in their human form," Flint said. "Thank you for your hospitality sir, and for your gift."

"Perhaps when this is over, you and your assistant can join us for a meal after all."

"I should like that very much." Flint donned his hat and long coat and set out to fetch Navarro.

"Ricardo!" he shouted. "Ricardo! Where the devil are you?!"

Flint sniffed. Whatever they were cooking smelled delicious, and regret flickered in his heart. He strode into the kitchen where several pots were on the burner, meat was in the oven, and Navarro stood at the counter, chopping vegetables and chatting up Julia. She was hanging on his every word.

"So then Silas is like, 'Ahh, have at you, vile witch! Your judgment is at hand!'"

Julia giggled. "Oh my God, my dad was like that too. You

should hear his Witch Hunter voice some time. He'll do it if you ask him."

"Mr. Navarro!" Flint barked.

Navarro put down the knife and turned to face Flint. He cleared his throat. "Yes sir, Captain Flint, sir," he said.

Julia smiled.

"That was an excellent impersonation, Mr. Navarro," Flint said, crossing his arms. "I recognized myself."

"Oh, uh, thank you sir, I was just, ah, telling one of our hosts about some of our exploits."

"I am afraid it will have to wait. We must make for the mayor's office, post-haste."

Julia's face fell. Navarro put a hand on her shoulder.

"Sorry Jules, I'm sure you know how it is."

She sighed. "Promise me you'll come back another time?"

"Definitely."

"Okay… Rico," she said, blushing. "Can I at least pack you two a to-go lunch?"

Navarro looked to Flint, who nodded.

"Great! I'll have them ready in no time. Now, out you two! Out! Out!"

Flint and Navarro made their way back to the parlor to wait for Julia.

"A lovely young woman," Flint said. "She has her mother's eyes."

"Yeah. Jules is something else," Navarro said.

"Were I in your shoes, I would tread carefully. Her father is more fearsome than most. And for the record…" He squinted at Navarro. "I have never said 'Have at you,' to any of the depraved fiends we have encountered."

9

Flint and Navarro flagged down a carriage outside of Oglethorpe's house. The horses whinnied and tapped the street with their hooves.

"Where can I take a Knight Templar today?" the driver called down from his perch.

"City Hall, if you please," Flint replied. He and Navarro climbed into the carriage, nodding to another man who was already inside. Once they were seated, the driver flicked the reins, and the horses set off at a leisurely pace. The carriage rattled as it went along the cobblestone street. Flint filled in his assistant on the discussion he'd had with Oglethorpe

"Huh," Navarro said. "Makes sense. So how do you want to play this boss?"

"Our first order of business should be to meet with the city council.

"What about the mayor? You think she's involved?"

"It is possible, but I find it unlikely. As a public figure, it would be difficult for her to leave the city proper undetected. Nevertheless, we shall inquire as to her whereabouts last night to be sure."

"So we're looking for someone who suffered a stab wound, doesn't like Wolf's Bane, and who's got something to gain if the SRTC comes here."

"Yes."

Navarro chuckled. "Well, at least we're narrowing down the list some."

Presently they arrived outside City Hall. They disembarked, paid the driver, and took a moment to behold their surroundings.

"Interesting," Flint said, gazing at the Greek columns at the top of the stairs.

"What's that sir?" Navarro asked.

"General Oglethorpe told me that the city's form of government was based loosely on the United States Constitution. I see that they also imitate its architecture. This building was closely modeled on the old American capitol." Flint reflected that the United States and its way of life were centuries in the grave, but its spirit lived on in North America. "Come," he said.

They entered City Hall. In the central rotunda was a marble statue of General Oglethorpe in his youth. Flint approached a bureaucrat in a grey suit and put his hand on his shoulder.

"I beg your pardon," Flint said.

The man turned. His eyes widened at the sight of Flint's hat and long coat.

"Oh!" the man said. "You're a Witch Hunter!"

"Is the city council in session?"

"Uh… yes, yes they are."

"Where?"

"They're over at the end of the East Wing," the man said. "But you can't go in right now, they're…"

Flint set off down the hall toward the meeting room, Navarro at his heels. Civil servants made way for him, some flattening themselves against the wall. Heavy double doors were at the end of the hallway, flanked by two police officers. One of them held up his hand as Flint reached the threshold.

"I'm sorry sir," the officer said. "The council is currently in a closed-door session. Members of the public can..."

"Step aside," Flint said.

The police officer blinked. "Sir, Witch Hunter or not, I have orders to..."

Flint glared at him. "Do you really mean to interfere with a servant of God who is carrying out the Lord's work?"

The officer swallowed. "Sir... I..."

Flint leaned in closer to the officer's face. The policeman swallowed again and blinked rapidly. Flint squinted, as though studying an insect in a jar.

"Interesting..." he murmured. "The subject is positively wilting before my eyes. What do you think Mr. Navarro?"

"You got something to be nervous about, Officer?" Navarro asked.

"Perhaps an hour or two on the rack would loosen that tongue," Flint said.

"You can go on in sir," the officer said.

"Splendid," Flint said, patting the cop on the shoulder. "Carry on, officer."

Flint pulled open the double doors. As he and Navarro stepped inside, they saw desks arranged in a semicircular fashion, four on one side and five on the other side of the central aisle. Eight of the desks were occupied by men and women of various ages, all dressed in business attire. As one, they turned around to look at the uninvited guests. At the front of the room was a middle aged woman with her hair up in a bun, dressed in a well-tailored pantsuit, whom Flint took to be Mayor Lisa Burns. On her left was a man and two young ladies, presumably her family. On her right, standing behind a lectern facing the council was an older gentleman in a suit and waistcoat. His hair was snow white, his face deeply crinkled, reading spectacles perched on his nose. He had been addressing the legislators and stopped when Flint and Navarro entered.

"What is the meaning of this?" Mayor Burns called out. "I left strict instructions that..."

"I do not offer apologies, Madame. It is urgent that I speak with you and the council. Alone," Flint said, looking at the older man and Burns' family.

The mayor's nostrils flared, her eyes widened. "Master Templar, may I remind you that you are a guest in my city, and I will not tolerate..."

The older man cocked his head. He called out, "Captain Silas Flint?"

Flint turned his attention to the man. "I am."

"I'll be damned," the older man said, chuckling.

"May I ask how it is that you know me sir?"

"I'm Harry Brown, with the Snake River Trading Company," the man said. "We've never formally met, but I saw you in Canyon Cove a few weeks ago. Thank you again for all of your help."

Flint dipped his head. "Mr. Navarro and I were simply doing our duty, sir."

Brown looked to Mayor Burns. "It's alright, this can wait." He gathered a sheaf of papers from the lectern. "My advice? Do whatever Captain Flint says." He stepped down from the dais and shook Flint's hand on his way out of the council chamber. All eyes were on Flint and Navarro as they made their way to the front of the chamber and ascended the dais.

Flint looked to Mayor Burns and her family. The mayor looked resigned, the husband indifferent, one daughter eager to listen, and the other daughter scowled at him.

"I am afraid I must ask your family to leave as well," Flint said.

"Now wait just a minute," one of the girls cried. "I'll have you know I am the Secretary for Health and Sanitation and I..."

"Good for you," Flint said.

The girl's face turned red. "You can't just..."

"It's alright Sonya," the husband spoke up. "We shouldn't interfere with Witch Hunter business. Come on Sara, you too."

"Aww..." Sara said. She got down off of the dais and headed for the exit. The husband got down too and extended a hand to Sonya. She scowled at Flint again and took her father's hand, delicately stepping down. She winced when her feet hit the floor. Her hand went to her side and rubbed a spot on her ribs.

"Are you alright, Miss?" Flint asked.

"Fine," Sonya snapped.

"May I ask how..."

"None of your goddamned business," she snarled. Her father patted her on the back and led her out of the chamber. Sonya moved with a pronounced limp. Flint studied them both carefully on their way out. They shut the doors behind them.

"That was my husband, Paul, and my daughters Sara and Sonya," Mayor Burns said. "Please forgive Sonya. She had a bad fall the other day."

"Did she now?" Flint said.

"Now, would you mind explaining what's going on?" Burns asked.

Flint faced his audience. "A foul darkness has befallen your fair city. I have reason to believe that a lycanthrope is responsible for the gruesome murders which have been plaguing you for these few months past."

A collective gasp rose from the assembled legislators. Then they all began talking at once.

"How?"

"Why?"

"What's being done to..."

"How could this..."

"Dear God..."

Flint held up his hands for silence. After a few moments, the audience calmed down enough for him to go on.

"Further, I believe that this depraved fiend is a greater lycanthrope."

"What's the difference?" a man asked.

"You got your lesser werewolves that can only change on the night of the full moon. And then you got the greater werewolves that can transform whenever they want to," Navarro said.

"Yes," Flint said. "A greater lycanthrope can not only transform at will but maintain their human psyches while in the form of the beast."

The crowed murmured. The color drained from the mayor's face.

"Underneath the full moon, the greater lycanthrope loses all control and gives in completely to the beast blood. This accounts for the monthly murders, for the werewolf craves human flesh above all else."

"Then that means..." Burns said.

"The beast exists in a state of uncontrollable fury under a full moon. Otherwise, even in its beast form, it retains the wits to makes plans. To target specific individuals."

"Holy shit!" screamed a female legislator. The hall broke down into panic with everyone yelling at once.

"Hey!" Navarro bellowed. The council chamber fell silent, and all eyes went to him.

"Thank you, Mr. Navarro," Flint said. "I surmise from your agitation that I do not need to explain the implications."

"The monster is targeting the council..." Mayor Burns whispered. She buried her face in her hands.

"I would like a vote," Flint said. "All in favor of inviting the Snake River Trading Company to open a new office within Oglethorpe?"

"What?" a man asked.

"You want a vote on that at a time like this?" a woman shouted.

"Humor me," Flint said. Three hands went up.

"And opposed?"

Three hands rose.

"I have reason to believe that the monster is targeting those of you who oppose the motion."

The crowd was stunned. All was silent for a few moments. Then the shouting began.

"Are you responsible for this?!" a man yelled at Mayor Burns.

"This was your idea!" another shouted.

Mayor Burns held up her hands, attempting to placate the angry legislators. "No! No, I have nothing to do with this! I would never…"

"Are you a werewolf?!

"Are you a witch?!"

"What?!" Burns yelled. "No! I have nothing to do…"

"Silence!" Flint shouted. The crowd obeyed, looking to him for guidance. "Mayor Burns… can you account for your whereabouts on the night of the most recent murder?"

"Yes!" she shouted. "Yes, I attended a fund raising dinner for the city library. You can ask anyone who was there! I went home at around 10 p.m. and went to bed. You can ask my daughter Sara, she was there, when I got home!"

"Very well," Flint said. He looked to Navarro, who nodded. He'd caught it too. The one daughter could vouch for Mayor Burns, but no mention of the other daughter or the husband.

"What are we supposed to do, Captain?" asked one of the council members.

"Ah…" said one man. "I know it sounds bad to bring it up at a time like this, but… if the werewolf is targeting us because of the SRTC… well, we could just vote to invite them in. Then it'll go away."

"Really?" a woman asked. "How about we vote to tell them 'thanks but no thanks?' That would take away its reason to kill us too."

"But we'd lose all of the jobs they could bring us!"

"We've got plenty of jobs from local businesses right now!"

"Enough!" Flint shouted, banging his fist on the lectern.

Everyone looked to him again. "I am afraid that a vote will not do. I believe that the lycanthrope lives among you. Even if it no longer has reason to target members of this council, it will continue its bloody rampages when the full moon rises. The monster must be put down, to answer for the crimes it has already committed, and to prevent it from killing again in the future."

Everyone considered his words. The mayor was the first to speak up.

"So what do you suggest we do?" she asked.

Flint pursed his lips. "Hmm... thus far the beast has targeted citizens who live outside the protection of the city walls. Does anyone here own property outside of the gates?"

Two hands went up. Flint pointed at one of them.

"You are?" he asked.

"Lawrence Grant, sir."

"Are you yay or nay?"

"I'm a yay, sir."

Flint pointed to the other legislator, a woman.

"And you?"

"Margaret Atwell, sir. I'm a nay."

Flint smiled. "I have an idea."

10

The setting sun cast City Hall in a soothing orange glow. Flint and Navarro stood at the forefront of a large assembly of guests: civil servants, local journalists, merchants and their lobbyists, and average citizens who were curious about this latest civic engagement. Standing atop the steps of City Hall were the Mayor, her family, the city council members and their families, and another woman Flint had not seen before, but he expected to find out soon.

"It is with heavy hearts that we mourn our friend and colleague Roger Child," Mayor Burns said. "Let us all bow our heads and offer a prayer to Almighty God for the repose of his soul." A moment of silence passed. Looking up, the Mayor resumed her speech.

"I want the citizens of Oglethorpe to know that we are doing everything in our power to capture the monster responsible for this crime and bring him to justice. In the meantime, I assure you that while he may destroy our bodies, he can never conquer our spirit if we stand together and stay strong. It is for that reason I have called you all here this evening." Burns beckoned for the woman to join her behind the lectern.

Putting her hand on the woman's shoulder, Burns said, "Angelica Hughes has deep roots in the city of Oglethorpe. Her family has been here since the General put down roots twenty years ago. She is a devoted wife, a loving mother, and has a distinguished career in the civil service. It is for these reasons, and for her sterling character, that I hereby appoint Angelica Hughes to fill the seat on the city council formerly held by Mr. Child."

The crowd applauded, Flint and Navarro joining in. Hughes raised her hand in acknowledgment.

"Thank you, Mayor Burns," Hughes said. "I offer my deepest condolences to Mrs. Child, and all of Mr. Child's children. Roger was a great man, both in the business world, and in the political arena. I cannot hope to fill his shoes, but I promise to honor his memory and his life of service by serving the people of the district we both called home."

Hughes went on to talk more about her background and her vision of where she wanted to lead her district, and the city, but Flint tuned that out. He scanned the crowd. Bureaucrats, passersby... there. A man with a clip board was taking notes on Hughes's remarks. Flint pushed his way through the crowd until he reached him.

"You are a journalist, I presume," Flint said.

"Huh?" The man looked up. "Yes, that's me. Marshall Adams, Oglethorpe Bulletin."

"I have a suggestion."

Adams stopped scribbling, giving Flint a worried look. "Am I in trouble? Look, I don't actually believe in astrology, I don't think she does either, I just went to see her for..."

Flint held up a hand. "Mrs. Hughes will be taking questions. You should ask her opinion on the Snake River Trading Company."

Adams raised an eyebrow. "No offense, but what does a Witch Hunter care about our economic squabbles?"

Flint stared at him.

Adams started to say something, stopped.

Flint kept staring.

"Uh..." Adams said. "The SRTC. Got it. Will do."

"Good man."

Flint patted Adams on the shoulder and took his leave to rejoin Navarro at the front of the crowd. Hughes was winding down her prepared speech.

"You think the werewolf is somewhere here, in the crowd?" Navarro asked.

"I cannot be certain, but I think it is likely," Flint said.

"You still got that Wolf's Bane? Now might be a good time to open up that bag."

"No. It may trigger a transformation into the beast. We cannot risk it with these many civilians about."

The crowd applauded again, and Hughes waved her acknowledgment.

"I can take a few questions at this time," she said.

A few hands shot up. Flint crossed his arms and waited. Adams was the third she called on.

"Hello Councilwoman Hughes, I'm Marshall Adams from the Oglethorpe Bulletin," he said.

"Yes, Mr. Adams?"

"Can we get your opinion on the recent proposal to invite the Snake River Trading Company to open up a new field office here in Oglethorpe?"

"That is an excellent question," Hughes said. Flint took a deep breath. What happened next could make or break this case.

"I will say up front that this is one area where Mr. Child and I disagreed," Hughes said. "Personally, I believe the SRTC would bring new wealth and new prosperity to our city. Obviously, the details will need to be hashed out between ourselves and Trading Company representatives. But I believe the benefits of a new field office in Oglethorpe would far outweigh costs. It is for those reasons and more that I will cast my first vote as a member of the city council in favor of the invitation later this week."

The crowd whispered among themselves. Flint smiled. He hadn't met Hughes before this evening's gathering, but she couldn't have played into his scheme better if he had coached her himself.

Hughes answered a few more questions, including one about whether she felt it was in bad taste to cast such a momentous vote so soon after the death of her predecessor. Flint found that she had a talent for speaking at great length without saying much. A necessary talent for any politician he supposed, but he still found it distasteful.

Burns took the lectern again. "I want to assure the people of Oglethorpe again, we will not be terrorized into submission. Your government stands with you. Thank you all, and God bless."

The crowd dispersed. Flint overheard fragments of conversation about the upcoming vote. He had asked the Mayor and the council to schedule it for Friday morning. Tonight was Wednesday.

Mayor Burns and Councilwoman Atwell approached Flint.

"It's done," Burns said.

"Indeed," Flint said. "I thank you and the council for your cooperation." He looked to Atwell.

"Do you understand your part in what comes next?" he asked her.

She gulped and nodded.

"Have faith, Mrs. Atwell. If God is for us, who can stand against us?"

"A seven foot tall, 800 pound hairy monster?" she replied.

"Captain Flint and I have seen worse," Navarro said.

"Mr. Navarro and I will be at your side throughout," Flint said to her.

"You really think he'll come out tonight?" Burns asked.

"If the lycanthrope was present among this evening's guests, it is highly probable. If not, it will learn of the vote in tomorrow's news bulletins and will have to strike." Flint chose not to reveal he was all but certain that the werewolf was among tonight's crowd. "In any case, I suggest you dispatch police officers to maintain a discreet security detail around the homes of council members within the city walls tonight."

"Already done," Burns said.

"So what now boss?" Navarro asked.

"Now we take our positions, and we wait," Flint said.

"I don't suppose…"

"No."

"You don't even know what I was going to ask."

"Indeed I do know what you wish to ask, Mr. Navarro."

"Come on, just one? You don't really think I'd get smashed before something like this?"

"No, I say! We must maintain our wits about us. Not one drop, do you hear?"

"Fine. Afterward though?"

Flint rolled his eyes. "Afterward, you may immerse yourself in your drunken iniquity."

Navarro chuckled. "Oh man, will I ever."

11

Flint checked his pocket watch. 9 p.m. He and Navarro were stationed inside a guest bedroom on the second floor of Margaret Atwell's mansion on the outskirts of Oglethorpe.

After the audience for Mrs. Hughes' acceptance speech had dispersed, Flint had several of the civil servants in attendance spread the word in their social circles that Mrs. Atwell would be spending the night in her country estate.

Navarro sat in a rocking chair, his bolt action rifle in his lap. He gazed around the room. The electric light was off, their surroundings illuminated by a flickering candle.

"Check it out Silas," he said, pointing at a photograph on top of the dresser.

Flint took the candle to the dresser for a closer look. A young Mrs. Atwell, in a black dress and mantilla, was standing next to His Holiness, Pope Gregory XXI. Flint estimated the photograph to have been taken in the 2490s.

"Remarkable," Flint murmured. "I have always wished to visit Rome. Its rebirth since the coming of the Great Magician is nothing short of miraculous." Simon Magus's first act of aggression in the Occult War was the sacking of Rome. The city had been leveled, churches and basilicas that had stood for millennia destroyed, but the people rebuilt, even during the Hundred Years Darkness that followed Magus's downfall.

"Me too," Navarro said. "I don't fancy a trip across the ocean though. Monsters on dry land are bad enough. The ones who come at you from underneath the water though?" He shuddered. "Scares the hell out of me. Those things are nothing but dead eyes and sharp teeth. Those that sail the oceans for a living? They got balls of steel."

Flint nodded. "Perhaps within our lifetimes mankind will fully restore the powered flight industry. I have always been fascinated by the notion of jet propulsion from the history books. One could travel from the western coast to the east in a matter of hours."

Navarro chuckled. "Yeah, but then you got to worry about dragons or gryphons or other flying beasties. And then I got the same problem I have on a ship: I can't shoot back. No sir, I'm happy keeping both feet on the ground for the rest of my life. Give me a strong horse, the open road, a dive bar, and a pretty girl at the end of the day, and I'm good to go."

Flint stifled a smile. He was often appalled by Navarro's debaucheries, but there was something to be said for simple tastes.

"Sir? Look," Navarro said, pointing at the window.

Flint went to the window and parted the curtains as little as possible while still giving him a view of the front yard and the dirt pathway leading to the patio. A carriage was slowly making its way toward Mrs. Atwell's mansion. It was small, nondescript, pulled by a single white horse. Flint tried to make out the driver's features, but the distance was too great and the lanterns lining the pathway too dim.

Flint left the room, went to the top of the stairwell leading down to the first floor.

"Mrs. Atwell!" he called.

The old woman came to the front parlor, looked up at Flint.

"Yes?"

"Are you expecting guests tonight?"

"No..."

"They will be arriving shortly."

"Oh God..." she whispered.

"Be of stout heart, Mrs. Atwell. Mr. Navarro and I stand

ready. I swear before almighty God and all of the angels and saints that no harm shall come to you."

"What do I do?"

"I suspect this person is someone you are familiar with. For now, behave as if it is a normal social visit. It may well be the case."

Flint returned to the bedroom and motioned for Navarro to join him. Together they crept to the end of the hallway, remaining behind the corner so they could not be seen from downstairs.

After a few minutes, there was a knock at the door. Mrs. Atwell took a deep breath, smoothed her dress, and went to the front door. She looked through the peephole. Whatever she saw, she quickly undid the bolt, turned the lock, and opened the door wide.

"Paul! Sonya! What brings you two to this neck of the woods at this hour?" she asked. Flint thought that she was either a convincing actress, or completely unawares.

"Hello Margaret," Paul Burns said. "Forgive us for dropping by at this hour, but Sonya and I have something we would like to discuss with you. It will affect the future of Oglethorpe for generations to come. May we come in?"

"Of course, of course," she said, motioning for them to enter. Paul was dressed in a black suit with leather gloves. Flint surmised that he drove the carriage personally. Sonya was dressed down in a simple blouse with denim jeans.

"Can I get you two anything? Coffee, tea, water… something stronger perhaps?"

"No, thank you," Sonya said. Atwell led her guests into a

living room off to the left of the parlor, away from the staircase. Flint heard them take seats.

"Now, what's this about?" he heard Atwell say.

There was a pause. "It's such a shame what happened to Mr. Child," Paul said.

"Yes, yes… horrible," Atwell replied. "I pray that the Witch Hunter is able to put down that vicious beast who attacked him."

"Speaking of," Sonya said, "What did he say to you all earlier this afternoon? Mother wouldn't talk much about it."

"Oh, well, you know, he formally introduced himself, gave us an update on his investigations, assured us he'd get to the bottom of this, told us not to lose faith. Just the usual platitudes."

"So he doesn't have any suspects?" Paul asked.

"If he does, he didn't mention it."

"Hmm. Terrible," Paul said. "But that's not why we're here tonight. We came to talk about the future."

"Oh?"

"Mrs. Hughes gave a good speech, I thought. She has a vision that one. A vision I happen to share. One that I think will be good for the city."

"Oh, I see," Atwell said. "You're here about the vote."

"The Snake River Trading Company is one of the biggest businesses in the West," Sonya said. "They've got offices all over this part of the continent. They bring good jobs, greater prosperity. We brought some graphs that can…"

"Yes, but at what cost?" Atwell said. "Now I admit they've done good. That Mr. Brown fellow is a decent sort, and even

I'll concede that he makes a good sales pitch. But the SRTC is a bit too large, if you follow my meaning."

"I'm afraid we don't," Paul said.

"All of that additional traffic will fuel uncontrolled growth. Local businesses can't compete with the SRTC's prices. Most of those families have been here since General Oglethorpe himself put down roots. What about them? Where do they fit in to your vision?"

"It's not like they'll be destitute," Sonya said. "You said it yourself: they're old money now."

"I'm sorry," Atwell said. "But my mind is made up. I will be voting no."

Another pause. "Your decision is final?" Paul asked.

"Yes, I'm afraid it is."

"Mmm. Pity," he said. "I'd hoped to do this the easy way."

"I didn't," Sonya said. Flint and Navarro looked at each other.

"What… what are you talking about?" Atwell asked.

"I'm afraid I haven't been completely honest with you Margaret," Paul said. "You see, the SRTC would bring more money into Oglethorpe. More money means more taxes. More taxes mean more cash flowing into City Hall that Sonya and I can divert into our little slush fund."

"What?!" Atwell cried.

Paul laughed. "Everyone thinks I'm content being a face-less bureaucrat living on a civil servant's salary. Even Lisa! I admit I have certain ambitions. And those ambitions don't come cheap."

"All of this… this is all about lining your own pockets?!" Atwell shouted.

"Not quite," Paul said. "Now don't get me wrong, I never say no to more money. But in this case, I need the cash to pay for my lessons. And to pay for a cure for my poor Sonya."

"What does that mean?" Atwell said.

"I discovered at a young age that I have a certain talent. I've tried to cultivate it on my own, but I never made much progress until I met three remarkable women who offered to teach me how to develop my talent."

Atwell said nothing.

"Sonya caught me... practicing, so to speak, and she wanted to join me. I love my other daughter dearly, but Sonya has always taken after me more. It occurred to me that as my power grew, I could use it to steer the course of this city's destiny. But as you well know, if nothing else politics is a clash of visions. I would persuade when I could, but sometimes a problem needs to just... disappear."

Atwell was silent.

"I went to my teachers and asked them for the perfect enforcer. Assassin, to be blunt. They granted my request in a way I never expected though: they chose my Sonya. And they gifted her with lycanthropy."

Atwell gasped.

"The beauty part is that she is able to retain her mental faculties when she transforms. Except when the moon is full. For those nights, I have to take her out of the city. She always manages to eat her fill, no matter what I do to restrain her though."

Sonya giggled.

"But with the upcoming vote, the time is fast approaching when we won't need her gift anymore. No offense Sonya my dear, but it's a real pain in my ass to try and restrain you on the full moon."

"None taken, father."

"I returned to my teachers and asked them to provide a cure when our business is finished. They promised me a cure was coming soon. And so here we are."

Atwell said nothing.

"For what it's worth Margaret, we've had our differences, but I've always liked you. This isn't personal."

Flint and Navarro took the steps two at a time, rushing to the living room. Flint drew his sword, which gave off its tell-tale glow. Paul and Sonya noticed them as they reached the arched threshold.

"What..." Paul said.

"Paul Burns! Sonya Burns!" Flint shouted. "In the name of God, I place you both under arrest!"

"What?! On what charges?" Sonya cried.

"The crime is your existence, monster!" Flint snarled. "And the sentence is death!" He reached into his shirt pocket and withdrew the plastic bag of Wolf's Bane Oglethorpe had given him. Tearing it open with his teeth, he flung it at Sonya. It hit her in the face, scattering its contents about her person.

The effect was immediate. Sonya screamed in agony. Her scream was cut short by a thunderous sneeze. She growled and hissed. Her eyes turned a sickly yellow as she howled and writhed on the floor. She coughed and blood spattered the floor. Her skin began to ripple and contort. Flint saw black hair sprouting from her skin.

"Sonya!" Paul screamed, rushing to her side.

"Mrs. Atwell! Get out of the way!" Navarro shouted. Atwell had stood transfixed in the midst of the chaos, but, regaining her senses, she rushed away from her guests.

"Get her out of here," Flint said. "Mrs. Atwell, make for the city! Notify the police!"

She nodded her understanding and Navarro hurried her out.

Sonya continued to thrash on the floor. Her limbs were elongating, her fingernails stretching into mighty talons. Flint drew one of his pistols with his off hand, aimed, and fired at the girl.

Paul raised his hand and the bullet veered enough to miss them both. His face a rictus of fury, Paul rose to his feet and pointed at Flint, a bolt of lightning firing from the tip of his index finger. Flint parried with his sword, the magical energy dissipated by the blessed steel.

"Father..." Sonya said, her voice degenerating into a guttural growl, her vocal cords no longer able to form human speech. Her face stretched, her jaws extending to form a muzzle, her teeth elongating into fangs.

Navarro returned at a sprint. He aimed his rifle, fired at Paul, but the warlock again deflected the bullet with a gesture.

"Just hang on Sonya!" Paul shouted. "You're almost there, just hang on a little longer!"

Flint strode forward, firing his pistol at his enemies, but Paul was too quick, deflecting each bullet with a gesture before they found their mark. He formed a fireball with one hand and hurled it at Flint, who again absorbed the spell with his sword. Navarro advanced, aiming and firing silver tipped bullets at Sonya, but Paul had erected some sort of energy barrier about the writhing lycanthrope.

Flint slashed with his sword, but Paul, levitating two feet off the floor, backed away from the blade. He landed on the wall, crawling on all fours like a great spider. He laughed, his face split by a manic grin.

"You're too late Witch Hunter," he said. "Sonya's ready to play."

12

The werewolf rose to its feet. The beast was seven feet tall and 600 pounds of fur and muscle, its talons like swords, its teeth like daggers, its yellow eyes focused on Flint with a fury born from the depths of Hell itself. The monster threw back its head and loosed an eardrum shattering howl that Flint swore shook the mansion to its foundations. Flint winced at the pain.

"Sonya, kill them both," Paul said. "Have fun." He blasted the window with a magical lightning bolt, the pane exploding in a shower of glass, and he floated out into the night.

The werewolf backhanded a wooden chair, which flew across the room and smashed into Navarro just as he was about to fire. The shot went wild, hitting the ceiling, and Navarro fell to the floor in a spray of wood and splinters.

The werewolf sprung at Flint, its leap almost carrying it to the ceiling, but Flint dove and rolled forward. Sonya crashed into a coffee table, and Flint fired two silver tipped rounds into her back. The werewolf squealed like a dog. Flint dropped the empty magazine and reached into a coat pocket for another, when he remembered the silver dagger given to him by the Weird Sisters. He'd grown accustomed to its weight and had nearly forgotten about it.

He sheathed his sword. The holy steel would protect him against direct magical assault, but this was a contest of man vs animal. He reloaded his pistol and withdrew the dagger.

"Your judgment is at hand!" Flint yelled, advancing toward Sonya. The werewolf whipped around, lashing out with its vicious talons. Flint saw it just in time, springing backward, the monster's claws tearing his shirt and waistcoat but failing to break his skin. He fired, the bullets hitting Sonya center mass. Her ear piercing screeches of pain echoed throughout the house.

Navarro's rifle boomed. The round pierced Sonya's side, her other side exploding in bloody fur and gore. The beast fell to one knee.

Seeing his chance, Flint rushed forward. Before the werewolf could strike, he plunged the silver dagger into her chest, burying it to the hilt.

The werewolf's howl was deafening. It broke off into a bloody gargle. Flint drew his second pistol, prepared to empty both magazines into the creature's face, but a hairy fist hammered into his side. Flint was hurled across the living room, crashing into Navarro, both men falling to the floor in a tangle of limbs.

The werewolf coughed and snarled. It attempted to rise but dropped to one knee again, its breathing labored. Before Flint or Navarro could climb to their feet, the monster crawled out the broken window left behind by her father.

"Sir?! Silas! Are you alright?!" Navarro shouted, kneeling at Flint's side.

Flint groaned and sat up. He winced at the pain in his side. The taste of blood filled his mouth. He feared his ribs were broken, but he gritted his teeth and climbed shakily to his feet.

"I have been better," he said. "Mrs. Atwell has horses, does she not?"

"Yes sir."

"Come! We cannot allow these depraved fiends to escape!"

13

Flint and Navarro saddled up and took off after their prey. The werewolf left behind a trail of blood. The beast was preternaturally fast, but the silver dagger in its chest and the silver tipped bullet wounds were taking their toll. Flint was certain that the beast would bleed out absent any magical healing abilities her father may possess.

"Where do you suppose she thinks she's..." Navarro said.

"Dear God," Flint said. Even at night, he could see where the trail of blood was leading them. The city. They urged their horses into a gallop. As they approached the wall, they could hear screaming and the rattle of gunfire within. They pushed the horses harder.

Arriving at the gates, they saw the two bloody corpses of the police officers who had stood guard.

"God *damn* those villains straight to Hell!" Flint bellowed. He ground his teeth, clutching at his ribs.

"Boss..."

"I will seek medical attention later. Right now we have to put down this animal once and for all!"

They pressed on. The blood trail continued to point the way. Crowds of terrified citizens fled in the opposite direction. Flint's heart went out to them. Lead bullets and steel blades were of no avail against the werewolf. Only the Witch Hunter's tools of the trade would suffice.

As they continued on their way, the tide of fleeing townsfolk grew thicker. The two men heard gunfire in the direction of the blood trail. Flint surmised that it had to be the Oglethorpe Police Department. Those brave souls had to know they stood no chance against the beast, and still they did their duty. They were worthy men and women indeed, serving as law enforcement for the city of...

"General Oglethorpe," Flint said.

"What about him sir?" Navarro said.

"I recognize these streets. I believe the lycanthrope is headed for the General."

As they went on, Flint's hypothesis was confirmed. The gunfire grew louder. They hurried through the familiar turns they had made that morning.

Presently they reached the General's street. OPD officers had barricaded off the central boulevard. The hairy, hulking form of the beast was visible now. It was moving slowly, blood flowing freely from its many wounds. The police officers fired everything they had at it: pistols, rifles, shotguns.

The lead core bullets impacted harmlessly, failing to pierce the beast's shaggy hide.

"Hurry!" Flint shouted. They galloped toward their final showdown.

14

Matthew Oglethorpe bowed his head in prayer. He could hear the police outside dumping magazines into the approaching werewolf. These men and women, who had dedicated their lives to the people of the city that had been named for him, were fighting and dying in a hopeless battle.

His mind went back twenty years. He was the hero who had slain the necromancer Arturo Vasquez. He was the Witch Hunter General, in command of hundreds of men who, like him, had pledged their lives to doing battle against the forces of darkness that had been ravaging their world for nearly five hundred years. He remembered feeling tired more than anything else, tired after a lifetime of killing the devilish fiends and fearsome monsters that plagued mankind. He remembered the loneliness of that life. Witch Hunters did not make a pledge of celibacy. In theory, they were free to marry, though few did in practice. Knights Templar of the Order of Saint Benedict did not have the greatest life expectancy. And not many women were eager to settle down with men who could be gone for months at a time, who could be killed any day by witches, werewolves, vampires, zombies, or any number of the horrors that Simon Magus had unleashed on the planet.

But then he had met Jane. He was 55, she 28. They fell in

love. She gave him the children he'd always wanted. And now his wife and his children were hiding in the basement. He remained upstairs. Sweat broke out on his brow.

"My Lord and my God," he whispered. "I give thee thanks and praise for the gift of my life. I thank thee for my beautiful wife and my dear children. Your people have given me honors that I do not deserve, for to you alone is due all honor and glory and praise."

The werewolf howled. It was rough, ragged. Captain Flint and Supernumerary Navarro must have wounded it.

"My God," Oglethorpe said. "I beseech thee, in the name of thy son Jesus Christ, and through the Immaculate Heart of the Blessed Virgin Mary... please. Grant these old bones strength one last time."

A few moments passed in silence. Oglethorpe opened his eyes. His mouth was set in a grim scowl. And he stood up from his wheelchair.

15

The werewolf reached the barricade just as Flint and Navarro arrived.

"Fall back!" Flint shouted to the police. "Your weapons are of no avail here! I shall slay the beast!"

"With all due respect Captain, you can go to Hell!" a familiar voice yelled back. Detective Mark Barnes reloaded his revolver and poured .357 Magnum slugs into the werewolf's chest. "This is our city, and we're not going down without a fight!"

The werewolf had slowed, but it wasn't out of the fight

yet. It lashed out with its hairy arm, its talons splitting open a police officer's belly. The man's intestines spilled out. He fell to his knees, grasping at the slick organs.

"Come Mr. Navarro. We must end this," Flint said.

The two men strode forth. Navarro made to aim his rifle but lowered it again. The werewolf was in the thick of the police officers, tearing them limb from limb.

"I think we're going to have to do this one up close and personal," he said. They continued toward the bloody melee. Navarro slung his rifle on his shoulder and drew his own pistol from his belt.

Onward they advanced.

"Aim for the head," Flint said. "I believe the dagger is still buried in its chest. God willing, I shall take it and bury it in the creature's eye."

"Jesus Christ, sir."

"Mind the blasphemy, Mr. Navarro."

The werewolf coughed great spatters of blood on to the street, but still it kept coming. The police were breaking. More and more were fleeing the scene.

"The judgment of God is upon you monster! And I am the instrument of His justice!" a voice yelled.

"Who the…" Navarro said.

"Look," Flint said, pointing.

The remaining police officers stopped and turned to stare at the figure that was approaching them. Even the werewolf fell still, cocking its head.

"Good Lord," Flint whispered.

"Holy shit," Navarro said.

Witch Hunter General Matthew Oglethorpe marched toward the scene. His gait was unsteady, but he was walking. He had donned the trademark long black coat and tall wide brimmed hat that he had worn in his youth. He carried a shotgun at the low ready.

"The children of God do not fear the night!" Oglethorpe yelled. "The children of Magus have no place in this world any longer!"

The police officers stared, their mouths hanging open in shock. Even Flint felt a tingle up his spine.

"You will not terrorize these innocent souls!" Oglethorpe bellowed. "Our Lord is the Prince of Peace, but I come not bringing peace. I come bringing the sword!"

The werewolf snarled and bounded toward the old man. Oglethorpe raised his shotgun and fired. The silver buckshot slammed into the beast's belly and it flew backward. Flint and Navarro leaped away from the towering monster that came hurtling toward them. It crashed to the ground.

Oglethorpe racked his shotgun, expelling the spent shell.

The werewolf's stomach was a bloody ruin, but still it writhed and attempted to climb to its feet.

"You've got to be shitting me," Navarro said.

Flint approached the werewolf. It tried to swipe with its claws, but the motion was weak, and Flint dodged with ease. He planted his foot on the werewolf's chest and it coughed, spitting up more corrupted blood.

"Your father will be joining you soon," Flint snarled. He reached down and yanked the silver dagger from the werewolf's chest, causing it to howl in agony. Flint rammed the dagger into the creature's left eye. The werewolf gurgled, twitched, and finally lay still.

16

Flint stepped away from the enormous carcass. His ribs ached with every breath. He took off his hat and ran a hand through his bristly hair. Navarro joined him at his side.

"God damn, sir," he said.

"Mr. Navarro…"

"I know, I know. But sometimes that's all you can say."

The police officers broke out in cheers. Half of them came forward to meet Flint, the other half rushed to Oglethorpe, who had apparently lost whatever newfound vigor he had possessed. Officers gently lowered him to a seated position on the ground.

Flint and Navarro made their way to him, cops following in their wake. Oglethorpe was breathing hard, but otherwise appeared none the worse for wear.

The two Witch Hunters looked at each other for a few moments. It was one of the few times in his life that Flint was at a loss for words.

Oglethorpe smiled. "Beware of the man who grows old…"

"In a profession where men die young," Flint said.

The police officers laughed and cheered.

"Young man," Oglethorpe called out. An officer stepped forward.

"Yes sir?"

"Would you be so kind as to bring me my wheelchair? I've fallen and I can't get up."

"Right away sir." He set off at jog toward Oglethorpe's house.

Flint squatted next to Oglethorpe. "The beast was Sonya Burns," he said.

"God have mercy," Oglethorpe whispered.

"What's more, her father Paul is responsible for her lycanthropy."

"What?!"

"And he is not alone. I heard him speak of his 'teachers,' who instructed him in the dark arts. As much as I should like to savor our triumph here, Mr. Navarro and I must continue the pursuit."

Flint rose. "Hear me!" he shouted to the assembled cops. "Sonya Burns was but a pawn. Her father, Paul Burns, is responsible for her transformation into the beast!"

The officers gasped and murmured.

"We cannot rest until the fiend is brought to justice!"

"That will not be necessary," a female voice said. Everyone turned to look at the source.

Three women in OPD uniforms stepped forward from an alleyway. They all appeared identical but for the color of their hair. One was snow white, the second jet black, the third a fiery red. With them, handcuffed and gagged, was Paul Burns.

Flint's eyes widened. "You," he said. They were the three sisters he and Navarro had encountered on their way to the city.

"Uhh…" Navarro said.

"The suspect was fleeing on horseback," Mallory said.

"We captured him a few miles south of here," Monica said.

"He is guilty of witchcraft and multiple counts of conspiracy to commit murder," Madeline said.

Detective Barnes stepped forward. "Um... I know every uni in the department, but I've never seen you three before."

"We are new to the force."

"We live to protect and serve."

"We will do our best."

They pushed Burns forward. Seeing the corpse of his daughter, he fell to his knees, his cries of anguish muffled by his gag. The three sisters turned to go.

"Wait!" Flint cried. They faced him simultaneously. He and Navarro broke from the crowd to meet them.

"What are you witches playing at?" Flint said.

"Whatever do you mean Silas?" Mallory asked.

"We do like to play games," Monica said.

"And there is a great game afoot," Madeline said.

"You were Burns' teachers," Flint said.

"Yes," they replied in unison.

"What the hell," Navarro said. "You take him in, teach him witchcraft, and then you turn on him? Why? He got a lot of innocent people killed!"

The sisters looked at each other. They appeared to be at a loss for words.

"We... had a change of heart."

"After Paul left us, we... realized the error of our ways."

"And now we must do penance."

"You cursed his daughter with lycanthropy!" Flint said.

"We gave him what he wanted."

"He asked us for a cure for her."

"And you delivered it."

Flint closed his eyes and sighed. He asked, "What is this great game you spoke of?"

"You'll find out."

"We will be watching you."

"We may even visit you again."

There was a flash of light. Where the three women had been, there were three ravens, who took to flight. Flint and Navarro watched them until they vanished from their sight.

"A 'change of heart,'" Navarro scoffed. "They're hiding something."

"Pay no mind to those devilish wenches."

"Well… you got to admit sir, that dagger of theirs did come in handy."

Flint scowled. "Come. Mr. Burns has an appointment with the gallows."

17

A hundred miles away, Charles Flint opened *In Realis Magicae* and set the book on a lectern. He'd spent the last several days devouring its contents. He'd finally found the spell he had been searching for. Charles smiled. He'd never attempted it before, but Nazari made for an excellent teacher. The powers below willing, he'd soon have another teacher. Assuming she was still alive of course. But Charles had a feeling that if anyone could survive being trapped in the void between worlds, it was her.

He extended his hands and began chanting. The language was never meant for human tongues, but fortunately, Nazari had transcribed a phonetic pronunciation guide. Even

Charles feared the consequences of getting one syllable wrong.

Sorcerous blue fire engulfed his hands. He felt his feet lifting off from the floor. Charles always loved this part. He drew his hands in a circle leaving behind trails of fire that formed a ring which hovered over the floor. As his chanting went on, the interior of the circle darkened until it was inky black. A blast of cold wind enveloped him.

He extended his will into the void. It was... harrowing. He could see nothing within the void but he sensed the presence of ancient evil that did not appreciate intruders into its realm. It sought to pull him in and Charles felt a temptation to leap into the void. He hoped that he found his quarry soon.

There. It was faint, but it was human. No, more than human. He sensed a great deal of power in this one. The power he sought would soon be his.

Charles concentrated on that human presence. He could not see it with his eyes, but in his mind it was like a shining beacon in the darkness. The presence sensed him now too and reached out.

"Come," Charles said. The presence obeyed. Charles sensed that the natives of the void were swarming to stop the human presence. Magical energy focused and exploded from the presence, and the eldritch creatures fled from its wrath. The presence moved closer.

Now. A human hand emerged from the void, beyond the fiery circle and into the room where Charles was conducting his ritual. The hand belonged to a woman. Charles reached out and grabbed it, giving it a firm pull.

The woman came tumbling out of the void. Charles

snapped his fingers and the black hole disappeared, the fiery ring soon following. The woman was breathing hard. Her raven hair was all a tangle. She wore the tattered remains of what had been an elegant ballroom dress. Charles reached out to her, but she flinched at his touch, pushing herself up on to her hands and knees and scrabbling across the room. Her eyes were wild with fright, looking every which way.

"It's okay," Charles said. "It's okay. You're safe now."

The woman finally focused her attention on Charles. She opened her mouth to speak but only a dry croak emerged.

"Of course, where are my manners?" Charles said. He extended his hand and a canteen flew into his grip from across the room.

"You must be dying of thirst," he said, offering the canteen to the woman.

She extended her hand for it.

"Go on, take it. I know you can do it. I imagine your powers were stretched to the breaking point in there, but this is a simple trick."

The woman glared at the canteen. It wobbled in Charles' hand. Then it flew to the woman's outstretched hand. She tore the cap off and began guzzling.

"Easy now," Charles said. "You'll make yourself sick, and healing magic isn't my forte."

The woman stopped drinking, and gasped. She coughed and shivered.

"Just relax. You're safe now."

She looked at Charles again. Her brow furrowed.

"You..." she said.

"Yes, me," Charles said.

"You... I... your face..."

Charles snickered. "Perhaps you refer to the family resemblance? I believe you've met my brother Silas. Allow me to introduce myself: Charles Julian Flint, at your service. I know who you are, Lilith Harkmoore. Or do you prefer to go by Lilian Turner now?"

The woman's eyes widened.

"Didn't see that coming, did you?" Charles asked. "To be honest Lilith, or Lilian, or whichever you prefer, I didn't rescue you from that abyss out of the kindness of my heart. You see, I've been reading the magnum opus of an old friend of yours, Abdul Hakim Nazari. You two knew each other back in the 21st century, didn't you?"

Turner said nothing.

"In his book, he mentioned something about how you developed a certain elixir. One that bestows eternal life. But Abdul never bothered to write down the recipe. I think teaching it to me would be an adequate repayment for my rescuing you from the void, don't you think? As a bonus, you get a second chance to do battle with dear brother Silas. If you're feeling up to it of course."

Turner smiled.

The Gloom
Of The Grave

1

Witch Hunter Captain Silas Flint and Supernumerary Ricardo Navarro rode their horses through the massive gates of Fort Marsing. The setting sun cast the massive stone fortress in an orange glow. Arriving at the stables, they dismounted and handed the reigns off to Robert Carrow, the stable master. Carrow had once been a Witch Hunter himself, but old age and injuries had taken their toll on him, and he was now content to work as the Chapter House's horse master and unofficial mentor to the new recruits.

"Evening Silas, Ricardo," Carrow said.

"Mr. Carrow," Flint replied, tipping his tall, wide brimmed hat.

"Evening Robert," Navarro replied.

"I understand you boys did some good work down in Oglethorpe."

Several days earlier, Flint and Navarro had investigated a series of murders that had taken place in the city of Oglethorpe, named for the city's most prominent citizen, retired Witch Hunter General Matthew Oglethorpe. The culprit had turned out to be a werewolf, and Flint's ribs were still sore from where the beast had hammered its fist into his side. Revealing nothing of his aches and pains, Flint said, "Our Lord saw fit to carry us through another trial. General Oglethorpe sends his regards."

Navarro chuckled. "Silas is being modest. He walked right up to a fucking werewolf and stuck a silver dagger in its eye. One of the most badass things I've ever seen him do."

Carrow smiled. "I'm happy I'm retired... but I'll admit, sometimes I miss going out in the field."

"I guess you'll be wanting to go see General Abernathy, right boss?" Navarro asked.

Flint nodded. "Indeed, I must make my formal report."

"Uh, well, if you won't be needing me sir..." Navarro's eyes looked to his left, toward the cantina frequented by all the Witch Hunter assistants. Even from this distance, Flint could hear the strains of music, laughter, and clinking of glasses.

Flint waved Navarro off. "Yes, you are free to drown your wits. I should have thought you drank your fill before we left Oglethorpe."

"Well sure boss, but that was a couple day ago now."

"Off with you!"

Carrow laughed as Navarro jogged toward the bar. "I remember when Abernathy put you two together. As I recall, you weren't happy with the arrangement at first."

Flint nodded. "He is a drunkard, a glutton, a womanizer, and God only knows what other iniquities he dabbles in. But Mr. Navarro has proven himself in the field a dozen times over in our five years together. I often exhort him to give up his debaucheries, but thus far to no avail."

"I'm not condoning it, but at the same time, I can't really blame him or any of the Supernumeraries for indulging when they can. This is a hard life. Harder for them in some ways."

"Hmph," Flint said. "I shall take my leave. Good evening to you, Mr. Carrow."

Flint strode toward the Great Hall, the central hub of Fort Marsing that led to Witch Hunter General Abernathy's office, and the living quarters for Witch Hunters who did not own homes elsewhere. Flint had sold off his family farm on the outskirts of Mount Angel when he moved east to join the Knights Templar of the Order of Saint Benedict. He'd wanted to be as far away from his childhood home as possible while still remaining within the Empire of Cascadia. Technically Fort Marsing was his home now, though in fifteen years, Flint estimated he'd spent more days in the field than within his living quarters here.

Flint passed the Witch Hunter's dining hall. Through the stone archway he could see several of his fellow Templars sharing a meal and glasses of wine, all of them more restrained than the Supernumeraries in their cantina. Several acknowledged Flint as he passed with nods of their heads, which he returned. Flint knew that he had a reputation for being a workaholic, even by Templar standards, and few of his fellow Witch Hunters could say they truly knew him. Perhaps someday he would confide in them, but for now, duty called.

Presently, Flint arrived outside General Abernathy's office. He knocked on the great oaken door.

"Enter," came the gruff voice from within.

Flint pulled the door open. Abernathy was seated at his desk, spectacles perched on his nose, reading a communique that he had pulled from the large stack of papers on his left. He put the paper down on top of a stack to his right and looked up at his visitor. He took off the glasses and rose from his seat.

"Captain Flint! Please, come in."

Flint entered the office. A ceiling lamp buzzed overhead. Both sides of the office were lined with bookshelves, all of which were packed with leatherbound tomes, icons of saints, and miniature statues of saints, with more books stacked on the floor next to the shelves. Shortly after Abernathy had been appointed General for the Fort Marsing Chapter House, he'd had electricity installed. It had been a challenge, wiring a fortress that had been modeled on an ancient European castle. Flint recalled his early days as a Templar when everything had been torches and gas lanterns. Some of the older Hunters grumbled about losing a time honored tradition, but Flint was grateful for the electric lights, which provided better illumination when he needed to work late into the night.

Abernathy went to meet Flint, shaking his hand, and indicating for him to take a seat in one of the wooden chairs placed before his desk. Flint took off his hat and seated himself, stifling a groan that threatened to escape his lips. He'd been examined by a doctor before leaving Oglethorpe. By some miracle, his ribs hadn't been broken by the werewolf's fury, but they still hurt.

After Abernathy took his seat, he said, "I've already received word about what happened in Oglethorpe, but I'm eager to hear your account. How is General Oglethorpe, by the way?"

"He is in excellent health sir, and he sends his regards to you and to everyone here," Flint said. He then went into his report, about how he and Navarro had encountered three sisters, witches all, on their way to Oglethorpe, how they had given him a silver dagger that had proven crucial in putting down the werewolf that had been terrorizing the city, how the werewolf was a young woman cursed with lycanthropy by those same three witches at the behest of her warlock father, about how the father had used his daughter in a campaign of targeted assassinations, and how the three sisters had themselves captured the father and turned him over to Flint's custody.

Abernathy remained silent as Flint spoke.

"The warlock was hanged outside of the city gates the morning after his apprehension. We took our breakfast with General Oglethorpe and his family, and then set out on the journey back to Fort Marsing," Flint said.

Abernathy said nothing. He stared off into space, drumming his fingers on his desk.

"Three witches…" he finally said. "The Weird Sisters. Did they prophesy that you would one day be the King of Scotland?"

Flint gave a wintry smile. "They did not, sir."

"What do you make of them?"

"I concede that their assistance proved useful on this case."

"But…?"

Flint frowned. "I strongly doubt that they offered it out of the kindness of their hearts. They knew my name. I suspect I shall see them again in the future. I do not like being used as a pawn, particularly by their vile kind."

Abernathy grunted. "It's not the first time a witch has been of use to us."

"How is Miss Fletcher, by the way?" Flint asked. Several weeks ago, the witch Zelda Fletcher had turned herself in to the Order and helped Flint and his fellow Witch Hunters destroy her former lover who had given himself over to demonic possession.

Abernathy sighed. "She is as you described when I met her: insolent, ill-tempered, no respecter of proper authority."

"But...?"

Abernathy smiled. "But she's grown on me. She's proven herself a fount of knowledge about local covens and where to find them."

Flint nodded. "I am glad to hear of it."

"She's asked about you too."

"Oh?"

"I think she's interested in going out into the field with you again some time."

"Hmph. We shall see," Flint said. "Speaking of that, sir, I am ready for my next assignment."

Abernathy raised an eyebrow. "So soon?"

"Evil never rests, sir, and neither can servants of the Lord."

Abernathy chuckled. "Spoken like a true Templar. But I'm afraid you may not have a choice this time, Silas."

"What do you mean sir?"

"I mean there's nothing left for you right now. I've dispatched Hunters to investigate all of the cases currently on the docket."

Flint blinked. He hadn't expected this. It happened from time to time, more available Hunters than available cases, but he never liked it.

"I... see," Flint said.

"You've been in the field constantly for the last few weeks," Abernathy said. "I daresay you could use some rest and relaxation. When was the last time you've been to confession?"

Flint thought for a moment. "It has been some time, sir."

Abernathy nodded. "Just so. Do that and take some time to recuperate. Don't think I didn't notice that you're favoring one side. You were injured on this last assignment."

"It's only a trifle, sir..."

Abernathy raised a hand, silencing Flint. "Relax. That is an order, Captain."

Flint sighed and nodded.

"If it's any consolation, Silas, I don't expect this lull to last long. You are dismissed. God be with you."

Flint stood and put on his hat. Clicking his heels, he dipped his head toward Abernathy. "And also with you, sir."

2

Flint returned to the Templar dining hall. Night had fallen outside. The tables were empty, and the kitchen was dark. It looked as though Flint would be on his own for supper. Another modern convenience Abernathy had introduced to the Chapter House besides electricity was refrigeration, for which Flint was equally grateful. After perusing the contents of the refrigerator and pantry, he made himself a ham sandwich, a salad with oil and vinegar dressing, and took one chocolate chip cookie for dessert. Flint had once read about a device called a microwave oven in his history books. He reflected that such a machine would prove quite useful in reheating food quickly, but it was lost technology, like so many of the other devices that had existed before the coming of Simon Magus.

As he dined, Flint considered what to do with his time

off from field work. Normally he shut himself in his living quarters to catch up on paperwork or spent his waking hours in the library. His mind kept returning to the Weird Sisters that he had encountered during the Oglethorpe case. And his brother Charles was still out there. God only knew what fiendish devilry he was plotting.

"Captain Flint?"

Flint looked up and saw Sam Breckenridge, a Supernumerary and courier for the Order. He was dressed in leather armor like Navarro's, a pouch hanging from his shoulder.

"Ah, Mr. Breckenridge," Flint said. "It is good to see you again."

"I hope I'm not disturbing you sir."

"Not at all. How may I help you?"

"Actually sir, I have a letter for you," Breckenridge said.

"Indeed? It was my understanding that there were no open cases at the moment."

"Oh, it's not from Mr. Archer, sir," Breckenridge said, referring to Knight Templar Andrew Archer, who had an uncanny talent for directing couriers to Witch Hunters in the field. "It's from a…" He dug around in his pouch, took out a letter, and looked at the return address. "It's from a Professor Karl Johansson."

Flint raised his eyebrows. "This is a surprise," he said, taking the envelope.

"Friend of yours?"

"More of an acquaintance. We met several years ago at an archaeological symposium. His lecture on twenty-first century communication devices was most compelling. We engaged in conversation and learned that we have a mutual interest in the history of the old United States. We have corresponded regularly since then, though my unpredictable schedule often makes it difficult to respond in a timely manner. I have not heard from the Professor in some time."

"Twenty-first century... communication devices?" Breckenridge asked.

"Yes. They were a combination of telephone, radio, and telegraph. One could establish audio communication with another person who had one, receive radio broadcasts, and send written messages, all with one machine. The truly remarkable fact is that these devices were small enough to carry in one's trouser pocket, and so ubiquitous that virtually the entire population of North America had one."

Breckenridge whistled. "Sounds like they'd make my job a lot easier."

Flint smiled. "Yes, I imagine that they would have. Unfortunately, the science and technical knowledge of the devices has been lost to time. Scholars have recovered several of them from archaeological sites, but they are all inoperative, and are little more than curiosities now."

"Well, I'll let you get to it then sir," Breckenridge said. "Let me know if he's found anything interesting!" He departed.

Flint tore open the envelope and began to read the letter:

> May 15, 2533
>
> Dear Silas,
>
> I pray that this letter finds you in good health. I apologize for failing to keep up with our correspondence, but I've been engrossed in my latest project, one that I think you will

find interesting: I have discovered the location of a United
States Air Force Base. Not only that, but from what my team
has uncovered so far, it appears mostly intact. I don't wish to
get ahead of myself, but I feel like this could be the archae-
ological discovery of the century! It is for that reason, old
friend, that I invite you to visit my dig site and get a taste
of twenty-first century American history. I know that your
vocation keeps you on the road much of the time, but I expect
I will be here for months, if not years, to come. Are you still
working with Ricardo Navarro? Please tell him he is wel-
come to visit as well. My dig site is located across the bor-
der in the United Mountain States, approximately 75 miles
southeast from your Chapter House at Fort Marsing. I hope
to see you soon, Silas.

Cordially yours,

Karl Johansson, Ph.D., University of Denver, UMS

Flint put down the letter. His heart raced in his chest. A
United States Air Force Base! Largely intact! He didn't know
how that could be possible. The United States government
had dissolved shortly after the fall of the Great Magician in
2076. So many of its military bases around the world had
been destroyed during the Occult War. The ones that had
survived were either stripped bare by scavengers over the
centuries or sealed off by governments interested in whatever
old world technology they could salvage. To discover another
one so close to Fort Marsing, one apparently untouched by
salvagers... this was a priceless opportunity. There was no

way the technology could still be operational after 457 years buried beneath the earth, but to see American made machines in one piece? Very few outside the ranks of government or academia could boast such an experience.

Flint thanked God for this providential development. He would not have to spend his time off in isolation after all.

The church bell rang. Flint folded the letter and put it inside one of his long coat's many pockets. He tried to clear his mind in preparation for Compline, the night prayers that were part of the daily routine at Fort Marsing. Rising from his seat, Flint made his way to the chapel, falling in with a group of Templars. He expected that his mind would still be distracted as he recited the prayers that had been a part of the Order of Saint Benedict for two thousand years but hoped that the Lord would understand.

3

Dawn rose over Fort Marsing. Flint barely took notice of the rising sun as it peeked through the window in his quarters. They consisted of one large room that served as his office, living room, and bedroom, with a privy in a separate, smaller room. A crucifix above his bed and a portrait of Saint Benedict behind his desk were the only decorations. Like Abernathy's office, Flint's room was packed with bookshelves, with more books stacked on the floor, on his bedside table, on the coffee table by the two upholstered chairs in the living room portion, everywhere. To the untrained eye, Flint's quarters appeared unorganized, but a closer look revealed the bookshelves were arranged by subject and author.

Even the books not on the shelves were so organized. He sat at his desk now, poring over a text he had pulled from the shelf devoted to secular history.

He found an atlas of the United States as it existed in the twenty first century. Fort Marsing was in the far eastern half of the Empire of Cascadia, a nation consisting of the former states of Oregon, Washington, and the western half of Idaho. Flint traced his finger along Highway 84 on the map. Johansson had said the Air Force Base was 75 miles southeast of Fort Marsing. By Flint's calculations, that would make it Mountain Home Air Force Base. Cascadia's eastern border was marked by the Boise River. From there, he would enter the United Mountain States, made up of the eastern half of the Idaho country, and the former states of Montana, Wyoming, and Colorado.

Flint shut the book and pondered his next move. There was no hurry; Johansson had said he would likely be there for months. His letter was dated May 15, seven days ago. Flint still wanted to get there, post-haste, before the UMS government took an interest and decided to seal it off. He checked his pocket watch. 6 a.m. He sighed. Was there even a point in seeing if Navarro was awake? Flint expected his assistant had drank himself unconscious last night, and would no doubt roll out of bed at the gentlemanly hour of 11 a.m.

The church bell rang. Flint grabbed his prayer book and made for the chapel. It was now the liturgical hour of Prime and the Templars were meeting for their morning prayers.

"Seven times a day I have given praise to thee, for the judgments of thy justice," Flint thought. The Templars were not bound by

the religious vows of monks, but since the Templars' founding in 2181, it was the standard practice for Witch Hunters to pray together when they were at their Chapter Houses.

"Silas?"

Flint tried again to clear his mind, but it kept presenting him visions of a bygone age when mankind could take to the skies, not through diabolical magic or deals with demons, but through its own ingenuity and the reason that God had gifted them.

"Silas?"

Magus was responsible for the deaths of billions. So many of humanity's brightest minds lost in a conflagration that had broken nations, remade the face of the earth, and set back mankind's technological progress by centuries.

"Silas!"

Flint's reverie was broken and he looked up. Witch Hunter Captain Reginald Withers had fallen into step beside him on his way to the chapel and Flint hadn't noticed. He chided himself for losing his situational awareness. Such lapses could get one killed in the field.

"Forgive me, Mr. Withers," Flint said. "My mind was elsewhere."

"Clearly. What's got the Ruin of Witches so preoccupied?"

Flint pursed his lips. The Ruin of Witches. He didn't know who started it, but the nickname had begun circulating after his encounter with the witch Lilian Turner in Canyon Cove the previous month.

"I am planning an excursion for today," Flint replied.

"You don't have an assignment either, eh?" Withers said. He did a double take. "Wait… Silas Flint, taking a vacation?"

"Not at all. This will be more of an educational endeavor."

"Thank God," Withers chuckled. "When Silas Flint takes time off from work, it will be a sign of the end times."

4

After Morning Prayers and breakfast, Flint went across the courtyard to the Supernumerary barracks. They served as assistants to Witch Hunters in the field, specializing in weaponry and interrogation techniques. Some wag had said their main purpose was to serve as pack mules for Templars. Many Supernumeraries went on to become Witch Hunters in their own right. Navarro certainly had the faith, the courage, and the fighting skill to become a Templar, Flint thought, if only he would reform his life enough to pass the requirement of being a Catholic of good moral character.

The hallways of the East Wing were silent and deserted. Flint reached the door to Navarro's quarters and knocked.

"Mr. Navarro!" he called. Nothing.

He pounded harder. "Mr. Navarro! Wake up, I say!" Still nothing.

He checked his pocket watch. 9 a.m. Early by Navarro's standards, but there should have been other men in the hallway. Had they all drunk themselves into a stupor last night?

Flint cocked his head. He heard the faint rattle of gunfire, the pinging of steel plates. Ah. Gunnery Sergeant Mendoza had his charges at the firing range. Supernumeraries were all officially equals, but the resident gunsmith and firearms instructor Miguel Mendoza had picked up the unofficial title several years ago. Even General Abernathy addressed him as

"Gunny" and deferred to his wisdom in all things relating to weapons.

Flint left the barracks and proceeded toward the gates. The bright sun and clear skies promised a pleasant day ahead. He wondered if the eternally dark clouds that obscured the Dead Lands would be visible from the Air Force Base. It occurred to Flint that he had never left Cascadia in his life, despite residing so close to the border with the United Mountain States.

Exiting the fortress, Flint strode toward the sound of gunfire, due south from Fort Marsing's gates. The firing rage consisted of a wide open field featuring a series of man-made berms, spaced at regular intervals of 100 yards, out to a maximum of 1000 yards. The targets were mostly steel plates, though some of the more artistically inclined Supernumeraries designed their own cardboard targets with witches, vampires, or other monsters drawn on them.

Flint could hear Mendoza's gravelly voice bellowing. "Ready... aim... fire!"

There was a thunderous volley from dozens of rifles.

"Ready... aim... fire!"

Another volley.

Flint approached the shooters, whose backs were to him. Mendoza spotted him.

"Cease fire... cease fire on the firing range!" he shouted, waving one arm in front of his face. The Supernumeraries lowered their rifles. "Check your targets!"

The riflemen slung their weapons and made their way downrange. Mendoza came forward to meet Flint, extending his hand, which Flint shook.

"Morning, Captain," he said. Mendoza was just a hair under Flint's own height of six feet, two inches. His hands were callused from a lifetime of working with weapons.

"Good morning to you, Gunnery Sergeant," Flint replied.

Mendoza chuckled. "Even I don't know when the men started calling me that," he said.

"The rank went extinct, but I cannot think of a better man to raise it from the dead like Lazarus from his tomb."

"If you're looking to get some practice in, you're welcome to join us."

"I may take you up on that, Mr. Mendoza. But first I must speak with my assistant. Is he here?"

"Yeah, he's somewhere out there." Mendoza cupped his mouth and yelled, "Navarro! Ricardo Navarro, where you at?!"

700 yards away, Navarro waved back.

"Get over here, *pendejo!*" Mendoza shouted. After a moment, he winced. "Uh, sorry sir," he said.

Flint smiled. "Think nothing of it."

Navarro jogged toward Flint and Mendoza, no doubt nursing a debilitating hangover. He arrived at the firing line, breathing hard. He saluted. "Ricardo Navarro, reporting as ordered, sir!"

"This isn't the Army, smartass," Mendoza said, though Flint could see he was suppressing a smile. "Captain Flint wants a word." He walked away to give the two men privacy.

"What's going on boss? We got a job?" Navarro asked.

"No, actually," Flint replied. "General Abernathy informed

me that all active cases currently have investigators assigned to them."

"You mean we get some time off?" Navarro pumped his fist. "Alleluia and praise God!"

"Hmph."

"Oh come on boss, we've been going hard for weeks."

Flint cleared his throat. "Yes, well… I will concede that our last few cases have been… trying."

"You should get out of here for a while. Get some rest and relaxation in."

"As it happens Mr. Navarro, that is precisely the reason I am here."

"Oh yeah?"

"Do you recall our meeting with Professor Karl Johansson several years ago?"

Navarro thought for a few moments. He snapped his fingers. "Oh yeah! He was the one did that lecture, the one about the, uh… uh… the smart… things."

"Smart phones," Flint said, nodding.

"What about him, boss?"

"He has written to me about his latest discovery; a United States Air Force Base. It is 75 miles from here. He informs me that so far, the facility appears largely intact."

Navarro's eyes widened. "An American base, still in one piece? Damn. You don't see those every day."

"Indeed not. He has invited me to see it for myself. And he extended the invitation to you as well."

"No shit? An Air Force Base… you think they got any of those fancy black rifles? Or what do you call them, jet planes?"

"It is possible, though I find it doubtful they would still be working after nearly 500 years."

"Yeah, but to see them all in one piece..."

Flint nodded. "A once in a lifetime opportunity."

"Hey," Navarro said. "The professor's not there by himself, right?"

"I should think not. He did mention a team in his letter."

"Like a team from his university?"

"Most probably."

Navarro smiled. "All right! College girls, here I come!"

Flint rolled his eyes.

5

Inside his quarters, Flint packed for his trip. He didn't know how long he would be gone, but the couriers would find him if a case came up. They always did, somehow. He folded several changes of clothes into his travel case: white dress shirts, black waistcoats, black trousers, black socks. His black long coat and tall, wide brimmed hat went with him everywhere. It didn't occur to him to leave behind his sword or his pistols. One never knew when the forces of darkness would rear their ugly heads on the road.

He was considering which books to bring with him when there was a knock at his door.

"Enter," he called, not turning around. He heard the door creak open.

"Hey Silas. Long time no see."

Flint knew that voice. Turning, he saw a young woman in leather body armor and denim jeans. Her long black hair was tied back in a ponytail. Her blue eyes had a peculiar hue, which Flint knew came from the magical power coursing in her veins. He raised an eyebrow. He would never admit it to her of course, but she had cleaned up rather nicely since the last time he had seen her, covered in demonic ichor, her hands raw and blistered from channeling too much magic too quickly.

"Miss Fletcher," he nodded.

Zelda Fletcher cocked her head. "That's it?"

Flint snorted. Then his face softened. "It is good to see you again."

"Uh huh," she replied. Then she smiled. "How's things?"

"Quite well, thank you. I understand you have been making yourself useful to the Order."

"Oh yeah, that's me," she said. "The fallen woman earning her redemption."

"Redemption is not earned, Miss Fletcher. It is a gift offered by the Lord."

"Yeah, well... I still feel like I got to earn it."

A few moments of silence passed.

"Is there something that I can do for you?" Flint asked.

"What? I can't drop by just to say hello to an old friend who got me out of jail?" She approached Flint and extended her hand. Flint took it. She reached and gripped his arm with her free hand. Flint narrowed his eyes.

"Whatcha got going on here?" she asked, nodding her head toward his travel case.

"Mr. Navarro and I are planning a field trip."

"Oh yeah? What are we going after this time? A witch? A coven of witches? A demon?"

"It is not a case, Miss Fletcher. It is an educational field trip."

"Oh." Her face fell. "Where's it at?"

"An old colleague of mine has discovered an American Air Force Base."

Fletcher's eyebrows went up. "No shit? You mean one that's not smashed to pieces?"

"Indeed."

"Huh..." She kneaded her hands, bit her lip. "I... uh... don't suppose..."

Flint stared at her.

"Well, I mean, if you've got plans... I wouldn't want to... uh..."

Flint said nothing.

Fletcher sighed. "Yeah. Okay. I get it. Well, have fun, I guess." She made her way for the door.

"Miss Fletcher..." Flint said.

She turned, a smile on her face.

"Give me back my pocket watch."

Her brow furrowed. "What are you talking about?"

"Miss Fletcher, my vocation is to recognize magic in all of its forms. That includes ordinary sleight of hand."

Fletcher laughed. "You've got it all wrong, I never..."

"Give me back my pocket watch and I will give you back your coin purse."

"What the..." Fletcher patted her belt. Her eyes went wide. "How did you..."

Flint smiled. "The same way that you did. You took my pocket watch when we shook hands, just as I took your coin purse," he said. He reached into his long coat and took out the pouch, dropping it into his other hand. "Misdirection does not work if your mark knows that it is coming."

Fletcher chuckled. She reached into her pocket, took out Flint's watch. They tossed their belongings to each other simultaneously.

"I was going to give it back," she said, blushing. "I was just testing you."

"I am sure," Flint said, returning the watch to his waistcoat pocket.

"But, you know, in all seriousness... um..."

Flint sighed. "I will save you the discomfiture, Miss Fletcher. You may accompany Mr. Navarro and I if you wish."

She exhaled. "Oh, thank God. I didn't want to impose, and, no offense, you're kind of scary sometimes."

"I am pleased to hear that, thank you."

Rolling her eyes, Fletcher said, "I've always wanted to see more of the world. And an American base? I've heard stories about what they were like."

"I imagine the reality will be most impressive."

6

Navarro heaved everyone's travel cases into the luggage compartment of the carriage, while Flint and Fletcher climbed aboard. The carriage would take them to the border city of New Meridian on the banks of the Boise River. From there, they would cross over into the United Mountain States and take Highway 84 southeast toward Professor Johansson's dig site.

Navarro entered the carriage, shutting the door behind him. The driver flicked the reins, and the team of horses took them out of Fort Marsing and on their way. The carriage rattled and shook.

"Five hundred years, you'd think people would pave some decent roads again," Fletcher muttered. The carriage dipped with a bang as it went over a pothole.

"The apocalypse disrupted supply chains some, you know?" Navarro said.

Flint said nothing, staring out the window.

"Thanks again for letting me tag along," Fletcher said. Flint grunted and gave her a slight nod.

"You into history?" Navarro asked.

"Yeah, I am actually," Fletcher replied. "I didn't get much formal schooling, growing up. I heard stories, and legends about what the old world was like. Like, did we really walk on the moon once?"

"The Americans sent several missions to the moon," Flint said, continuing to stare out the window.

"Fucking amazing... hey, where we're going, you think they have space rockets there?"

Flint shook his head. "No. Those missions originated from La Floride."

"Where's that?"

"It is a peninsula approximately two thousand miles southeast from Cascadia."

"Oh..."

Navarro chuckled. "I hear it's nice down there, if you don't mind all the voodoo shamans and Santeria cultists."

"Hmph. I'd still like to go there some day," Fletcher said.

"I'm hoping that where we're going, they got some of those jet planes," Navarro said.

"You think they still work?" Fletcher said.

Flint broke in. "It is unlikely. Even if the internal mechanisms were still functional, the fuel has a limited shelf life."

"Can't we just put some more gas in them?"

"If I saved up for a few years, I might afford a gallon or two," Navarro laughed.

"Even if we possessed the necessary funds, it is my understanding that the fuel for ancient aircraft required specialized treatment. Automobile gasoline or kerosene would not work."

Fletcher looked out the window. "Why is gas so damn expensive anyway?"

"Much of the old world's supply of oil came from the area surrounding the Holy Lands," Flint said. "Simon Magus wreaked such destruction upon that region of the world that the industry never fully recovered. The inhabitants of those lands were more focused on bare survival, and the practical knowledge of oil extraction, with the accompanying technology, was gradually lost through the generations."

"Yeah," Navarro said. "Plus the oceans are filled with giant tentacle monsters. That'll drive the old insurance up."

Fletcher sighed. "It's too bad. I've always wanted to ride in an automobile."

"Canyon Cove isn't too far from the Fort, they have…" Navarro stopped as Flint nudged him with his elbow. "Oh… uh, never mind." Flint and Navarro had witnessed the destruction of much of Canyon Cove's automobile fleet during the Lilian Turner case the previous month.

"The city of Salem has more automobiles," Flint said, referring to the capitol of Cascadia. "Enough to offer a public transportation system."

"It's a great place to visit, but I wouldn't want to live there. The taxes are murder," Navarro said.

Fletcher looked at the two men seated across from her. "How do you guys know so much?"

"I have been a student of history since my childhood," Flint said. "The Order also provides a rigorous academic curriculum for all aspiring Templars."

"Lot of what I know, I picked up from Silas. Plus experience in the field," Navarro said.

"I never got that growing up," Fletcher said.

"It is never too late to pursue an education, Miss Fletcher."

She laughed. "Silas, come on, it's okay to call me Zelda."

Navarro chuckled. "Good luck with that. I been with him five years and he hardly ever calls me Ricardo, let alone Rico."

"I fail to see what is wrong with maintaining a certain sense of decorum."

"There's decorum, and then there's having a stick up your..."

"That will be enough, thank you," Flint said, cutting her off.

Fletcher smirked. "Okay, okay. Why don't you tell us more about where we're going?"

Flint straightened up in his seat. "I believe the site was formerly known as Mountain Home Air Force Base. It is approximately twelve miles southwest of a town called Rattlesnake Station. We shall hire another carriage once we reach New Meridian, and it shall deliver us to the town. From there, we shall rent horses to carry us for the rest of our journey. I suspect the roads are nonexistent in that part of the United Mountain States."

"I hope the base still has some of those black rifles stored away somewhere," Navarro said. "I hear those things are pretty light, and they got thirty round magazines."

"Even if they are present, it is unlikely that you would be permitted to take one, Mr. Navarro."

"Hey Zelda, how's your marksmanship going?"

Fletcher shrugged. "It's going alright, I guess. I'm still better with fireballs and lightning though."

"Miss Fletcher…"

"I know, I know," she sighed. "I don't know why you're complaining though. I saved your ass back in New Rome with magic."

"She's got you there boss," Navarro said.

"Be that as it may, your rehabilitation program forbids the use of magic."

"I don't see what the big deal is if I'm not hurting anybody. Or at least nobody who doesn't deserve it."

Flint scowled. "The 'big deal' is that magic is, by its very essence, unnatural. It violates the laws of science and is an abomination in the eyes of God."

Fletcher spread her arms. "Unnatural? Really? What about guns? Or automobiles? Or jet planes or space rockets? They aren't found in nature. We built them."

"Here we go," Navarro said, rolling his eyes.

"All of those devices were invented by man through the gift of reason God bestowed on him at the dawn of creation, using the natural resources of the world God made for us.

Magic circumvents the physical laws God made to govern our world."

"It's not all bad!" Fletcher replied. "Do a lot of witches and warlocks go batshit crazy? Yeah. But magic can be used to heal yourself and others, it can provide electricity or fire when you don't have other stuff to make…"

"You said it yourself, Miss Fletcher. I will concede that magic is not always directly harmful to others. However, it always harms the spirit of its wielder. It gnaws at the mind, burrows into the soul, drawing the witch ever closer to the powers below. It drives them 'batshit crazy,' as you so color-fully put it."

Fletcher and Navarro's mouths dropped open simultaneously.

"Boss… are you feeling alright? That's the first time I've ever heard you swear."

Fletcher clapped her hands. "I didn't think you had it in you!"

"You will note that I was quoting Miss Fletcher," Flint replied. "I find swearing to be vulgar, but in this case, the term she used was apt."

Fletcher smiled at him. "You are full of surprises, aren't you?"

"More than you know."

7

Mark McCloskey and Jennifer Barrett made their way through the corridors of a building on Mountain Home Air Force Base. Their flashlights cut a swathe through the darkness, revealing only dust, cobwebs, and an endless procession of doors. Most were locked, and Professor Johansson had been insistent about not smashing or picking them yet. The doors that were open led to offices with desks, filing cabinets, and those flat plastic shells with keyboards on one side and panels of black glass on the other.

"What exactly did those things do?" Barrett asked.

"Professor Johansson said they're called computers," McCloskey replied. "It'd be quicker to say what they couldn't do."

"Too bad they don't work anymore."

"Yeah, well, I doubt anything works well after almost five hundred years."

McCloskey and Barrett were both doctoral students studying North American Archaeology. When Professor Johansson had announced the discovery of a previously unknown American Air Force Base, they'd leaped at the opportunity to join his excavation team.

"What do you think?" McCloskey asked. He turned a doorknob. Locked.

"I don't know," Barrett said. "I was kind of hoping..."

"That we'd find working jet planes? Computers?"

She laughed. "Kind of, yeah. In my head I know it's not going to happen, but..."

"I know how you feel. But I think this is the reality of archaeology: a lot of poking around in old buildings."

"This one is kind of spooky."

McCloskey tried another door, and this one opened. This office was occupied. A human skeleton lay slumped over the desk, an ancient pistol clutched in one bony hand, a hole in its skull with bone fragments scattered about. Faded spray paint adorned the wall behind it. It spelled out LET IT ALL END.

The two graduate students looked at each other.

"Yeah... yeah, it is kind of spooky," McCloskey.

"Poor guy," Barrett said. "It must have looked like the world was ending back then."

McCloskey approached the desk. Gingerly stepping around the skeleton, he opened one of the desk drawers. Pens, paperclips, thumb tacks, rubber bands... and a typed sheet of paper.

"Jen, come take a look at this."

As Barrett stepped forward, McCloskey took the paper out of the desk. Holding it in one hand, he aimed his flashlight at it and began to read.

July 19, 2076

It's over. We just received word. Washington is overrun. Air Force One is down, the President unaccounted for. They say Magus is dead, killed in Italy, just like in Bible times. It's such bullshit. In the movies, TV, you kill the big bad and that's it, happily ever after. But this is real life. Magus might be dead – I don't think anything can really kill him – but all of these goddamn witches and wizards and monsters are still on the loose.

Why God? Why? Why is my family dead? Why is the world destroyed? The preachers all say it's the end times, that Magus is the anti-Christ, and to trust in you. I tried, God. I tried to believe in you, to trust you. Magus is a guy

from the Bible. If he's real, you must be real too, right God?
Then why have you done this to us if you're all knowing
and all loving and all that happy horseshit?

Well, frankly God, I don't care anymore. My family's
dead. My country's dead. There's nothing and no one left for
me here. What do I have to live for now? We got turned back
to the stone age, and we still have to fight? No, to hell with
that. I'm done. The preachers say suicide is a sin, but hey,
what's one more after all I've done, all I've been through?

If anyone ever reads this, my name is Captain Greg But-
ler, United States Air Force. A pilot for a military which no
longer exists, that serves a nation which no longer exists. I'm
sorry.

"God," Barrett whispered.

McCloskey made the sign of the cross. "Rest in peace,
Captain Butler."

Barrett rubbed her arms. Her breath began to fog.
"Mark... let's get out of here. We need to tell the professor
about this."

McCloskey shivered. "Why did it get so cold all of a sudden?"

"Mark, please."

"We only have a few more doors to check. We'll finish up
and then get the hell out of here."

They left the office and continued down the hallway. As
they expected, most of the doors were locked. They reached

the final two doors at the end of the corridor. McCloskey turned the knob but it was unyielding. Locked.

Barrett's door opened with a creak.

"Oh shit!" she gasped.

"What is... oh. Jesus Christ," McCloskey whispered.

He counted three human skulls. The rest of the skeletons' bones were scattered everywhere. Femurs were splintered. Ribs were shattered. McCloskey knelt for a closer look. There were marks on some of the bones. He squinted, aiming his flashlight.

"They look like... teeth marks," he said.

"Do you think...?"

"Could be anything. Some animals got in here, ate the bodies."

"What kind of animal does this kind of damage?"

"Jennifer... look."

She pointed her flashlight at the spot McCloskey indicated. More writing on the back wall. It read THE MAJOR IS NOT HIMSELF.

"What do you make of that?" McCloskey asked.

"Mark, we've checked all the doors. Let's go." Their breaths continued to fog.

"Yeah... yeah, I think you're right."

There was a bang from the corridor that made them jump.

"What was that?" Barrett whispered.

"Stay behind me," McCloskey said. He went back into the corridor, Barrett close on his heels. He shone his flashlight down the hall, but the darkness felt more oppressive somehow. It swallowed the light only a few feet in front of them, not at all in the same manner as when they had entered the building.

"Hello?" McCloskey called. Silence.

"Hello?" he called again. Nothing.

"Mark, I'm scared," Barrett said.

"Come on, let's get out of here."

They crept forward as quickly as stealth would allow. Darkness encroached upon them, the light from their flashlights dimming. They flickered.

"Oh Jesus," Barrett whispered.

"Don't panic, just keep moving forward."

They passed an open doorway. Barrett turned her head to look inside and she gasped, dropping her flashlight.

"What?! What's wrong?!" McCloskey whispered.

"There was somebody in there!"

He shone his flashlight into the office. There was nothing but the desk, filing cabinets, and computer.

"I'm telling you, someone was in there! I saw a silhouette or a shadow or something. It was a person, I swear!"

Deciding to forgo stealth, the two graduate students started running. Only a few more feet to the exit...

A hand reached down from the ceiling, grabbing Barrett by the hair. She screamed as the hand yanked her up off the floor and into the darkness.

"Jennifer!" McCloskey screamed. He shone the light up at the ceiling. Her screams echoed in the hallway, growing distant.

"Jennifer, where are you?!" He ran back the way he had come, following the sounds of Jennifer's cries. They were cut off, replaced by a wet gurgling.

"Jennifer!"

The gagging noises stopped, and all was still and silent. Dust motes drifted through the cone of light cast by McCloskey's flashlight.

"Jennifer?"

Something came crashing down from the ceiling. McCloskey screamed and stumbled, dropping his flashlight. It spun in a lazy circle on the floor. It stopped, the light aimed at the fallen object.

Barrett's glassy eyes stared into nothingness. Her neck was a bloody ruin but McCloskey still saw the two ragged holes in her flesh.

Before he could scream, the hand reached down from the ceiling and pulled him off the floor. Like Barrett's before him, McCloskey's screams of pain and fear were cut off by a strangled squeak. Slurping echoed throughout the hallway. Then all was still and silent again.

8

"Rattlesnake Station!" the driver called.

Flint, Navarro, and Fletcher disembarked from the carriage. Navarro unloaded their travel cases from the luggage compartment while Fletcher stretched and Flint observed their surroundings. Rattlesnake Station wasn't a town so much as a travel hub. It lay in a valley at the foot of a mountain range. There was a locomotive station, numerous horse and carriage rental services, hotels, saloons, and a smattering of cottages and farms. The streets were packed with merchants, bankers, businessmen, and itinerants, who flagged down carriages, rushed to the locomotive station, rode horses out of town. It was small, but as one of the few settlements along this stretch of Highway 84, it saw much international traffic.

"Awfully busy, huh?" Fletcher said.

"It is not without its charms," Flint replied.

"Can I ask you something?"

"What is it, Miss Fletcher?"

"What's with you and the no contractions? It's always 'I will or I cannot.'"

Flint raised an eyebrow. "Are you in some sort of rush?"

Fletcher scoffed. "Don't you just hate it when somebody answers a question with a question?"

"If that is all, we must secure horses for the remainder of our journey. Come along Miss Fletcher, Mr. Navarro."

The trio made their way to the nearest stable. The stablemaster sat on a wooden stool, leaning against a post, his hat pulled down over his eyes against the afternoon sun. His jaw worked like a cow chewing its cud. Horses snorted and tapped their hooves inside their stalls. Fletcher wrinkled her nose.

"I beg your pardon," Flint said.

The stablemaster looked up. His skin was like old leather. He spat a wad of tobacco juice into the dirt.

"Help you?" he asked

"My companions and I should like to rent three horses, if you please."

The stablemaster smirked. "Ain't from around here, are you?"

"Indeed not. We are visitors from Cascadia. Knight Templar Captain Silas Flint, at your service. May I present my assistant, Supernumerary Ricardo Navarro and our... ward, Zelda Fletcher."

"What the fuck?" Fletcher blurted. "Ward? I'm a 24 year old woman for God's sake, you're making me sound like some little lost orphan girl."

The stablemaster chuckled. "Jed Everett," he said, giving Flint a brief handshake. "You're a Witch Hunter huh?"

"Yes, that is the more common name."

"You headed down south to Mountain Home?"

Flint locked eyes with Everett. "Yes, actually."

"Good. Do us a favor and burn it to the ground."

The trio exchanged glances.

"Why would we want to do that?" Navarro asked.

"The place is cursed."

"Ahh shit," Navarro groaned. "I should have known this trip was too good to be true."

"What is the nature of this curse?" Flint asked.

Everett lowered his voice. "There's stories of an old military base buried out there. You ask me, it was buried for a good reason. All them soldiers who was there went crazy when the United States went down. Started killing anyone they could get their hands on. Then each other. Then themselves."

Flint leaned in. "Go on."

"Ever since the war ended, that land's been a magnet for all kinds of crazies. Couple of witches have hidden out there over the years. Something to do with all the bad juju around."

"Yes," Flint nodded. "The forces of evil are often drawn to locales that have seen mass insanity and bloodshed."

"Couple of weeks ago, some professor from Denver and a bunch of his kids came through here. Folks warned them like I'm warning you, but they went on their merry way." Everett snorted and spat another wad of tobacco juice. "Damn eggheads. I'm all for learning history and such, but sometimes it's best to forget the past."

Flint stroked his chin. "You said several witches had taken up residence over the centuries."

"Yeah. I don't know all the details, but I heard the worst of them all was... uh... Carey... Carey something."

"Is this Carey still active?"

"Oh no, no. This was right after the war, back when the Hundred Year Darkness had just begun. Most recent witchcraft I know about was back when my granddad was a kid. It's been quiet since then, but anyone with a lick of sense steers clear of that whole area. People who go out there don't usually come back."

"Well, if it's so dangerous, why do you live here?" Fletcher asked.

"Can't speak for the others, but my family's been here since this was Idaho, and I expect we'll live here until the Good Lord sees fit to come back."

"Do you get a lot of witches or monsters rolling through town?" Navarro asked.

"Occasionally. Same as everywhere else I suppose. Witches are usually more interested in finding that base. On top of everything else, they say the place is haunted. I don't know if that's true or not. If it is, the ghosts stay there. Best to leave them alone, I say."

"Fascinating..." Flint said. "Nonetheless, we shall rent the horses, if you please."

Everett shrugged. "Suit yourself."

Flint removed his purse from his coat pocket and tossed three silver coins to Everett. The stablemaster stared that them, his mouth agape.

"I trust that is enough," Flint said.

"Uh... yeah... that it is... I might have to get into the safe to get your change."

"Think nothing of it, Mr. Everett."

Fletcher nudged Navarro. "How much do you guys make?" she whispered.

Navarro grinned. "Not as much as you're thinking. Silas comes from money."

"Really? Why'd he become a Witch Hunter then?"

"That's... that's a tough one. I wouldn't feel right sharing it without running it by him first. Let's just say he joined up for personal reasons."

"Maybe I'll just ask..."

"I wouldn't."

"What's the problem?"

"He doesn't like people prying. And coming from you, he really might take it the wrong way."

"Me?"

"Not you, personally. From... you know, a witch."

"Former witch."

"Either way, if I was you, I'd leave it alone for now."

"Fine."

Flint rejoined them a few moments later. The sun dipped

below the mountain range on the horizon and their shadows grew long. He checked his pocket watch. 7 p.m.

"What's the plan boss?" Navarro asked.

"Let us secure lodgings for the night. We shall resume our journey..."

"At first light?"

Flint gave a wintry smile. "We are not on a case. You may sleep in until... shall we say 8 a.m.?"

"You're getting soft in your old age!"

9

Flint sat alone at a table in the hotel restaurant, dining on a rare steak, oven roasted asparagus, and a glass of red wine. He took a sip and looked around the dining room. The Church's presence was thin in the United Mountain States but the other patrons still recognized the hat and coat of a Witch Hunter, and they gave Flint a wide berth. An old juke box filled the room with an inspirational tune from the twentieth century, something about a tiger's eye. Flint preferred live performances, particularly of mid-twenty fourth century songs, but he had to admit that the musicians of the 1980s knew how to stir the emotions.

Navarro and Fletcher had ordered hamburgers and were sitting at the bar, drinking and laughing together. Flint pondered what Everett had told him. Professor Johansson had not mentioned any supernatural goings on in his letter. Everett said the last time a witch had befouled the city was when his grandfather was a child. Perhaps the legends were only that, legends. Flint snorted. He could count on one hand the number of times that had proven the case over his career. He prayed this time would be one of the rare exceptions. Like Navarro, he hoped to see an intact jet plane.

"Excuse me, sir?"

Flint looked up. Standing before his table were two young men, clean shaven, dressed in black pants, and white shirts with black ties.

"Yes?" Flint asked.

"We couldn't help but notice that you were eating alone. Would it be alright if we joined you?" one of them asked.

"I prefer solitude, thank you."

"Ok, no problem. We'll leave you in peace. But before we go, I'd like to intro…"

"I know who you are, Mormon."

"Oh, you've heard of us?"

"Yes. Here from Deseret on a mission, I presume."

"Yes sir," the other young man said.

"Do you recognize my attire?"

The two boys looked at each other.

"Actually sir, that was one of the reasons we approached you. We wanted to ask… what's with the pilgrim outfit? If you don't mind us asking."

Flint smiled. "I am a Knight Templar of the Order of Saint Benedict. A Witch Hunter, to use the common phrase."

"Oh! You're Catholic!"

"Yes. I myself used to find it ironic that we wear the garb of an extinct Protestant sect, but the imagery holds a prominent place in the collective memory of North America, as you have just demonstrated."

"We don't have any Catholics or Witch Hunters back home."

"How unfortunate. Now, as much as I appreciate theological disputation, I have more immediate concerns to ponder. Leave me."

The two boys waved their goodbyes and went to ply their trade elsewhere. Flint admired their spirit, if not their doctrine. Deseret, formerly known as Utah, had recovered quickly after the war, thanks in part to the Mormons' strong social cohesion. The rest of North America had barely survived the Hundred Years Darkness that followed the Great Magician's downfall.

Speaking of the Hundred Years Darkness, Everett had said that the witch named Carey was active during that time. God only knew what diabolical sorcery the harlot had worked on the common people. That could explain the haunted nature of the Air Force Base, Flint thought, if the rumors were true. Normally, human souls went to their judgment after death, but sufficiently powerful magic could keep them tethered to this world.

"Hey."

Flint stifled a growl. What in God's name did a man have to do to eat in peace? Scowling, he looked up and saw Fletcher. She swayed a bit on her feet.

"Miss Fletcher," Flint said, nodding.

"What's a matter, Silas? You too good to drink with me and Rico?" she slurred.

He raised an eyebrow. "I should think that you have had enough."

She giggled. "I've only had one in dog beers!"

Flint's gaze was icy. "Is there something that I can do for you, Miss Fletcher? Walk you to your room perhaps?"

"What?! No! This party is just getting started!" She sat down at Flint's table.

"Oh yes, please, do join me," he said.

"Don't mind if I do." She belched. "Hey, can I ask you something?"

"If you must."

"You come from money, right?"

Flint said nothing for a few moments. "In a manner of speaking."

"What's that supposed to mean?"

"I inherited a modest sum from my parents when they... passed away, along with their property. I sold everything when I pledged myself to the Order."

"So you got money. I haven't known you long but you're one of the smartest guys I've ever met. So I got to know..." She hiccupped. "Why'd you become a Witch Hunter? I mean you could have done anything, gone anywhere."

Flint said nothing.

"Oh shit. I wasn't supposed to ask that, was I?" Fletcher said.

"No. You were not."

"I didn't mean anything by it. I just want to... you know... I want to... uh... Oh, God damn it." She put her head down on the table, her face buried in her arms.

"Mr. Navarro!"

All heads turned at Flint's outburst. Navarro left a lovely young woman he'd been chatting up at the bar and approached Flint's table at the double.

"Problem sir?" he asked. Flint had seen him match Fletcher drink for drink, and he appeared none the worse for wear.

"Please escort Miss Fletcher to her room. I believe she has had more than enough merriment for one night."

"Hey, Zelda," Navarro said. He shook Fletcher's shoulder and she groaned in response. "Let's get you to bed, yeah?"

"I'm sorry Silas," Fletcher mumbled. She allowed Navarro to drape her arm around his shoulders, and he guided her out of the restaurant.

Flint drummed his fingers on the table. He'd lost his appetite.

10

The next morning, the trio saddled up and set out for Mountain Home Air Force Base. Flint found the sunrise to be particularly beautiful as it peeked over the snow capped mountains on the horizon. Navarro hummed a tune to himself. Fletcher moved her horse parallel to Flint's.

"Hey," she said. "About last night..."

"Do not mention it," Flint replied.

"I just wanted to say, uh, you know, I'm sorry. I was drunk and Navarro told me not to ask about it, and then I went and..."

"I meant that literally, Miss Fletcher. Do not mention it."

"Oh. Okay." She fell back until she was side by side with Navarro.

"Told you so," Flint heard Navarro say.

"Is he really mad?" Fletcher asked.

"He'll get over it. But yeah, I wouldn't ask him about his past again if I was you. He'll share whenever he feels comfortable with you."

"Does that guy ever feel comfortable?"

"I can hear you two," Flint spoke up.

They both fell silent. Flint was used to being asked about his past. He'd had to speak on it at length when he arrived at Fort Marsing as an 18 year old boy, all but demanding to join. But he was not ready to speak about it to a witch, reformed or otherwise. She did not need to know about Charles.

The landscape around Rattlesnake Station had rolling grassy hills with groves of trees dotted here and there. As they proceeded to the southwest, the grass thinned, the soil becoming dried and cracked. The trees grew bare, their bark gnarled and blackened. Flint thought the only thing missing was the cawing of crows. As if on cue, a crow lighted upon a dead tree and squawked. Even the sunlight seemed dimmer.

"Whoa," Fletcher said, looking around. "This place is bad. I can sense a lot of dark magic around. It's like it's got into the soil."

Flint grunted in reply. Fletcher had told him when they met that she could feel the presence of magic and overhear the thoughts of others in her mind. He didn't like it, but he believed her when she said there was nothing she could do about it. The Lord gave everyone a cross to bear.

"You'd think somebody as smart as the professor would see there's something wrong with this place," Navarro said.

"Professor Johansson can be rather narrowly focused at times," Flint said.

"Hey Zelda, one silver dollar says we end up fighting some kind of monster before we leave," Navarro said.

"No… no, I don't I'll take that one."

They rode on, the land remaining still and barren. Flint shielded his eyes and squinted. He could make out something on the horizon, standing out against the otherwise empty landscape.

"I believe we are nearly there," he said.

Several minutes passed, the clopping of hooves the only sound, when an icy wind blew over them. The horses spooked, and Flint struggled to control his mount. The animal's eyes were rolling in its head, its breath fogging in the now frigid air.

"Jesus!" Fletcher shouted.

"What is it?!" Navarro said.

Fletcher's eyes were wide, her face a shade paler. She pointed all around them.

"There are people," she whispered.

Flint looked around and saw nothing but cracked dirt and tumbleweeds.

"These… people… how do they appear?" he asked.

Fletcher took a few deep breaths. "Sorry, they just startled me. One minute there was nothing, and then all of a sudden, boom, here they are."

"Miss Fletcher?"

"Oh, right, ah… by people I mean ghosts. It's like I can see them but also see through them… what's the word?"

"Translucent."

"Thanks."

"What are they doing?" Navarro asked.

"They're just standing there, staring at us. A bunch of them are dressed the same. Some look like they're in pajamas with these weird patterns on them. Some are wearing suits with a bunch of little rectangles on their chests. Patches on their shoulders."

"Hmm…" Flint said. "I believe you may be seeing the spirits of American military personnel."

"I fucking hate ghosts," Navarro said, shivering.

Fletcher turned to him. "Don't you, like, hunt witches and warlocks and monsters for a living?"

"Those things I can shoot. But what can you do about a ghost?"

"What else, Miss Fletcher? Can you sense their intentions?" Flint asked.

Fletcher closed her eyes and inhaled deeply. She frowned.

"They're all thinking the same thing: 'help us.'"

"What kind of help does a ghost need? They're dead," Navarro said.

"Yes," Flint said, "But they should not be here. I believe that some fell sorcery is keeping these poor souls tethered to this world."

"I knew it. I knew we'd end up working."

"Calm yourself Mr. Navarro. There may be nothing that we can do for these men and women. But I suggest we remain on alert."

"Doesn't this freak you out?" Navarro asked Fletcher. "I can't even see them and they're giving me the creeps." His breath fogged as he spoke.

Fletcher looked all around her. "I've seen a lot of spirits since I learned magic. But never this many in one place. And never all thinking the same thing over and over. That's what's creeping me out."

"The dead are all quite single-minded," Flint said. "Come. Let us proceed to the dig site. We may find our answers there."

After much coaxing of their spooked horses, the trio moved on. The chill followed them. Flint pulled his long coat a little tighter.

"They're keeping pace with us," Fletcher said.

"I suspected as much," Flint replied.

"How do you do it Zelda?" Navarro asked.

"Do what?"

"Well, you can hear people's thoughts, right?"

"Yeah, but not in the way you're thinking."

"What do you mean?"

"I mean it's just sort of there, as background noise. Like when you're hanging out at the bar and everyone's talking? It's kind of like that. I know they're talking but I can't make out specific words unless I really focus on one person. And if I really focus on them, they feel it. I've heard it's like fingers poking around in your brain."

"And you can hear ghosts too?"

"Yeah."

"Doesn't it drive you crazy?"

She shrugged. "You get used to it, learn how to tune it out. It's either that or go mad."

"Can you read our minds right now?"

Flint turned around to glare at Fletcher. "Do not even think about it."

She raised her hands. "Easy there, hoss. I can hear Rico

easy. But ever since we met, I could never get a bead on you. It's like you're not even there. I don't know how you do it, honestly."

"Templars receive extensive training in mental discipline. We have long been aware that many witches share your talent. We are able quiet our minds sufficiently that mentalists are unable to penetrate unless they exert their full power."

"That's… kind of impressive."

"Hmph."

11

The trio continued in silence. The chill gradually dissipated as they grew closer to their destination. Flint saw a patch of black up ahead. It stretched into the distance. He started when he realized what he was seeing: a paved asphalt road. Intact. There were no holes, no weeds, no broken fragments.

"Remarkable," he said.

"Didn't think roads like these existed anymore," Navarro said.

"How come?" Fletcher asked.

"The material is bound by a type of pitch called asphalt. It has been difficult to acquire since the war."

"And those yellow stripes?"

"Automobiles would travel along either side of the yellow lines in opposite directions."

Fletcher nodded. "Makes sense."

They directed their horses to the right half of the road and proceeded. The sunlight returned to its normal hue as they left the badlands further behind.

"Are the ghosts gone?" Navarro asked.

"Yeah, they disappeared a while back," Fletcher said.

"Maybe this won't turn into a case after all, eh boss?"

"We shall see," Flint said.

Flint could make out buildings up ahead, along with a large blue sign. The sign featured two wings superimposed above a star and read U.S. AIR FORCE Mountain Home Air Force Base Main Gate. Past the sign was a small building, and a roof held up by columns.

"I believe that hut is where the gate guards were stationed," Flint said. "And automobiles would pass between those columns."

"Shit looks brand new," Navarro said.

"Yes. I begin to think it is unnaturally so."

"There's power here," Fletcher said. "It's getting stronger the closer we get."

"What kind of power?" Navarro asked.

"I don't know… some kind of magic I've never felt before, but it's been here a long time. Feels like centuries."

"Could it be that this power has been used to artificially preserve this area?" Flint asked.

"Maybe… I've heard of spells that can slow down time within range of the caster, even stop it. Whatever this is, it's beyond me."

"Can we stop and take a look inside that building?" Navarro asked.

"Very well," Flint said.

They dismounted and made their way to the guard station. Flint could see evidence of the archaeological team's work: a sign posted on the door read, "University of Denver Archaeological Site Authorized Personnel Only." Flint considered Johansson's invitation to be his authorization, so he turned the knob. The door opened with a creak.

The first thing he noticed were the mummies. Three desiccated corpses were sitting in swivel chairs before a work station with glass panels stretching up to the ceiling, which Flint took to be computer or television screens. The area was surrounded by tape that had University of Denver printed on it. The bodies were wearing green grey uniforms that looked like the "pajamas" Fletcher had mentioned earlier. The second thing he noticed was the graffiti on the walls. Much of it was meaningless to him, but two examples stood out: one message read MAGUS LIVES! The other said, WATCH OUT FOR MAJOR BOOTHE.

Navarro went to the work station. He poked at a few buttons, but nothing happened.

"Guess they haven't had electricity in a while, huh?"

"I should think not."

"Hey," Fletcher said. "I could... supply some electricity, if you know what I mean." She held up her index finger which crackled with sorcerous lightning.

"I do not believe that would work," Flint said. "Machines such as these were designed to be insulated from power surges. And I will thank you to cease your blasphemous witchcraft."

Fletcher shrugged, the energy dissipating from her fingertip.

Flint continued to survey the room. There were desks,

plastic clamshells with keyboards (laptops, that was the word), and photographs on the wall. He approached for a closer look. They were photographs of military personnel in blue uniforms, colorful rectangles above their left breast pockets. Flint recalled that they were called ribbons and represented medals that the owner had been awarded throughout their career. One photograph caught his eye.

A stern looking woman with her steel grey hair up in a bun glared at the camera. Two stars were on the shoulders of her uniform jacket. She had more ribbons than any of the other personnel on the wall, even more so than the man above her who had four stars on his shoulders. Something about that woman rubbed Flint the wrong way. He felt a tingle run up his spine. He leaned in closer to read the plaque beneath her picture. It read MAJOR GENERAL NEVEAH CAREY. Beneath the name was Director of Logistics Operations.

Flint furrowed his brow. Was this the witch Carey that Everett had mentioned back in Rattlesnake Station? He knew from his history books that after the appearance of Simon Magus in 2055, and through the end of the Occult War in 2076, the United States government was riddled with the Great Magician's converts and acolytes. If this was the same Carey from Everett's story, then Flint guessed that a general in charge of logistics could have wreaked untold havoc with the American military establishment.

"What'd you find sir?" Navarro said, coming to Flint's side.

"I have solved one mystery," Flint replied, pointing at the photograph.

Navarro squinted at the plaque. "Carey... you think that's the witch Everett was talking about?"

"Either she was the witch herself, or perhaps she had a daughter."

"Nasty looking piece of work."

"Yes. I cannot explain why, but I feel evil positively radiating from this portrait."

"I don't see anything else in here worth checking out. I'm ready to go sir."

"Let us be on our way then."

They left the portraits on the wall and went to where Fletcher was digging through desk drawers, no doubt for something valuable to conceal and sell later on. She turned to face them at the sound of their footsteps.

"Nothing in here but a bunch of junk. Let's... what the fuck?!"

Flint whirled around. There was nothing.

"What's wrong?" Navarro asked.

"That picture... it smiled."

Flint looked over his shoulder at her. "Which photograph?"

"That one." She pointed at Carey.

Flint went over to it again and scrutinized it from various angles. Carey's image was as he had left it, her glare frozen in time forever. But the more he looked at it, the more he felt a weight pressing on his chest. His head began to throb. The longer he gazed into the picture's eyes, the more he felt as though he were teetering at the edge of an abyss. It was only a photograph but there was something... uncanny about this portrait. He felt certain now: Carey had been a witch, which meant this photograph had been taken some time between 2055 and 2076.

"I don't see anything," Navarro said.

"Come," Flint said. "Let us find the professor and his team." Navarro and Fletcher left the building. Flint looked at Carey's portrait one last time before he followed, shutting the door behind him.

12

They climbed back onto their horses and proceeded south. Flint observed that not only was the road in perfect condition, but the street signs also bore no signs of wear or rust. They were currently on Gunfighter Avenue. On their left was a building called Pizza Hut.

"Pizza? Soldiers could just get pizza anytime they wanted to?" Fletcher asked.

"The proper term is Airmen," Flint said. "In theory they could, but I expect that they had to maintain certain physical fitness standards."

As they moved further south onto the grounds of the base, Flint saw houses on either side of the road. They were modest one- or two-story dwellings. Like everything else he had seen thus far, they appeared to be in pristine condition after nearly 500 years.

"Is this a military base or a town?" Navarro asked.

"It is both," Flint replied. "The Americans designed their military outposts to be self-enclosed communities. Personnel and their families lived on the grounds in these houses we see before us."

"Wait... some 18 year old kid could join up, and they just gave him a house? Damn."

"I do not believe it was quite that simple, but the United States was fantastically wealthy."

"How much did these guys get paid?" Fletcher asked.

"I do not know how to convert the value of American paper currency into modern money. By the late twentieth century, American money was no longer backed by gold or silver."

Fletcher blinked. "Their money was just paper?"

"Paper backed by the 'full faith and credit' of the United States government. Obviously, it became worthless when the American federal government dissolved."

"Shit," Navarro said.

"Yes. That contributed much to the suffering of the Hundred Years Darkness: the common people were thrust into a dark new world with no way to obtain goods and services save for bartering. It is only through the grace of God that humanity survived."

They traveled on, Navarro and Fletcher looking all around them. Flint focused on the road, looking for signs of Professor Johansson's encampment, or any sign of his archaeological team. Something caught his eye. There, up ahead. He saw rows of tents spread out on a grassy field near a series of buildings. As they grew closer, he saw a sign in front of the largest building that said they were entering the grounds of Mountain Home Air Force Base Junior High School.

"Why are they in tents? They got luxury homes all around them," Fletcher said.

"They no doubt wish to preserve everything as much as possible," Flint said.

"Plus they probably don't want to sleep in dead people's beds," Navarro said.

Flint saw movement in the encampment. His hand reached for one of the pistols on his gun belt. He relaxed when he saw young people in khaki shorts and polo shirts. These had to be Professor Johansson's students.

The trio moved their horses off the road and onto the field where other horses cropped at the grass. They dismounted and untied their travel cases from the saddles. Flint flagged down a young woman carrying what looked like a tablet of glass and plastic.

"Young lady," he said.

Her eyes widened when she saw Flint. "Oh shit... am I in trouble?"

"Not at all. I should like to know where Professor Johansson may be found, if you please."

"Right... over there," she said, pointing at the largest tent, a bemused look on her face.

"Thank you."

The tents were arranged by rows and columns, making navigation simple. The professor's tent was pitched atop a small rise in the ground.

"Did you see that look on her face?" Navarro asked.

"I'm pretty sure it was because of the way he talks," Fletcher said.

Flint ignored them and pressed on. He pushed aside one of the command tent's flaps and stepped inside. Rows of tables held recovered artifacts from the base, including tablets similar to the one the girl had been carrying, some sort of plastic rectangles with metal protrusions, moldering books, wires, tools, military medals, and what looked to be a rifle that was entirely black. Professor Johansson was in the back, speaking to a group of students who were jotting down his words on notepads. A black man leaned against one of the posts holding up the tent, his eyes hidden by dark sunglasses, a shotgun slung across his back. He looked up as Flint and his companions entered the tent and began walking to them.

"Help you?" he asked when he arrived.

"Knight Templar Captain Silas Flint, at your service," Flint replied. "May I present my assistant, Supernumerary Ricardo Navarro and our..."

Fletcher glared at him.

"Our associate, Zelda Fletcher."

The black man gave each an appraising look. He nodded and said, "Ezekiel Austin, head of security. You can call me Zeke. What brings you here, Knight Templar Captain Silas Flint?"

"We are here at the invitation of Professor Johansson."

"Just a minute." Austin went to the professor. Flint couldn't make out the words, but Johansson looked over Austin's shoulder. His face lit up when he saw the trio.

"Silas! Ricardo! So glad you could make it!" he cried, coming forward to meet them. Austin appeared to relax and resumed his position, crossing his arms and leaning against the wooden post.

Johansson shook hands with Flint and Navarro. He looked at Fletcher.

"Who's your new friend?" he asked Flint.

"May I introduce Miss Zelda Fletcher. Miss Fletcher, this is Professor Karl Johansson of the University of Denver."

She gave Johansson a brief handshake. "Pleased to meet you sir."

"You're wearing a similar outfit to Ricardo's. Are you a Supernumerary as well?"

"It's complicated."

"Please, please, come in," Johansson said, spreading his arm to take in his team's findings. "I have much to show you."

Navarro pointed at the black rifle on the table. "Is that what I think it is?"

Johansson chuckled. "Yes, you are looking at an American M4 assault carbine. Weaponry is not my forte, but Zeke should be able to answer any questions you may have. He's something of an enthusiast. Mr. Austin?"

Austin came to Navarro, and they went to the table to give the rifle a closer look. Flint and Fletcher followed Johansson as he gave them a brief tour of the tables.

"What are all those tablets?" Fletcher asked, pointing.

"Ah, an excellent question," Johansson said. "They're machines many Americans owned for business purposes or for personal use."

"Machines? How? I don't see any moving parts."

"By the late twenty-first century, humanity had miniaturized much of their machinery. These had no moving parts. Everything is on the inside."

"What did they do?"

Johansson laughed. "What couldn't they do? These could hold calendars, letters, music, encyclopedias…"

"Sounds like magic," Fletcher said.

"'Sufficiently advanced technology is indistinguishable from magic,'" Johansson said. He stroked his chin. "That's an old saying, but I can't recall who said it. Oh well, no matter."

"Do they still work?" Fletcher asked.

"Alas, no. As near as we can tell, they are powered by some sort of advanced batteries. Professor Matheson at the University of Sacramento down south managed to find an intact wire that plugs into these machines in order to recharge them. Unfortunately, the contents were protected by a numeric password. Even if we could crack it, I don't think it would do much good."

"Why not?"

"I'm not sure... the screen said, 'no service,' and we have no idea what kind of service it means. The Americans had an extraordinarily complex society and economy. The chief drawback is that if even one of the components is missing, it can set off a chain reaction that collapses the entire edifice. We no longer have the technology to make this technology, and likely several more regressions after that."

"Huh," Fletcher said. She looked around the tent. "If you don't mind, I'm going to go take a look around on my own."

"Of course, of course."

Fletcher wandered off and the two men resumed their walk.

13

"It's good to see you again, my friend," Johansson said.

"I feel the same professor," Flint said.

"How's the life of the fearless Witch Hunter?"

"It has been trying as of late, but I am in good health."

"Glad to hear it, glad to hear it."

"I am curious Professor... are you familiar with the legends that surround this area?"

"Hmm? Oh yes, the locals in Rattlesnake Station told us all about them, at great length."

"I take it you did not find them worth heeding."

"It's a calculated risk, to be sure, but there has not been evidence of witches or witchcraft here for generations. I think the scholarly rewards far outweigh the potential risks."

"I am not so certain," Flint said.

"What do you mean?"

"My companion, Miss Fletcher, is a witch."

Johansson's jaw dropped. "What?!"

Flint raised a hand. "Former witch, I should say. She is an insolent drunkard, but she provided invaluable assistance in a case several weeks ago and is working to amend her life."

"I... see..." Johansson said. He chuckled. "Silas Flint, friends with a witch. Truly these must be the end times."

"'Friends' may be too strong a word. In any case, she brought something interesting to my attention on our journey here: this entire area is haunted. She claims to have seen the spirits of hundreds of American military personnel, all begging for help."

Johansson thought for a few moments. "Do you believe her?"

"I do."

The professor was silent for a few moments more. "Haunted... that would explain a few things."

"Such as?"

"Nothing concrete. I myself haven't experienced anything strange. But some of the students have reported odd happenings: unnatural chills, shadows. Some claim to have heard voices."

Flint nodded. "What else?"

"It may be nothing. This base is large and it's easy for many of my students to get so caught up in cataloguing that they lose track of time but... two of my Ph.D. students, Mark McCloskey and Jennifer Barrett? The night before last they went out to investigate an unusual structure at the far end of the base where the jet plane runways begin."

"This structure, how is it unusual?" Flint asked.

"The architecture for one. This base was built in the twentieth century, with additions made up until the end of the Occult War. Most of it I recognize as twentieth and twenty-first century designs. But this one, it's not like anything I've ever seen before. It's like some sort of tower, but not like the ones air traffic controllers use. Not only that, it... well, it hurts to look at it. Like it doesn't belong here. I don't mean just on this base, but here in this world."

"Where are Miss McCloskey and Mr. Barrett now?"

"I don't know. I haven't seen them since then."

Flint raised his eyebrows. "That did not strike you as ominous?"

Johansson shrugged. "As I said, it's not unusual for students to be gone for a long time. They're all adults. Sometimes they take their bedrolls with them and just sleep wherever they happen to be when night falls." He hesitated. "Although I must admit, this is the first time anyone has been gone for longer than a day."

Flint checked his pocket watch. 12:30 p.m.

"If they do not return by dusk, I suggest you order Mr. Austin or one of his guards to commence a search for the missing students. My associates and I will join them."

"As you wish."

"Another matter," Flint said. "Have you by any chance recovered personnel files on anyone who served here?"

"Not yet. By the twenty-first century, Americans relied heavily on computers to take care of everything. We haven't discovered the physical copies of any personnel files yet. May I ask why?"

"I am interested in learning more about the background of a Major General Neveah Carey. Am I pronouncing the name correctly?"

Johansson chuckled. "As far as I know. 'Neveah' is 'Heaven' spelled backwards."

"Please let me know if you or any of your students discover the physical paperwork."

"Of course. Now, if you'll come with me, I have something I think you'll find particularly interesting..."

14

Flint sat before a crackling firepit as the sun touched the horizon. The work had mostly finished for the day, and students crowded around other firepits, eating dinner and sharing drinks. Johansson had taken him on a tour of a jet plane hangar, GUNFIGHTER COUNTRY spelled out in capital letters above the façade. Unfortunately, there were no intact jet planes. A few carcasses littered the interior, stripped for parts over the centuries by scavengers brave or foolish enough to trespass in this haunted place. Flint was pleased to find that a Catholic church, St. Mary's, still stood between the Junior High School and Stephensen Elementary School. There was no Sacred Host within the tabernacle, but it was still good to know there was some hallowed ground here.

Flint was eager to see and learn all that he could, but at the same time his mind was preoccupied. Fletcher's words had touched him deeply. He couldn't see them like she could, but he was curious if the spirits she had seen were watching him now. What kind of help did they need? And could he provide it? Then there was the question of General Carey. If she was a witch, then she may have been responsible for keeping those souls tethered to the earthly plain. On top of that, students had gone missing in some mysterious tower that Johansson said didn't belong here. It looked as though Flint may have a case to work after all.

Navarro and Fletcher approached and took seats in folding lawn chairs on either side of Flint. Each of them had a paper plate loaded with roasted chicken and mashed potatoes, along with a bottle of ale.

"Hey Silas," Fletcher said.

"I trust you both found today educational," Flint said.

"Sure did sir," Navarro said. "That black rifle I was looking at earlier? The stock is made of plastic. Plastic! Can you believe that shit? I feel like I'd break the damn thing if I had to hit someone with it."

"Why would you hit someone with your rifle? You're supposed to shoot them with it," Fletcher said.

"Sometimes you run out of ammo."

"A plastic stock makes the weapon much lighter, does it not?" Flint asked.

"Yeah, I guess so. Zeke said the bullets were smaller too. 5.56 millimeters. Too small to take down a deer, let alone a werewolf or a wendigo."

"I believe the Americans only worried about human enemies for most of their nation's existence."

"Don't get me wrong, it's a nice rifle, but I think I'll stick with good old 7.62 millimeters. A rifle should have power, you know?"

Flint nodded. "And what did you discover, Miss Fletcher?"

She took a deep pull from her bottle of ale. "There's a golf course here. A fucking golf course! And a bowling alley! It's like a damn luxury resort. How come you guys don't have stuff like this at Fort Marsing?"

Flint smiled. "As I said earlier, the Americans were rich beyond the dreams of avarice. No other empire in human history has ever rivaled them in power or scope. I do not expect the world will ever see their like again."

"If they were so powerful, why'd they fall so quickly?"

"That has been the subject of scholarly research for almost 400 years. If you like, I have a number of tomes on the subject at Fort Marsing, and I should be happy to..."

Zeke Austin strolled up to their firepit before Flint could answer. He nodded to each of them in greeting.

"Mr. Austin," Flint said.

"McCloskey and Barrett aren't back yet," he said.

"What's going on sir?" Navarro asked.

"Professor Johansson has lost two of his graduate students.

Their last known locale was a certain tower at the end of the jet plane tarmac."

"Me and a couple of my people are going to check it out," Austin said.

"My companions and I shall join you."

Austin's eyes were not visible behind his dark glasses, but Flint was sure the man was giving him a skeptical look. "We can handle it."

"I am afraid I must insist. I have reason to believe sorcery is at work in his area. If that is the case, I fear that you and your men are not equipped to deal with it."

Austin stared at Flint for a few moments, then shrugged. "Suit yourself." He walked away from the firepit toward the command tent.

Flint rose from his seat, adjusted his gun belt and his hat. "Finish your meals. Quickly," he said. Navarro and Fletcher each took a few more bites, chugged what was left of their ale, and rose to join Flint as he strode toward their horses.

"Does this always happen? You end up working on your time off?" Fletcher asked.

"Yeah, pretty much," Navarro said.

"The Knights Templar and Supernumeraries of the Order of Saint Benedict are ever ready to answer the Lord's call to action. We should be grateful and honored that God has seen fit to bless us with so many trials."

"Oh I am boss, I am." Navarro said. "Sometimes I wish God wasn't so confident in us."

"'The harvest is indeed great, but the laborers are few.'"

"With these hours, I can see why," Fletcher said.

Flint ignored her as he climbed up into the saddle.

Presently, Austin and two others, a man and a woman, joined them on horseback.

"This is Jefferson Jones, and Shannon Elmore," Austin said by way of introduction. Jones and Elmore wore dusters similar to Flint's long coat. Both had two pistols on their belts and shotguns slung across their backs, like Austin. They nodded greetings toward Flint.

Flint introduced himself and his companions in return. "Lead on," Flint said to Austin. The riders steered their horses westward toward the runways. Around them, college students continued to eat, drink, and socialize after their long day.

"How many students are present?" Flint asked.

"About a hundred, give or take," Austin said.

"No offense, but why do a bunch of college kids need armed security guards?" Fletcher asked.

"Professor says it's because of all the artifacts lying around. We've been here a few weeks and we've had to scare off a few salvagers," Austin said.

"How'd you get into the security business?" Navarro asked.

"For the paycheck. I'm a bounty killer by trade. Professor put out an ad for security for this little expedition of his. For what the University's paying, I'm glad to take a break and babysit a bunch of college kids."

Navarro turned to Jones and Elmore. "Same for you two?"

"Yeah," Jones said.

"Me and Jeff go way back," Austin said.

"I'm a country girl," Elmore said. "Work on my dad's farm up near Rattlesnake Station. I like getting paid to watch other people dig in the dirt instead of doing the digging myself."

"Mr. Austin, have you or either of your companions encountered any unexplained phenomenon in your time here?"

All three nodded.

"I usually hang around the school, where the whole team is camped out," Austin said. "I've walked around inside the school and sometimes I see shadows. Like the kind of shadows people would make. Only nobody's there."

"It's almost June but some of those buildings, you walk through certain hallways, go in to some of the rooms, it's like a meat locker. Can see your breath and everything," Jones said.

"Sometimes I swear I can hear voices. Not like the 'I'm going crazy' kind of voices. Others who were with me heard them too," Elmore said.

"What did they say?" Fletcher asked.

"Only words I can always make out are 'help us.' Sometimes it's laughing. A woman laughing real mean like."

"Professor Johansson informed me that it is not unusual for students to wander off on their own," Flint said.

Austin nodded. "Yeah, true enough. Usually no longer than a day. First time we've ever had to go looking for them."

"What is the shortest route to this tower?"

"We're going to take Gunfighter Avenue south. It turns into Central Avenue near the Credit Union building. We keep going straight until we reach Liberator Street, then we take a right and keep going until we get there."

15

They rode on in silence. Summer was nearly upon them

and the sun was late in setting, the twilight illuminating their surroundings. Automobiles were parked alongside the curb on this street, their designs smoother and sleeker than the models that had been manufactured since the twenty first century. The gasoline would have spoiled or evaporated centuries ago, but Flint still felt tempted to see if they still functioned. There were store fronts, offices, chapels, everything one would find in a small town. Flint would have found it almost idyllic if not for the deserted streets and the utter quiet.

"Silas?" Fletcher said.

"Yes?"

"They're back."

He could feel it now: the icy chill.

"Who's back?" Austin asked.

"Ghosts," Navarro said.

Austin, Jones, and Elmore reined in their horses. They looked all around them.

"I don't see anything," Jones said.

"You, uh, need to have the talent for it," Fletcher said.

"Can you sense anything from them?" Flint asked.

"The same thing as earlier: 'help us.' Some of them are pointing down the street, the way we're headed."

"The hell is this all about?" Austin said.

"Uh... well... the thing is..."

"Miss Fletcher is a witch," Flint said.

Austin and his companions all stared at Fletcher.

"Former witch," she said. "But I still have certain gifts that I, ah, can't get rid of."

Austin turned to Flint. His eyes were hidden by his sunglasses, his face neutral. He asked, "You trust her?"

"I do," Flint said.

A few moments of silence passed. Austin shrugged. "Works for me."

"Me too," Jones said.

"I'm fine," Elmore said.

"Well, that was easy," Navarro chuckled.

"Way I see it, if she was trouble, you'd have burned her by now," Austin said.

"Miss Fletcher has many shortcomings, but none that warrant burning at the stake. Yet," Flint said.

"Hey!"

"Let us be on our way."

They turned right on Liberator Street and proceeded to the northwest. The sun was still visible over the horizon, continuing its descent. Flint estimated the temperature to have been in the mid-70s at base camp, but now he wished his long coat was thicker. The horses were skittish and it took some struggle to urge them forward. Fletcher rode up beside Flint.

"Hey," she said.

"What is it? Has there been a change in the spirits' behavior?"

"No... no, they're still standing there on both sides of the street, staring at us. I, uh, wanted to ask you something."

"Yes?"

"Did you mean what you said back there? You really trust me?"

Flint was silent for a few moments. "I trust that you are committed to reforming your heretical ways concerning magic."

"Oh." Her face fell. "Is that all?"

"For now."

She sighed. "Okay. Well, it's a start, I guess." She fell back in alongside Navarro.

Austin chuckled.

"Does something amuse you, Mr. Austin?" Flint asked.

"'There are none so blind as those who will not see.'"

"I fail to see what that quotation has to do with anything."

"Of course you do."

They reached the end of Liberator Street and the runway was in sight. Austin handed Flint a pair of binoculars.

"It's off to the side, over in that direction," he said, pointing. Flint put the binoculars to his eyes. There it was. He thought it looked less like a tower than a ziggurat. The base was the largest portion with each additional floor on top of it growing smaller and smaller until it reached the top floor which looked to be the size of one room through the binoculars. Flint realized what Johansson had been talking about now. Even at this distance, there was something profoundly wrong about the structure, though he could not think of a specific reason. It felt uncanny somehow. Flint did not share Fletcher's talent for sensing the supernatural around them, but even he knew there was foul sorcery about.

Fletcher shivered. "Christ, what is that? Feels like sandpaper in my head."

"We are nearly upon our destination," Flint said. The horses were growing more skittish as the sun continued its descent. He felt something brush his cheek. It was like a human knuckle, but he saw nothing.

The six managed to get their horses going toward the

tower. As they crossed the runway tarmac and the tower grew larger, Flint could see that the base of it was comprised of an ordinary twentieth century-style office building. It was with the upper floors that the drastic changes began. They appeared to be black stone of some sort, perhaps marble. No lights appeared in any of the structure's many windows. Flint, Navarro, and Fletcher all had flashlights given to them by students back at basecamp. Flint hoped he would not need to fire his pistols into the dark.

There were no hitching posts on the tarmac. After everyone had dismounted and secured what they wished to take from the saddlebags, the horses bolted away from the tower.

"What do we do now?" Elmore asked.

"We do what our Blessed Lord Himself once did: we walk," Flint said. He drew his sword from his hip. As he expected, the blessed steel gave off a powerful white glow.

"The fuck is that?" Austin asked.

"Every Templar is given a blade that has been blessed by the Holy Father himself," Flint said. "They are most effective against the creatures of the night. One of their other attributes is they shine more brightly when the forces of darkness are present."

"Shit," Jones said. The three security guards unslung their shotguns and held them at the low ready. Navarro drew the tomahawk and pistol hanging from his belt. Fletcher had a sidearm as well but she made no move to draw it yet.

"Let us go," Flint said. He pulled open the glass front door to the office complex portion of the tower. The glow from his sword illuminated the interior well enough. He stuck his flashlight into a coat pocket and drew one of his pistols to carry in his off hand. The floor creaked as the six entered the entryway. Dust motes swirled in the lights cast by the group. Ahead there appeared to be a reception desk with a mummified corpse seated before an old computer and a telephone. Beyond the desk there stretched a long hallway with doors on either side. Most were closed but a few lay open.

"Man, this is creepy," Navarro said.

"Probably not so bad with the lights on," Elmore said.

"Speaking of which... uh, Silas?" Fletcher said.

"What is it?"

"I know a spell that could shed some light on the situation."

"Miss Fletcher..."

"It doesn't do anything bad, I promise. It's just... well, I really don't want to wander around in the dark in here."

"I'm with her," Jones said. The others all chimed in with their assents.

Flint scowled. "This is not a democracy, but I will allow it. For now."

Fletcher held her arms out to her sides, the palms of her hands facing upward. She closed her eyes and whispered something. Two balls of fire appeared in her hands. She opened her eyes and brought her arms forward. The two fireballs left her hands and sped down toward the end of the hallway, leaving an orange light that lingered in their wake. It was not bright, but they could see clearly now. Everyone clicked off their flashlights.

"Must be nice having a witch on your side for once," Elmore said.

"Hmph. Let us begin the search."

"You're welcome," Fletcher said.

16

Flint moved past the desk, down the hallway, his sword and pistol held at the ready. The others followed, scanning their surroundings, looking for anything amiss.

"How long's this light going to last?" Austin asked.

"As long as I focus on it," Fletcher replied.

Navarro tried one of the doors.

"It's locked, sir," he said.

Flint looked to Austin.

"Professor doesn't want anybody damaging artifacts or buildings." He shrugged. "I figure finding two missing kids is more important."

Flint nodded to Navarro who backed away from the door, then advanced on it, aiming a kick at the lock. The door smashed open and he looked inside.

"Shit," he said.

"What is it, Mr. Navarro?"

"Look."

Flint made his way to the door and peered inside. Human bones were strewn everywhere, ankle deep. They piled up against filing cabinets on either side of the room, and underneath a desk in the center. Graffiti on the wall read BLOOD IS LIFE and IT'S MAJOR BOOTHE.

"Jesus Christ," Austin said when he caught a glimpse of the interior.

"Mind the blasphemy Mr. Austin," Flint said. He entered the office, the bones clattering around his feet as he moved.

On a hunch, he went toward the first filing cabinet on his left. Peering at the tag on the front, it read AB-AR.

"What are you looking for boss?" Navarro asked.

"I am not sure."

"Can we get out of here please?" Elmore said, her voice quavering. "This is seriously scaring the shit out of me."

"One moment," Flint replied. He scanned the other filing cabinets until he found one labeled CA-CO. After a brief struggle, he pulled the drawer open with a grinding noise. Inside were manila folders, each one with a name tag. He found one labeled CAREY, N. He pulled it out and opened it. There was General Carey. It was a different photograph than the one in the guard station, but she had that same glare. The first sheet of paper was divided into boxes. They held her name, her date and place of birth, and many numbers and abbreviations that meant nothing to Flint. He flipped the page to the other side of the folder. The second page consisted of one sentenced typed single spaced, repeating until the bottom of the paper: YE SHALL BE AS GODS. There were other pages inside, and they all contained that single sentence.

"Okay, well, that's normal," Navarro said, reading from behind Flint's shoulder. He closed the folder and put it back in the filing cabinet. They rejoined the others outside.

"Find something?" Fletcher asked.

"Possibly," Flint said. "Let us continue for now."

By the light of Fletcher's witchfire, they went further down the hallway, kicking in doors that were locked, always finding more human bones and graffiti. In one office, Flint saw IT'S MAJOR BOOTHE scrawled on the wall again. That was the third time he had seen that name, and he wished that he had thought to check the personnel files for anything on this Major.

"Sir? Take a look at this," Navarro said. He held up a splintered femur. Flint took it and scrutinized the part Navarro had indicated. There were markings on the bone. Markings that could only be made by fangs or claws.

"Hmm…" Flint said. "I am forming a hypothesis, but we shall need more data."

"What are you talking about?" Austin asked from across the hallway.

"I suspect that spirits are not the only supernatural beings present."

"Guys?" Fletcher called. She was ahead of the group and all eyes turned to her. She pointed. "Look."

Flint strode forward. A crumpled body lay further ahead. He hurried to its side, the others in his wake. It was the shriveled corpse of what appeared to be a young man. The body was clothed in the same polo shirt and khaki shorts favored by the other archaeological students. The flesh was desiccated, like every drop of moisture had been sucked out. Flint used the tip of his sword to turn the head to one side. There. The flesh was brittle but there was no mistaking the two holes in its neck. Elmore gasped.

"It is as I feared," Flint said.

The corpse screamed.

The others screamed in fear and surprise, backing away from the body. It stretched its head toward Flint, as if trying to rise from the floor. Fletcher's magical lighting flickered.

"Do not lose the light!" Flint shouted at her. He fired his

pistol into the corpse's head and its screams fell silent, its head lolling, this time truly dead.

"The fuck was that?!" Jones shouted. Austin had taken his sunglasses off and his eyes flitted everywhere, on the alert for more threats. Elmore was hyperventilating.

"A ghoul," Flint said.

"Huh?" Austin said.

"Surely you all know of vampires?"

Everyone nodded.

"When a vampire feeds on a human being, its corruption passes on to them. If they taste of the vampire's blood, they become vampires themselves. Those who are completely drained of their blood become ghouls, eaters of the dead. Truly they are among the vilest of the Great Magician's children."

Austin stepped forward to get a closer look at the corpse. "I'm guessing this was McCloskey."

"Wait a minute," Fletcher said. "Vampires make ghouls. So that means…"

"There is a vampire present on the base," Flint said. "And I believe I know who it was in life."

"We need to get out of here," Elmore said.

At that moment, they heard heavy breathing and shuffling further down the hallway. They saw a silhouette with long stringy hair. Its gait was unsteady, but it caught sight of them and moved forward with purpose, snarling and gnashing its broken teeth.

"Kill that unclean monster!" Flint shouted. He strode forward to meet it. It had been a young woman in life. She had the same desiccated look as McCloskey, empty sockets where her eyes should have been, her teeth broken stumps where she had been gnawing on bones. Her arms reached out for Flint, but with one stroke of his sword, the ghoul's head flew from its shoulders, rolling away as the body fell to its knees and then to the floor.

Flint heard a woman scream behind him. Turning, he saw a panel had opened up in the hallway's ceiling. A hand with long talons was reaching down from the blackness above, the arm in a blue jacket sleeve. It had grabbed Elmore by the hair and was pulling her off the floor, up into the ceiling. Austin and Jones fired their shotguns at the apparition, Navarro and Fletcher joining with their sidearms. There was an animal cry of pain and the hand released Elmore. She fell to the floor in a heap.

Flint rushed to join them, Austin and Jones kneeling by Elmore's side. She was crying now.

"Miss Elmore... Miss Elmore! Hear me!" Flint cried.

She got control of her sobbing long enough to look at him.

"Did the creature's talons break your skin? Are you bleeding?"

In a panic, she ran her hands through her hair and over her scalp. Her mouth agape, she shook her head no. Flint exhaled in relief.

"What was that?!" Austin yelled.

"I believe that was Major Boothe," Flint said. "I have seen his name appear several times since our arrival. Were you able to see him in the darkness?"

"I caught a glimpse," Jones said. "Vampires are supposed to look like us, right? Well, he sure as shit didn't. God... he was like a man... bat... thing."

Flint nodded. "Normally vampires do indeed appear human. When they are starved for blood, however, their inner monsters come to the fore. Combined with his centuries of isolation, I daresay he is little more than a rabid animal now."

"What do we do?!" Austin said.

Flint pursed his lips. "I suggest that you three return to base camp at all possible speed. Inform Professor Johansson of what has happened and that my companions and I remained behind to put an end to this blasphemous abomination."

"I should come with you," Austin said.

Flint shook his head. "No. Our weapons are loaded with silver tipped bullets. Your lead buckshot is of no avail against this child of Satan."

"But…"

"Do as I say!" Flint roared. His face softened. "The students are your responsibility. Have them all take shelter inside St. Mary's."

"The church? Why?" Jones asked.

"Assuming the local bishop did not deconsecrate it, it remains hallowed ground, and the vampire will not be able to set foot inside if it escapes from here."

Austin scowled, then nodded. "Alright. We'll play it your way."

"Good. God be with you."

Austin and Jones helped Elmore to her feet, and they ran for the entrance. Flint, Navarro, and Fletcher watched them until they were out the door and out of sight.

"Miss Fletcher, you are not a sworn member of the Order. You are not required to accompany Mr. Navarro and I."

She blushed. "Yeah, well, it's not like I've got anything better to do than hunt a five hundred year old batshit crazy vampire. Besides, somebody's got to keep the lights on."

"Amen to that," Navarro said.

"Very well. Do not get carried away with witchcraft."

"Yeah, yeah."

"What's the plan sir?" Navarro asked.

Flint took his flashlight and shined it upward through the panel where Major Boothe had reached for Elmore. It wasn't an airduct; it opened onto the floor above them.

He clicked off and put the flashlight away. He stroked his chin before saying, "More than a hundred human beings are within the confines of this base, and yet so far the vampire has only attacked those who entered this building."

"What do you suppose that means?"

"I do not know. For now, we press on. That panel opens to the floor above us. We will clear this building floor by floor until we find this monster and send it to Hell where it belongs."

17

They reached the end of the hallway. The door on their right was open. Flint peeked inside and saw more graffiti: THE MAJOR IS NOT HIMSELF. *He most definitely is not,* Flint thought. Navarro tried the opposite door. Finding it locked, he kicked it open, revealing a staircase going up. A shower of dust rained down from above. The smell of mold, decay, and death assaulted their nostrils.

The trio looked at each other and nodded. Flint took point, with Fletcher behind him and Navarro bringing up the rear. Going up stairs was always the most dangerous part of clearing a building. Fletcher whispered something Flint couldn't make out. A ball of witchfire hovered past him, lighting the way, casting everything in a soft orange glow. He slowly put his foot down on the first step, probing for any spots that might creak. The vampiric Major Booth would undoubtedly smell them no matter how quietly they moved, but God only knew what other monstrosities awaited above.

Step by step, they advanced to the next floor. At the top they arrived on a landing. A steel door was open before them. Beside it was a smooth glass panel with a hand shaped depression along with some sort of numerical keypad. A locking mechanism perhaps? Flint didn't know how the technology worked exactly, but he'd read accounts of machines that somehow recognized hand and fingerprints. A buzzing sound echoed beyond the door.

Leading the way, Flint pulled the door open wider. Before them was another hallway, similar to the one they had just left. Electric lights in the ceiling flickered.

"Boss," Navarro whispered. "How does this place have electricity?"

"I do not know," Flint replied.

"Guys..." Fletcher said. They turned to face her. "This... I... I don't know how this is possible but... the ghosts? Some of them are in here. They're... they're the ones powering the lights."

"That doesn't make any sense," Navarro said. "How can dead people power anything?"

"It's like they're being drained somehow. I remember near the end, Francisco saying that the strongest magic is fueled by blood and souls," Fletcher said, referring to her former lover whom she had helped Flint destroy weeks ago.

"Indeed it is, little one."

Fletcher's eyes widened, her jaw dropped. "One of them's talking to me now. She sounds..."

"Miss Fletcher... we heard her too," Flint said. Navarro nodded in agreement.

A pale blue light appeared at the end of the hallway. It formed into a ball and floated toward Flint and his companions. He held his sword at the ready in his right hand, aimed his pistol with the left. Navarro holstered his pistol and tomahawk and unslung the bolt action rifle on his back. Fletcher stood transfixed by the approaching sphere.

It glided toward them and Flint could now see that it was witchfire. His sword glowed ever brighter as the dark magic drew nearer.

It stopped ten feet away. The fireball stretched and contorted, forming into the outline of a human being. The fire slowly burned off. Standing before them was the translucent, shimmering figure of an old woman in trousers, a single breasted suit jacket over a button up dress shirt. Her jacket had a series of rectangles over the left breast pocket. There were two stars on her shoulders.

"General Carey, I presume," Flint growled.

The spirit of General Carey smiled. "I'd say 'in the flesh,' but, well, as you can see..." she said, spreading her arms.

"Alive or dead, your judgment is at hand, witch!" Flint shouted.

Carey crossed her arms, gave Flint a coy smile. "No, I don't think so. Alas, it's true that my body gave out long ago, but I've gone to considerable lengths to prevent that judgment your God is always going on about."

"He is the God of all creation, witch, and I am the instrument of His divine wrath!"

Carey laughed, cold and cruel. "Tell me boy, what can you do to someone who is already dead?"

"With God, all things are possible." Flint holstered his pistol. He reached into one of his long coat's inner pockets and withdrew a crucifix, holding it before him.

"Where was God when Magus appeared?" Carey sneered. "The Great Magician proved that God is weak and impotent. Magus showed us the true power, to become gods ourselves, to..."

Flint took a few steps toward Carey's apparition. The crucifix in his hand began glowing in sync with his sword. Carey winced and shielded her eyes, her form flickering. She backed up a few steps.

"Your foul sorcery is no match for the power of the Holy Spirit! *Ex Umbris Ad Lucem!*" Flint bellowed.

The ghostly flesh on Carey's face melted away, her eyes liquified, until all that remained was a grinning skull with a fringe of stringy hair. The uniform too was undergoing a transformation, great tears and ragged fringes forming along the seams.

"Enough!" Carey screamed. An invisible force pushed against Flint, driving him backwards. He bent his knees and leaned into the force, the soles of his boots squealing on the linoleum floor. Navarro aimed and fired his rifle, but the silver tipped bullet harmlessly passed through Carey's spirit.

Blue flames appeared in Carey's eye sockets. She focused her burning gaze on Navarro and raised one hand.

"Burn," she said. A jet of flame spewed forth from her palm.

"No!" Fletcher cried. She held up both her hands and a wall of light appeared before Flint and Navarro. Carey's fire struck the barrier and dissipated harmlessly.

Carey cocked her head. The invisible force she had summoned continued to push Flint backwards even as he struggled to maintain his forward momentum.

"You're one of us," Carey said.

Fletcher spat. "Everyone makes mistakes."

"Stupid bitch," Carey replied. "Magus brought us the gift of magic, and you're throwing it away to work with these little pissants?"

"If you're trying to convince me to switch sides, you need to work on your sales pitch."

Carey laughed. "Oh I can do much better than that." She flicked her hand, and Flint was lifted off his feet and thrown down the hallway. He rolled with his impact on the floor as best he could, but the pain in his ribs flared. He gritted his teeth and stifled a groan as he pushed himself to his feet.

"I have to admit, I'm impressed," Carey said. "It's been a long time since I've seen a man with your kind of grit."

"I am Knight Templar Captain Silas Flint," he said, clutching his side. "You are a traitor to your country and your God, and I swear in the name of the Father, and of the Son, and of the Holy Spirit, that I shall be your final ruin, heretic!"

Carey snickered. "Poor little boy, play acting as some kind of Witch Hunter." Her skull moved up and down, taking in Flint with her fiery eyes. "Why do you wear that ridiculous pilgrim Halloween costume?" She looked at Flint's pistols. "Those guns... they look like Makarovs. Oh, that is rich. A man of God carrying Soviet pistols." She averted her gaze toward the steel door at the end of the hallway, which slammed shut.

"Catch me if you can, boy," Carey said. "Major Boothe is eager to meet you." Carey's apparition condensed into a ball of blue fire and flew away from them to the end of the corridor and disappeared around the corner.

Navarro and Fletcher rushed to Flint's side.

"You alright sir?" Navarro asked.

"I will have to be," Flint said. He grunted and clutched at his ribs.

"Hey Silas," Fletcher said. "I can fix that easy."

"No."

Fletcher blinked. "Excuse me?"

"I do not wish to receive whatever unnatural healing you are offering."

She glared at him and muttered, "Stubborn son of a bitch."

Navarro glanced back the way they had come. "I'm going to go out on a limb and say the door's locked."

"No doubt," Flint said. "Our only way out is through. We must put an end to this devilish fiend."

"But how? She said it herself, she's already dead."

"Miss Fletcher... in your studies of the dark arts, did you ever encounter anything that could account for Carey's soul remaining on earth beyond death?"

"Uh… well, you understand I never got into that kind of magic, messing around with life and death. But I did get a few bits and pieces from Francisco before, you know, he became a demon."

"Go on."

"He said something about how killing someone and harnessing their soul could magnify a witch or warlock's power. You'd need some kind of talisman or make a deal with a demon to channel and contain that kind of power. Most magic users couldn't handle that much energy without getting burned themselves."

"What do the talismans look like?" Navarro asked.

Fletcher shrugged. "They could be anything: a doll, a statue, a medal, a ring, a wand… hell, you could use a wrench if you know the right enchantments."

"So we're looking for a needle in a haystack."

"More like a needle in a pile of needles."

"Hmm…" Flint said. "I do not believe it will prove quite so difficult."

"What do you mean sir?"

"Consider: Carey's spirit, and all of the spirits Miss Fletcher has attested to, seems confined to this base. Two: the vampire Boothe is mad with thirst, and yet he remains here in this structure. This leads me to believe…"

"Whatever the talisman is, it's in here," Navarro said.

"Correct. It is possible that Major Boothe has been on guard duty for nearly five hundred years."

Carey's mocking laughter echoed through the hallway. Flint raised his sword, ready for any magical onslaught.

"You're smarter than you look Captain," she said, her

voice distorted, seeming to come from everywhere and nowhere. "I granted Eric the gift of vampirism during the war. Even undead, he takes his mission seriously. Perhaps too much... the poor dear went feral... one hundred, two hundred years ago? It's difficult to keep track of time here."

"Then allow me to be of assistance: your time has run out, harlot!"

"We'll see. In the meantime, I'd like to introduce you to my children."

18

Zelda Fletcher looked to her left, right, up, down, scanning for threats as Mendoza had taught her. *Oops,* she thought, *guess I better draw my gun first.* She pulled her gun from the holster on her belt, holding it in a two handed stance. It was identical to the models Flint and Navarro carried. What had Carey called it – a Makarov? Sounds Russian. Weird.

Flint and Navarro scanned the hallway as well. Fletcher wanted to shake the lanky Witch Hunter. What the fuck was his problem? He'd clearly gotten hurt on his last mission, and he refused her healing magic because... what? It was unclean? Impure? Unnatural? She hoped the stubborn asshole wouldn't drop out of the fight on account of his busted ribs or whatever the problem was. She had a feeling that she'd need him if she was going to survive what came next. *Look at him,* she thought. His face was all sharp angles, with those high cheek bones, those icy blue eyes, that mouth always set like he sucked lemons. She couldn't recall ever hearing the man laugh once in all the time they'd known each other. The other Hunters at Fort Marsing she'd spoken to all said that Flint was intense even by Templar standards. She'd have to...

She shook herself. What was coming over her? There wasn't time for... whatever it was she was feeling.

Every door in the hallway burst open simultaneously, showering the floor with dust, plaster, and bits of stone. She raised her gun, aiming it at one of the open doorways. *Breathe, Zelda, remember to breathe.*

Groans came from every room, cries of misery and burning hunger. There, movement. A figure emerged from the doorway on her left. It looked like a shriveled corpse, wearing a tattered blue suit with gold bars on its shoulders. The eyes were wrinkled white pearls, its lips rotted away, exposing the jagged stumps that were its teeth. It hissed and rushed toward Fletcher. She aimed her gun, took a deep breath, squeezed the trigger. The pistol bucked in her hands as it fired, the silver tipped bullet entering the thing's forehead, the back of its skull exploding in a shower of bone, ichor, and brain matter. The things moans were cut off. It fell to its knees, and face-planted on the floor, dead for good this time.

More groans came from every doorway to the end of the hall.

"Look out!" Navarro yelled. He aimed and fired his rifle, the boom echoing throughout the hallway, as one of the ghoul... zombie... thing's head disintegrated from the high powered round. Fletcher heard a high pitched whine in hear ears. Shit. That was one thing the story tellers never mentioned: the goddamn pain in your ears after firing guns indoors.

More ghouls emerged from every room. Each one was wearing one of those blue suits – uniforms? – or those weird mottled green pajamas. They hissed and growled and roared as they smelled something they'd missed for centuries: fresh meat.

"Destroy these abominations!" Flint shouted. With the sword in his right hand, he sheared off half of a ghoul's skull, the brains and blood spilling over the linoleum floor. He aimed and fired the pistol in his left hand, drilling another ghoul through the forehead.

Navarro slung his rifle and drew his tomahawk and pistol from his belt. He roared in defiance of the oncoming horde, burying the blade into one creature's face, shooting down one, two, three more as he yanked the axe from the ghoul's forehead.

"Praise Jesus!" Flint bellowed, slicing and shooting his way forward.

Holy shit, Fletcher thought. She brought her mind to the present, focused on the task at hand. She aimed and fired, the bullet striking a ghoul in the shoulder. It stumbled backward a few steps. Then it focused its blank gaze upon her and shrieked. It advanced on her, arms outstretched, eager to take her down and tear into her soft flesh with its jagged teeth.

She aimed and fired again. This time the bullet entered the creature's eye socket and exploded out the back of its head. It fell to the floor.

Not bad, child, not bad.

Fletcher shook her head. Great. On top of everything else, now a dead witch was whispering in her mind.

We both know you're not going to survive this with that little peashooter. You've got the power, little girl. Why not use it? Carey hissed.

Fletcher hesitated. It was enough for more ghouls to emerge from the offices, separating her from Flint and Navarro who continued to slash their way forward. The hungry monsters had her surrounded. At this close range, she was able to score headshots with ease. Her pistol's slide locked open. Empty. She pushed on the heel release, removing and pocketing the empty magazine, reached into one of the pouches on her belt for a fresh one.

She felt one of the creature's claws scrape across her back, her body protected by the thick leather armor on her torso.

Fuck this, she thought. She put on the familiar pattern like a well fitted glove. Sorcerous energy gathered around her, filling her with that addictive giddiness that came from commanding the elements. Fire ignited on the palms of her hands. She laughed with the sheer exhilarating joy of it. The flames exploded from her, expanding in a circle, enveloping the mob of ghouls. They shrieked, and backed away from her, their bodies engulfed in sorcerous fire. Their cries tapered off to whimpers as they fell and were still. The crackling of flames echoed in the hallway and the foul stench of burning flesh made Fletcher's eyes water.

"Who wants some more?!" she screamed. A nimbus of blue fire surrounded her.

"Miss Fletcher…"

She could feel it, oh the power was so intoxicating. Earth, fire, air, and water were hers to command, to shape as she willed.

"Miss Fletcher…"

She was grateful to the Templars, and especially to Silas, for giving her a second chance. But holy shit, this was such an amazing feeling. She'd go forth and burn the earth, purging it of all the monsters, and necromancers, and all of the witches and warlocks who had made her life a living hell. Her lips stretched into a manic smile, and she cackled, imagining the pain and terror she would wreak on her fellow witches. Silas would surely…

"Zelda Fletcher!"

She blinked. She remembered who she was, where she had come from. The fire died. She looked around her. There were no moans, no growls, no hisses. Ghoul corpses were strewn everywhere. The hallway flickered with the burning bodies that surrounded her, putrid smoke wafting in the air. She looked to Flint and Navarro. The latter looked impressed. Flint narrowed his eyes and frowned at her.

"Uh… sorry. I got a little carried away," she said.

"Indeed," Flint replied. "I will overlook it this time, but you must control yourself in the future. I should hate to see you go mad and be forced to summarily execute you."

"And I should hate to be executed," she said, mimicking Flint's voice. Navarro snorted.

"Come," Flint said. He turned and proceeded down the hallway. Navarro approached her.

"When we get back to Fort Marsing, you got to do that

impression for the other guys," he whispered, chuckling. She grinned. Navarro left to follow Flint.

Fletcher was about to go after them, when something caught her eye. On the floor was Flint's pocket watch. *Must have dropped it when he took that tumble.* She bent down to pick it up. She flipped it open, thinking to check the time, but what she saw surprised her.

There was the watch of course, which told her it was almost 9 p.m. On the inside of the front lid was a picture. It was taken on a sunny day, pink blossoms on the tree in the background. Before it there was a family: the mother, the father, and two little boys. The father was on the left, strikingly handsome, dressed in a flannel shirt and jeans, with a full head of black hair parted on the side, a trimmed beard, soft blue eyes, and a warm smile. The mother was a petite blonde, demure, but with a dazzling smile that was all pearly white. She had one hand on the shoulder of the smaller boy on the right, who had an unruly mop of brown hair and looked shyly at the camera. The taller boy stood between his parents, also wearing flannel and blue jeans. He too had black hair and blue eyes. He favored the camera with a wide toothy grin.

Fletcher did a double take. *Holy shit.* Could this be the Flint family? And was Silas smiling like he was happy? She never would have believed it if she hadn't seen it with her own eyes. She snapped the watch shut, stuffed it into one of her pants pockets, and hurried to catch up to Flint and Navarro.

Something was wrong. Fletcher kept jogging but the hallway kept stretching ever onward, far further than it should have from how it appeared outside. The electric lights continued buzzing and flickering overhead. There: she could make out something just within earshot. Screaming.

To hell with what Silas said. She willed herself off the floor, levitating a few feet above the linoleum, and picked up speed, hurtling down the hallway, past open doorways which revealed more trashed offices, and broken corpses. The screaming grew louder. If it was Silas or Rico...

Blue light flickered through an open doorway and out into the hall. Fletcher touched down on the ground just outside the door. Silas and Rico were still nowhere to be seen, so she summoned fire in one hand, lightning in the other, prepared for whatever or whoever waited on the other side. She peeked around the doorframe. Her mouth fell open, the magic dying on her fingertips.

She gazed into a yawning black abyss. A column of icy blue light stretched upwards and out of sight. Trapped in the column's orbit were souls. Men and women in uniform slowly twisted and writhed in the void, their wails of pain and despair assaulting Fletcher's ears. She staggered and leaned against the doorframe for support. All their anguish and sorrow flooded her mind and tears welled up in her eyes.

"God..." she whispered. Bolts of energy emanated from the column, keeping the souls tethered to it.

You there, a male voice whispered in her mind.

Who are you? Fletcher asked.

It's upstairs, the voice said, sounding like it was in sheer agony. *Top floor.*

You mean whatever's keeping you here? The talisman?

Help us!

"Zelda!"

Fletcher jumped and screamed in surprise. She turned around, and there was Navarro, Flint behind him. Silas was as stone faced as ever. Rico looked concerned.

"You still with us?" Navarro asked.

She looked through the doorway again, but there was nothing but an ordinary office with a desk and filing cabinets. She sniffed, only then noticing the burned ghoul corpses in the hallway. She was back where she had started. Had she moved at all? Was that all some kind of crazy vision or dream? She patted her jeans pocket and felt Flint's pocket watch inside. At least that had been real.

"What happened?" she asked.

"We were gonna ask you that," Navarro replied.

"Mr. Navarro and I reached the staircase to the next floor before we noticed you were not with us. We retraced our steps and discovered you here, in some sort of daze," Flint said.

"You okay?" Navarro said.

"It's even worse than I thought," Fletcher said, and informed them of what she had seen.

"The fuck?" Navarro said. "Why would Carey do that? Besides just being a stone cold bitch, I mean."

Flint's eyes widened, his mouth twisted in fury.

"She has enslaved thousands of souls... kept them from passing on... tying them to this plane to fuel her wicked designs... this is *unholy* beyond words!" he snarled. "Neveah Carey! Hear me! We are coming for you! And in the name of God we will send you to the fiery abyss! Onward!"

He stalked off toward the stairway, sword and pistol at the ready. Fletcher stared after him, her mouth agape.

"Gonna catch flies like that," Navarro chuckled, before going on his way.

It took her a moment to get it. She straightened up and followed them.

You really know how to pick 'em Zelda, she thought to herself.

19

The trio crept up the stairwell. Fletcher had summoned another ball of fire to light their way, the orange glow casting long shadows. Flint kept his gun trained toward the top of the stairs.

"Seriously, why would she do that?" Navarro asked again.

"Only thing I can think of is she was casting some kind of spell that needed a whole lot of power," Fletcher replied. "I don't know if it went right or wrong though."

"It does not matter," Flint said. "We must put an end to this devilish horror and liberate the innocent souls she holds captive."

The reached another landing at the top. There was another steel door with a glass panel and numeric keypad by the door frame, but this door was shut. Flint pushed down on the handle, which had no give. Locked. He exhaled.

"What now?" Navarro asked.

Flint furrowed his brow. He put his hand on the glass

panel. A bar of light moved up and down beneath his palm. The panel glowed red, and a buzzer sounded.

"I don't think it likes us," Fletcher said.

"Apparently not," Flint murmured. He poked at a few numbers on the keypad, not expecting anything.

"You know how that thing works boss?" Navarro asked.

Flint crossed his arms. "I believe this machine is designed to recognize handprints."

"Of people who work here?"

"Yes.

"And I'm guessing the numbers on that pad are like the dial on a safe?"

"I would assume so."

"I guess it's too much to expect it'd be written down somewhere," Fletcher said.

Flint looked up. "Perhaps not. Miss Fletcher, you are able to see and hear the spirits that haunt this facility."

She nodded.

"I get it," Navarro said. "Could you ask them for the combination?"

"I can try. They're in a lot of pain."

Flint nodded. "With God's help, we shall end their suffering."

Fletcher closed her eyes and took a deep breath.

20

She opened her eyes and it was light. Flint and Navarro were gone. She heard footsteps ascending the stairwell.

Looking down she saw a man in a blue uniform carrying a briefcase.

"What the fuck..." she whispered. She then realized she was exposed up here, with nowhere to hide. If this soldier – Airman? – tried to do her harm, she'd have no choice but to...

He reached the top of the stairwell, taking no notice of Fletcher. He pressed his free hand onto the glass panel by the door. It glowed green and a chime sounded. He opened the door and passed through.

Must be another vision, Fletcher thought. Deciding to experiment, she reached out to touch the door and her hand passed through. She moved forward, phasing through the solid steel, and there was the officer again, striding down the hallway, his black shoes tapping on the linoleum. Fletcher levitated off the floor and followed him. The hallway was filled with black smoke. Passing by one open door, Fletcher looked inside and saw two Airmen throwing papers into a burning garbage can, some of the smoke billowing out an open window. Fletcher squinted. Through the window she could see the sky was purple, and not because of the setting sun.

This is the war, she thought. *This has to be during or right after the Occult War.*

She left and flew after the Airman she had been following. He stopped before a door and knocked.

"Enter," came a female voice from within. Fletcher saw a plaque on the door which read, MAJOR GENERAL N. CAREY, LOGISTICS. She entered in the Airman's wake.

There was General Carey, her steel grey hair up in a bun,

her blue uniform immaculate. Her back was to them, hands behind her back as she stared out a window. The purple skies held dark clouds which swirled and twisted into skulls and screaming faces. She wasn't sure, but she thought she saw winged figures soaring in the sky. Fletcher shivered. She knew the basics of the Occult War's history – how could anyone living not know it, when it gave birth to a new world? She never expected to witness a piece of it.

The Airman saluted. "Major Boothe, reporting as ordered, ma'am," he said.

"At ease. Shut the door."

Boothe set the briefcase on the General's desk and went to close the door. He passed through Fletcher like she wasn't there, which in a way, she wasn't.

Boothe returned and stood before Carey's desk, his hands behind his back. Carey turned away from the window to face him.

"What's the situation?" she asked.

Boothe looked ashen as he said, "It's confirmed. Simon Magus is KIA."

Carey nodded. "And Washington?"

"From what our sources could gather, it's currently under siege by forces loyal to Harkmoore. They expect it to fall within a few weeks."

Carey nodded. "Eric, listen to me. Even if Magus is gone, his work goes on. This isn't the end. We can't surrender now."

Boothe sighed. "I understand. It's just... what can we do now? Without Magus, it feels like it's every man for himself. Or every woman for herself."

Carey scowled. "God didn't let Moses reach the Promised Land, but I'm not about to let that son of a bitch do that to me."

Fletcher winced. Her own relationship with God was complicated, but it still felt wrong to hear Him willfully insulted like that.

"What are you talking about ma'am?" Boothe asked.

Carey opened the briefcase. She removed what looked like a bundle of sticks tied together in the form a human being with arms and legs attached to a torso.

"This, my friend, will allow us to remain on earth as long as it takes," Carey said.

"What is it?"

"Right now, it's just a doll. When I'm finished with it, it will keep my soul in this world even after my body dies. But I'm going to need power. Lots of power. I can't do this on my own Eric. That's why I need your help."

"Just tell me what you need ma'am."

"I've never tried a spell of this magnitude before. What I need are souls."

"How many?"

"All of them. Everyone here."

Boothe was silent for a few moments. "That... could take some time."

Carey smiled. "Fortunately, I know of a way to both give you all of the time in the world, and to give you the power you need to do this for me."

"What does it involve?"

"I know of a spell that can bless you with the gift of vampirism, without the need for drinking a vampire's blood. I'd cast it on myself, but I need to continue my work during daylight."

Boothe said nothing.

"Eventually, my body will give out," Carey said. "But with your help, my spirit can stay here on earth until I can find a newer, younger body."

Boothe said nothing.

"This doll is the key. I don't know if I'll be able to continue using magic after I die, but it's enough if I can stay here. What I'm asking you to do is kill everyone here and stand guard over this doll until I am reborn. Then our work can continue."

Boothe said, "How will we find you a new body to possess?"

Carey smiled. "Oh, I'm certain they'll come to us. You can sense the power here, can't you? Other witches will come. If nothing else, you can go hunting in Boise. But you must stay here. Do you understand? You must guard this doll with your life. Or unlife, rather."

Boothe slowly paced a circle around the office. After he returned to where he'd started, he smiled.

"I understand ma'am. I'm ready."

Carey smiled and clapped him on the shoulder. "Good man, Eric. The United States is done for. I don't know what's coming next, but we'll get through it together."

Boothe nodded.

"One thing you have to understand though. The men and women serving here? They're good people but make no mistake. They are the enemy now. If they knew that we stood with Magus, they wouldn't hesitate to kill us. You can't hesitate either."

"I understand."

Carey barked a laugh. "I just realized: Magus was like our Moses. He won't live to see us enter Eden, but we can't let his death be in vain, not after everything he's done for us."

"I'm ready ma'am."

"Good. Someday I'll be able to possess some pretty young thing." She made eye contact with Fletcher. "Like that one over there."

Fletcher gasped and the scene dissolved before her. She was back in the stairwell, her witch fire illuminating everything with its orange glow. Flint and Navarro were back.

"Did you learn anything?" Flint asked.

"How... how long was I gone?" she said.

The two men looked at each other.

"You never left," Navarro said. "It's been maybe ten seconds since you closed your eyes."

Fletcher was quiet for a few moments.

"Were you able to speak with any of the spirits?" Flint prompted.

"No... I got a history lesson though." She summarized the scene she had witnessed. When she finished, she said, "This was a bad idea. I shouldn't have come here."

"Nonsense," Flint said. "Were it not for you, we may never have learned of the fiend's wicked plans. I shall not allow her foul spirit to touch you."

Fletcher felt something stir in her chest. "You really mean that?"

"Of course. You are a ward of the Order and a valuable asset."

God damn it. "Oh, right, sure," she said, rolling her eyes.

"We know we're looking for a doll now," Navarro said. "But we've still got no way to open that door."

"I believe I have a solution that will kill two birds with one stone, so to speak," Flint said.

21

Flint led his two companions back down the stairs to the second floor. They would need room to maneuver for this part of his plan. He had complete confidence in Navarro to handle himself, but he wasn't so sure about Fletcher. Her ability to see and hear spirits had proven an asset thus far, but he could see how the witch Carey could also exploit it as a weakness. She had nearly lost her senses with that magical outburst earlier. Flint wouldn't hesitate to put her down if she went mad, either through lust for power or through Carey's machinations... but he felt sad when he considered the possibility.

They reached the halfway point between the opposite ends of the hallway. The acrid stench of burning flesh still lingered in the air.

"You sure you want to do this part sir?" Navarro asked. "I don't think he's the picky type."

"That is quite all right, Mr. Navarro. I am ever ready to shed my blood for the Lord. Your tomahawk if you please."

Navarro pulled it from his belt and handed it to Flint. He took off his long coat and handed it off to Navarro. Flint undid the buttons on the sleeve of his white dress shirt and rolled it up, exposing his forearm. He rested the blade on the fleshiest part, taking care not to press too hard. He couldn't afford to lose too much. He drew the tomahawk's blade across his skin. A red line appeared and blood seeped out. Flint turned his arm, allowing the fresh blood to drip onto the floor.

"Mr. Navarro, hand me the salt."

He dug around in the inner pockets of Flint's coat, withdrawing the pouch of blessed salt Flint always kept with him. It had served him well during their adventure in Canyon Cove, and he suspected he would have need of it again. Navarro tossed it to him. Flint caught it and was about to stuff it into the pocket of his black waistcoat when he realized something was missing.

"My watch," he said, patting the waistcoat. "Where's my watch?!"

"Oh!" Fletcher said. "I almost forgot. You dropped it when…"

A blood curdling scream echoed from above, along with a crash. Flint drew his sword and one of his pistols, Navarro readied his rifle. Fletcher summoned a ball of fire that hovered above the palm of her hand.

"No flames!" Flint said. "We need this leech intact!"

The fireball disappeared, and Fletcher drew her sidearm.

They heard footsteps descending the stairs. Fletcher's magical lighting didn't extend to the end of the hallway, which remained shrouded in darkness. The footsteps stopped. Two glowing red eyes appeared in the darkness. The creature hissed at them. Flint could make out words.

"Blood is life." The words were in a low growl. "Blood is life, blood is life, blood is life, blood is life…"

The vampire stepped into the light.

His Air Force shirt and jacket hung in tatters on his emaciated torso. His hands were tipped with gruesome black talons. Most horrifying of all was his face. His nose had flattened, the nostrils expanded, like those of a great bat. His ears had grown long and pointed. The sclera of his eyes was black, the irises a flaming red. His mouth opened to reveal enormous fangs.

"Blood is life!" the creature shrieked as it charged them.

"We shall put you out of your misery, monster! Open fire!" Flint yelled. They aimed, but just as they fired their guns in unison, Major Boothe was gone, and in his place was a colony of squealing bats.

"Ah! Damn it!" Navarro shouted. He swung his rifle like a baseball bat, striking the flying mammals as they swarmed around him. Fletcher summoned electricity to her fingertips, the chain lightning jumping between several bats but not slowing them down. Flint made wide swings with his sword, cutting down the animals, their bloody bodies falling to the floor. One landed on his bleeding forearm, but before it could bite down, he clubbed it with his pistol, and it flew off with a shriek.

As Navarro and Fletcher struggled, Flint sheathed his sword and took out the pouch of blessed salt from his waistcoat pocket. He reached inside and hurled a handful into an oncoming swarm. The Major screamed in pain, the salt sizzling as it struck the bats. They all came together, morphing back into the crazed vampire.

"Blood is life, blood is life, blood is life," he chanted. He threw back his head and roared, "Blood is life!"

"Now Mr. Navarro!"

Flint reached inside his shirt and pulled out the small crucifix he wore around his neck, a Saint Benedict medal embedded where the beams met, above the image of Christ's shoulders. Navarro drew a larger crucifix from a pouch on his belt.

Major Boothe cringed, shielding his face with his arms. "Blood is life, blood is life." His voice was trailing off into a whimper.

"There shall be none where you are headed, leech," Flint said, advancing on the Major.

An icy chill blasted the hallway. Carey's mocking laughter echoed in their ears.

"That's cheating," she said.

An invisible force slammed into Fletcher, sending her hurtling down the hallway, away from the melee. Her magical lighting vanished. All that was left were the flickering electric lights above.

"Zelda!" Navarro cried. Flint glanced down the hallway to where Fletcher lay crumpled in a heap. Their lapse in concentration proved enough for Major Boothe to break free. With a snarl, he got down low the ground and launched himself at Flint. The vampire's shoulder plowed into him, and Flint cried out as the pain in his injured ribs tore through him, clouding his vision in a red haze. Together, Witch Hunter and vampire crashed to the floor. Flint managed to hold on to his pistol despite his agony. He pressed it into Boothe's side and pulled the trigger again and again, the silver tipped bullets causing his flesh to sizzle and burn. He fired nine rounds into the Major's side until the slide locked open on empty. Boothe howled and cried, clutching at the bloody hole in his side, the ichor staining Flint's dress shirt. He launched his hips up, hurling Boothe off of him.

The vampire did a handspring and landed on its feet. At that moment, Navarro came up behind him and buried his tomahawk into the vampire's head. The Major roared and spun to deliver a backhanded slap, but Navarro ducked out of the way. He brought his rifle up and cracked Booth across the jaw with the wooden buttstock. Black blood and shattered teeth spewed from the vampire's mouth as he was spun around by the force of the blow. Navarro fired his rifle from the hip, into the Major's back, the high powered rifle round exploding out of his belly and over Flint's body where he still lay on the floor.

Flint kicked up off the floor, gritting his teeth against the pain in his side. His extra magazines were in his long coat pockets, so he holstered his empty pistol and drew his second. He unsheathed his sword, the blessed steel shining brightly in the gloom. While the Major was still stunned, Navarro grabbed the handle of his tomahawk and gave it a twist, wrenching the vampire's head around.

"Blood is life!" Boothe shrieked, ramming his elbow into Navarro's gut. He fell to his knees, gasping and wheezing for breath.

"Here, beast! Here is your blood!" Flint shouted, exposing his bloody forearm. Boothe's blood red eyes locked onto Flint's. Flint gave him a grim smile in return. Even if the vampire was in full possession of his sanity, his mind tricks would not work on Flint.

He brought his blade down in an overhead arc. Before it could bury itself in Boothe's shoulder, the vampire dodged, and delivered a heel kick to Flint's sternum that sent him flying down the hallway. Flint crashed to the floor, groaning in pain. His teeth were stained red with his own blood.

"Blood is life, blood is life, blood is life, blood is life, blood is life..." the vampire mumbled as it advanced on the fallen Witch Hunter. Flint rose to one knee, breathing hard.

"Blood is life, blood is life, blood is..." The vampire's words were cut off as an office chair slammed into its back, making him stumble. He turned around in time for a filing cabinet draw to smash into his face.

Fletcher was advancing on him, one hand outstretched. Debris from the rooms adjoining the hallway unerringly zeroed in on Major Boothe, smashing into him.

"Leave him alone!" she screamed.

The vampire began walking toward her. The objects did not slow him down, but they provided a distraction, and that was all Flint needed. He spat a mouthful of blood onto the floor as he rose to his feet. Moving as quickly as he could, he came up behind Major Booth and ran his sword into his back, through his heart, and out his chest. The vampire's corrupted blood sizzled and smoked as it contacted the blessed steel. Boothe's eyes opened wide as saucers, and he looked down at the glowing blade in his chest.

"Blood... is... life..." he said, his voice gurgling.

"No blood, no life," Flint replied. He ripped his sword from the Major's back and brought it around in a sweeping cut that sent Boothe's head flying from his shoulders. The head rolled away from the body which pitched forward and was still.

Flint dropped his sword and it clattered onto the floor. He staggered to the wall and leaned against it, sliding to a seated position on the floor. Every breath was agony. Fletcher rushed to his side.

"Silas!" she cried, putting her hand on his shoulder.

"I... I am fine," Flint wheezed. "There is still... work to be done." Navarro joined them, having regained his breath.

"Silas, I'm making an executive decision," Fletcher said.

"No," he said.

Fletcher slapped him in the face. Navarro looked almost as stunned as Flint, who stared at her, his mouth agape.

"Shut the fuck up!" Fletcher screamed. "You stupid, stuck up asshole!" Her eyes watered with tears. "You stupid, stuck up, crazy brave asshole! You're going to die if I don't fix you! And God damn it, I won't let you die here, you hear me?! So keep your fucking mouth shut and let me do it!"

The hallway was quiet save for Flint's ragged wheezing. He stared at her for a few moments, before giving a slight nod.

She put her hand on his chest and whispered to herself. Flint felt warmth envelop his body. His breathing returned to normal. Even the cut on his forearm sealed before his eyes. The pain was gone.

Fletcher removed her hand and looked at him. "How do you feel?" she asked.

Flint said nothing for a few moments.

"Silas?" Navarro asked.

Flint ran his hand over his close cropped hair. "I seem to have misplaced my hat again. Be a good assistant and fetch it for me, would you Ricardo?"

Navarro smiled. "Yes sir."

Flint got to his feet. Navarro brought him his tall, wide brimmed hat. Flint went to where Navarro had dropped his long coat, put it on, and adjusted his hat. Fletcher and Navarro watched him in silence. He removed the empty magazine from his pistol and loaded a fresh one, pulling the slide back and letting it slam home. He returned to his companions.

"Miss Fletcher... thank you."

She gave him a warm smile and nodded. "You're welcome."

"But let us not make a habit of this."

She laughed. "Then just don't get hurt anymore."

"Hmph." He picked his sword up off the ground. "Now... Mr. Navarro, raise that filthy beast's arm."

22

Flint pressed Major Boothe's severed hand against the glass plate. The bar of light moved up and down beneath the palm. The panel turned green, and a chime sounded. Navarro pushed down on the handle and the door swung open.

"Miss Fletcher, take this," Flint said, handing her the crucifix from his inner coat pocket. "It will be of use if Carey attempts any fiendish sorcery against us." She took it and nodded.

Flint led the way into the third floor hallway. All was

quiet. Fletcher cast another spell to illuminate their surroundings. From what the trio could see, this hallway was identical to the second floor, with doors on either side.

Navarro looked to Fletcher. "You said her office was at the end of the hall, right?" She nodded.

"We must ensure each room is clear before we proceed," Flint said. He kicked in the first door on his left. He entered, sweeping the room with his pistol. Nothing.

"Clear," he called.

"Clear," Navarro called back from the office across the way.

Wait. Perhaps not. Flint caught movement in his peripheral vision. It was on the other side of the window. He saw nothing but blackness outside. He moved for a closer look. There was faint light out there. He got closer, squinting into the darkness. It looked like... people. No, not people. Spirits. They swirled, were tossed and turned by some invisible force. All of their faces were rictus masks of pain and fear.

"You see something sir... holy shit," Navarro said, joining Flint at his side.

"I could not have put it better myself," Flint replied. Fletcher came in as well and gasped at the sight.

"You can see them too?" she asked.

"Yes," Flint said.

"It looks like they're going up," Navarro said.

Flint recalled that from the outside there appeared to be a small room at the top of this structure.

"I believe I may know where Carey and her accursed idol can be found," Flint said. Between the three of them, they checked every room, all of them empty, the tormented souls outside continuing to swirl and rise past the windows.

"Kind of suspicious she's not talking to us anymore," Navarro said.

"I can kind of sense her," Fletcher said. "She's focused on something else right now."

They reached the end. There was no door facing the hallway, no stairs leading up. On their left was a door with a plaque: MAJOR GENERAL N. CAREY, LOGISTICS. Flint led the way into her office.

It appeared to be like any other twenty-first century office. A window looked out into the darkness, revealing more souls being pulled upward. There were photographs on the wall of other men and women in uniform, and a portrait of Jeffrey Simmons, the last President of the United States.

"Search this room," Flint said. The trio spread out, poking around at bookshelves, filing cabinets, looking behind the photographs. Flint went to the desk. He opened the drawers, found nothing but pens, paperclips, and files containing the details of long dead personnel. On a hunch, he reached underneath the desk's central drawer. There. He felt a button. He pushed it. A panel opened up in the ceiling, and a ladder lowered itself to the floor.

"This is obviously a post-war addition," Flint said. "We go up."

23

He grabbed on to the first rung and hoisted himself up.

As he climbed higher, he heard Navarro's and Fletcher's boots tapping against the metal rungs. All was blackness.

Flint's hand bumped against the ceiling. They'd reached the end of the ladder. He pushed up, revealing they'd reached a trap door. It swung open with a creak, releasing a cloud of dust. He climbed up out of the shaft, standing aside to make room for Navarro and Fletcher. She cast her illumination spell and the hallway lit up. The walls appeared to be made of black marble. Along every inch were intricate carvings. Runes.

"Jesus," Navarro said. "What is all this shit?"

"I can't read them, but there's a lot of power here," Fletcher said.

Flint drew his sword and pistol. This hallway was shorter than the others. The air stank of must and decay. He crept forward. There were no doors on the sides, but God only knew what horrors may lay in wait. He could see a doorway at the end which held more stairs to climb. They reached the door and began their ascent. Alcoves in the walls held either human skulls or demonic idols.

"When we complete our mission, I shall see this structure razed to the ground, and let the archaeology be damned," Flint growled.

At the top of the steps was another door. Fletcher closed her eyes for a few moments.

"She's in there," she said.

Flint looked at his companions and holstered his pistol. "Our firearms will be of no use against spirits," he said.

Navarro slung his rifle and took his crucifix from his belt. Fletcher gripped hers harder.

"Our faith will be our shield. We must find this doll and destroy it. Understood?"

They nodded.

Flint pushed the door open and beheld a scene of absolute horror. On the far side of the room was a blood stained altar atop a raised dais. A circular section of the floor lay in a depression. In the center, a column of light rose from a carved pentagram bearing the familiar goat's head of Baphomet. Shrieking souls swirled in orbit around the column of unholy witchfire. Levitating before it was the spirit of Neveah Carey. She had not bothered to restore her human appearance, her exposed skull grinning, her stringy hair fluttering about her.

"Your nightmarish reign is over, Carey!" Flint bellowed over the cries of the dead and the unnatural winds that whipped through the chamber. "Tonight you face your long overdue judgment!"

Carey's apparition faced them, fires burning in her eye sockets.

"You've killed poor Eric," she said, her voice echoing.

"I shall see to it that you are reunited in Hell!"

Carey turned her gaze toward Fletcher.

"Thank you for bringing my new vessel to me. Your reward will be a quick death, and an eternity in my service."

"You will not touch her," Flint said.

Carey pointed at Flint, a bolt of lightning firing from her fingertip. Flint held his sword to parry, the blessed steel absorbing the magic.

"Come, my children!" Carey shouted. "Kill these pitiful creatures!"

Darkness fell within the room. Flint held his sword high,

the glow holding the shadows at bay. Fletcher cowered behind Navarro who held his crucifix aloft, giving off its own white light. The darkness pressed in, the sphere around them shrinking.

"Help us..." Fletcher said. "Help us! Help us set you free!" her voice rising to a shout.

Carey laughed. "These souls can't help you, child. They are mine to command, forever!"

There was a shift in the wind. The souls stopped their twisting and writhing. Flint could make out one figure, a woman, with two parallel bars on each shoulder of her jacket. Her face was a rictus of pain. She struggled as if against an invisible straitjacket.

"No!" Carey screamed. "You cannot do this! You are mine!"

Flint advanced toward Carey, crucifix in one hand, sword in the other.

"These souls belong to God alone!" he yelled. "They are not yours to imprison!" Carey shrank away from Flint.

The spirit of the Air Force woman managed to point at the altar for a second before she was gone, carried off by whatever dark magic held her prisoner.

"Silas! The altar!" Fletcher shouted.

Flint glanced at the altar. There. He could see the doll on top of it, propped up against the wall.

"Ricardo! Keep this demon at bay!"

Navarro rushed forward, Fletcher close on his heels. He held the crucifix before him.

"Our Father, who art in Heaven, hallowed be Thy name..." he said. Carey's spirit twisted and writhed.

"Thy Kingdom come, Thy will be done, on earth as it is in Heaven…" Fletcher joined in.

Carey threw her head back and shrieked. The glow of the crucifix grew brighter.

"Give us this day, our daily bread…" they said together. The winds grew stronger, Fletcher's long hair whipping about her. Flint made his way toward the altar, struggling against the sorcerous winds blowing against him. He felt like he was trying to run underwater.

"You cannot do this!" Carey screamed.

"And forgive us our trespasses…"

Carey's cries echoed throughout the chamber. Flint felt them in his chest and he winced at the pain in his ears.

"As we forgive those who trespass against us…"

"He's not real!" Carey shouted. "He's not real! He abandoned us! He abandoned me!"

"And lead us not into temptation…"

Flint was almost there. Just a little further.

"But deliver us from evil!"

"Nooooo!"

Flint cried out as he swung his sword. It cleaved through the doll, slicing it in two.

There was a great clap of thunder. The darkness vanished. The column of witch fire exploded in a shower of blue sparks that slowly floated to the floor.

All was silent for a few moments. Carey didn't have a face for Flint to read, but he had a feeling she was transfixed in horror.

Demonic laughter echoed in the chamber. Flint saw shadows circle the room, shadows with wings, and two horns curling up from their heads.

"No…" Carey whispered.

One of the shadows stopped in front of Flint. Two red eyes materialized where its face would be. And then a third, larger eye opened in the center of its forehead.

"Ah, Captain Flint," it said. "So good to see you again."

"Robin Redcap!" Flint said. Redcap was a demon he had encountered in Canyon Cove last month.

"I'd love to stay and catch up," the demon giggled. "But business before pleasure. My masters give you their thanks. We've wanted this one for a long time."

"No! Begone!" Carey's spirit cried out.

"Come Neveah," Redcap said. "Your new home awaits."

The shadows closed in on Carey's soul. They grabbed on to her and began dragging her down, down through the floor.

"No! Please! I take it back! I take everything back! I believe! Oh God, help me! Help meeee!" she shrieked.

"Too late," Redcap laughed. "You made your choices, and now you must live with them and with us for eternity."

Carey's cries were cut off as her head passed through the floor.

"So, what have you been up to lately?" Redcap said to Flint.

"Begone, demon! Return to the fiery abyss!"

Redcap laughed. "Stay safe, Captain. We're all looking forward to your reunion with Charles." The demon's shadow passed down through the floor and was gone.

A few moments passed. The three looked around the chamber. All was still and quiet.

"Is it over?" Navarro asked.

"Not quite," said a voice.

"What?!" Flint said.

A shimmering, translucent figure appeared before them. It was a man in an Air Force uniform, his chest bedecked with ribbons, what appeared to be eagles on his shoulders. He saluted the trio.

"Colonel Harry Adams, United States Air Force," he said.

"Knight Templar Captain Silas Flint. My assistant Supernumerary Ricardo Navarro, and our associate Zelda Fletcher."

The colonel nodded his head. "I don't have long, but I wanted to thank you all on behalf of the men and women of Mountain Home Air Force Base..." His voice broke. In a sob he cried, "We're free."

"Rest in peace Colonel," Flint said. The soul slowly faded from sight.

Fletcher's face brightened. "They're gone. The ghosts... they're all gone now," she said, smiling.

Flint pulled his long coat tighter. He adjusted his hat. He couldn't sense these things the way Fletcher could, but he felt... lighter somehow. He realized that the entire time they had been inside this accursed place, it had felt like a great weight was pressing down on their shoulders. But it was gone now.

He turned to face his companions. "Thank you both," he said. "I do not believe I would have survived this encounter if not for your assistance."

Navarro grinned. "Just doing my job, boss."

Fletcher blushed and looked away.

"Come," Flint said. "Never have I so eagerly wished to depart."

24

"Fire in the hole!" Austin yelled. He depressed the plunger. The explosives detonated with a thunderous boom. Carey's tower collapsed in a shower of stone, wood, and dust.

The morning sun warmed the tarmac with its golden rays. After a memorial service for the late Mark McCloskey and Jennifer Barrett, Flint had ordered the tower destroyed. He stood now with Navarro, Fletcher, Johansson, Austin, Jones, and Elmore. The college students stood off at a distance to watch the fireworks.

"I'm so sorry, Silas," Johansson said.

Flint patted him on the shoulder. "You could not have known."

"Yes, I could have. The locals warned me away from this place, and I ignored them."

"And thousands of imprisoned souls are now free to pass on to their eternal reward," Flint said. "Do not blame yourself for the deaths of your students. The vampire and the witch are responsible, and they have paid for their crimes against God and man."

Johansson said nothing.

"What will you do now?" Flint asked.

The professor sighed. "I want to continue our work here, but... I feel like it wouldn't be right, somehow."

"You must always do what you believe to be right, of

course. I have a suggestion: request that your university establish a scholarship in the names of your fallen students."

Johansson nodded. "Yes... yes, I will do that. My heart goes out to their families, but... it's an unfortunate truth that archaeology is much more dangerous than it used to be. I think I'll continue the dig. It's what they would have wanted."

Flint nodded and left to see the others. Navarro was chatting up Elmore, who seemed none the worse for wear after her encounter with Major Boothe. She laughed at a joke his assistant cracked. Flint shook his head. The man was incorrigible. He seemed to make new girlfriends everywhere they went.

Austin and Jones nodded to Flint. "Nice work, Captain," Austin said.

Flint nodded in return. "And you as well, Mr. Austin."

"Me? I didn't do anything, besides get the shit scared out of me."

"You and your companions sheltered and stood watch over these young people all throughout the night. That is no small thing."

"Yeah, well..." Austin said.

"We don't get paid if the boss dies," Jones said.

"What will you do once your contract here is complete?"

They both shrugged. "Probably go back to bounty hunting," Austin said. "Seems a lot safer than the shit you have to deal with."

"Hmm," Flint said. "I feel the same about your profession."

"Huh?"

"It is my solemn duty to exterminate the forces of darkness wherever they may be found. I find dealing with mundane criminals to be rather depressing. I expect nothing but pure evil from demons and witches, and I always know to put them down. Men who willfully choose a life of crime are a different matter."

"If you say so, Captain."

Flint chose to leave Navarro to his rakish ways with Elmore, and he went to join Fletcher.

"Silas," she said.

"Miss Fletcher," he replied.

Her face brightened. "Oh! I almost forgot again." She reached into her pants pocket and took out Flint's watch. "You dropped it in there." She held it out to him.

He took it from her and put it back in his waistcoat pocket.

"Thank you. This… it's sentimental value is priceless."

"About that…"

Flint stared at her.

"I… uh…"

"You opened it," he said.

She nodded and spread her arms. "In my defense, I honestly just wanted to check the time."

Flint took a deep breath, exhaled. "I presume you have questions."

"Yeah, of course. If you feel comfortable sharing. With me."

Flint gave her an appraising look. "I suppose you have earned that much, Zelda."

She blushed.

"I warn you, it is a dark tale that does not have a happy ending. Walk with me." He held out his arm. Fletcher looped hers around it and they began to stroll.

"My parents were Robert and Janet," Flint said. "And the other boy is my younger brother Charles..."

25

Far to the northeast, in the territory formerly known as Montana, a ring of fire appeared in the middle of a thick forest. Birds took flight, and deer fled in terror. Within the ring a black hole appeared. Charles Flint and Lilian Turner stepped out of the void and onto the forest floor. Their portal shrunk and vanished behind them.

Charles looked all around them. The leafy canopy was thick enough to shield them from the glare of the morning sun to some degree, spackling the trees with patches of light. He frowned.

"You're sure this is the place?" he asked.

Lilian shrugged. "As sure as I can be. The land has changed a bit in almost five hundred years."

Charles stretched out his senses, searching for anything with a trace of magic. There. It was faint, but he sensed something, a kind of magic he hadn't encountered before.

"It's over here," he said, leading the way, Lilian close behind him. She had discarded the ball gown she had been wearing when Silas Flint had kicked her into the demonic abyss, and now wore a blouse, jeans, and hiking boots. It was quite a change from her life of wealth and luxury in Canyon Cove, but it wasn't the first time she'd had to begin again with nothing.

"What exactly is this spell I'm sensing?" Charles asked.

"Think of it as a kind of cryogenic treatment," Lilian said.

"I don't know what that word means."

Lilian bit down a sarcastic reply and said, "Oh... right, I guess you wouldn't. Back in the twentieth and twenty-first centuries, they developed a technology called cryogenics. The theory was that people who had terminal illnesses could be frozen in pods and thawed out once science had developed a cure for whatever they had."

"Fascinating," Charles said. "I never thought I'd get to learn about ancient history from someone who's lived it."

Lilian laughed. "Five hundred years is not ancient. I refuse to believe that."

"You don't look a day over three hundred, my dear."

Lilian, with the help of Simon Magus himself, had developed an elixir that stopped the aging process in the year 2059. Chronologically, she was 503 though she still appeared to be a woman of 29.

"Anyway," she went on, "After the Occult War began, several members of the American national security establishment joined us. They had access to places we thought would come in handy, and together we developed a spell to suspend time. And before you ask, no, it's not possible for us to travel through time. At least, no one has ever figured out the trick, if it is possible. But we learned how to have time travel through us. Or not travel, in this case."

"And that's where we're going."

"I hope so, anyway. A lot has happened since Magus fell."

They pressed on. The magic Charles had sensed was growing stronger. He couldn't wait to see it for himself. Lilian had told him something of it before they departed, but he still couldn't quite wrap his mind around the science of it. Lilian had lived then, and even she didn't understand all of it, the knowledge requiring years of specialized education. He suspected it was more technology that had been lost over the centuries, the kind of technology the twenty-sixth century simply couldn't make or reverse engineer anymore. Still, he had some ideas. The science may be lost, but he thought that magic might be able to bridge the gaps.

"I think we're here," Lilian said.

Yes, this had to be it. The ancient magic nearly overwhelmed Charles's senses with its potency. He looked around. It was a patch of forest that appeared no different from all the rest. Wait. There. He saw something metal protruding from a small rise in the ground. He approached it, pushed aside the leafy branches of the bush with his mind. It looked like some sort of hatch. The metal was covered in rust, and covered in leafy tendrils, but he could blow it open if it came to it.

"Welcome, my friend," Lilian said. "A gift from the old world. Say hello to a small piece of America's nuclear arsenal."

The Deepest Circle

1

Ricardo Navarro sat at the bar inside the cantina located on the grounds of Fort Marsing. His fellow Supernumeraries were gathered around in a semicircle as he held a small box in his hands. It had a grille on the front, with two knobs on the side, and a folding antenna in the back. Professor Karl Johansson had allowed Navarro to take it with him as a souvenir when he, Zelda Fletcher, and his boss, Witch Hunter Captain Silas Flint, had departed from Mountain Home Air Force Base far to the east.

Supernumerary Cassandra Henson peered over Navarro's shoulder.

"You really think it still works?" she asked.

"It should," Navarro said. "You should have seen that place. A dead witch from the twenty first century did some magic shit and kept the whole area preserved. Almost five hundred years old and it all still looks brand new."

"What's it run on?" asked another Supernumerary, Pablo Ruiz.

"Old world batteries called Energizers," Navarro said.

"Can you recharge them?"

"Dunno."

"So if they go dead, that's it?"

Navarro shrugged. "Maybe, but I don't see why modern batteries wouldn't work."

"Well, turn it on then," said the bartender, retired Supernumerary Alfred Carruthers. "I'm not getting any younger."

Navarro unfolded the antenna and extended it as far as it

could go. He thumbed the power knob on the side, and the radio spewed static.

"We have a heartbeat!" Navarro said.

"Are there any radio stations around here?" Henson asked.

"We might be able to pick something up from Canyon Cove or New Meridian, maybe," Ruiz said.

Navarro thumbed the tuning knob and the red needle moved from left to right between two sets of numbers, the top set called FM and running from 88 to 108, the bottom set called AM with a range of 550 to 1720. As near as he could tell, the radio was currently set to AM. He wasn't well versed in the science of radio, but he believed that in the old days, stations could claim exclusive broadcast rights on certain frequencies. How the old world managed to enforce that, he had no clue.

The needle crept forward. Static continued to pour from the radio. Wait... he thought he heard something. The Supernumeraries crowded in closer, straining to hear.

"Think we got someone..." Navarro said. He inched the needle further forward.

"I say again, repent!" a voice blared from the radio. "Will the Lord find even one faithful man on earth when He returns? Simon Magus was God's punishment on a wicked and sinful people, yea, and even now, the Children of Magus butcher our children, rape our women, and devour the souls of..."

"That's enough of that," Carruthers growled. Navarro moved the needle past the furious preacher's broadcast. Although he was a lifelong Catholic, Navarro had to admit that other churches often had the Catholic Church beat when it came to preaching. He memorized the number of that broadcast for later.

He moved the needle forward again. The static abated and another voice began coming through.

"I daresay the Emperor is being positively derelict in his duty," said a man's voice. "A witch in Canyon Cove, a were-wolf in Oglethorpe… are there witches in Salem? In Astoria? What about further north? My sources are telling me there's evidence of a coven in…"

"Shit," Navarro said, as he scrolled past the station. This wasn't turning out the way he'd hoped, but maybe the FM side would have some good music. He noticed movement in his peripheral vision. Looking up he saw three Supernumer-aries near the swinging doors at the front entrance. He thought he knew all his fellow Witch Hunter assistants, but these three he didn't recognize. They all wore the trademark leather body armor and denim jeans of the Supernumeraries. All three were Hispanic women, identical to each other, equally gorgeous. The one in the center held a piece of card-board above her head, which she slowly moved back and forth. Written on it in black marker was 1530 AM.

Navarro furrowed his brow, looked down at the radio's needle. He was about to say something to the Supernumer-aries crowded around him when the realization struck him. He had seen those three before. Silas had called them Weird Sisters, claimed they were white girls with white, black, and red hair. He looked up again, but they were gone. He scanned the cantina, looking for any trace of their presence.

"What's up?" Henson asked. Several of the Witch Hunter

assistants turned around to look at where Navarro was peering.

"You see something?" one of them asked.

"No… no, nothing important," Navarro said. It wasn't that he doubted his friends would believe him. When you were sworn into the Knights Templar of the Order of Saint Benedict, you saw enough weird shit to last a lifetime within your first few years. He and Silas had encountered those three witches on a mission to the city of Oglethorpe two months ago. They'd proven helpful then, but the two still didn't trust them. They were up to something, and their plans involved Silas and Ricardo somehow. He'd have to tell Silas about this later. In the meantime, they wanted him to tune in to 1530 AM. He gave a grim smile. He was about to ask himself what could it hurt, but those were famous last words if ever he'd heard them.

He thumbed the knob and the needle inched toward 1530. His eyes were focused on the radio but he heard the bar quiet around him. The static decreased as he got closer. He reached the spot where 1530 should be. The static stopped. All was silent as Navarro looked at the radio, not knowing what to expect. A jazzy tune began playing. He heard a saxophone, a piano, and drums. The blues wasn't Navarro's favorite genre – he preferred more upbeat tunes – but the music affected him, nonetheless. It spoke to him of remembering better times that were lost forever. He nodded along with the beat, unaware of himself.

"What do you guys think of…" He looked up. His fellow Supernumeraries were frozen in place. Some held mugs of beer halfway to their mouths. Others were staring at him, not moving, not blinking.

"The fuck…" he muttered. He got up from his stool, leaving the radio on the bar. He snapped his fingers in front of Henson's face, but she continued to stare, unblinking, at the spot where Navarro had been sitting. He put his hand on Ruiz's chest and pushed. The man didn't budge. He was like a statue bolted to the floor.

"What the hell?!" Navarro shouted. "Cass! Pablo! Alf! What's wrong with you? What's happening?!" His heart pounded in his chest. Christ, what had he done? Why did he have to tune to that station? Those damn witches had everyone frozen or suspended or something, and he was responsible for it.

The music ended. After a few moments, a jingle played. Seconds after that a female voice broke in.

"This is Mallory Proctor," it said.

"Joining her is Monica Proctor," said another woman.

"With special correspondent Madeline Proctor," said a third.

Navarro closed his eyes. Shit. He'd left his rifle in his quarters. He still had his pistol and tomahawk on his belt, but if it came to a firefight, he had no idea if… if whatever these witches had done to his colleagues made them bulletproof. He'd have get up close and personal if they tried anything.

"We mean you no harm, Ricardo," said Mallory.

"You won't need your weapons," said Monica.

"Not yet anyway," said Madeline.

He opened his eyes, looked all around him. He put a hand on his temple. "What... are you reading my mind?"

"Of course," they said in unison.

"You are easy to read," said Mallory.

"The fuck is that supposed to mean?"

"You are a man of simple tastes," said Monica.

"And simple pleasures," said Madeline.

"Not like poor Silas," said Mallory.

He scowled at the radio. "You were in here a minute ago. You wanted me to tune to this station."

"Indeed," they replied in unison.

"What did you do to the others?"

"Fear not."

"They are unharmed."

"We have taken you sideways in time so we could chat in private."

Navarro blinked. He rubbed his forehead. "Oh, is that all?" He blew out a breath, and returned to his stool at the bar, taking the radio in his hands. "So what do you want now?"

"You and Silas will be journeying west soon," said Mallory.

"You both want to leave the past behind," said Monica.

"But the past makes us who we are," said Madeline.

Navarro growled in frustration. "What is it with you and being mysterious? Huh? Is it too much trouble to just come right out and say what you're after? Are us mere mortals too dumb to follow your higher purpose or your master plan or whatever?"

The radio was silent.

"I mean you've got the bar frozen in time. You took me 'sideways,' whatever that means. If you're powerful enough to do that, what do you need me and Silas for?"

The radio was quiet for another few moments.

"You are sworn to obey your superiors," Mallory said.

"You follow orders even when you do not understand them," Monica said.

"So it is with us," Madeline said.

Navarro opened his mouth, paused, and shut it again. That was a surprise.

"We ourselves do not fully understand."

"We know that you and Silas play an important part in events to come."

"We have power, yes, but we are forbidden from direct intervention."

Navarro blinked. "Forbidden by who?"

"It does not matter. We have been shown a great vision."

"A vision of two brothers."

"Light and shadow, at the edge of the world, beneath weeping skies and an ancient flag."

Navarro's eyes widened. "Charles..." he whispered. Silas didn't like talking about his younger brother, but Navarro knew that Charles Flint had become a formidable warlock, bent on delving ever deeper into the realms of sorcery and demonology.

"You should take your new radio with you when you depart," Mallory said.

"Music can brighten even the most arduous journeys," Monica said.

"Don't forget to turn on the news," Madeline said.

Navarro snorted. "I don't suppose you've got any more presents for us?" They had given Silas a silver dagger during their mission to Oglethorpe that had proven crucial in in solving the case.

"You will receive a package within the next two days," they all replied.

"Hope you didn't scare the courier too badly when you gave it to him."

"You are a good man, Ricardo Navarro," Mallory said.

"You are a man of faith and courage," Monica said.

"Do not grow too cynical. Silas will need you," Madeline said.

Another jingle sounded from the radio. "The Proctor sisters, signing off," they said. Another jazz tune began.

"Hey, you finally found some music!" Henson said.

Navarro looked up. The other Supernumeraries had been unfrozen. Most were still crowded around him, but he could hear the clink of glasses and the murmur of conversations again. His eyes darted around the bar.

"You alright, Rico?" Ruiz asked.

"Yeah... yeah, I'm fine."

Carruthers closed his eyes, nodded his head along with the beat of the jazz tune. "Not bad," he said. "Sounds twenty-fourth century, I think."

"Well, at least there's one music station," said Henson.

"Why not try the FM side?" Ruiz said.

"Tell you what," Navarro said. "Why don't you guys mess around with it for a bit?" He handed off the radio to Henson and Ruiz. "It's just, ah, I'll need that back at closing time."

"Yeah, of course." The crowd focused on Henson as she began experimenting with the knobs and antenna.

Carruthers raised an eyebrow at Navarro. "I know that look," he said.

"What look?"

Carruthers chuckled. "You just saw something that was not of this world, am I right?"

Navarro grinned. "You could say that."

"Want to talk about it? I saw a thing or two in my day."

"Sure."

"Drink?"

"Ah… no, not right now."

"Jesus Christ, what the hell did you see?"

Navarro told his story, from the first time he and Silas had encountered the Weird Sisters - the Proctors - on their way to Oglethorpe, how the witches had assisted them during the case, and their latest conversation. When he had finished, Carruthers scowled.

"Frozen in time? Damn witches… it ain't natural."

"You don't seem any worse for wear. You still got your charming personality."

Carruthers snorted. "So what are you going to do?"

Navarro shrugged. "Gonna tell Silas about it, of course. After that, I don't know. They said we'd be getting a package soon. And we'd be heading west. I'll bet you a round of drinks that we're going to get a case somewhere out there."

"Nah, don't think I'll take that one. A man's gotta make a living."

"Interesting," Silas Flint muttered to himself. He stood within his living quarters, hands behind his back, facing the portrait of Saint Benedict of Nursia above his desk. Navarro was seated on one of the cushioned chairs in the part of the quarters that served as the living room. He had headed over to the Templar wing of Fort Marsing shortly after recounting his story to Carruthers and repeated it for Flint's benefit.

He turned to face Navarro. "They said we would be journeying west soon."

Navarro nodded. "Yeah."

"They did not say why though."

He shook his head.

"Hmm…"

"What do you think boss?"

Flint was silent for a few moments. "Actually Mr. Navarro, I should like to hear your opinion."

"They got some brass balls showing up at our Chapter House."

"Indeed. I suspect that is why they chose to suspend time, to 'take you sideways.' I am curious, how did that feel?"

"I felt fine. Little shook up that they can do that. The others just carried on like nothing had happened."

Flint paced back and forth before his desk. "They know about Charles," he said.

Navarro nodded. "Yeah. 'Two brothers, light and shadow, at the edge of the world, beneath weeping skies and an ancient flag.' They got a gift for the dramatic, I'll give them that."

"The edge of the world…"

"I'm guessing that's metaphorical, but I got no idea what it could mean."

"Nor do I. Do you happen to have the radio with you?"

Navarro opened a pouch on his belt, took out the radio, and handed it to Flint. He extended the antenna, turned it on. The other Supernumeraries had left it tuned to an FM station that specialized in popular Spanish language music.

"1530 AM, correct?

Navarro nodded.

Flint switched bandwidths, thumbed the knob to the appropriate station. The static was broken by a soft jazz tune. The piano tinkled a melancholy beat, the drums adding contrast, the saxophone broke in with the occasional solo. The music made Flint think of his family farm, of his father, so strong and full of dreams about what his precocious boys could accomplish to bring honor to the Flint name, of his mother, so gentle, yet possessed of an iron will and a rapier wit, of his younger brother, a shy lad who hungered for knowledge and was driven by a burning ambition to surpass his older brother in...

Flint shook his head.

"You alright sir?" Navarro asked.

"Yes... I am fine. This music, I recognize it. 'Star Spangled Blues,' composed by one Johnny Crowe in 2376, to commemorate the three hundredth anniversary of the fall of the United States."

"If you say so sir. This kind of Jazz isn't exactly my style. Always makes me feel down, you know?"

"Yes, I believe that is the intention behind this particular genre." They both fell silent, let the song continue. After another few minutes, it concluded with a flourish on the piano.

"That was 'Star Spangled Blues,' by Johnny Crowe," said a male announcer. "The United States may be gone, but she is not forgotten on 1530 AM, Cascadia's number one station for classical music. I'm your host Nick Sanderson. Coming up we've got..."

Flint turned the radio off. "I wonder why the Proctors chose this particular station."

Navarro shrugged. "Maybe they like the blues."

Flint snorted. He handed the radio back to Navarro. "I suggest you keep it with you for now."

"You think they're trying to help us again."

"I do not know. Your account made them out to be obeying orders from some higher power. Or lower power, in this case. They proved themselves useful in the Oglethorpe incident. Perhaps they mean to lend their assistance again, however indirectly."

Navarro nodded. "Don't suppose you know where we can hear the news on this thing? I found a talk show earlier, but I don't know if that qualifies."

"It is my understanding that most radio stations report the news at the top and the bottom of every hour." Flint checked his pocket watch. 10:51 p.m.

"You want I should tell General Abernathy about what happened?"

"I shall inform him in the morning. You and your compatriots appear unharmed. So far the witches have offered nothing but platitudes and vague prophecies."

"And a special delivery."

"Yes… and that. For now, we shall carry on as normal. I suspect you are eager to return to the cantina."

"Eh, I was actually thinking about calling it an early night boss."

Flint raised an eyebrow. "Have my entreaties finally penetrated your endless appetite for debaucheries?"

"I wouldn't go that far sir. Watching time get frozen, talking to those three again, prophecies and mysterious packages and shit… feel like I should keep a clearer head for now."

"Hmph. It is a start, I suppose."

3

The next morning, Flint knelt in the pews with hundreds of other Witch Hunters, all packed into Fort Marsing's chapel (it was called a chapel, but Flint had seen Cathedral churches with smaller interiors.) An elderly Benedictine monk stood before the altar, his back to the congregation. He slowly raised the Sacred Host. Bells rang, signifying that Christ was now present in the Sacrament. To the priest's right, a monk fulfilling the role of Deacon swung a thurifer, the incense wafting through the rays of sunlight shining through the stained glass windows.

My Lord and my God, Flint thought, bowing his head. The priest lowered the Host, setting it on the paten, the gold dish reserved for use during Mass. The priest took the chalice in hand, preparing to consecrate the wine into the Blood of Christ. Flint looked up and nearly shouted aloud.

At the bottom of the steps leading up to the altar were the Weird Sisters, the Proctors. They wore the same ankle length dresses from his first encounter with them outside of Oglethorpe two months ago. If he recalled correctly, the white haired one was Mallory, Monica had black hair, and Madeline was the redhead.

You dare... you DARE defile the Holy Sacrifice of the Mass with your vile presence?! I'll see you all burn for this sacrilege! Flint thought, his face twisting into a furious snarl.

"You may speak aloud, Silas," Mallory said.

"Although you need not repeat what you just thought," Monica said.

"Is that any way to greet old friends?" Madeline said.

Flint looked around, bewildered. The priest should have consecrated the chalice by now, but he stood frozen in place. The Witch Hunters on his right and left were similarly rooted to the floor. They had suspended time, just as they had for Navarro last night. He rose to his feet.

"How dare you! Release them and begone! Or I shall shoot you down where you stand!"

The three witches smiled in unison.

"We will not be long."

"We needed to speak with you."

"And it is not meant for Ricardo's ears."

Flint scowled at them. "Say what you have come to say, and leave."

"It is vital that he make peace with his father."

"You will need Ricardo at his best to face what is to come."

"Charles and Lilian will awaken a sleeping giant."

"What?!" Flint cried.

"We shall take our leave now."

"We suggest you get back on your knees."

"Only a Godless heathen would be on his feet during the consecration."

The sisters shimmered and became translucent. Flint knelt in his pew again by the time they vanished. The priest resumed the Mass. Once again, Flint could hear coughs, sniffles, the clearing of throats, and the other noises all congregations had made since the days of the Roman catacombs. The priest raised the chalice above his head. The kneeling acolytes rang bells, letting the world know that the Precious Blood was now present.

Flint tried to quiet his mind, but it raced with questions and possibilities. Navarro's father? Flint knew that Navarro's family endlessly worried about him choosing such a dangerous profession, but he wasn't aware of any conflict between Ricardo and his father, Angelo. More unsettling was their knowledge of Charles and... could it be they referred to Lilian Turner? Flint had hurled her into a yawning demonic void in Canyon Cove three months ago. Looking back on it, he always harbored a suspicion that she had survived. Now it seemed the Weird Sisters had confirmed his fear. If Charles had fished her out of that Godless abyss, and they were now in league together, God only knew what fiendish devilry they could accomplish together.

The rest of morning Mass proceeded uninterrupted. Flint received the Sacred Host on his tongue and returned to his pew. He would have to speak with Witch Hunter General John Abernathy as soon as possible.

"Benedicat vos omnipotens Deus, Pater, et Filius, et Spiritus Sanctus," the priest said, delivering his benediction to the congregation and making the Sign of the Cross.

"Amen," they replied. The priest turned to face the altar again to quietly recite the Last Gospel. Flint chided himself for being distracted and prayed that the Lord would understand. The priest knelt before the altar, the congregation kneeling in their pews.

"Saint Michael the Archangel, defend us in battle," everyone recited together. "Be our protection against the wickedness and snares of the devil. May God rebuke him, we humbly pray. And do thou, O Prince of the Heavenly Host, by the power of God, thrust into Hell Satan and all the evil spirits who wander through the world seeking the ruin of souls. Amen."

The priest quietly departed, followed by his Deacon and the altar servers. Flint often thought he should develop a devotion to St. Michael. The prayer the Witch Hunters had just recited was granted to Pope Leo XIII in a vision over six hundred years ago and was declared to be an official part of the Mass in 2251 by Pope Pius XV. Flint thought he was going to need as much angelic and divine intervention as he could get.

The Templars began filing out of the chapel, pew by pew. Flint remained standing in his place, allowed the other Witch Hunters in his pew to squeeze by him. General Abernathy was always the first inside and the last to leave. The chapel slowly emptied. The other Templars would be headed to their living quarters or the library for research, some would be departing for field assignments, still others to the gun range, the fencing strip, or the weight room. Over the centuries, Fort Marsing had expanded to the point of being a self-contained community, not unlike an old American military base.

Lady Templar Diana McFarlane nodded to Flint as she passed him in the central aisle of the chapel. She was the unofficial leader of the women's division at Fort Marsing and had taken the repentant witch Zelda Fletcher under her wing when Flint and Navarro had brought her in two months ago. There weren't nearly as many women who took up arms for the Order as men, either as Supernumeraries or Templars, but the few who did had all proven their worth as far as Flint was concerned.

Witch Hunter General Abernathy approached. He was dressed identically to the other Templars, save for the gold epaulettes on the shoulders of his long coat, signifying his rank. He was a trim man in his late fifties, a fringe of gray stubble circling his otherwise bald head. Flint went out to meet him in the aisle.

"General Abernathy," he said.

"Captain Flint," Abernathy replied.

"I have troubling news sir."

His nostrils flared. "Walk with me. We can discuss it on the way to my office."

The two men exited the chapel and put on their tall, wide brimmed hats which more than any other of their accoutrements signified the Witch Hunter profession.

"Now, what's this about Silas?" Abernathy asked.

"The Weird Sisters that Mr. Navarro and I encountered on our way to Oglethorpe have returned. They were here, at Fort Marsing."

"What?! When?"

Other Witch Hunters in the hallway outside the chapel looked up at Abernathy's outburst. He waved off their concern and they returned to their conversations.

"How is it that three witches were able to infiltrate a Templar Chapter House?"

Flint summarized everything that Navarro had told him and told of his meeting with the Sisters during Mass. Abernathy's eyes widened in shock.

"They can freeze time?" he whispered.

"I am not sure," Flint replied. "Mr. Navarro said that they described it as 'going sideways.' I suspect that it means the target is made to be… adjacent to the flow of time, like standing on the bank of a moving river. From my point of view, you all appeared to be frozen at a particular moment, like a photograph."

Abernathy said nothing as they progressed toward his office. Arriving, he opened the heavy oaken doors and motioned for Flint to enter first. Abernathy followed and shut the door behind him.

"Have a seat," he said, walking toward his desk. Flint went to one of the wooden chairs Abernathy kept for guests. The General's office was crammed with overloaded bookshelves, the walls crowded with paintings and photographs of momentous occasions in the Chapter House's history. On one side of his desk was the gold and white of Vatican City's flag, on the other the blue, white, and green of the flag of Cascadia.

Abernathy took his seat. He put his elbows on his desk and steepled his fingers. "They said you would be headed west soon?"

"That is what Mr. Navarro reported."

Abernathy leaned back in his chair, drumming his fingers on the desktop.

"Is something troubling you sir?" Flint asked.

"Yes, a great many things are troubling me," Abernathy replied. "As it happens, yesterday evening I received a letter from the west, for my eyes only."

Flint raised an eyebrow.

"It came from Fort Ingalls."

Flint inhaled deeply. Fort Marsing was in the far east of Cascadia, largely considered a backwater by the rest of the country, and most of the other Chapter Houses of The Knights Templar of the Order of Saint Benedict. For the Chapter House in the capitol city to send Abernathy an eyes only letter…

"You may as well hear what it says," Abernathy said. "I was going to need an investigator anyway, and since you're here…"

"I take it the situation is dire if the imperial capitol is reaching out to us."

"You could say that. General Hickock believes there is a traitor in their midst."

Flint blinked. "Sir… he believes that one of his own has fallen away and joined with the powers below?"

Abernathy nodded. "He doesn't have any hard evidence

yet, but they've experienced a series of devastating setbacks in the field. We all know the risks of this vocation, but Salem Templars and their Supernumeraries are dying in unprecedented numbers. Witches and their minions always seem like they are two steps ahead of them."

Flint closed his eyes and sighed. "Either they are facing witches of unparalleled genius..."

"Or someone on the inside is feeding them information about our movements. Or killing them themselves."

Flint scowled. Witch Hunters betraying their oaths, turning against the Children of God and joining the Children of Magus was not unheard of, but this would be the first time such a thing had happened in his lifetime if General Hickock's suspicions were correct. "What is it that the General proposes?"

"He feels that he can't trust anyone in Fort Ingalls right now. He's experimented with spreading false information about field operations to try and determine the source of the leaks, but so far has had no luck."

"Yes, many witches and warlocks have the talent to read the thoughts and intentions of others," Flint said, thinking of Zelda Fletcher. Her talent had saved the day at Mountain Home Air Force Base, but if a Witch Hunter had the talent and used it for nefarious purposes, the consequences would be catastrophic. Witch Hunters were trained to resist the mental influence of witches, but even the most dedicated among them could not keep up that level of focus indefinitely, particularly if they didn't know from whence the probes were coming.

Abernathy nodded. "Exactly. What he proposes is an outsider to come and investigate. Someone with no ties to Fort Ingalls. It is his hope that fresh eyes will be able to discern what he has not."

Flint steepled his fingers. "Is it your desire that I be these fresh eyes, sir?"

Abernathy sighed. "It was. After hearing your story about these three witches, I'm not so sure anymore."

"What do you mean sir?"

"What I mean is that I'm getting eaten alive by doubts. Did they predict that I'd ask you to do this? Did they plan for it to turn out this way? I've never questioned my gut feelings in my life, and it's not a pleasant experience, I assure you. If I send you west, would I be playing into their hands? Or would I be playing into their hands if I didn't?"

Flint raised his hand in a placating gesture. "We cannot afford to second guess ourselves in times such as these, sir. I concur that there is a danger here. These Proctor women assisted Mr. Navarro and I in Oglethorpe, but I still do not trust them. There is no doubt that they have an agenda that only they and God know. But whatever it is, we must trust in the Lord to lend us the strength we need to defeat whatever devilish trickery they have in store for us."

Abernathy grinned. "Spoken like a true Templar. Alright. I'll send you and Ricardo to Salem. We'll worry about whatever the Sisters are planning later."

"Very good sir. I have a question though: will not the Templars in Salem be aware that I am there to investigate their comrades?"

"They may suspect, but General Hickock anticipated that. First, you and Ricardo won't be the only ones moved there for temporary duty. Second, you'll have a cover story: due to your exemplary work in Canyon Cove and Oglethorpe, the Order feels that your talents would be better employed in the heart of the Imperial Capitol, closer to the Emperor himself."

Flint said nothing.

"It's not that far from the truth. General Hickock has read copies of several of your case reports, and he is quite impressed by your work."

"I do not wish to be transferred to Salem," Flint said.

"Fear not. As I said, it's a cover story, and you will be returning to us when your mission is complete. You aren't escaping my authority that easily."

Flint gave a wintry smile.

"I haven't forgotten your desire to be as far from Mount Angel as you can be," Abernathy said.

"I appreciate that sir."

"The Order takes your personal preference into account, but bear in mind there may come a day when you have no choice in the matter."

"I understand."

Abernathy nodded. "There was something else I wanted discuss: this mysterious package they said you would receive."

"Yes… what it could be, I have not the foggiest idea."

"It makes me wonder if the witches sent it themselves, or if it's from someone within either of your social circles."

"Either is a distinct possibility sir."

Abernathy snorted. "I suppose there's nothing to be done

for it but to sit down, shut up, and wait. Never my first choice."

"If it is any consolation sir, apparently it will be arriving soon."

"Yes, there is that. As I recall, the last gift they presented to you may have saved your life."

Flint hesitated. He hated to admit it, but it was the truth. "I would say so."

"Do you believe we should wait?"

Flint thought for a moment. Time was of the essence if there was a traitor at the Salem Chapter House interfering with field operations. If he and Navarro left immediately, they might miss their package, but then again, the Order's couriers had a preternatural talent for finding Templars in the field.

"I feel that Mr. Navarro and I should leave immediately. If there is indeed a traitor in Salem's midst, then any delay could cost other Templars their lives."

"Very well. If your package arrives after your departure, we will direct it to Fort Ingalls. You and Ricardo should make your preparations. Make your way to the Cascadia Express station southwest of here and take the first available locomotive to Salem."

"Very good sir. If there was nothing else…?"

"Be extra vigilant, the both of you. My gut tells me this one will be bad."

"Of course, sir."

"God be with you."

Flint rose from his seat. He clicked his heels and dipped his head. "And also with you, sir."

4

Flint strode across Fort Marsing's courtyard. He had made haste to the Supernumerary wing after his meeting with Abernathy, but Navarro was not in his quarters. After asking around, he'd learned that his assistant was at the cantina. Flint checked his pocket watch. 9:30 a.m. He doubted that Navarro was drinking, but nonetheless offered a short prayer to St. Matthew Talbot in his mind.

As he approached the cantina, he could hear a man's voice coming from inside, a voice he didn't recognize. "It's the bottom of the hour and time for your news update," it said. "Our top story: Witch Hunter General Jeremiah Hickock asks for prayers as the Hunter death toll continues to climb. This morning the bodies of Templar Captain Hosea Hughes and his assistant Supernumerary Isaac Montoya were found..." Flint pushed open the swinging wooden doors and stepped inside.

"Templar on deck!" the bartender, Alfred Carruthers, bellowed.

"As you were," Flint said, before the Supernumeraries could rise from their seats. The cantina looked half full, with men and women seated at the tables or at the bar, enjoying breakfasts of eggs, bacon, and sausage, washing them down with mugs of coffee. In the corner, Navarro was sharing a table with two other Supernumeraries. They all wore the same unofficial uniform of leather body armor, denim jeans, and steel toed boots. Navarro's companions were Cassandra Henson and Pablo Ruiz, if Flint recalled correctly. Navarro's radio was in the center of the table, continuing to play the news update. Flint went up to the bar. Carruthers had retired from active duty as a Supernumerary shortly after Flint had taken his oath as a Templar. He was tall and lanky with a white horseshoe mustache.

"Morning, Captain Flint," Carruthers said, nodding. "Get you anything?"

"I should like coffee, if you please. Black."

Carruthers grinned. "A man after my own heart," he said. He removed a mug from a rack underneath the bar and poured Flint some coffee from a carafe that sat on a percolator on the countertop behind him.

"I take it that Mr. Navarro has become the entertainment," Flint said. The news update was over, and now the radio played an upbeat Spanish tune.

"Yup. Now it's just a matter of getting everyone to agree on a station to listen to."

Flint took a sip of his coffee. "Mr. Carruthers… may I ask you a personal question?"

Carruthers raised an eyebrow. "You can ask anything you like Captain, but I reserve the right to answer that it's none of your damn business."

Flint smiled. "I understand."

"Go ahead then."

"You served as assistant to General Abernathy in his younger years, correct?"

"Sure did. John and I worked together for thirty years, right up until he got promoted to General. I figured that was as good a time as any to retire. Being in the field as a Supernumerary is a young man's vocation."

"May I ask why you never undertook the trials to become a Knight Templar yourself?"

Carruthers thought for a few moments while Flint took another sip of coffee. He put his hands on the bar and said, "John used to ask me that all the time. Thing is, Templars have to deal with a lot more politics than us. You've got to play nice with mayors, cops, bureaucrats, bishops, Cardinals, the Emperor if you're really unlucky…"

Flint nodded.

"I was never interested in any of that. I joined up to fight. My job was to protect my partner, kill monsters, and crack witch skulls. I was damn good at it too if I do say so myself. Just give me a rifle and point me in the right direction. You boys in black can handle the rest. Besides, I never could get the hang of the High Speech. 'Have at you, vile witch,' just doesn't sound right coming from me. Now…" He leaned in closer to Flint. "What's eating you Captain? You didn't come to our side of the Fort just to listen to me reminisce."

Flint was silent for a moment. "Mr. Navarro and I work together."

"Yup."

"I confess that it is not easy for me to confide in others."

"So I've heard."

"Has… has Ricardo ever spoken about his father with you?"

Carruthers furrowed his brow. "Hmm… not so much as I recall. Name's Angelo. He's some kind of small business tycoon. Other than that, not much."

"You are not aware of any… difficulties between them?"

"Can't say that I am. Any particular reason you're gossiping about it with me instead of asking him?"

"There are complicating factors at work."

"Them complicating factors wouldn't happen to be them witch sisters of yours, would they?"

Flint looked up. "You know of them?"

Carruthers nodded. "Yeah. Rico told me all about them messing around with time last night."

"They appeared to me at Mass this morning."

"No shit?"

"Indeed. They told me that it was vital that Mr. Navarro make peace with his father, and that this was not meant for his ears."

Carruthers was silent for a moment. "You gonna listen to them? About not telling him?"

"I am not sure. I do not trust them, but I cannot deny that they proved themselves useful during our visit to Oglethorpe."

"Wise man once said, 'Trust but verify,'" Carruthers said. "My advice? Do whatever your gut tells you to do. If they really mean to help you, they'll figure out a work around if you break one of their little rules. And if they mean you harm, put a silver bullet in them for me."

"Ha!" Flint barked, causing several Supernumeraries to look up at the rare display of humor from the infamously dour Witch Hunter. He finished his coffee. "Thank you for your assistance Mr. Carruthers. I shall take your words under advisement. Now, I am sorry to interrupt this morning's entertainment, but duty calls for Mr. Navarro and I."

"Any time Captain. Where you boys headed off to this time?"

"Salem."

"God damn," Carruthers said, making the sign of the cross. "I'll say some extra prayers for you two."

Flint rose from his bar stool and strode to Navarro's table. Henson and Ruiz nodded to Flint and left the table to give them some privacy.

"Morning sir," Navarro said. "I'm guessing we got a case?"

"Indeed Mr. Navarro, we do. This time we shall be traveling to Salem."

Navarro whistled. "That's going to be a long... hey. Wait..."

Flint nodded. "Yes. The Sisters' prophecy. We are traveling west."

Navarro furrowed his brow. "Salem has its own Chapter House though. How come we're being sent out there?"

"General Hickock suspects that there is a traitor in their midst."

"I just heard about that on the radio." He shook his head. "Two dozen Hunters and assistants dead in two months. Yeah, that makes more sense if some bitch has gone over to the dark side."

"Our mission is to investigate Fort Ingalls for this traitor and put them to the torch."

Navarro chuckled. "If we were cops, we'd be the rat squad."

"I am aware of the poor reputation of internal affairs investigators, thank you."

"I didn't mean anything by it. When do we leave?"

"As soon as we are ready. We shall be taking the locomotive for this journey."

Navarro nodded. "You got it boss." He started to rise from his table when he hesitated. "Oh, I just remembered… the Sisters. They said we'd be getting a package soon."

"I remember, Mr. Navarro. However, this mission cannot wait. We shall depart as soon as possible. If we miss this package, General Abernathy informed me that it will be forwarded to Fort Ingalls."

"Alright, good enough. I'll go get my stuff."

5

Flint and Navarro stepped down from their carriage. The Marsing Train Station was less busy since the destruction of the city of New Rome months ago, but it was still a bustling scene. A clock tower tolled the hour, locomotive whistles screamed, conductors called out destinations and departure times, and travelers pushed their way onto their trains, businessmen in tailored suits and waistcoats, hobos in tattered rags who had earned or stolen enough money for a ticket, all hurrying toward home or away from it, toward new opportunities or away from ignominious failures. Navarro went to remove their travel cases from the carriage's baggage compartment while Flint proceeded to one of the ticket booths. No matter their walk of life, everyone in the station recognized Flint's hat and long coat. They parted ways like the Red Sea, allowing him to the front of the line. Whatever their religious background, or lack of it, they knew the

Witch Hunters were their first and best line of defense against the forces of the night.

"Good afternoon, Sir Templar," the ticket master said when Flint arrived.

"Good afternoon," he replied. "My assistant and I require two tickets to Salem, on the soonest available departure, if you please." He reached into one of his long coat pockets and took out his coin purse. He flipped a silver coin into the booth.

The attendant caught the coin and dropped it into a safe box. "Two tickets to Salem," he repeated. He tore off two red tickets from a thick roll and handed them to Flint, who put them into his waistcoat pocket.

"First class seats, sir," the attendant said.

"That was not necessary, but I thank you," Flint said. Navarro came to Flint's side and handed him his travel case. Flint gave Navarro his ticket. They pushed through the turn stile next to the ticket booth and entered the station proper.

"Platform seven..." Flint whispered to himself. He looked around. The brick hallways echoed with the tramp of hundreds of feet on the linoleum floors. It was crowded, but the people still gave the two men a respectful berth. The hallways converged into a central rotunda where station attendants manned telegraphs and a giant board with each platform's arrival and departure times where they would add or remove plaques announcing that a train was on time, delayed, or canceled. Flint saw a sign in the shape of an arrow pointing toward platforms one through nine.

"Come along, Mr. Navarro," Flint said. "I trust that you brought your radio?"

"Sure did," he replied. "Everybody at the bar was disappointed it's going away so soon, but they'll survive with the jukebox until we get back."

"I should think that they would have all of its selections memorized by now," Flint said as they made their way toward platform seven.

Navarro laughed. "Oh yeah. It's got a lot, but I think we've heard them all. I like twentieth and twenty-first century music, but eventually you want something new, you know?"

Flint smiled. "Ironically enough, I believe the problem is that your model is too new."

"What do you mean sir?"

"I once read that when the technology was in its infancy, it played physical record discs instead of the... programmed songs, I believe is the correct term. Presumably, one could remove old discs and supply new ones."

"Huh. Who'd have thought Fort Marsing would splurge on the fanciest music machines for us humble assistants?"

Presently, they reached Platform Seven. An attendant held up his hand and the two men stopped.

"I can get your bags for you gentlemen," he said. "Heading to Salem?"

"Indeed," Flint replied. He and Navarro handed off their travel cases, which contained changes of clothing, additional magazines for their pistols, and other tools of their violent trade. They climbed aboard and presented their tickets to one of the conductors. He scrutinized them and looked back up at the two men.

"First class, gentlemen, right this way," he said, motion-

ing for them to follow. He led them down the carpeted hallway of the train car. Through the windows on his left, Flint
saw passengers disembarking from recently arrived locomo-
tives. The Marsing station was the furthest east that railroad
tracks had been laid since the end of the Occult War and the
founding of the Cascadian Empire. The largest settlements
were Canyon Cove to the north and New Meridian to the
east, near the border with the United Mountain States. From
here, travelers could hire horses, carriages, or walk. Otherwise, the eastern half of Cascadia was mostly forests, grassy
plains, and mountains.

The conductor led them through several train cars, toward the front near the engine car. He stopped outside a
wooden door and slid it open, motioning for them to enter.
Flint and Navarro passed through the doorway and looked at
their travel arrangements. Navarro gave a low whistle. Two
adjoining rooms were separated by a thin plywood wall.
Each room had a couch, a table and chairs, and a twin bed.

"Dinner is at six," the conductor said. "Dining car is two
cars back from where we started."

"What is our estimated time of arrival to Salem?" Flint
asked.

"We have two scheduled stops in Burns and Bend. Other
than that, assuming the tracks are clear, estimated arrival is
11:30 p.m."

"Very good."

"Can I get you gentlemen anything else?"

"That will be all for now, thank you."

The conductor tipped his hat and shut the door behind
him. Flint removed his hat and tossed it onto the table. He

shrugged out of his long coat and draped it over a chair before sitting down. Navarro unslung his bold action rifle and ducked into his room. Flint removed a book from one of his coat pockets: *The Witch Hunter's Guide to North America.* He had read it many time over the course of his career, but he always returned to it, like an old friend. He'd wished that he'd had the presence of mind to take his Bible out of his travel case before handing it off to the attendant. There was something the conductor had said before he left that stuck with him, but he couldn't quite put his finger on it.

Navarro returned to Flint's room. "Hey, Silas?" he asked.

"What is it Mr. Navarro?"

"The conductor said we'd be stopping in Bend…"

"He did."

"I know we're kind of in a hurry on this case, but… well, do you think it would be okay if we got off there? Catch a later train, or maybe head out in the morning?"

"Whatever for?"

"Well, it's been a while since I've seen my family and…"

Of course, that was it. Navarro's family lived in Bend. Flint remembered now that Navarro had mentioned it when they were paired together five years ago, but otherwise the man didn't speak much about them. Flint's mind returned to what the Weird Sisters had told him, and Carruthers's advice. The Proctors had said that their message about Navarro making peace with his father was not meant for his ears. Carruthers had said that if they truly meant to be of help, they could work with or around whatever he decided to do. That clinched it for him.

"Mr. Navarro, may I ask you a personal question?"

"Do it."

"Are you on speaking terms with your father?"

Navarro blinked. He opened his mouth, shut it again. He furrowed his brow. "Yee-aa-hh," he said, drawing out the word. "Why wouldn't I be?"

"The Proctors appeared to me at Mass this morning."

Navarro sat down in the other chair, rested his elbows on the table. "What'd they have to say this time?"

"They said that it was vital that you make peace with your father."

Navarro leaned back, rubbed a hand over his thick black hair. He shrugged, spreading his arms wide. "Make peace with papa?"

"That is why I asked you about your relationship."

"That doesn't make any sense though. Papa and I get along great."

"You are certain? You rarely speak of your family."

"Not much to tell really. My mama passed away when I was twelve, papa remarried a few years later. I'm the oldest, the only son. I got two sisters and two half sisters. I don't get to see them often, but we write each other at least once a month."

"Forgive me, but could you tell me again what it is that your father does for his vocation?"

"He's got his own construction business. He and mama founded it together, and now my step-mama is the one who does the books and answers the phone, stuff like that."

Flint steepled his fingers. This was proving more difficult to solve than he'd anticipated. Perhaps Angelo Navarro held on to some sort of resentment toward his only son that Ricardo was not aware of.

"Curious," he said out loud.

"Hell yeah it is," Navarro replied. "I don't know what those three are talking about." He looked up at the ceiling. "Hey, sisters, if you can hear me? Just talk normal, say what you really mean."

"In any case, to answer your earlier question, yes, we shall disembark in Bend and pay a visit to your family. Perhaps their words will become clearer."

"Thanks boss. Heh… now that I think about it, I'm looking forward to introducing you to each other. I've told them a lot about you."

Flint raised an eyebrow.

"Only the stuff having to do with our cases."

Flint nodded.

"Well, sir, if there's nothing else, I'm going to go check out the dining car, see what's for lunch. You want me to get you anything?"

Flint waved him off. "No, thank you. Before you depart, however, I should like to keep your radio with me."

Navarro opened a pouch on his belt and removed the portable radio, handing it off to Flint. Navarro gave him a jaunty salute and left the room, shutting the door behind him.

Flint checked his pocket watch. 12:25 p.m. It was nearly the bottom of the hour, which meant it was time for the news. He adjusted the dial to 1530 AM and turned the radio on. It was the tail end of another jazz piece, one that Flint did not recognize this time. This song made him imagine a world free of witchcraft, monsters, devil worship, and all of the other horrors unleashed by Simon Magus nearly five hundred years ago. It made him feel hopeful for the future. He could never hope to exterminate every foul sorceress on earth, or even in Cascadia, but he could fulfill his duty here and stand before God at the Final Judgment and say that he had done His will.

The song trailed off. A three note jingle played.

"This is Mallory Proctor."

"With special correspondent Monica Proctor."

"Joining them is Madeline Proctor."

"And now for the news," they said in unison.

Flint scowled at the radio. "I begin to share my assistant's frustration with your indirect manner of speaking."

"You left before you received your package," Mallory said.

"And you told Ricardo something he was not meant to hear," Monica said.

"Tsk tsk. Whatever shall we do with you Silas?" Madeline said.

"You could explain yourselves. Or leave us in peace. I am in favor of one or both of those possibilities," Flint said.

"We are not at liberty to explain."

"Nor can we leave you be, however much we would like to."

"Orders are orders."

Flint raised an eyebrow. "And who, pray tell, would command the likes of you three to insert yourselves into the life of one sworn to hunt your kind?"

"It does not matter."

"Suffice it to say, one with a dark sense of humor."

"He is making our lives difficult, and so are you."

Flint gave a tight smile. "It pleases me to hear that."

The three sisters gave a deep sigh together. If he could have seen them, Flint imagined they would be rolling their eyes.

"We must make special arrangements now," Mallory said.

"More innocent people will suffer," Monica said.

"It's a pity you could not wait," Madeline said.

Flint gripped the radio, scowling at it. "If you three mean to harm the innocent, I swear I shall…"

"Not us."

"Your foe who awaits you in Salem."

"We suggest you spend the night in Bend."

Flint furrowed his brow. "But if the traitor in Salem is going to work their wicked schemes, should we not…"

"The Proctor Sisters signing off," they said together. Another three note jingle played, and the voice of Nick Sanderson broke in.

"That was our news at the bottom of the hour. Get ready for thirty minutes of uninterrupted classic music on Cascadia's number one station for…"

Flint turned the radio off. Curiouser and curiouser. The sisters confirmed to him what they had told Navarro: they were constrained by some higher power who commanded them to come into his life. Carruthers had been right; he had disobeyed their requests, but they were going to work around it. At a price. Other things they had said seemed contradictory: more innocent people would die, but he and Navarro should spend the night in Bend. Would it not be more prudent to push on to Salem that very night if lives were at stake?

He snorted in frustration. There was nothing to be done for now but be patient and enjoy the ride to Bend as best that he could.

6

Charles Flint sat before an ancient console deep within an underground bunker. The console had a glass screen, a keyboard with numeric keypad, and various gauges whose needles all rested at zero. He had with him an ancient tome bound in cured human flesh called *In Realis Magicae* – On The True Nature of Magic – and written by Abdul Hakim Nazari, a handpicked disciple of Simon Magus himself. Charles would never admit it to anyone other than himself, but he felt that his magical studies had left him woefully unprepared for the power promised by Nazari's long dead hand. The damned Witch Hunters, including his brother Silas, had seen to it that witches and wizards had a low life expectancy, which made it difficult to find experienced teachers. Most of what he knew of magic came in bits and pieces picked up from a petty magical criminal here, a paranoid recluse there… wholly unsuitable for the scope of his ambitions.

But then several months ago, he'd picked up a startling rumor: a practitioner of the dark arts within the city of New Rome had somehow acquired a copy of *In Realis Magicae*. The man had been a small time gangster, using his powers to steal valuables from the well-to-do, mug travelers, and rob trains. Then he'd merged with a demon and leveled New Rome before Silas and his little friends could put him down. Stranger still, he'd heard that the Witch Hunters had been assisted by a witch who had actually turned herself in to them. Charles snickered. What a pathetic wretch that woman must be. She had the power to bend reality to her will, and now she was making a pretense of renouncing that power. Idiot. She'd return to the fold soon enough, or wind up getting burned at the stake. Nobody willingly gave up that kind of power. It was intoxicating, addictive.

He heard clattering from the next room. His... friend? No, that was too strong a word. His associate, Lilian Turner, was poking around at the ancient machinery, digging through files, textbooks, and notes. She had been born Lilith Harkmoore in the year 2030. She was 503 years old now but didn't look a day over 29 thanks to a magical elixir she had concocted with the help of Simon Magus, a recipe which she had taught Charles to thank him for rescuing her from the demonic abyss into which Silas had hurled her months ago.

"What are you up to in there?" Charles called. Turner appeared in the doorway. Her long black hair was tied back in a ponytail, her blouse and jeans stained with dust and grime. Back in the twenty-first century, she and several members of the American military establishment had cast a spell over numerous bunkers like the one they were in now, both to prevent their enemies from using them and to preserve the contents from the ravages of time.

"Just checking out the computers, seeing what we have to work with. It's been a long time since I've been in here."

"These... computers... I understand they need access to the... the..."

"Internet."

"Yes, thank you. I thought they needed the internet to reach their full potential."

"Normally, yes. These were designed to have no links to the outside world though. The American government didn't want to risk hackers getting in."

Turner often spoke rapidly in jargon that Charles didn't fully understand, even when she tried to explain it. The chronological gap was simply too wide. It would be like trying to explain the internal combustion engine to a caveman. Charles smiled. He supposed that made him the caveman in the analogy.

"It's funny," Turner went on. "This was before even my time, but I read that up until the 2020s, these bunkers ran on 1970s era technology, with floppy disks, spools of tape, landline phones... all analog."

"Why? I thought the Americans had a mania for technological advancement."

"We... they did, but they also subscribed to the philosophy of 'if it ain't broke, don't fix it.' But they did fix it eventually. They updated their nuclear missile silos with cutting edge technology and kept tinkering with them up until the end of the Occult War."

Turner often demurred when Charles asked her about the pre-war world but he couldn't resist. "I have..."

Turner rolled her eyes. "Ask your questions. I'll answer what I can."

"Whatever happened to this internet?"

She laughed. "That's what IT men are for."

He furrowed his brow.

"Never mind," she said. "I'm honestly not sure how it began. Magus used it to great effect to spread his teachings in the early days. I remember when the first video appeared. Magus asked for a volunteer to come forth and be baptized. It was an Israeli school teacher, a perfectly ordinary woman. He sprinkled her with his elixir, and then she was conjuring fire and lightning on her fingertips."

"Amazing," Charles said.

Turner nodded. "Once people saw with their own eyes that magic was real and that Magus could gift that power to anyone, billions flocked to his banner. Once the war began, one of his first acts was to disrupt global communication systems. I don't know all the science of it – or the magic for that matter – but suddenly we couldn't access the internet. No matter what address you typed in the bar, the same page came up, one that read only 'Ye shall be as gods.' The war went on, people would restore it, it got disrupted again, and back and forth it went until Magus was gone. After the war ended, the survivors had more pressing issues to worry about, such as food, water, and electricity before they went about restoring a way to look at pornography and cat videos. After two or three generations they began to wonder why they ever needed it. Then they forgot that they ever had it."

Charles smirked. She'd tried explaining the internet to him before, and as he understood it, it compiled all the accumulated wisdom of mankind onto machines small enough to carry in one's pocket, but hardly anyone ever used it that way, instead using it to seek out vain amusements. Such a degenerate people didn't deserve such a wondrous invention. "Another question: if Magus was so powerful…"

"How did he fall? I've asked myself that hundreds of times since then. Understand that I wasn't present when it happened. I haven't left North America since I was still an ordinary mortal. Seems like the only thing everyone agrees on is that it happened in Italy. Other than that, consult a hundred sources and get a hundred answers."

"I have to ask: what was he like? You met him in person."

Turner smiled. "I've had centuries to think about it, and it's still difficult to put into words. He was like the ten most charismatic men in human history rolled into one. He had this way of speaking to you that made you feel like he was an old friend that you've dearly missed, even if there are thousands of other people present. He offered humanity a brighter future. He could lead us back into Eden. He was going to right the wrong that God had wreaked upon Adam and Eve, the wrong He holds us responsible for even though we weren't even born yet. I'd have followed that man into Hell itself."

Charles felt tempted to skewer her by asking, *So why didn't you,* but said instead, "I understand he made it to the Gates of Eden."

She nodded. "He and his Host did battle with the Archangel Uriel. They failed."

"But his work goes on."

"Yes." She sighed. "At least, I like to think it does. If there are any other witch or wizard survivors of the Occult War, I haven't met them. I sometimes wonder if I'm the only living witch on earth who heard the Gospel of Magus from the man himself."

"I take it that you haven't found many new recruits."

"No," she said. "What I said earlier, about Magus? When he was gone, it was like someone had flipped a switch. It was everyone for themselves. Every middling hedge wizard and fortune telling hag fancied themselves warlords, all trying to carve out their own petty fiefdom from the ruins. Although…" She laughed. "I suppose I shouldn't throw stones. I made a go of it myself at first. My followers and I overran Washington, D.C. a few months after Magus's defeat. The United States of America… born July 4, 1776, died July 5, 2076."

Charles nodded. He recalled that Silas's favorite history book growing up had been *300 Years and a Day: The Story of The United States of America.* "Why did you give it up?" he asked. "The warlord life, I mean."

"Because I grew tired. Tired of defending my territory from every boy and girl who could cast a few spells and thought to earn their reputation by overthrowing the great and terrible Lilith Harkmoore. And then to top it all off, the Church got her sheep organized."

"The Witch Hunters."

"Yes. Nothing was ever the same after that. Even I'll admit that the Hundred Years Darkness was brutal, but we could practice the craft openly. Then the Church proclaimed a new Crusade against us. Before, we'd occasionally encounter a few lone wolves with rifles who wanted to be heroes. They were never a problem. Then the so called

Knights Templar came, with swords that could absorb our spells... suffice it to say, they pushed us back. It was around the late twenty-second century that most of us decided to begin practicing in secret. And here we are."

"And here we are indeed," Charles said, rising from his seat. He paced back and forth, hands behind his back. "The Witch Hunters are an organized fighting force, while we remain an unorganized rabble torn by paranoia and infighting."

"It's not paranoia if they really are out to get you."

He smiled. "Yes, I suppose that is true. Out of curiosity, how is it that you ran afoul of my brother?"

Lilian scowled. "I hate to admit it, but I only have myself to blame. It was a few months ago. I had been living in Canyon Cove for the last twenty years. Silas and his little assistant came to town on... Victory over Magus Day. They were simply passing through, and I thought it would be a good opportunity to strike against the enemy when their guard was down. My pupil at the time tried to talk me out of it, but I didn't listen."

"What did you think of him?"

"He's as arrogant, self-righteous, and bloodthirsty as any Witch Hunter I've ever met. But he has an uncommonly strong will. I couldn't break him, even when I conjured up his most painful memory. He even managed to turn my late husband against me."

"I figured into his most painful memory, didn't I?"

She nodded. "As a matter of fact, you did. You've heard my story. I'd appreciate hearing yours."

Charles felt a tug in his mind. A soft blue glow emanated

from his hip pocket. Reaching in, he withdrew a small blue jewel that resembled a fine cut sapphire. The gem's glow pulsed with his heartbeat.

"That shall have to wait, my dear," he said. "I need to speak with an associate of mine."

"Shall I leave you two alone?"

"That won't be necessary. In fact, I'd like you to listen."

He set the jewel on top of the console, waved his fingers over it while whispering a spell. A column of light rose from the jewel and spread out, wide enough to encompass a human being. Within the column there appeared the silhouette of a woman. She wore a flowing long coat that reached the top of her ankles and a tall, wide brimmed hat.

"Good afternoon, Alice," Charles said.

The woman, Alice, nodded in acknowledgment. "Good afternoon, Master Flint."

"I trust you have more good news?"

Alice shrugged. "That remains to be seen."

Charles raised an eyebrow. "Oh?"

"I believe Hickock suspects there's a serpent in his garden."

Charles sighed. It was bound to happen sooner or later. For all of his vices, Hickock wasn't stupid, unfortunately. "Does he suspect you?"

"I don't think so, but he's guarding his thoughts more carefully than he used to. It's getting more difficult to read him without him noticing. I'm still able to access case files and written orders… except for a letter he sent the other day."

"Do you know where it was sent at least?"

"Yes… to the Chapter House at Fort Marsing in the east. Addressed to General Abernathy, eyes only."

Charles's nostrils flared. Fort Marsing. Silas.

"I can't be certain of course, but if I had to guess…"

"He's asking for an outside investigator to visit Salem," Charles said.

"Right," Alice said. "How would you like me to handle this?"

Charles paused. There were hundreds of Witch Hunters stationed at Fort Marsing. It was improbable that out of those hundreds of Knights Templar, Abernathy would send Silas. He chuckled to himself. Improbable but not impossible. Charles had followed his brother's career for the last several years and the elder Flint had demonstrated an irritating talent for prevailing no matter how steeply the odds were against him.

"Sir?" Alice asked.

Charles shook his head. "When exactly did the letter go out?"

"Two nights ago."

More than enough time to go from Salem to Marsing. The investigator was no doubt on their way now. He or she would catch a train at the Cascadia Express station near the fort. "Carry on for now. Kill as many Templars as you can."

"The investigator too?"

"If he manages to discover your identity, then yes, kill him. But hold off for now. Discrediting him, humiliating him, breaking him… yes, I think that would serve our purposes just as well. Better, perhaps."

Alice paused. Her silhouette disguised her facial expressions, but Charles expected her to look skeptical. "This... this sounds personal, sir."

"I don't know what you're talking about. You have your orders."

"Of course, Master Flint." Alice's image shimmered and faded from sight. The column of light returned to the jewel and winked out. Charles took it off the console and stuck it back in his pants pocket.

Lilian crossed her arms. "So... Master Flint, is it?"

Charles smiled. "Yes... I met Alice several years ago. She's a Templar at the Salem Chapter House who was ordered to bring me in, believe it or not. It turned out that she had a talent for magic that she never knew about until I gave her a push. I offered to teach her how to use her new power, and she agreed."

"You must have been very persuasive."

"I like to think so. I explained my long term plans to her and how she could have a place in them. For now, her talents are best used to undermine our mutual enemies from the inside. I gave her the codename 'Alice' because she's stepped through the looking glass, so to speak."

"Your long term plans..."

"Indeed. And since we're on the subject, now is the perfect time for me to offer you a proposal."

Lilian snorted. "Don't misunderstand me. I'll always be grateful to you for saving me from the abyss. But I've taught you the recipe for my life-extension formula. I've brought you to this bunker. We're more than even, as far as I'm concerned."

"Yes, absolutely," Charles nodded. "You are free to go whenever you please."

Lilian began to turn.

"I'm curious though," Charles went on. "What will you do when you leave this place?"

She stopped, turned to face him again. She thought for a moment, then shrugged. "Same thing I've done for the last few centuries I expect. Find a new city to take up residence. Practice the craft in secret. Try to recruit new students."

"Marry again?"

She shook her head. "Someday, maybe... but not for a long time. Not after my last husband."

"I'll tell you what," Charles said. "Why not stay for a bit longer? At least hear me out. If you decide you don't want to be a part of my plan, then we'll shake hands and go our separate ways. But I'm confident that you'll want to stick around. A witch of your power and experience on my side would be invaluable."

Lilian said nothing.

"And it's not like you've got anywhere else to be right now."

She sighed. "You got me there. Alright, fine, Charles Flint. Tell me about these big plans of yours. After five hundred years of life, I'm certain that I've heard them all before, so you'll have to work at it to impress me."

Charles laughed. "You may have heard the plan before... but you've never heard it from me before."

Flint checked his pocket watch. 7 p.m. The sun hung low in the sky, but the summer heat had not let up. The train gave out a long whistle as it began slowing. The trip had been uneventful, and Flint offered a short prayer of thanksgiving to God. Through the window, Flint saw the first signs of civilization since the stop in Burns hours ago. The Bend train station was at the eastern edge of the city. Already Flint could see various hotels, saloons, general goods stores, gun shops, massage parlors (*Brothels more likely,* he thought), and everything else the discerning traveler could need. Flint snorted. The Occult War should have proven beyond any reasonable doubt that God existed, and His laws must be obeyed, yet the large cities continued to remain dens of iniquity. Aristotle had called man the rational animal, but Flint thought the rationalizing animal would be nearer the mark. The train shuddered to a halt, the engine giving one final blast of steam.

"Bend!" one of the conductors yelled outside in the hallway. "All passengers destined for Bend! The train departs for Salem in one hour! All passengers destined for Bend…"

Flint adjusted his gun belt, straightened his hat. He slid the door to his compartment open. Navarro was no doubt in the dining car, either enjoying an adult beverage or chatting up a pretty female passenger, most likely both. Flint made his way down the hallway toward the nearest exit. He didn't know his way around the city, so there was nothing for it but to wait for his assistant. He exited the car and stepped off onto the platform.

Other passengers disembarked with him. They gave him

a wide berth, casting nervous sidelong glances as they hurried on their way. The Church's political influence was stronger in the western half of the Empire, but Flint suspected that the faith was weaker. The west was wealthier than the east. Flint could literally smell it in the air: automobiles were more commonplace here along with their accompanying smog. It was one of several reasons why he avoided the west whenever he could.

He looked around and saw Navarro several car lengths away, speaking to a conductor. The conductor stepped back onto the train. Flint made his way through the crowds to join his assistant. When he arrived, the conductor came back down with both of their travel cases.

"Mr. Navarro," Flint said, nodding.

"Hey boss," he said. "Just getting our stuff, and we can be on our way."

"Is our destination far from here?"

"Yeah, afraid so. We should probably try to catch a cab."

"Very well. Lead the way if you please."

They slung their travel cases over their shoulders and Navarro led Flint out of the station toward the city street. Several automobiles were parked by the curb, uniformed drivers holding up signs with family names on them. When Flint had visited Mountain Home Air Force Base, he had seen several twenty-first century automobiles that had been magically preserved along with the rest of the base. Automobiles manufactured since the end of the Occult War had sharper angles and rougher machine marks, not at all like the smooth curves of the older models.

Navarro stopped at a section of the curb where there

were no waiting autos. He looked back the way they had come. Putting two fingers in his mouth, he gave a shrill whistle. He waved his hand.

"Hey! Taxi!" he shouted.

A boxy automobile painted with black and yellow checkers pulled up to the curb. The driver was an overweight, unshaven man wearing a flat cap and smoking a malodorous cigar. He blew a large cloud of smoke out the driver's side window before giving Flint and Navarro a skeptical look.

"Where you holy rollers headed?" he asked.

"River West," Navarro said.

"You got it," the driver replied. Leaving the engine running, he got out of the cab, went to the back, and opened the trunk. Navarro handed off both of their travel cases to the driver. He put them into the trunk as the two men got into the back of the cab. Flint's nose wrinkled at the stench of the driver's cigar smoke. He had nothing against tobacco use per se, but the cab stank of years' worth of what was no doubt the cheapest brand on the market.

The cabbie got back into the driver's seat and shut the door. "You guys mind?" he asked, holding up his cigar.

"You may indulge if you wish," Flint said. "I do not believe it could make this vehicle smell any worse."

The cabbie laughed, stuck the half-smoked cigar back in his mouth, and lit it with a flick of his lighter. He manipulated the gear shift lever and the cab pulled away from the curb and into traffic. Navarro leaned back and draped his arm over the back of the seat.

"I think you're going to like my papa sir," he said. "Very devoted to the Church."

"That is good to hear," Flint replied. "I hope that we are not imposing by visiting unannounced."

"Oh, you kidding? They'll probably shit a brick."

"Er… I take that to mean they will be pleased to see us."

Navarro laughed. "You got a gift for understatement boss. I haven't come by to visit since… since we took out whatshername. You know, that witch up north in Hermiston."

Flint nodded. "Samantha Quinn. That was a near run thing. I am pleased that you were able to make the time."

They were silent for a few moments. The cabbie, despite his rough appearance, proved to be a skilled driver. Flint had never visited Bend before, and he took in everything through the smoke begrimed windows. The sun would not be setting for another hour or two, but streetlights and neon signs were lit up on every block. Young couples dined on outdoor patios, drunkards gathered outside of bars to smoke cheap cigarettes, local police walked their beats. Up ahead on the left, Flint saw an imperial barracks, guardsmen standing at attention outside the gates, the blue, white, and green flag of Cascadia hanging limp in the summer twilight. The bulk of the Empire's population resided in the western half of the country, along with a more visible imperial presence. Flint could count on one hand the number of times he'd seen the Emperor's Finest in the east.

"You alright sir?" Navarro asked.

Flint shook himself from his reverie. "Yes, I am fine."

"First time to Bend?"

"Yes."

"What do you think?"

"Hmph. I see an abundance of wealth and a paucity of faith."

Navarro chuckled. "You say that about every big city, boss."

The cabbie cleared his throat. "You, ah, you boys aren't here on official business, are you?"

Flint looked up. "Should we be, master driver?"

"Nah," Navarro said. "Here to visit family."

"That's a relief," the cabbie said. "I, uh, just wanted you to know that, ah, my family and I attend Mass every Sunday, and there's never been any witchcraft in either branch of…"

"Yes, yes, I trust that you are a faithful son of the Church," Flint interrupted. "How near are we to our destination?"

"Not too much further," Navarro said.

The cab stopped at a red light. The driver looked at them in his review mirror. "You mind if I ask you fellas a question?"

"If you must," Flint said.

"How is it you always know where to be?"

"I beg your pardon?"

The light turned green, and the cab pulled forward. "Ok, like, for example? When I was a kid, there were rumors about this witch who lived in Awbrey Butte. One night, me and my friends saw storm clouds, lightning and shit, circling above her house and only her house. Not a cloud in the sky otherwise. Next morning, a Witch Hunter and his, ah, what do you call them? One of his sidekicks was with him."

"We're Supernumeraries," Navarro said.

"Yeah, sure."

Flint gave a tight smile. "The Knights Templar of the Order of Saint Benedict possess the finest system of couriers in the world. Even we are often surprised by their talent for locating us in the field. No doubt a courier found your Witch Hunter near this place and redirected him here."

"Can't you just use the phone or the telegraph or something?"

"Sometimes we do, sure," Navarro said. "Wires can be cut though, and we don't got as many technicians in the east. Couriers though, they'll crawl through Hell if that's what it takes. They always find us, no matter where we are."

"Huh," the cabbie said. "It's like my dad always said, 'Don't fuck with the guys who deliver the mail.'"

"Indeed," Flint said.

The cab rattled over a bridge that spanned the Deschutes River which ran through the center of the city. Flint wondered what Bend had been like before the Occult War remade the face of the earth. He knew that the former Oregon country had been one of the less populated regions of the old United States. Now it was the seat of an Empire that was the richest nation in the west. He supposed that Columbia in the far eastern half of North America might be wealthier still, but he had no desire to traverse the Dead Lands to find out.

"River West," the driver called. "Now where to?"

Navarro gave him an address. After another few turns, the driver eased the cab to a stop outside a white two story house with an immaculate lawn and a rusty brown pickup truck in the driveway. Flint gave the driver a silver coin as they exited the cab. The driver popped the trunk, and they took out their travel cases. The cab pulled away from the curb, diesel exhaust and the driver's cigar smoke billowing in its wake. Navarro coughed.

"Been out east so long, my lungs are growing back," he said.

Flint didn't think that was the way the human body worked but said nothing. "I shall defer to you tonight Mr. Navarro. Lead the way."

"Uh, actually sir, I was wondering if you would do me a favor?"

"Oh?"

Navarro leaned in to whisper in Flint's ear. When he had finished, Flint raised an eyebrow.

"Surely you jest."

"That's the idea."

Flint sighed. "Very well."

8

Charles paced back and forth. Lilian was seated before one of the computer consoles, leaning back in her chair. She'd asked Charles to explain his plan to her. He'd done it for dozens of other witches and wizards over the years, but none of them matched the accumulated wisdom of Lilian's five hundred years of life. He would have to put his best face forward. If his suspicions were correct, he needed her to unlock a crucial aspect of his plan. He knew he would figure something out if she demurred, but all the better if she cooperated.

"Tell me," he said, "What became of all those petty magical warlords you mentioned earlier? Where did all of Magus's followers disappear to?"

She shrugged. "After the Witch Hunters were founded, many of us went into hiding. Some decided to build cabins in the woods or to live in caves to continue practicing their craft. Others, like me, stayed in the cities, practiced in secret. Many of the others got married, had children. That's how the talent for magic has been passed down throughout the centuries."

Charles stopped. He looked at her. "I've known I had the talent for magic ever since I was a boy. Are you saying...?"

She nodded. "Yes. Somewhere in your family tree there was a witch or a wizard before you."

Charles threw back his head and laughed.

"Is that really so funny?" she asked.

He pinched the bridge of his nose as his laughter subsided. "No... I was just thinking of how poor Silas would react if only he knew he had an 'unclean' ancestor." Charles knew that neither of his parents nor his brother had the spark for practicing the dark arts, but oh how things would be so different if any of them had.

"You were saying?" Lilian prompted.

"Yes... I myself was always curious about that, where they went. Men and women who have the power to bend reality, to influence the mind, to raise the dead, to reshape matter as they will... and yet we hide in the shadows and keep our talents a secret."

"Abuse a dumb animal enough and eventually it will fight back," Lilian said. "I know where you're going with this. You think we should rule the world, keeping the populace in check through sheer terror. I can assure you from personal experience that that strategy never ends well. Not even I can fight off an entire city single handedly, let alone a nation or a continent."

Charles smiled. "You're half right. I do think that we should rule, but nothing so grandiose as world domination. Not yet anyway."

Lilian crossed her arms. "Go on."

He had her now. "We keep to ourselves. We are isolated, hiding in our lairs, hoping that no one catches on to our experiments. But eventually the Witch Hunters come for us. We live alone and we die alone."

"That's the nature of this life."

"But it doesn't have to be," Charles said. "The Templars work in pairs: the Witch Hunter and the Supernumerary. They live in their Chapter Houses alongside hundreds of their compatriots. We, on the other hand, are solitary creatures. We think we're more than a match for two ordinary men or women armed with some ancient firearms and a fancy blade. Sometimes that is true. More often it's not."

Lilian frowned, no doubt thinking back on her encounter with Silas and his little assistant.

"But suppose," Charles said, gesturing with his hands, "Just suppose... we didn't operate alone?"

"What do you mean?"

"What I mean is that we practitioners of the dark arts need greater coordination. We need to support and sustain one another."

"To what end?" she asked. "As I said, I haven't had much luck in passing on the teachings of Simon Magus. Some want to rule, like you. Some want to be left alone to pursue research and experiments. Some are content living like ordinary human beings. That is another truth that I can attest to from experience: organizing witches and wizards is akin to herding cats."

"All true. We all have a common enemy however: the Witch Hunters. They have been so successful in their work partly because they have the strength of numbers. They share a common purpose. They work together so that the unwashed masses can be free to live their pointless little lives."

Lilian raised an eyebrow. "So... what, you want to found your own Order?"

Charles shook his head. "You're not thinking big enough."

"I'm not following you."

"You were born in the United States of America. Correct me if I'm wrong, but it was originally thirteen colonies. One of their mottos was, 'Join or Die.' They all shared a common enemy: their mother country of England. They fought together. They bled together. And thirteen separate colonies joined to form..."

Her eyes widened. "A nation."

"Exactly."

"A nation... with you at its head, I presume?"

He smiled. "Well, I wasn't going to bring it up yet but..."

She laughed. "Charles Flint, the wizard George Washington."

"How many men can claim to be the father of their country?"

She was silent for a few moments, thinking. "Well," she said at last, "I have to admit that I admire your ambition. However, I see a few problems with your little scheme." She began ticking them off one by one with her fingers. "First, you have no army. A nation only exists to the extent that it can project power. Second, even if you had an army, you have no territory for it to defend. Third, even if you had an army and territory, the Church would never allow a nation of magic users to exist. It would call for another Crusade and they would win, through either conquest or attrition."

Charles nodded. "All good points. Now, allow me to retort. You already know of Alice, but she is not the only one of my followers in high places. I have allies within the governments of both Cascadia and the United Mountain States. Thanks to them and to your old friend Nazari..." He patted his copy of *In Realis Magicae*. "I think that I will be able to expand my recruitment efforts by an order of magnitude."

"Go on."

"Secondly, I believe the territory in which we find ourselves right now will suit my purposes quite nicely."

"We're in the middle of the United Mountain States."

"A minor detail. And thirdly, I don't think the Church would call for a Crusade against us. Not after a demonstration."

She furrowed her brow. "A demonstration of what?"

"That's where you come in. If you're willing, that is."

"Me? What is it that you think I can do for you?"

"You're looking at it," Charles said, spreading his arms.

"What are you... no."

"Yes."

"Impossible."

"Why? You said it yourself when we arrived here: you and your allies preserved this place, these weapons, for a rainy day. Look around you Lilian. A storm is gathering. And we shall be at its center."

Lilian took a deep breath. "With all due respect, I don't think you fully understand the nature of nuclear weapons. Yes, you're right, we did preserve several bunkers like these throughout North America, partly to ensure our enemies couldn't use them. But those allies of mine are long dead. I don't have the technical knowledge to operate these systems by myself. And even if I did, what would be the point?"

"The point, my dear, is insurance. Eventually I will publicly proclaim the birth of my new nation. And you're right, the Church and the nations of the world will be outraged that our kind might have a home of our own. But they will not dare risk a war with me when they witness the full destructive power of the old world. I read history too, and there was a term for it back then: Mutually Assured Destruction. Except in this case, I would maintain a monopoly on these weapons."

"You don't know that. The United States was not the only old world nation that possessed nuclear weapons."

"That is a risk I am willing to take."

"That's fine for you, but again, I don't think you fully understand the nature of these weapons. They're not simply bombs. They would leave the entire area radioactive. You could annihilate your enemies with the push of a button but all you would get for your trouble is poisoned, uninhabitable land."

"I admit that the thought of destroying the Witch Hunters in one stroke is sorely tempting, but you're right. If I destroyed a city – I believe the slang term is nuked? – then the nations of the world would indeed declare total war. I believe I would prevail in the end, but I'm not interested in ruling over the ashes. What I'm proposing is simply a demonstration. The target I had in mind is within the Dead Lands. This would accomplish two goals: everyone gets to witness a terrific explosion for one. I understand these devices leave behind clouds in the shape of mushrooms? And second, I kill a few thousand undead. Who could quibble with that?"

Lilian said nothing.

"Think of it," Charles said. "A nation of our own. You would be free to spread the teachings of Magus, if that is what you wish. Our kind would be free to live their lives and practice their craft openly, never having to look over their shoulder, never having to worry about the damned Witch Hunters."

Lilian said nothing.

"My new nation would be the shining jewel of the north. An oasis of light and wisdom. A beacon to show mankind the way to the future. And we are the future Lilian. Magic has made us the next step in human evolution. And thanks to your elixir of life, we will live forever, lead our people forever."

She rose from her seat. She looked around the bunker, at the ancient consoles that still looked brand new after being preserved in magical amber for five hundred years. Charles controlled his breathing. He had a feeling she knew more about these systems than she let on. He had no doubt that he would learn how to use them as well, given time. And thanks to her magical elixir, he had all the time in the world now. But with her help, he could avoid much of the error that came with trial and error.

Finally, she turned to face him. The corners of her mouth quirked upward in the beginning of a smile.

"Well," she said, "I guess the first thing we need to do is turn the computers on."

9

Angelo Navarro sat at the desk in his study. Before him was a sheaf of papers detailing the latest project his construction firm had taken on: a Chapter House for the Knights Templar of the Order of Saint Benedict. Southern Cascadia's territory was divided roughly in half, with the Fort Ingalls Chapter House covering the west, the Fort Marsing Chapter House handling the east. The Emperor had personally requested that a third Chapter House be established on the outskirts of Bend. An additional Chapter House, centrally located, would ease the case loads of both east and west, and hopefully make life a bit easier for his only son, Ricardo.

Ricardo. Angelo took off his reading glasses and leaned back in his chair. It had been four months since he'd last seen his son in person. The last letter he'd received had been two weeks ago. Ricardo and his partner Silas had been invited to check out an old American military base that was still in one piece. Angelo shook his head. If he knew his son, he'd surely run into trouble out there. There was no way anything American-built could still be intact after nearly 500 years, not through natural means.

He heard sizzling come from the kitchen, the delicious aroma of beef wafting through the living room and into his study. It was nearly dinner time, and Lucía was preparing carne asada. She wasn't as good a cook as his dearly departed first wife, Magdalena, but near enough that he couldn't help thinking of her at every meal. He loved Lucía dearly – she had given him two beautiful daughters – but he still missed Magdalena every day.

There was a knock at the door. Not a gentle rap, but the pounding of a fist. He furrowed his brow. He wasn't expecting any visitors. "I'll get it," he called.

The pounding resumed. He began to worry. Whoever it was, it sounded like they had urgent business. "Alright, alright, I'm coming," he shouted. He opened the door and looked up into the eyes of a giant.

No, not a giant. The man's hat made him look taller than he was. And what a man. Icy blue eyes glared at Angelo from beneath the brim of that Templar hat. He was a trim figure but still broad in the chest and shoulders. He wore a long black coat over a white dress shirt, black waistcoat, and black trousers. On his belt were two small pistols and a sword. He was a young man but the deep frown lines in his angular face made him look older. His mouth was set in a thin lipped scowl, as though he felt defiled at setting foot on Angelo's doorstep.

"Angelo Navarro," the man said.

Angelo opened his mouth to speak but nothing came out.

"Angelo Navarro, I have something for you," the man said, stepping inside. Angelo backed up a few steps, at a loss for words. A Templar? Here? What on earth was going on?

The man stopped. His scowl eased a bit, the corners of his mouth turning up in the ghost of a smile. "May I present your son, Ricardo Navarro."

"Hey, hey!" Navarro yelled as he strode through the doorway. The elder Navarro, Angelo, stood stock still, mouth agape. Flint had to admit that the resemblance was uncanny. Angelo's hairline was receding. He had a thick mustache. There was more crinkling about the eyes. But otherwise, he and Ricardo could have been twins.

"Ri... Rico?" Angelo whispered.

"Hey papa," Navarro said, smiling.

"Rico!" Angelo cried. He rushed forward and enveloped his son in a mighty bear hug.

"What's going on out there?" called a female voice from deeper inside the house.

"Lucía! Look who's back!" Angelo yelled. A petite woman emerged from the kitchen, thin, with mocha skin and lustrous black hair.

"Rico!" she shouted, going to join her husband and stepson. "Girls! Girls! Get down here now!"

Footsteps pounded upstairs, making their way to the stairwell. Flint saw two teenage girls at the top of the stairs. Their eyes widened when they saw Flint.

"What's going on ma..."

"Rico!"

The girls squealed in delight and tore down the staircase, ran to Navarro, both embracing him at the same time, knocking the wind from him.

"Oh, hey, easy there," Navarro laughed. "I'm not getting any younger."

Flint stood at a respectful distance. He felt a tug at his heart. The scene reminded him of happier times from his youth when his own family was intact. Only God knew when or if he would ever experience this kind of joy again.

Navarro disengaged from his half-sisters. "Papa, mama, Daniela, Elena... I'd like to introduce you to my partner: Captain Silas Flint."

Flint clicked his heels, acknowledged the Navarro family with a nod. "At your service."

The older half-sister gave Flint an odd look he couldn't quite understand, a look he'd gotten from Zelda Fletcher on several occasions during their trip to Mountain Home Air Force Base weeks ago. "Uh... hi..." she said, blushing.

The younger half-sister stepped forward to give Flint a vigorous handshake. "Elena," she said. "Don't mind Daniela. She gets tongue tied around..."

"Shut up!" Daniela hissed.

"A pleasure," Flint replied to Elena.

"Captain Flint!" Angelo said, giving Flint another handshake. "Rico has told us so much about you!"

"Only the interesting parts I trust."

Angelo chuckled as Lucía came forward. "Oh Captain, I was just preparing dinner. Please, won't you join us?"

"It would be my honor, Mrs. Navarro."

"Please, call me Lucía."

Navarro laughed. "Good luck with that mom. It's like pulling teeth to get him to call me Ricardo."

"Girls," Angelo said. "One of you get on the telephone, invite your sisters over. Call your grandfather too." Daniela and Elena left the front parlor, pushing each other, arguing over who would get to use the phone.

"Please, please, come in," Angelo said, motioning for Flint and Navarro to make themselves at home. Navarro unslung the bolt action rifle from his back, unbuckled his gun belt which held his pistol and tomahawk. Flint shrugged out of his long coat and hung it and his hat on a row of hooks next to the front door. Angelo led them into his study. Flint was impressed by the number of bookshelves surrounding the desk. A cursory glance at the book spines revealed many technical manuals for construction, carpentry, electrical wiring, plumbing, and roofing. Another shelf was packed with devotional manuals, lives of the saints, and history books. Angelo led them to a closet which held a safe. He turned the dial until the safe clicked and he pulled open the large metal door. Inside was an ancient shotgun, a pistol, and boxes of ammunition. Flint and Navarro handed him their weapons. Angelo hesitated when Flint handed him his sword.

"May I?" he asked.

Flint nodded.

Angelo slowly withdrew the blade from its scabbard. To the naked eye, it was an ordinary, double edged arming sword. He squinted at the letters engraved on the blade near the hilt.

"C.S.S.M.L…" he read aloud. He turned the blade over, saw the letters on the other side. "N.D.S.M.D…"

"Crux Sacra Sit Mihi Lux, Nunquam Draco Sit Mihi Dux," Flint said. "May the Holy Cross be my light, may the dragon never be my guide."

Angelo turned the sword around in his grip, studying it from different angles. "These swords, they can absorb magic?"

"Yes," Flint said. "When a candidate passes the necessary trials to become a Knight or Lady Templar, they are presented with a sword that has been blessed by the Holy Father himself. If you will observe the cross guard, you should see more letters."

"P.P.L.XVI."

"This particular sword was among the first to be blessed by His Holiness Pope Leo XVI. I took the Templar oath shortly after he was elected to the papacy."

Angelo gave the sword another once over before sliding it back into its scabbard and placing it in the gun safe. "What about you Rico? Will you ever receive such a blade?"

Navarro shrugged. "I will if I ever take the trials."

Angelo raised an eyebrow. "Will you? Take the trials?"

"Maybe. Some day. I don't know."

"I see."

Flint said nothing.

"Well!" Angelo said, clapping his hands. "Enough of that for now. You two must be exhausted after your journey. May I get you a drink?"

"I shall have a glass of red wine, if you have any," Flint said.

"And you son?"

"Don't suppose you got any Newport Ale?"

Angelo laughed. "Of course. It's become my favorite as well. Come! Come, I want to hear all of the good stuff you leave out of your letters."

"You got all night?"

Twenty minutes later there was another knock at the door. Angelo's two daughters by his first wife entered accompanied by their husbands. Behind them was an elderly gentlemen whom Flint imagined Navarro would strongly resemble in another fifty years or so.

"Captain Flint," Angelo said. "May I present my other daughters: Rita Callahan and her husband Alex, Maria Salazar and her husband Antonio. And this tough old buzzard is my father, Ernesto Navarro."

"Mucho gusto," Ernesto said, extending his hand.

"El gusto es mío, señor," Flint replied, giving Ernesto a firm handshake. *"We may continue in Spanish, if you prefer."*

Ernesto chuckled. "You speak Spanish like a Spaniard," he said in thickly accented English.

Flint smiled. "My Spanish language instructor hailed from Barcelona."

"Captain Flint, it's a real honor," said Rita, giving a curtsey while Alex stepped forward to give Flint another handshake. "Rico's told us a lot about you."

"So I have heard," Flint said, giving his assistant the side eye.

"Only the most exciting parts," Alex said.

"Now that you're here, he can tell us the embarrassing parts!" Maria said.

Flint's nostrils flared.

"Don't worry about it, Captain," Antonio laughed. "It's all in good fun."

"Yes, quite."

"Well, if that's how you feel sir, then I got some good ones for everybody!" Navarro said, laughing.

The Navarro family shifted their attention to him, and Flint took the opportunity to look around the living room. A family photograph was on the coffee table. There was Angelo, looking considerably younger, alongside a beautiful woman, presumably his first wife. Between them was a young Ricardo, his hair slicked back, wearing a tiny suit, flanked by Rita and Maria who were both in white dresses. Their First Communion, perhaps?

On a table next to the recliner was another family photograph. This one had an older Angelo with Lucía, Ricardo, Rita, Maria, and two girls who appeared to be nine or ten years old: Daniela and Elena. Lovely family. He had no doubt that they had their fair share of ups and downs, like any other family. He didn't think they came anywhere close to those of his family.

"Captain Flint?"

He looked up. Lucía had brought him another glass of red wine.

"Thank you, Mrs. Navarro," he said, accepting the offered glass.

"Please, call me Lucía. I insist."

"Very well... Lucía. You may address me as Silas."

"I will Silas," she replied, smiling.

"I was admiring your family photographs."

She nodded. "Angelo is a good man. He works hard to take care of us."

"How did you meet?"

"Through my brother, Ignacio. He and Angelo worked together for several years. After Magdalena passed away, Angelo was depressed for a while. Ignacio helped him through it, and I'd watch the kids while they were out. Eventually, Angelo and I fell in love."

Flint nodded. "I expect that Ricardo will endeavor to embarrass me tonight. If you would care to share anything with which I may return fire, I would be most appreciative."

She laughed. "Oh don't worry about that Silas. You'll hear plenty over dinner."

10

Alice was perched on the ceiling like a great spider, hidden among the wooden rafters. Below her she could hear Knight Templar Enrique Marquez and his assistant Supernumerary Henry Fields creeping further into the abandoned warehouse. She was taking a big risk by personally handling this mission, but it had been too long since she'd felt the warm gush of blood.

That's it, dear, whispered the voice of her dead mother in her mind. *Make them bleed. Make them suffer.*

Alice smiled. Charles Flint had taught her how to commune with the dead, and ever since their fateful encounter years ago, she'd been able to communicate with the spirit of her long dead mother, burned at the stake when Alice had been only five years old. She'd been a witch of considerable power with her husband, Alice's father, none the wiser. Her father had tried to convince her that she'd died in an accident, to cover up the truth of what really happened back then. It would have destroyed her father's career at its start, if it were more widely known that he'd been married to a witch. And she'd believed him, her young mind not able to conceive that her daddy might lie to her. But Flint had taught her to use the power that had laid dormant, undeveloped within her. And now, by all the powers below, she would make the Witch Hunters pay.

I'm very proud of you darling. I love you very much, her mother said.

Alice wasn't her real name, but she'd grown to think of herself as Alice more and more. Flint said it was a literary reference, to some ancient book called *Alice in Wonderland.* She'd never read it, but Flint's summary of it made the pseudonym feel right. Since she'd accepted her true nature - stepped through the looking glass, he'd called it - the life she had known as a Lady Templar felt like a part to play. She couldn't wait for the birth of Flint's new nation. No more pretending to be a faithful woman of God. No more hunting her own kind. Soon these apes would know what it was like to be the hunted.

The floor creaked below her. Marquez had drawn one of his guns, bracing it against his other hand which held a flashlight. Fields had duct taped a flashlight to the barrel of his shotgun. She stifled a giggle. This was going to be fun. Marquez was an especially self-righteous prick, even by Templar standards.

"This place gives me the creeps," Fields said.

"Steady, Mr. Fields," Marquez replied. "This warehouse has no doubt been the site of countless diabolical rituals. There may be demons about."

"Looks like nobody's been here in years."

"Witches often hide in plain sight. Be on your guard."

Alice struggled not to laugh aloud. Oh, if only he knew! Perhaps it was time to give her intrepid Witch Hunters something to investigate. She pointed at a spot behind some old wooden crates stacked near the wall.

"What was that?" Fields whispered.

"It came from over there," Marquez whispered back, aiming his flashlight at the crates. He turned off the flashlight, stuck it in one of his long coat pockets. He drew his sword, the blessed steel shining brightly in the darkness. "Your judgment is at hand!" he bellowed, striding forth to meet his foes.

Alice felt a tingle up her spine, despite her contempt for the man. There was something about the High Speech that stirred every human heart. Since her embrace of her magical heritage, a new feeling emerged from the depths of her soul: fear. She shrugged it off. These two buffoons had no idea that she was here. They had no idea she was their sworn enemy now.

Below her, Marquez was nearly upon the stack of crates, Fields close on his heels. Alice pointed at the wall on the opposite side of the warehouse.

"Who's there?!" Fields shouted. He aimed his shotgun toward the imagined source of the sound. Flint had begun her education with simple mind tricks such as making her target hear sounds that weren't there. She didn't find them particularly interesting, but she had to admit that they were most useful. Witch Hunters were trained to resist the simpler spells; indeed, Hickock kept his guard up almost every waking hour now. But when they weren't expecting them, when they couldn't see their foe, they could be caught unawares. Speaking of which…

Marquez reached the stack of crates and found nothing. Fields made his way toward the opposite side of the warehouse, shotgun held at the ready. "Mr. Fields…" Marquez said.

Fields stopped, looked back toward his partner.

"We are being toyed with."

Shit. Time to end this.

All good things, her mother's voice whispered.

Alice crawled along the ceiling toward Fields. That shotgun was going to be a problem if he got a bead on her. Flint had taught her to deflect individual bullets, but buckshot was much trickier. She whispered a spell and drew her hands in a circle. A ring of fire manifested on the floor between Fields and Marquez.

"What?!" they cried, almost in unison.

An ear splitting roar echoed throughout the warehouse. Within the ring, the floor disappeared, leaving an opening into the void between worlds. An arm reached up through the portal, its skin a mottled grey, rippling with muscle, its fingers tipped with talons like steak knives that dug into the concrete floor. Flint had warned her against making deals with demons – they always found a way to get you in the end, he'd said – but the more dimwitted ones were little more than beasts. Just set them loose and watch them tear your enemies to pieces.

Fields braved the flames, rushing to the edge of the portal. He aimed his shotgun straight down and pulled the trigger. The boom left Alice's ears ringing. The demon screamed, the arm withdrew back into the void. Fields racked the weapon, fired again, repeating until his shotgun was empty. Now.

Alice swooped down from the ceiling, soaring toward Fields. She had changed out of her Templar uniform, and was dressed in a flowing black robe, her face covered in a black scarf. Fields caught movement in his peripheral vision and looked up.

"Shit!" he cried. He dropped the shotgun and moved to draw his pistol, but Alice was upon him. She drew her sword across his throat. A thick red line appeared, and blood gushed forth. Fields looked shocked. His hands went to his throat, and he gurgled as he sank to his knees. Alice wished that she could savor the moment, but business came before pleasure.

Marquez's pistol barked as he fired at Alice, but she easily dodged. He drew his sword and marched toward her.

"Murdering harlot! I'll see you burn!" he shouted.

She alighted upon the floor. Marquez was fast approaching. Magic was no good against his sword. She'd have to do this the old fashioned way. She drew her pistol, aimed, fired.

Marquez flinched and grunted in pain as the bullet tore into his right shoulder. Son of a bitch managed to hang on to his sword. Alice fired again and again. She had to be careful not to kill him just yet. She wanted him to see this.

Marquez sank to the floor, two bullet wounds in his shoulder, another in his leg. His fingers relaxed and he let go of his sword. Alice smiled. She never understood why Supernumeraries wore body armor and Templars didn't. Probably not fashionable or something.

Marquez tried to push himself up. He made to draw his second pistol with his good arm, but Alice extended her hand, and the pistol flew from his holster and into her grip.

"How... how did you..." he started.

Alice walked up to him and kicked him in the ribs. He grunted in pain. She drove her heel down into his leg wound and Marquez screamed in agony.

"How did I get my hands on Templar weapons?" she said. "How do you think, Enrique?" She tore the scarf away from her face.

His eyes widened, his face went pale. "You..."

"Yes, me," she said. She conjured a ball of fire in her hand. "Me, me, me." She threw the fire into Marquez's face. He screamed and screamed until the flesh had burned away, leaving only his grinning skull behind.

Alice smiled and shuddered with sheer pleasure. God, she had been missing out for entire life until she had met Charles.

Well done, my dear J...

"Mother..." she said out loud. "Call me Alice."

11

"So then Silas says, 'Your father will be joining you shortly,' and boom! Rams the dagger right into the were-wolf's face," Navarro said. His family's mouths hung open in shock. Flint took a sip of wine. He had decided that this, his third glass, would be his last. It was all well and good to drink with friends – and Navarro's family had gone out of their way to make Flint feel at home – but a Knight Templar must keep a clear head.

"Is that really how it happened?" Daniela asked Flint.

"I recall saying those words, yes," he replied.

"Jesus Christ…" Angelo said. Flint gave him a sharp look. "Oh, uh, sorry. It just… well, we're not always able to tell when Rico is exaggerating or not."

"Only when it's funny," Navarro laughed. He took a swig from his beer bottle. "But yeah, Silas has his moments when he's a real fuckin' badass."

"Ricardo, language," Lucía said. "More fajitas, Silas?"

"No, thank you, I am quite full. You are an excellent chef, Mrs. Navarro. I cannot recall the last time I saw Mr. Na… er, Ricardo partake of Mexican cuisine."

Ernesto looked to his grandson, raised an eyebrow. "Is true?" he asked.

Navarro shrugged. "It's just not the same when I'm not here. Nobody else can get it quite right."

"I'll take that as a compliment," Lucía said, smiling. "Would you like some more, Rico?"

"Yes, please and thank you."

"You make me wonder if the Order feeds you, son," Angelo chuckled.

"In his defense, our field rations are not the most palatable."

"That's an understatement," Navarro said. "Hard bread, beef jerky, water... I, uh, might overindulge real food and drink whenever we're in the big city."

"Now it is you who are making an understatement," Flint said. The entire family roared with laughter.

When it had died down, Rita asked, "What brings you two out here, by the way? Did you get some leave time?"

Flint and Navarro looked at each other. Flint cleared his throat. "We are on our way to Salem. I am afraid that I am not at liberty to say much more than that."

"Salem!" Elena cried. "Oh wow! That's so cool! Will you get to meet General Hickock? Oh! Will you get to meet the Emperor?"

"We shall indeed meet with the General. I do not believe we will be having an audience with His Majesty." He hoped not anyway. "We must be on our way tomorrow morning."

"You and Rico are welcome to stay with us tonight," Angelo said.

"I thank you both for your hospi..."

There was a knock at the front door. The table fell silent, everyone exchanging confused looks.

"Dear?" Lucía asked.

Angelo furrowed his brow. "I'm not expecting anyone else. Are you two?"

Flint and Navarro both shook their heads.

"Huh. Well, I'll go see who it is. Excuse me." He pushed

himself away from the table and left the dining room. The family sipped their drinks, poked at their food, kept quiet. Flint took another sip of wine. One possibility occurred to him, and he prayed that the Proctor sisters wouldn't ruin tonight's conviviality.

Angelo returned to the dining room accompanied by a familiar face: Supernumerary Samuel Breckenridge. He was dressed in the customary leather body armor, denim jeans, and steel toed boots. His mail satchel hung over his shoulder.

Flint rose from his seat. "Mr. Breckenridge. What on earth brings you out this far?" he asked.

"How'd you know we were here?" Navarro asked.

Breckenridge smiled. "There's kind of a weird story behind that."

"Girls, one of you bring up another chair," Angelo said. Elena got up and left the dining room. "You are welcome to join us. We still have plenty of food left. Beer?"

"Oh yes, please," Breckenridge said. Elena returned with a folding metal chair.

"Sorry," Angelo said. "Kind of a full house."

"I'll survive." Breckenridge took a seat between Navarro and Maria.

"Um... should we leave?" Alex asked. "Is this classified Templar business?"

"No, I don't think that'll be necessary," Breckenridge said. "Just have a delivery for these two."

"You mentioned unusual circumstances?" Flint said.

"Oh, yeah." Angelo twisted the cap off a fresh bottle of beer and handed it to Breckenridge. Lucía passed him some tortillas and spooned carne asada strips and peppers onto his

place. He made himself a taco and took a large bite. "Mmm…
oh wow. This is amazing."

"Mr. Breckenridge?" Flint prompted.

"Right. I was just about to head out of Marsing to go deliver a letter to Captain Withers and his assistant. Then Sir
Archer himself comes running up to me, says there's been a
change of plans."

Flint raised an eyebrow. Knight Templar Andrew Archer
oversaw Fort Marsing's couriers. Every order, every communication passed through his office. Flint had never met
the man face to face, and only interacted with him through
written communiques. Archer's letters made him out to be a
man of extraordinary powers of deduction, always knowing
where every Witch Hunter and Supernumerary was at all
times.

"He hands me this package," Breckenridge said. He
opened his satchel and removed a small parcel wrapped in
brown paper, handing it off to Flint. It was addressed to Silas
Flint and Ricardo Navarro, care of Angelo Navarro, along
with the correct address. The return address only read MP3.
One corner of Flint's mouth turned up.

"He gives it to me, and he says, 'Get this to Captain Flint
and Mr. Navarro as quickly as possible. You should still be
able to catch a train.' So I got on the next train to Bend, and
here I am. That's not the weird part though."

The Navarro family was hanging on his every word.
Even the stolid Ernesto looked to be paying close attention.
"And that would be?" Flint asked.

"I asked him what the hurry was. He says three Lady
Templars came to his office. He'd never seen them around

before, and Sir Archer knows everyone. But he said they made a compelling argument that you had to have this package before you reached Salem. How they knew you'd be here, he has no idea." He finished off his beer with one last swig.

Navarro whistled. "Didn't think anybody could stump Archer."

"Yes..." Flint murmured, turning the package over in his hands. Whatever it was, it was light. He shook it, heard nothing moving. At least it wasn't ticking. The Navarro family all began speaking at once.

"So cool..."

"How'd they know?"

"What's this all mean?"

"Who are these Lady Templars?"

"Do you think I could..."

Flint and Angelo both raised their hands for silence and conversations tapered off. Flint looked to his assistant. Navarro appeared to be carefully considering what to do next. Flint wasn't sure himself. MP3 had to be Mallory, Monica, and Madeline Proctor. Flint was grateful that they hadn't made an appearance tonight, but he was unsure what to do with this package.

"You gonna open that or what?" Elena asked.

"Elena!" Lucía said. "That package is for Silas and Rico. It's none of our business what's in it."

"You remember those weird sisters I mentioned, that we met on our way to Oglethorpe?" Navarro said. His family all nodded. "I'm pretty sure it's from them." They all gasped and drew back a bit. Ernesto made the sign of the cross.

"You think it's another dagger or something?" Antonio said.

"Maybe it's a new gun," Daniela offered.

"Only one way to find out," Navarro said.

Flint took a deep breath. There was indeed only one way to find out. "Mr. Breckenridge? Might I make use of your letter opener?" The courier opened a pouch on his belt and handed the blade to Flint. He cut the string tied around the package, slit the tape, and pulled the flaps open. Amidst the shredded newspaper padding there was a folded sheet of paper and another smaller box. Flint unfolded the paper and saw a note written in a flowing cursive script.

Didn't your mother ever teach you to listen to your elders? You will need this in Salem. Keep it safe. You'll know when the time is right to use it.

We rmn yr mst Obt. Servants

-MP3

Flint scoffed, crumpled the note.

"What's going on sir?" Navarro asked.

"See for yourself." He tossed the ball of paper to his assistant who caught it with one hand. He unfolded it, his family crowding around him to read over his shoulder. Flint returned his attention to the smaller box inside the parcel. He took it out, removed the lid. His eyes widened when he saw what was inside.

"What is it?" Navarro asked.

Flint pulled out a set of rosary beads. A Saint Benedict medal was embedded in the crucifix at the end of the silver chain. The beads were all black. He held it up for all to see.

"Beautiful," Maria said.

"Those sisters, they're witches, yeah?" Angelo asked. Flint and Navarro nodded. "Why would they send you a holy rosary?"

"Not just any rosary," Flint said. He reached into one of his trouser pockets and took out a small leather pouch. Unzipping it, he pulled out another rosary. It was identical to the one he had received from the sisters. "Every Templar is given a rosary along with their weapons when they take the oath."

"So who does that one belong to?" Lucía asked.

"I do not know," Flint replied. His own rosary bore the dings and scratches of being on the road for fifteen years. The other appeared to be in nearly mint condition. He scrutinized it more closely. Some Templars inherited rosaries that had been passed down through several generations of Witch Hunters. His own had been a gift from his mentor, Captain Ross Williams, his initials etched into the first bead above the crucifix. There. The rosary the sisters had sent him had initials on the first bead: AB. On the second bead as well: GS. There were more initials on the next few beads as well, enough for ten Ave Marias and one Pater Noster. Whoever this rosary belonged to, it had been passed down for possibly a century or more.

"What do you think boss?" Navarro asked.

"Most curious," he said. For now, he tucked the rosary into a waistcoat pocket. The clock on the dining room wall began to chime. 9:30 p.m.

"Mr. Navarro."

"Yeah?" Navarro, Angelo, and Ernesto replied in unison.

A ghost of smile passed over Flint's face. "Ricardo. I suggest we board the first available train to Salem in the morning."

"That'll be at six a.m.," Angelo said. "Daniela, Elena, one of you should spend the night in the other's room tonight so…"

"That will not be necessary," Flint said.

"Yeah, me and Silas sleep on the hard ground when we're in the field. A couch or the recliner will be just fine."

Conversation resumed but Flint's mind was elsewhere. The rosary the sisters had sent him was clearly Templar design, but why did they believe he would need it? Did it belong to someone at the Salem Chapter House? Was its previous owner still alive? The clock chimed 10:00 p.m.

"We should probably start heading out," Alex said. "I have an early start tomorrow."

"Same here," Antonio said.

The guests rose from the table and began filing out. Navarro hugged Rita and Maria and shook hands with his brothers in law. Ernesto shook Flint's hand.

"Take care of my grandson," he said in Spanish.

"Of course," Flint replied.

"Keep your rosary and it'll keep you."

"Always."

Breckenridge came next. "Is there anything you want me to pass along to Fort Marsing, sir?"

"Inform General Abernathy that Mr. Navarro and I should arrive in Salem early tomorrow. And… give my regards to Zelda Fletcher."

After the guests had left, Angelo put his hands on Flint and Navarro's shoulders. "Gentlemen, would you care to join me for a cigar outside?"

"Sure thing papa."

"Thank you," Flint said, hoping Angelo had a better blend than their cab driver. He and Navarro stepped outside while Angelo went to his humidor. It was a pleasant summer evening, the sun finally giving way to full dark. Flint stood with his hands behind his back, looking out at the neighborhood. He heard the smell of barbecue and the sound of laughter and music coming from several houses on the block. He thought that this was the reason why he'd devoted his life to the cause of rooting out witchcraft: so that ordinary people, God's children, could enjoy normal lives.

"Don't know what those three are talking about," Navarro said, his words slurred a bit. Flint hadn't kept track of how many drinks his assistant had enjoyed, but he sounded close to his limit.

"I take it you mean the Proctors."

"Yeah. You see how my family is."

Flint nodded. Navarro did indeed seem to have a close knit family. Perhaps the sisters were mistaken.

Angelo stepped out onto the front porch and handed the two men their cigars. He lit up his own, then passed his lighter to Navarro. Flint took several short puffs while he lit his cigar, finishing with a longer drag, holding the smoke in his mouth for a few moments before exhaling. It was a light, mild blend that he found quite smooth.

Angelo blew out a large puff of smoke. "So," he said, "Are

either of you able to tell me anything more about your trip to Salem?"

Flint thought for a moment. "Do you follow current events, Mr. Navarro?"

"Call me Angel. And yes, I read the newspaper every morning with breakfast."

"Heard about anything going on in Salem?" Navarro asked.

"Well, His Majesty has ordered another Chapter House for your Order. Guess whose construction firm got the contract?"

Navarro shouted and clapped his father on the back. "Congratulations papa!"

Flint took a deep drag, exhaled. "I too offer my congratulations. This is a most prestigious endeavor. The people of God and the Knights Templar shall remember you for generations to come."

Angelo gave him a curious look. "May I ask you a personal question, Captain?"

"Of course."

"Do you always use the High Speech? I don't think I've heard you use one contraction since you've arrived."

"I do," Flint said. "It did not come naturally to me at first when I pledged myself to the Order. Through practice, however, it has become my customary mode of conversation."

"How long were you a Supernumerary?"

"I never was."

Angelo looked up at that. "Oh? I thought you all started out that way."

"Normally that is indeed the case. However, when I presented myself to Fort Marsing for consideration, my... personal circumstances convinced them that my talents would be better employed by becoming a Templar sooner rather than later."

Angelo looked to his son. "How about you, Rico? Do you plan on taking the trials any time soon?"

Navarro looked down, puffed on his cigar. After a few moments he said, "Not any time soon, no."

"May I ask why?"

He looked up to his father. "Well... I don't know. I'm happy where I am. Silas is a good partner."

Angelo smiled. "Hmm. I was just thinking of how impressive you'd look in your own coat and hat."

"To answer your earlier question," Flint said, "You have no doubt read about the unusually high number of casualties at Fort Ingalls."

"Yes I have... are you two being transferred there? Are they that shorthanded?"

Flint and Navarro made eye contact. He hated the idea of lying to Angelo, but he couldn't risk compromising their cover story. "Yes. I am afraid so."

"Dear God," Angelo said, making the sign of the cross. "What is happening to this world?"

"Evil never rests, and neither can servants of the Lord."

The three men were silent for a few moments, enjoying their cigars. Angelo looked up and said, "Will this be a permanent transfer?"

"Nah," Navarro said. "We're just going to be there until... until the, ah, situation stabilizes."

"Hmm. I was just thinking, you'd be closer to home. Hey."

He snapped his fingers. "When this new Chapter House is complete, do you suppose you could transfer here? It's going to take them a while to recruit more local people."

Navarro thought for a moment. "Maybe," he said, shrugging. "It depends on the needs of the Order."

"But you could request it, right?"

"I could."

Flint blew out a puff of smoke. If Navarro did put in such a request, it could mean the end of their five year partnership. Flint himself had no intention of leaving Fort Marsing permanently absent a direct order.

"Then you could visit more often," Angelo said.

"I get out here as often as I can papa. Even if I were stationed here, there's no guarantee you'd see me more often. I'm on the road a lot."

"I know, I know. Speaking of which… are you seeing anyone? In your last letter, you mentioned a girl named Julia."

"Oh, uh, right," Navarro said, running a hand through his hair. "Well, you know, I write to her when I can."

"And that girl you met in Canyon Cove, Maria?"

"She was just visiting. Come to think of it, I have no idea where she's really from."

"Hmm." Angelo blew out a puff of smoke.

Flint said nothing.

"I imagine it's difficult to start a family in this sort of life," Angelo said.

"Yeah, it can be, but some of the guys manage it."

"What about you?"

"What about me?"

"Are you ever going to settle down, Rico?"

"Yeah, some day. I'd like to."

"You're 28 years old."

"So?"

"So maybe it's time to give it more serious thought."

Navarro looked at his father. "Who says I'm not? I'm just… committed to the work, is all."

"And I respect that. Truly, I do."

"Then where's all this coming from?"

Angelo closed his eyes, took a deep breath. "I'm just worried about my only son. I won't be around forever you know."

"Papa, you're not even fifty yet."

"I just… I want you to be happy. But I miss you. You're in a dangerous profession. You don't get a fancy sword that absorbs magic. And I'm terrified that I'll have to bury you like I had to bury your mother."

Navarro put a hand on his father's shoulder. "That's not going to happen papa. I promise."

"Your vocation is to protect Captain Flint," Angelo said, waving his cigar in Flint's direction. "But who protects you?"

"God," Flint said. "Along with all of the angels and saints."

Angelo looked to Flint. "Do you have a family, Captain?"

Navarro's eyes widened a bit. Flint was silent for a moment before answering, "No."

"I apologize if that's a sore subject," Angelo said, "But my advice holds for you too. Don't wait until it's too late. It's good to have the Lord on your side, but family is important too."

Flint nodded. "I agree completely."

They fell into a companionable silence again. Flint checked his pocket watch. 11 p.m.

"Well, I guess you two should get some rest," Angelo said. "Don't mean to keep you up."

"Hey. Papa," Navarro said. He embraced his father. "Don't talk like that. I'm going to be around a long time, and so are you."

Angelo smiled and hugged his son back. He put his cigar in an ashtray by the front door. "Good night son. Captain."

After he had gone inside, Flint and Navarro set their cigars in the ashtray as well. "I had no idea he felt that way," Navarro said.

"I am glad that you were able to clear the air, so to speak," Flint said.

"Yeah... I hope so anyway. So... you want the couch or the recliner sir?"

12

Charles Flint paced back and forth. Lilian Turner was underneath a console, reconnecting wires, flipping switches, and checking the power supply. Charles understood machinery that he could see, touch. But these computers were beyond him, probably beyond any living human being on earth. Lilian claimed that she wasn't a specialist in this sort of technology, but Charles thought she was either lying or knew more than she realized.

"What should I expect when these machines are operational?" he asked.

"It's going to talk to us," she replied.

Charles's brows went up. "I'm sorry?"

"The computer will speak to us."

"Is it... is it alive?"

She shook her head. "No. Back then, scientists tried to create true artificial intelligence, but the Occult War put a stop to all of that. Who knows, they may have succeeded eventually. The computer can understand and respond to voice commands, but it's not truly alive."

"Still... remarkable feat of engineering."

"I have no idea..." she grunted as she pulled a cable out and plugged it into the back of a console, "I have no idea if this is even going to work, or how it will respond when we tell it the entire presidential line of succession is dead and the United States is gone."

"We shall cross that bridge when we get there. How much longer?"

"That should do it," she said, coming out from beneath the console.

"Excellent. Activate it."

Lilian held up her index finger. It crackled and sparked as she summoned a bolt of sorcerous lightning. She extended her arm to the ceiling, and the lightning shot forth in a continuous stream, arcs of electricity coursing throughout the bunker. She lowered her hand. A soft hum came from the walls. The monitors flickered to life.

The two companions looked around. "What happens now?" Charles asked.

"It should start to..."

"INTRUDER ALERT."

The monotone male voice seemed to come from everywhere and nowhere. Charles raised his hands which crackled with magical energy.

"INTRUDER ALERT," the voice repeated. Hatches opened in the ceiling. Mechanical arms lowered into sight, each tipped with gun barrels.

"Oh dear," Charles said. He and Lilian raised their hands, shields of magical energy forming around them. The guns opened fire, a never ending stream of bullets shattering against the duo's barriers. A part of Charles's mind realized he was experiencing automatic fire for the first time.

"Still think this was a good idea?" Lilian shouted over the gunshots.

"I'm open to suggestions," Charles yelled back.

"Let me try something." Maintaining her shield around her, she stepped away from Charles. The ceiling mounted machine guns did not track her, focusing their fire on Charles, who was beginning to sweat from the pressure of maintaining his barrier. She lowered her hands, the magical barrier around her disappearing.

"What are you doing?!" Charles shouted.

"Testing something! The computer still recognizes me!" She took a deep breath. And then she spoke in a man's voice. "Computer!" she yelled. The voice was that of a much older man, raspy from a lifetime of smoking.

The machine guns stopped. The walls hummed and buzzed. Then the computer spoke: "Recognize voice pattern: Harkmoore, David R., General."

"Computer, recognize authorized user, Harkmoore, Lilith S., authorization Harkmoore alpha seven one eight delta."

The computer beeped and buzzed. "Recognize authorized user Harkmoore, Lilith S., confirmed."

"Computer, add authorized user, Flint, Charles J., authorization Harkmoore alpha seven one eight delta."

"New authorized user Flint, Charles J. Do you accept?"

Lilian smiled at him. "It's talking to you," she said, in her own voice.

Charles lowered his defenses, looked up at the machine guns in the ceiling. "Yes, yes, I accept."

"New authorized user confirmed. Welcome back Miss Harkmoore, Mister Flint."

"Computer," Lilian said. "Update personnel file. Harkmoore, Lilith S. Change name to Turner, Lilian S."

The computer beeped. "Personnel file updated. Welcome Miss Turner."

Charles wiped his brow. "What was that earlier? When you changed your voice?"

Lilian smiled. "It was a little trick I picked up back then. My father was a general, a member of the Joint Chiefs of Staff. The computer can't tell the difference between his real voice or a magical facsimile. Came in handy quite a few times during the war."

"I can imagine. Is it really so easy to give me access, to add me as a... recognized user?"

"Well, keep in mind this area was heavily fortified and packed with a military garrison back then. Otherwise, yes, if you know the right voice pattern and the right codes."

"Can I speak to this machine?"

"You're an authorized user now. Go ahead."

Charles looked up at the ceiling. "Computer?"

There was a chime.

"What would I need to do to fire a nuclear missile?"

"Nuclear missiles may only be fired through a direct order from the President of the United States."

"Computer," Lilian said. "Please verify the date and time."

The walls beeped. "The date is November 12, 2075. The time is 16:32 hours."

She nodded. "Yes... yes, that does sound familiar. Computer. Update internal clock: the date is June 9, 2533, the time is 23:15 hours."

"Internal clocks reset."

"Computer, remind me, what is your name?"

Charles raised his eyebrows. "It has a name?"

"In a manner of speaking."

"I am Rob," the computer replied.

"Rob?" Charles scoffed.

Lilian nodded. "Yes. The civilian models were Alexa and Siri. Very handy to have around." Turning her attention back to the computer she said, "Rob, things have changed a bit over the last few centuries..."

13

Salem. Capitol of the Empire of Cascadia, and largest city in northwestern North America, a sprawling megalopolis of five million souls, and a testament to mankind's will to survive. The rolling hills and green pastures of the countryside had given way to a cityscape as far as Flint's eyes could see, the train decelerating and moving through Salem's concrete jungle at a more leisurely pace. He checked his pocket watch.

8:50 a.m. They'd made excellent time. There were fewer bandits and predators out west capable of hindering a loco-motive, but even then, attacks on travelers were more common than the Empire cared to admit.

The slower pace allowed Flint to study his surroundings more carefully. It was not his first trip to Salem but knowing that there could be a traitor within the Chapter House made him suspicious of every window, every alley, every nook and cranny. He remembered that the train's terminus lay in the Grant neighborhood, from which one could see the Imperial Palace. From there they would have to backtrack to reach Fort Ingalls, either on foot or by hailing another taxi. The morning sun shone through a thick cloud of smog which perpetually enveloped the city from the automobiles and the factories.

The train's brakes squealed as it pulled into the Cascadia Express station. End of the line. Travelers who wished to proceed further west would have to make the journey by au-tomobile or carriage. Flint was considered wealthy by his fellow Templars, thanks in large part to his selling off his family's farm when he pledged himself to the Order, but even he blanched at the cost of owning and driving an auto-mobile across the nation. The price of gasoline would burn through his savings in no time.

Navarro slid open the wooden door that separated their first class compartments. He yawned and stretched. Flint didn't condone his assistant's heavy drinking, but he had to admit the man could hold his liquor.

"Morning sir."

"Good morning to you Mr. Navarro."

He looked out the window. They passed by another barracks, imperial soldiers even thicker on the ground in here in Salem than in Bend. He and Navarro both made the sign of the cross at the sight of the Cathedral of Saint Benedict. Centuries ago, Salem had been a part of the Archdiocese of Portland, but after the destruction of that city during the Occult War, the Church's seat of power in the northwest shifted to the capitol of the newborn Empire of Cascadia. Flint idly wondered if he would have to meet with His Eminence, Santiago Cardinal Benítez.

The train continued advancing at a snail's pace for another few moments before coming to a shuddering halt, a final blast of steam spewing from the smokestack. Navarro peered out the window.

"Can't believe they can fit so many people in one city. Place makes Bend look like a country village," he said.

Flint shifted. Being so close to his hometown of Mount Angel made him uneasy enough, but now he had to be on his guard even more so. "It is a pity that we cannot take the time to sightsee. I have always desired to see the Imperial Palace more closely."

"What, you can just stroll on in?"

"No, but they offer guided tours of the public areas."

"Hope we don't have to go there on business."

"I know precisely how you feel."

They received their travel cases from one of the conductors and stepped off the train. The other passengers and the citizens crowding the platform didn't pay as much attention to Flint as they did elsewhere, Witch Hunters being a more common sight in the imperial capitol. The train station too was far busier than any other they'd visited. From here passengers could catch a nonstop express train to Olympia, the regional capitol of Cascadia's northern province, or south to Ashland along the border with the Kingdom of Pacifica and the Free State of Jefferson.

"I'll go get us a taxi," Navarro said. He began walking toward the terminal gate when he stopped. "Sir?"

"What is it?" Flint asked. He looked in Navarro's direction. Standing near the archway to the station's central terminal was a hulking bear of a man, stout, but Flint suspected the fat covered hard muscle. The stranger wore a long black trench coat, a black fedora pulled low over eyes hidden by sunglasses, a scarf wrapped around the lower half of his face. The man held a sign that read FLINT.

Flint and Navarro looked at each other. Together they strode toward the man. It was a rare occasion when Flint had to look up to make eye contact with anyone.

"Captain Flint?" the man asked, his voice muffled by the scarf, difficult to hear over the murmur of conversation, the sound of rolling travel case wheels, and the steam blasts that permeated the station.

"I am Knight Templar Captain Silas Flint, and this is my assistant Supernumerary Ricardo Navarro, at your service sir. May I ask who you might be?"

"Come with me please," the man said. Something else was odd about his voice. It was as though he was trying too hard to enunciate.

"Are you with the Order?" Navarro asked.

"Just follow me please." He turned on his heels and began walking.

Flint looked at Navarro, who shrugged. They followed the stranger through the station. Speakers on the walls announced arrival and departure times. The hallways reeked of cigarette smoke, cheap alcohol, urine, and smog. Private security made their rounds, revolvers on their hips. No one batted an eye at the bolt action rifle on Navarro's back or the sword on Flint's hip. He hadn't noticed any weapons on the giant who had greeted them at the terminal, but Flint thought he could have concealed a rifle inside that trench coat.

The man stopped. He whispered in the ear of a security guard. The guard nodded, began walking, the giant following him.

"We in trouble already?" Navarro asked.

"We shall see," Flint said, following the man. The security guard led them down a hallway, away from the public areas. He stopped at a door, reached for the keyring on his belt, unlocked the door. Opening it, he motioned for the trio to enter. The stranger ducked inside. Flint rested a hand on one of his pistols and followed, Navarro close on his heels, gripping the tomahawk on his belt.

The room was well furnished with a refrigerator, couch, easy chair, wardrobe, king size bed, and a radio sitting atop a dresser. Flint was impressed. This was more lavish than many hotels he'd visited.

The stranger had his back to them as he removed his fedora, revealing long grey hair that tumbled down over his shoulders. He took off his sunglasses, pulled the scarf away from his face and turned around, a large grin splitting his bearded face.

"Surprise!" he said in a rich country drawl.

Flint immediately clicked his heels, bowed his head. Navarro snapped to attention and gave a crisp salute. "General Hickock, sir," Flint said.

"In the flesh, big as life, and twice as ugly," Hickock chuckled. He stepped forward to shake their hands. "I only wish we were getting to meet under better circumstances."

"I presume that is why you greeted us in disguise," Flint said.

"Sure is. Don't know how much good it does. I'm kind of hard to miss," Hickock said, slapping his belly.

"The situation is that grim then?"

Hickock closed his eyes, took a deep breath. "Two more were killed last night: Enrique Marquez and Henry Fields."

"Last night?!" Navarro said, nearly shouting. His face grew ashen. "Holy shit... it's my fault..."

"The hell you talking about?" Hickock asked.

"If we hadn't stopped to visit my family... we could have gotten here last night... could have saved them."

Before Flint could open his mouth, Hickock put both hands on Navarro's shoulders, stooped down to look him in the eye. "Hey. None of that now. This ain't your fault. It's the fault of that God damned snake in the grass I got in my house. You fellas getting here late last night wouldn't have made a lick of difference. So, no blaming yourself. That's an order."

Navarro was silent for a few moments before looking up to meet Hickock's gaze, nodded. "Yes sir."

"Good," he replied, clapping Navarro's shoulder hard enough to make him stumble. The General went to his easy chair and sat down, the furniture creaking under his bulk. He indicated the couch. "Have a seat."

Flint and Navarro sat down, facing Hickock. The General said, "You like the place? The station keeps a few rooms like these available for travelers who get delayed for whatever reason. I decided to keep this one permanently. Now it's my little home away from home."

"It is quite charming, sir," Flint said.

"Y'all ain't the only ones I've invited to Salem. Couple of guys are transferring here indefinitely from up north around Olympia. You two, on the other hand, I wanted to talk to in private, away from prying eyes and ears."

Flint felt sympathy for the man. It was a terrible thing, not knowing who to trust, particularly when in a leadership position. "Have you any suspects?" he asked.

Hickock sighed. "I've narrowed it down some, but the pool is still too big for my liking. It's somebody higher up, that's for sure. Somebody I talk to regularly."

"How do you figure sir?" Navarro asked.

Hickock leaned forward. "At first, I didn't suspect anything unusual. A Hunter and his assistant dying on a case is tragic, but it happens. We know what we're signing up for. But then more started dying. Dying in ways that could only be accounted for in one way: somebody on the other side knew where they'd be, snuck up on 'em and..." He drew his thumb across his throat. "And the damnedest thing is, as soon as I started to suspect something was rotten in the state of Denmark, killings stop for a bit. I start to relax, think maybe some of my boys and girls got unlucky. Then they start up again, and more of 'em too."

Flint steepled his fingers. "You fear that the witch or wizard in your midst is reading your thoughts."

"Either that or they're reading all of our mail," Hickock said. "The theologians talk about custody of the senses, but this is something else. I hate to say it, but I don't know who I can talk to freely anymore. I tried leaking some fake info: sending the boys out to random locations, making up case numbers, that sort of thing. So far, the snake hasn't taken the bait."

"And that's what makes you think it's someone higher up, somebody who knows what you're doing," Navarro said.

"You got it. So that takes the potential suspects down from a thousand to maybe a hundred."

Flint nodded. The thousand Templars and support staff could probably be employed within the city of Salem alone, but they were expected to cover all southwestern Cascadia. The harvest was plentiful but the laborers, as ever, were few.

"General Hickock," Flint said. "Before our departure from Fort Marsing, General Abernathy told me that you are familiar with some of my written reports."

"Sure am. Hell of a job you boys did out in Canyon Cove and Oglethorpe."

"Do you recall my account of the Weird Sisters?"

Hickock raised an eyebrow. "Yeah... what about 'em?"

Together Flint and Navarro told of their encounters with the Proctors over the previous two days, of hearing them on Navarro's radio, and of the package they had received last night. Hickock stroked his beard, thought for a few moments.

"Mind if I take a look at that there rosary?" he asked.

"Of course." Flint removed it from his waistcoat pocket and handed it to Hickock. The General squinted at the beads for a moment, before snorting in frustration.

"Shit," he muttered. He withdrew a pair of reading glasses from his shirt pocket and put them on before returning his scrutiny to the rosary.

"Definitely one of ours," he said to himself. "AB... GS..." He continued reading the initials aloud until he reached the end: "HF."

"Have you any idea who the owner might be?"

Hickock shook his head. "Afraid not. I suppose I could get some of the boys in personnel to do some research, try to match them initials to our departed brothers and sisters, trace who it's been handed down to."

"That's assuming it belongs or belonged to someone here in Salem," Navarro said.

"Yeah, there's that too. Why don't you hang on to it for now Captain?" He handed it back to Flint who returned it to his waistcoat pocket. "Something else I want to know. You say you got a radio on you?"

"Yes sir," Navarro said. "A souvenir from Mountain Home Airforce Base out in the UMS." He opened a pouch on his belt and handed the radio to Hickock.

"Shoot," he said, turning it over in his hands. "Never seen one like it before. Hell, this could fit in my pants pocket."

"It is an American device of pre-war manufacture," Flint said.

"How's that possible? That'd make it, what, 450 years old at least?"

"It is a long story. If you like, I shall request that General

Abernathy send you a copy of my report for you to read at your convenience."

"I might do that, I might do that. You mind?"

"By all means."

Hickock thumbed the power switch. The radio was still set to 1530 AM and the room was filled with the notes of another melancholy jazz tune. Hickock looked at the dial. His brow furrowed. He switched the radio off and handed it back to Navarro.

"I want to try something," he muttered. Hickock went to the larger radio on top of his dresser. He turned it on, adjusted the tuning dial. When he'd finished, the room was filled with static.

"1530 AM," he said.

Flint and Navarro looked to each other.

"The station sounded familiar when you mentioned it but I couldn't put my finger on it at first. Then I remembered: they went out of business when I was a kid."

Navarro shrugged. "Still probably the least weird thing about those three."

Hickock chuckled. He pulled a watch out of his trouser pocket. "Alright boys, this is how it's going to go. I gotta get back to the Fort. It's about 9:30. We're having a little ceremony to welcome you new people at 11. I hope you brought your fancy duds?"

The two men nodded.

"Alright, good enough. Head on over to the Fort, get changed, and be out on the field by 10:45. Once that's done, there's an old warehouse on the corner of Market and 17th. That's where Marquez and Fields were ambushed. It's probably still crawlin' with po-lice, but comb the scene anyway, see if you can find anything they missed."

"The city police department is involved?" Flint asked. There was an unwritten rule in the Empire that secular police departments handled the more mundane variety of criminals while the Templars investigated supernatural crimes. He was puzzled at why the Salem Police Department was inserting itself in this matter.

"Orders from the Minister of Justice," Hickock said. "Says he 'has concerns about a parallel law enforcement agency' and that he wants greater coordination between us and the cops. I got nothin' against it in principle, but you know how the police can be."

Flint nodded. Secular law enforcement often didn't have the appropriate tools for engaging with witches, monsters, or undead. Some brave souls still attempted to do their duty, most fled at the first sign that their lead bullets would not avail them. "We shall depart for Fort Ingalls immediately."

"Outstanding. I took the liberty of paying for your cab, should be waiting for you at the curb outside. I'm going to put my disguise back on and head out. Wait ten minutes or so, then you two follow suit." Hickock donned his hat and sunglasses, wrapped the scarf around his face, and headed out.

Flint checked his pocket watch. 9:31 a.m.

"You ever meet General Hickock before?" Navarro asked.

"This is the first time I have met the man in person, but I am familiar with several cases that he investigated in his youth. I tell you frankly, it is a miracle he has lived so long."

"Sometimes I think the same thing about you, boss."

"Hmph."

"I was just thinking, he seems so different from General Abernathy."

"Yes. General Abernathy comes from a more well established family. It is my understanding that General Hickock was born into more modest circumstances."

"I was kind of expecting him to be… you know, more stuffed up."

"I suspect we shall encounter more of that among the ranks."

14

Alice swore to herself in her mind. She was standing at attention atop a raised dais in the courtyard of Fort Ingalls. Surrounding her were the other higher ranking Templars and Supernumeraries that kept the Chapter House running smoothly. In front of her, Witch Hunter General Jeremiah Hickock stood before a lectern, facing hundreds of assembled Templars and Supernumeraries. Everyone was in their dress uniforms and she felt a bead of sweat drip down her back in the morning heat. The Templar dress uniform consisted of a heavier black long coat with scarlet trim and a Maltese Cross stitched on the back, with leather gauntlets, steel body armor with a cross embossed on the chest and Saint Benedict medals in each of the four points, a steel pauldron over the right shoulder, a stiff felt hat with silver buckle and another Saint Benedict medal in center. Supernumerary dress uniforms were a grey tunic and trousers, leather boots, gloves,

and a peaked cap with braiding and a gold trimmed Saint
Benedict medal in the center.

"Good morning," Hickock spoke into the microphone, his
voice echoing off the ancient brick walls. Alice had read that
before the war, Fort Ingalls had served as a mental hospital
run by the former state of Oregon. She suppressed a smile.
How fitting that the Church would turn a madhouse into the
headquarters for their hired butchers.

"It is with a heavy heart that I have gathered you all here
today," Hickock said. Alice kept her face neutral but felt like
sneering. The man was a rude country bumpkin playing at
wise leadership. Her father was ten times the man he was.
Had her mother still been alive, she could have no doubt laid
waste to this pitiful gathering.

Thank you... Alice, her mother's voice whispered in her
mind. *But you give me too much credit. I was powerful, but not
that powerful.* She returned her attention to Hickock's speech.

"I regret to inform you that two more of our brothers
have gone on to their eternal reward: Enrique Marquez and
Henry Fields."

Murmurs arose in the crowd, Templars and their assistants exchanging worried looks, others scowling in fury, no
doubt vowing to burn the vile witch responsible for killing
their comrades. *If they only knew,* Alice thought. Charles had
said that he wanted the investigator humiliated and discred-
ited, and to only kill him if he discovered her identity. That
didn't make sense to her. Why not kill him before he got
that far? Hickock already suspected that there was a traitor
in his midst. What difference would it make if the investiga-

tor had an accident? She blinked, focusing on Hickock again.

"The darkness rises, but as ever, we, the devoted servants of our Blessed Lord and His Holy Church, shall send His enemies back into the fiery depths of Hell, for the light shineth in darkness, and the darkness comprehended it not."

She struggled not to roll her eyes. Please. A few lines from Scripture would always get cheap applause from these peons. Sure enough, a wave of applause rippled through the crowd. She wondered if anyone else suspected that one or more of these new faces was a member of the rat squad. Several ideas came to her then. In a way, Templars – and the witches they hunted – had it easy. They knew who their enemies were. Rooting out corruption was a different matter. Alice supposed she was a traitor from a certain point of view, but she thought of it more as being loyal to her true self, to her true brothers and sisters who practiced the dark arts. Hunting for traitors was like trying to catch a shadow. One never knew who one's enemy really was. He could be anyone: one's partner, one's commander, one's best friend. Hickock looked like he was about to make introductions, so Alice brought her mind back to the present moment.

"The harvest is plentiful, but the laborers are few. For that reason, I have invited brothers and sisters from other Chapter Houses throughout the Empire to replenish our ranks. The Lord has called them, and they have answered. They come to us from Olympia, from Marsing, and all points in between. I am pleased to introduce your new brothers and sisters in arms. Together we shall..."

Blah blah blah, Alice thought. It's a pity that the General didn't do field work anymore. She'd have loved to have gotten her claws into the big oaf. Still she supposed she should be paying attention to the roll call. Twenty-four men and women stepped forward, standing apart from the crowd, and Hickock began reading off their names. One of them had to be...

"Silas Flint and Ricardo Navarro," Hickock said.

Alice's eyes widened, though not so much that the other staff on the dais noticed. Silas... Flint? Her master's orders, his attitude, all made sense now. Yes, she could see the resemblance between them. The Witch Hunter Flint made for a grim figure, even by Templar standards. He looked as though he never smiled, his face creased with deep frown lines, not at all like Charles's wicked grin. But there was no doubt in her mind that they were family, most likely brothers. Could Captain Flint be the one sent to root her out? Oh, this was perfect. As soon as this little ceremony was over, she'd have to contact Charles and let him know that his own brother was here. Hickock looked like he was winding down.

"Let us bow our heads, and beseech Almighty God to look with kindness upon we, His unworthy servants, to let His face shine upon us..."

Where was God when you were burned at the stake mother?

He was acting through these peasants, playacting at being good little Church boys and girls.

Don't worry. I'll make them all pay.

I know you will, daughter.

The crowd said "Amen," in unison. There was no applause this time. They had to resume their work of persecuting innocent practitioners of magic. But it was difficult to focus on the work in front of you when you had to worry about the scheming behind you. Perhaps she could take advantage of that. Maybe it was time to begin spreading rumors that the rat squad was among them.

15

Flint and Navarro stood at attention as General Hickock made his way down the line, shaking hands with each of the Templars and Supernumeraries that had transferred to Salem, offering words of encouragement. Out of the corner of his eye, Flint could see a bead of sweat running down the side of Navarro's face from underneath his peaked cap. He knew that Navarro hated the dress uniform, but fortunately for him, Supernumeraries rarely had to wear them. Flint rather liked the more formal Templar dress, even in the summer heat, but he had to admit that the steel chest plate probably wasn't the most practical garment for everyday wear.

Hickock reached Flint. The General was an even more formidable figure in his Templar dress uniform, a gold sash across his chest plate denoting his rank. He shook Flint's hand, the strength of his grip not diminished at all by the thick leather gauntlets. He leaned forward to whisper in Flint's ear.

"Get changed, get out to that warehouse."

"At once sir."

"God be with you."

"And also with you."

After Hickock had spoken to Navarro, Flint motioned with his head for his assistant to follow him. Together, they crossed the courtyard, making their way through the crowds of Templars and Supernumeraries, splitting off to go to their respective wings of the massive fortress. Flint had studied something of Fort Ingalls's history on the train ride to Salem. The grounds were once the home of the Oregon State Hospital, a home for mentally ill criminals. Shortly after the founding of the Cascadian Empire and the Knights Templar of the Order of Saint Benedict, the old hospital had been torn down to make way for the Order's second and largest Chapter House within the old Oregon country. The architecture and floor plans were similar to Fort Marsing writ larger to accommodate the greater number of personnel. Flint would have to...

"You there. Captain Flint."

A woman's voice. Flint stopped, looked over his shoulder. A Lady Templar was hurrying to catch up to him. Long blonde hair flowed down her back from underneath her felt hat, her coat flapping about as she jogged toward Flint. He kept his face neutral but dearly wished that this would be quick. There was work to be done, a traitor to be found.

"I am Silas Flint, at your service, madame," he said, clicking his heels.

"Captain Jessica Steiner," she said, extending her hand. Flint gave it a brief shake. "May I ask where you've transferred from?"

"Fort Marsing," Flint replied. "I beg your pardon Captain

Steiner, but my assistant and I must be on our way, post haste." He resumed walking toward his assigned quarters.

"So soon?" Steiner said, keeping pace with Flint. "You just got here."

Flint considered his next words. He didn't want to lie, but he couldn't tell the truth either. A lie of omission, a half-truth would have to do. This mission was turning him into a Jesuit, and it made him feel dirty. "We have been given our first case."

"What, did the General give it to you out on the field?"

Flint said nothing and continued walking. Steiner kept following him.

"We're going to be living and working together Captain Flint."

He said nothing, kept walking.

"Oh." She stopped. "Now I get it. You're here to investigate all of those fatalities we've been having."

Flint continued forward. Steiner rushed to catch up.

"For what it's worth, I think the General's right. I think there is a traitor here."

Flint said nothing.

"Just be careful, okay? I don't like it but I can see his reasoning. Some of the others might not take it so well, an outsider coming in to investigate us." She stopped, watched Flint continue. "If you need help, I'll be around."

Flint reached his temporary quarters. Save for the crucifix and portrait of Saint Benedict on the walls, it was devoid of all decoration or personal touch. He had tossed his travel case onto the bed, not bothering to unpack everything before heading out to the courtyard. As he changed into his field uniform, he pondered Steiner's words. His intuition told him that she was sincere in her desire to assist him, but there was no way for him to be certain. Her words echoed in his mind. He himself would have been distrustful of any outside investigators that came to Fort Marsing. He felt sick at the idea of a Templar turning against God, and this wasn't even his home. He could scarcely imagine how he would feel if the traitor was in Fort Marsing instead.

He changed into his black trousers, white shirt, and black waistcoat. After donning his long coat and adjusting his black hat, he snapped on his gun belt, his sword and two pistols on his hips. He made the sign of the cross and offered a brief prayer to the Holy Spirit to grant him the strength and grace that he would need to see this through to the end.

16

Charles ran a hand through his hair. The nuclear missile bunker had living quarters with showers, a mess hall, and refrigerators packed with twenty-first century food and beverages, all magically preserved along with the rest of the facility. He looked at a carton of milk. The expiration date read 12/16/75. He had no idea how old it was when it had been frozen in time. He sniffed. It smelled alright. And if worse came to worse, food poisoning was nothing a simple spell couldn't cure. He and Lilian had spoken with the computer, Rob (he still couldn't believe a machine could not only speak but had a name), late into the night. It had been a fascinating experience, but the machine's literal-mindedness had proven frustrating.

He heard Lilian's footsteps enter the dining hall. She joined him in the kitchen and opened one of the other refrigerators.

"What looks good?" Charles asked. "I admit I'm unfamiliar with some of these choices."

Lilian chuckled. "I never realized how much I'd missed some of this stuff until coming back here." She took out a purple can from the fridge, opened it with a crack, took a swig. "Mmm. Real Dr. Pepper."

"I take it that's some kind of soda?"

"Yes, my favorite. No one in the twenty-sixth century can get the recipe quite right."

"Is there any coffee?"

She took another swallow and pointed at a machine on the countertop. "Yes. Over there."

Charles approached the machine. There was a clear plastic container on one side, half filled with water. A bowl of what looked like plastic thimbles sat on the other side. There was a handle on the front of the device. He pulled up, revealing a depression inside that looked just large enough for one of the plastic thimbles. Charles saw a sharp looking needle at the bottom of the depression.

If there was a coffee making machine here, the mugs had to be nearby. He waved his hand and all the cupboards opened simultaneously. There. He took out an oversized mug from the cupboard directly above the machine. On one side of the mug was an American flag, on the other GOD BLESS THE USA. He peered at the machine from different angles. There was a small metal platform beneath the section where the depression was. He put the mug there. Out of the corner of his eye, he could see Lilian watching him.

"Need some help?" She asked.

"No, thank you. This machine seems simple enough." He took a plastic thimble, inserted it into the depression, and pulled the lever down. The thimble popped as the needle punctured the bottom. The buttons on top of the machine began flashing green. He didn't know what the symbols meant, but he decided to push the largest button. The machine hummed and gurgled. The kitchen was filled with the rich aroma of black coffee. The machine went quiet, the last few drips of coffee splashing into his mug. He took it off the platform, held it under his nose, took a deep sniff.

"Ahh," he said. He raised it in salute to Lilian, who acknowledged him by raising her can of Dr. Pepper. Charles took a sip. He scowled after he swallowed.

"Hmph," he said.

"Not to your liking?"

"It's… adequate. I guess I was expecting the wonders of twenty-first century science to produce a better tasting cup of coffee."

She laughed. "It's a secret military facility. I don't think gourmet coffee was high on their priority list."

"Beggars can't be choosers I suppose."

Lilian took out some eggs and bacon from the refrigerator and began to prepare breakfast while Charles took a seat in the dining hall. He and Lilian had informed the computer last night that the President of the United States was long dead along with all his successors, that the United States itself and its government was long gone, and that he, Charles, would soon be the legitimate ruler of a new nation which would encompass the bunker. Rob seemed to accept everything with equanimity, but it still wouldn't give Charles access to the nuclear arsenal.

"You're almost as irritating as Silas," he'd said at one point.

"I do not know to whom you refer," the machine had responded.

Lilian swore that the machine was not alive, that it did not possess its own consciousness, but Charles was beginning to wonder. There had to be a way to penetrate the computer's stubbornness. The trick would be in the wording of his commands, of that he was certain.

He felt the sapphire-like jewel in his pocket buzz and he felt the familiar tug in his mind. He took out the jewel and put it on the table, uttering the incantation. The column of light arose and Alice's silhouette materialized inside.

"Report," he said.

"We just finished with a little ceremony in the court-yard."

"And?"

"It turns out Hickock invited two dozen new people to fill in for our dearly departed brothers and sisters."

Charles smiled. Twenty-four wasn't much, but the outlying Chapter Houses would be stretched thinner the longer Alice continued her work. Rome wasn't built in a day.

"One of them was a Captain Silas Flint."

Charles froze, his eyes widening.

"Are you two...?"

"Yes," Charles said, regaining his composure. "You have seen my older brother."

"I thought I saw a resemblance."

"The resemblance is only physical, I assure you."

"I don't know which of them is the internal investigator but I'll..."

"It's Silas."

Alice cocked her head. "How can you be sure?"

"Because I know him. He is exactly the kind of fire breathing zealot Hickock would want to carry out that sort of mission."

"Do you want me to kill him?"

Charles felt an uncharacteristic hesitation. The safest course, for him, would be to have Alice contrive some way to kill him and be done with it. He had a suspicion that if Silas survived long enough, they would come face to face, and only one of them would survive. And yet... and yet he was reluctant to give the order. If Silas died now, he would never see Charles's plan come to fruition. He would never know that he, Charles Flint, would be the ruler of an entire nation, a nation that the Witch Hunters could never hope to defeat. Silas would never know the despair born of powerlessness.

"Sir?" Alice asked.

Lilian emerged from the kitchen, carrying two plates of scrambled eggs and bacon. She set Charles's plate in front of him. He made eye contact with her, and she shook head no.

"No," Charles said. "No. My previous orders still stand. If it's you or him, then put him down. Otherwise... string him along. Find a way to embarrass and humiliate him."

"I'm open to suggestions."

Lilian rolled her eyes. "He's looking for a traitor, isn't he? So give him one."

Alice's head turned to look at Lilian. "Who are..."

"She's with me," Charles interrupted. "You should listen to your elder."

Alice was silent for a moment. "I think I have an idea."

"Get to it then."

Her silhouette dematerialized; the column of light vanished. Charles stuck the jewel back in his pocket. Lilian nudged him with her elbow.

"I'm liable to begin taking offense at all of these references to my age."

"I'd have thought you'd have a thicker skin after 500 years." He poked at his breakfast with his fork. "Do you think I made the right decision?"

Lilian paused. "I do," she said after a few seconds. "I thought to kill him the moment I learned that he had arrived in Canyon Cove, and that proved to be my downfall."

"I wasn't going to mention it, but that thought crossed my mind as well."

"And besides, you promised me a chance for a rematch."

He chuckled. "Yes, that I did."

They dined in silence. After they had finished their meal, Charles rose from his seat. "Well," he said. "Let's see if we can't get this stubborn machine to listen to reason."

17

Flint and Navarro stepped out of their cab. This section

of the city consisted mostly of slums, boarded up shops, homeless encampments, and other signs of decay. Salem was the jewel of the West, but even it had its share of humanity's detritus. A good place for a witch to practice her diabolical craft, Flint thought. Isolated and packed with souls no one would miss. The warehouse where the murders took place was surrounded by police vehicles and marked off with yellow tape. Navarro had changed back into his leather body armor, blue jeans, and boots, his chest crisscrossed with ammunition bandoliers for the bolt action rifle he slung across his back.

"I hope the cops are as simpatico here as they are back east," he said.

"We shall see," Flint said. He led the way toward the warehouse's entrance. The first thing he noticed were the smells: sulfur, blood, and burnt flesh. He balled his fists. The deepest circle of Hell was reserved for traitors, and he vowed to send them there with all possible speed. Flint and Navarro stepped under the police tape blocking the doorway. A uniformed officer approached them, his hand held up.

"Sir, this is an active crime scene, I'm afraid I have to..."

"Stand aside," Flint said.

"Sir, I'm going to have to ask you..."

Flint glared at him.

"Uh..." the officer said.

Flint pinned him with his gaze.

"Sir..."

"It's alright Jerry, let 'em through," another voice called from further inside the warehouse.

The officer swallowed, stepped aside. "Right this way sir."

Flint brushed past him, Navarro close on his heels. The stench was growing stronger. There was a black ring burned into the concrete floor up ahead. Added to the myriad smells was ozone which could only mean sorcery. The body of Henry Fields lay in a pool of blood on the floor next to the ring. Further away, Flint saw a trail of blood lead to the body of Enrique Marquez. More blood spread out from underneath Marquez's body. His head was devoid of flesh, his face a blackened grinning skull. Two gurneys were standing by. Police officers with oversized cameras snapped pictures of the bodies. A black man in a bespoke suit approached Flint and Navarro.

"Detective Elijah Earle," he said, extending his hand.

"Knight Templar Captain Silas Flint, and my assistant Supernumerary Ricardo Navarro, at your service sir," he replied, shaking the detective's hand.

"You from Fort Ingalls?"

Flint caught himself before he said Fort Marsing. "Indeed. Please tell me what you know."

"Not much," Earle said, spreading his hands. "We got the call earlier this morning. Homeless guy came in and reported the bodies. My guys got here a short while ago. Speaking of which, how did you know about this? We haven't even had a chance to file a report."

"Our couriers have their ways," Navarro said.

Earle shrugged. "It's just as well. Soon as I saw the bodies, I figured they'd send a Witch Hunter. No ordinary human being could do… this." He winced as he glanced at Marquez's body.

"No. They could not," Flint said. "What evidence have you discovered thus far?"

"I admit I don't know much about this magic shit," Earle said. "We were kind of hoping you guys could explain some of what we've found."

"I shall answer what I can."

"Okay. First thing is that circle in the middle of the floor. Whatever it was, it melted through the concrete, which means it had to be burning at several thousand degrees."

Flint stooped to examine Fields's body. His throat had been slit, his face frozen in an expression of shock.

"First vic was carrying a shotgun. He emptied it into something. Or someone. We've found all of the shell casings, but no slugs or buckshot anywhere."

"I can explain," Navarro said.

Flint raised an eyebrow. "By all means, Mr. Navarro."

"Okay, this burn mark is in a perfect circle, yeah?"

Earle nodded.

"The concrete's melted, so like you said, it was several thousand degrees. I don't see any other signs of heat damage. There's only one kind of fire that can do that. Some witches are able to open portals. Let's 'em travel... thousands of miles, like stepping through a doorway. But they can open portals to other places too. Places that aren't part of this world."

Earle was silent for a moment. "That aren't of this world... you mean like..."

"Hell," Flint said. He looked around him and noticed that the other police officers were staring at them, hanging on

Navarro's words. Some looked like they'd gone a few shades paler.

"Mr. Navarro is correct. Our witch opened a portal during her encounter with our brothers. Judging by the circumference of the circle, I daresay that it meant to accommodate something significantly larger than a human being." He pointed at a series of parallel grooves at the edge of the circle. "You will notice these claw marks in the floor."

"Jesus Christ…" Earle said.

Flint gave him a sharp look.

"Oh, uh, sorry."

"I cannot be certain, but I have formed a hypothesis regarding the missing buckshot: Mr. Fields fired his weapon straight down into the portal. Whatever attempted to pass through was slain, or the portal was shut before it could enter our world."

"Fired into the portal? How? If the fire was hot enough to melt concrete, this guy should have been burned to a crisp getting that close."

"Hellfire does not always obey the laws of physics as we understand them," Flint said.

Earle swallowed. "You know, the Minister of Justice has been saying he wants us to work together more closely. As far as I'm concerned, you boys in black are welcome to all this shit. Doesn't obey the laws of physics… how the hell can you conduct an investigation when science doesn't apply?"

"You get used to it," Navarro said. "You have to be more open minded."

Flint shifted his attention to Marquez's body. The black skull stared sightlessly up toward the ceiling, the jaw hanging open. He noticed three bullet holes in the body: two near his right shoulder, one in his right leg. The bloodstains told him that he had been shot while still alive.

Navarro and Earle joined his side. "This one seems more straightforward. Three gunshot wounds and… well, his head. He started over there…" The detective pointed to where the trail of blood began. "…And made it to this spot. He fired his weapon twice. We found two shell casings near his body, and two slugs over on the far wall. Over here, we found three more shell casings which we think are from the killer's weapon." Earle snapped his fingers and beckoned a uniformed officer to join them. The policeman handed Earle a small bag, which he opened for Flint and Navarro to have a look.

The two men look inside. They closed their eyes and sighed, almost in unison.

"All five are identical," Earle said.

"Yes," Flint replied.

"They're ours," Navarro said.

"Come again?"

Flint pointed at one of the pistols on his belt. "All Templars carry the same model of pistol, chambered for the same cartridge. Those three ammunition casings also came from one of our pistols."

"We haven't found the gun," Earle said.

"I do not expect that you will."

The detective's eyes widened. "Are you saying what I think you're saying?"

"I must ask you to keep this in the strictest confidence, Detective."

Earle crossed his arms. "My partner and I are lead on this case. I'm willing to work with you here, but if you have any information that can…"

"There is a traitor in our midst."

Earle's brow furrowed. "A traitor… like in Fort Ingalls?"

Flint nodded. "Yes. General Hickock only had suspicions before, but you and your officers have provided the evidence. These shell casings prove that one of our own is responsible for this crime and for all of the other tragedies that have befallen of us as of late."

Earle sighed. "I've read in the papers about all the people you've lost over the past few months."

"Yes. Sent to investigate unusual happenings only to walk into traps."

"You sure you want in on this, Detective?" Navarro asked. "Our perp is a trained Templar who can also summon demons and throw hellfire from their hands."

Earle ran a hand over his head. Just then a white man in a suit approached the trio. He was middle aged, his body just beginning its turn to fat. "I've canvassed the area, Eli. Don't expect much, it's mostly homeless and junk…" He stopped, looked at Flint and Navarro. "Uh… am I interrupting?"

"No, no, not at all. Jay, I'd like you to meet Templar Captain Silas Flint and Super… supernu… his assistant, Ricardo Navarro. Gentlemen, this is my partner, Jay Marsten."

They exchanged handshakes. Marsten asked his partner, "What's going on?"

Earle thought a moment. "This is between us four."

Marsten nodded. "Okay, sure."

"Captain Flint here says our killer is a witch. And a Templar."

Marsten's jaw dropped. "Holy shit..."

"Yeah."

"This is an internal Templar affair, but we welcome the assistance of the Salem Police Department," Flint said.

"Yeah... yeah, of course," Earle said.

"Minister Edwards' orders," Marsten said, referring to the Cascadia Minister of Justice Benjamin Edwards.

"Splendid," Flint said. "Mr. Navarro and I shall be hunting for our traitor from within Fort Ingalls. I am willing to share our findings with you in exchange for your findings at other crime scenes where our brothers and sisters have fallen."

"Sure thing," Earle said.

"Who gets to make the collar though?" Marsten asked.

Flint scowled. "When we find this person, I will personally put them to the torch. It is not up for debate."

The two detectives looked at each other. "Ah... yeah, agreed," Earle said. He couldn't have fought Flint on the matter even if he'd wanted to; by the laws of the Church and the Empire, the Knights Templar of the Order of Saint Benedict were judge, jury, and executioner of those found guilty of practicing the dark arts.

"One more question Detective," Flint said. "Have you done an inventory of the deceased's possessions?"

"Yeah, everything's been catalogued."

"Did you find a rosary on Captain Marquez's person?"

Earle shook his head. "No. He had his weapons, crucifix and Saint Benedict medals, what looks like a bag of salt, other religious stuff, but no rosary. Why?"

Flint stroked his chin. "I am not certain yet. I shall have to acquire more evidence. Come along, Mr. Navarro," he said, turning on his heels. "Detectives, we would be most obliged if one of your officers would give us a ride back to Fort Ingalls."

18

Alice sensed no one else in the hallway, but she looked both ways out of habit. At this time of day, the Templars would be taking an early lunch, in the training pits or the library, or out in the field. Satisfied that she was alone, she approached one of the doors in the hallway. This next part would be tricky. It was a minor spell that would be over in a few seconds. The risk was small, but it was possible that a Templar might detect it, if he happened to have his sword drawn at the right moment. She scowled. God saw fit to give impart His blessing upon Templar blades, making them glow when in the presence of magic. God helped those who murdered her mother, who would murder her given the chance. Where was God when she needed Him?

God turned his back on us... Alice. He rejected us and we reject him, her mother's voice whispered in her mind.

"They want to follow Him, then they can die for Him," Alice said aloud. She stopped, chided herself. She had to be more careful. It was the joy of her life, being able to hear her mother's voice again, but if anyone overheard her conversing out loud with the voice in her mind, it could prove her undoing. Focusing her attention on the task at hand, Alice recited the spell Charles had taught her, exerting her will upon the lock. After a few seconds, there was a click as the tumblers fell into place and the deadbolt slid back. She smiled. If these murdering zealots were so keen to obey God's law, then why did they put locks on their doors?

She pushed the door open with her mind and stepped inside. That woman Charles had with him had suggested giving Silas the traitor he was looking for. It wasn't a bad idea, but Alice thought it would only delay the inevitable. As soon as she began killing again, the Templars would know they had fallen for a frame job and the hunt would be on again. Charles's reluctance to kill Silas outright made more sense now that she knew that they were brothers, but it still seemed unnecessarily risky to leave him alive. If Silas was even half as smart as Charles, he'd find her sooner or later. She'd only caught a glimpse of Silas, but enough to know that Charles was wrong about one thing: the Flint brothers shared more than just a familial resemblance. She sensed that Silas would be as relentless in pursuit of his goal as Charles was for his. If anything, more so. The elder Flint looked to her as if he never smiled.

She looked around the living quarters. Some Templars accumulated a large enough collection of books and religious trinkets that they spilled onto the floor, but these quarters had room to spare. The bed was perfectly made, the bookshelves were half full, the desk was clear save for one notebook and a mug filled with pencils and pens.

Alice held out her hand, exerted her will, and the crucifix on the wall slowly rotated until it was upside down.

Much better, her mother said.

She smiled. Alice hadn't put on gloves for this task. Why bother when you didn't need to use your hands to move objects? She drew on more of her power, her long coat spreading open around her body. From one of the inside pockets came rosaries, dozens of them, all taken from Templars she had killed over the last few months. It was a Templar tradition that each new member be gifted a rosary from their mentor once they took the oath, each previous owner engraving their initials upon one of the beads. She'd thrown hers away long ago and took her victims' as trophies. It amused her that these trinkets, handed down through generations of killers, now commemorated her exploits as the greatest killer of all. It pained her to lose them, but she reassured herself that it was only temporary. When she left to rejoin Charles, she'd break them out of evidence to take with her.

Where to put them though? They needed to be hidden but not so well hidden that Silas couldn't find them. Alice had her own secret hideaway where she kept her spell books, alchemical ingredients, and other tools of the witch's trade, but where would her patsy keep trophies? She decided on the desk. Alice waved her hand and one of the drawers opened. The rosaries levitated toward the open drawer and Alice released them from her mental grip, the beads dropping inside.

That taken care of, Alice considered her next step. Framing someone was turning out to be a more difficult task than she'd anticipated. The evidence had to point to her victim but be subtle enough that it wouldn't give the game away.

Remember your training, her mother said. *What are all of the things Templars look for?*

Of course. Alice had been so focused on physical evidence that she'd forgotten the other senses as well.

"Thank you mother," she said.

Be cautious. Do it quickly.

Alice summoned more magical energy into herself, a nimbus of unholy blue fire enveloping her body. She felt the power course through her like an electric current, her every nerve alight with that pleasant tingling that came with the use of magic. She levitated off the floor. The lighting dimmed. Her fingertips crackled with energy. She wanted laugh at the joyous rapture she always felt when the power was strong with her but suppressed the urge. Instead, she focused on the years of her life wasted pursuing the favor of a God whose servants had murdered her mother in cold blood for daring to use this great power.

That should do it, her mother said.

Alice let go of the power and she lowered to the floor which was now discolored from the surge of magic. She sniffed. The quarters now reeked of ozone. Perfect. The rosaries of dead Templars on the one hand, evidence of magic performed within these walls on the other...

Daughter.

She thought about her next steps. Her patsy would be thrown into the dungeons for sure. If all went well, she might even be burned at the stake. That would count as a kill, wouldn't it? Charles would be pleased.

Alice.

In any case, Fort Ingalls would be down another Templar. Then Alice would kill more. Silas would be humiliated for arresting an innocent woman. Well, innocent of Alice's crimes. Perhaps Master Flint would look on her with new eyes, not as a master toward his student, but as man looks at a woman...

Jennifer!

Alice frowned. "I told you mother, from now on call me..."

The door opened. Alice felt the blood drain from her face, her mouth falling open. In walked the owner of these living quarters, Captain Jessica Steiner. She shut the door behind her, deep in her thoughts. She had advanced several steps into her room before she looked up and noticed Alice.

"Ma'am?" Steiner asked. "What are you doing in here?"

"I... I was looking for you, actually," Alice said, recovering.

Steiner cocked her head. "Looking for me?" She laughed. "I thought it was your job to know where all of us are at all times."

"Oh... er, yes, but I... well, even I get distracted sometimes."

Steiner nodded. "I hear you. But here I am. What did you need ma'am?"

"I... I need you to... I need you to join Captain Flint. He, ah, he's going to need assistance with his... current case."

"I knew it," Steiner said.

"Knew what?"

"He's the one investigating all of the recent deaths in the field."

Alice nodded. "Yes. Yes, he is."

"I introduced myself to him earlier. Very intense, that one. It's going to…" She sniffed. "What is that smell?"

A bead of sweat ran down Alice's temple. "I'm sorry?"

Steiner sniffed again. "Ozone… how can you not smell it?"

Alice said nothing.

Steiner looked down at the floor. "The stone… what happened to it? It's stained."

Alice said nothing.

Steiner looked her in the eye. "I locked my door ma'am. How did you get in here?"

"I…"

"It's you!"

Before Steiner could finish drawing her sword, Alice raised her hand. A sorcerous lightning bolt struck Steiner in the chest. She flew across the room and hit the wall, cracking the stone with the force of the impact, and fell to the floor. The stench of burnt flesh mixed with the overpowering ozone. Alice fired another lightning bolt directly into Steiner's face to be sure, the Lady Templar's once beautiful features now a smoking ruin.

Alice's heart was racing. Sweat streamed down her face. She panted as if she'd just run a marathon. Her hands were bright red, burning after channeling so much energy.

Calm down Alice. Breathe.

"Mother, I'm ruined!

Others will have heard the commotion. You need to get out of there now.

Alice wrapped her long coat tighter around her body. She pulled down the brim of her hat over her eyes. She ran to the door, pushed it open, and rushed from Steiner's room.

Hurry but don't run. Go back to your office.

She made it to the stairwell and began ascending. Another Witch Hunter was coming down from the upper floors.

"Good day to y... oof!" he said as Alice plowed past him without an acknowledgment.

Shit shit shit. Her mind raced. That idiot would no doubt smell Steiner's corpse when he got down to her floor. It was over. She was found out. She'd have to flee tonight. No, she'd have to flee now. All of Charles's meticulous scheming to get a mole into the upper echelons of Fort Ingalls, it was over now. He'd surely...

Jennifer. Listen to me.

Alice continued up the stairs but said, "Mother..."

Fine. Alice. You can still salvage this.

"How?"

The rosaries are still in Steiner's room.

"Oh no no no..."

SHUT UP AND LISTEN TO ME.

Alice slowed her pace, almost reeling from the force of her mother's voice in her mind.

"Mother, I..."

Do not speak to me out loud.

She continued up the stairs at a normal pace, tried to slow her breathing.

Go back to your office and resume your duties for now. You of all people know that spells sometimes go awry. Young witches and warlocks biting off more than they can chew. Steiner was conducting experiments, trying to cast spells that were beyond her skill, and she paid the price.

But mother, Alice thought, *I was seen coming up the stairs.*

He doesn't know you came from Steiner's floor.

Alice reached to top of the stairwell. She opened the door and stepped out into the hallway, making her way toward her office, jamming her hands into her coat pockets. Supernumeraries called out greetings to her, their arms loaded with papers, letters, and files, as she passed them by. At the end of the hallway was Alice's office. She opened the door, passing through into the entryway. Her assistant, Supernumerary Audrey Willis, sat at her desk working on an ancient typewriter, a rotary telephone by its side, with several filing cabinets filling out the rest of the cubicle.

Willis looked up. "Good afternoon ma'am."

Alice stuck her hands back in her coat pockets. "Good afternoon, Audrey," she replied.

Willis cocked her head. "Are you alright ma'am? You look like you've been out for a run."

"I was. One must get one's exercise in, especially when you sit at a desk all day."

Willis smiled. "I was thinking the same thing. I think I've gained ten pounds."

"Any important messages?"

"General Hickock dropped off some orders. I'm typing them up now. I swear, translating his chicken scratch handwriting should be a paid position all by itself. Other than that, nothing super important."

"Fine… that's fine, Audrey. I'll be in my office. Screen my calls. I have work to catch up on."

"Of course, ma'am."

Alice let herself into her office, shutting the door behind her. She leaned against it, gave a great sigh, and slowly sank to the floor.

Everything will be fine J… Alice. Everything will be just fine.

19

Flint and Navarro thanked the uniformed officer and got out of the police cruiser. In his mind, Flint went over the report he would give to General Hickock. It still galled Flint to think that a man or woman could make a solemn oath to God and His Holy Church and then turn their back on Him, on the Church, on their brothers and sisters in arms. There was no longer any doubt that the killer was a Templar. Now it was time to begin the difficult task of narrowing down the suspects. Hickock had said that it had to be someone in the upper echelons, someone he saw frequently. That still left an enormous list of people to go through. Perhaps…

"Sir?"

Flint looked up. Navarro was pointing at the open gates of Fort Ingalls. From here, Flint could see into the courtyard.

Witch Hunters and Supernumeraries were running toward the central tower.

"What in the world?" Flint said. "Come. Something has happened."

The two men jogged through the gate, across the courtyard, catching up to another Templar.

"What has happened here?" Flint asked.

"Captain Steiner… she's been killed," the man replied, hurrying on his way.

Steiner… Good God. Flint remembered her from earlier in the day. An attractive blonde woman whom he had brushed off on his way to get changed for his journey to the warehouse. The crowd grew thicker as they got closer to the tower. Flint and Navarro pushed their way forward. He caught glimpses of shock, sadness, anger, and fear on the faces of dozens, hundreds of men and women. There were more than a few dirty looks as he used his elbows to make way.

They climbed the staircase to the third floor. General Hickock was standing in the hallway outside of an open door. A team of Supernumeraries were going in and out of the door, wearing gloves, having discussions in small groups. Flint and Navarro approached the General.

"General Hickock sir," Flint said, clicking his heels.

Hickock acknowledged him with a distracted wave. "Captain Flint," he said.

"What happened here?" Navarro asked.

"I'll tell you what happened," Hickock growled. "I think we may have found our snake in the grass."

"Sir?" Flint asked.

"Walk with me." Hickock reached into his long coat, took out leather gauntlets, pulled them over his hands. A Supernumerary handed rubber gloves to Flint and Navarro who put them on and followed Hickock through the doorway. Flint saw Steiner's body on the floor. Her face looked like burnt hamburger, her chest similarly ruined. The stench of ozone and burnt flesh made his eyes water. Further inside, he noticed scorch marks and a brown discoloration in the grey stone floor.

"I am afraid I do not understand sir," Flint said.

"We found something in her desk," Hickock said, pointing. Flint and Navarro went to Steiner's desk where they saw many rosaries laid out. All of them had the black beads and Saint Benedict medal crucifix.

Flint picked one up and scrutinized the beads. He saw several sets of initials. He put it down and picked up another. More initials.

"Taken from fallen Templars," Flint murmured.

"Damn right," Hickock said. "Twenty-four dead men and women, twenty-four rosaries."

Navarro furrowed his brow. "What happened to her?" he asked, pointing to Steiner's body.

Hickock gave it a glance. His shoulders slumped a bit. "I admit we're a little fuzzy on that part. I'm sure you noticed the smell of witchcraft on your way in. We were thinking that maybe Steiner was doing some experiments, pushing herself too far, lost control."

Flint approached Steiner's body, knelt for a closer look. The sword on her hip was halfway out of its scabbard. He looked up, saw the cracks in the wall. The stench of ozone was stronger here, nearly overpowering the smell of her burnt flesh. He studied her hands closely.

"General, Mr. Navarro, join me, if you please," he said. After they joined him, he pointed at Steiner's hands. "You will notice that the hands are intact. The magical energy necessary to wreak such destruction would have left telltale burn marks, which as you can see, are not present."

He rose, pointed at her chest. "Further, you see that there are two separate wounds: one to the chest and one to the face. The flesh between the clavicle and the top of the neck is also intact. It is exceedingly unlikely that two separate wild bolts struck her in the two places which would prove instantly fatal and only those two places."

"Unlikely, but not impossible," Hickock said. "There's still the Templars' rosaries."

"True," Flint said. As the saying went, possession was nine tenths of the law.

"I think she's being framed," Navarro said.

"Oh?" Flint and Hickock said simultaneously.

"Think about it," Navarro said. "There's the stuff Silas mentioned. If she was casting spells strong enough to do this, her hands would be burned. Plus look at her sword," he said, pointing. "It's halfway out of the scabbard. That doesn't happen by accident. She was drawing it when she died."

Hickock stroked his beard. "That would explain a lot. There's no sign of forced entry that we could find. Killer picks the lock, or uses a spell or something to get in. They plant the rosaries. Steiner comes in, catches the killer in the act, and ends up dead."

"Has anyone touched anything since the body was discovered?" Flint asked.

"Only with gloves," Hickock said.

"I propose that we inspect the room for fingerprints. It is possible that the killer may have left some behind."

"I'll get my guys on it," Hickock said. He stopped just as he was about to leave. "Captain Flint... you still got that rosary on you, the one you got from the sisters?"

Flint took it out of his waistcoat pocket and handed it to Hickock.

"I think I'll get the research boys to check into this too," he said. "Maybe it belonged to another victim, one we don't know about."

"Very good sir," Flint said.

"In the meantime, you two canvass the gawkers outside. Find out if anyone saw Steiner receiving a visitor, or someone in the hallway." He gave them a nod before striding outside.

After he had departed, Flint said, "I am impressed Mr. Navarro."

"With what sir?"

"That is the second time today that you have exercised your observational skill. You are improving."

"Oh, uh, thanks boss."

"Does it have anything to do with the talk that you had with your father?"

Navarro was silent for a moment. "Maybe."

"Should you ever wish to undergo the trials to become a Templar yourself, I should be happy to recommend you...

assuming you also cease your gluttonous and fornicating ways."

"I'll keep that in mind sir," Navarro laughed.

"Come, let us see if we can locate any witnesses."

They left Steiner's room. They passed a pair of Supernumeraries with fingerprint dusting kits. Even if they found prints that weren't Steiner's, Flint thought, it would be a painstaking process to compare them to every set of prints that Fort Ingalls had on file. It was a start though.

They soon reached a crowd of onlookers, all appearing in turn solemn, sorrowful, or angry.

"May I have your attention?" Flint called out. Their conversations ceased, all eyes focused on him. "My assistant and I have been tasked with investigating this incident. Did any of you see or hear anything unusual today before Captain Steiner met her demise?"

The crowd looked at each other. Some shook their heads. One Templar stepped forward.

"You're one of the new men, are you not?"

"I am sir," Flint replied. "Captain Silas Flint, at your service."

"Why'd General Hickock ask you to investigate?"

Flint blinked. "He did. That is all you need to know."

"It's one of us, isn't it?" The Templar continued. "He thinks one of us is a witch. He brought you in to investigate us." Murmurs arose in the crowd.

"Hey!" Navarro called. They fell silent again. "We're all on the same side here. We all want to find out who's been killing our brothers and sisters. Don't even start this bullshit about seniority, or territory, or rat squads."

The Templar's mouth fell open. "How dare you take that tone with…"

"He is right," Flint said. "There is no doubt that the killer is among us. One of our pistols was used to wound Captain Marquez before he died, in a most excruciating manner. If you wish to make the killer pay, I suggest you set aside your personal feelings and assist in any way that you can."

The Templar scowled but kept his mouth shut. A hand went up in the back. "Captain Flint?"

"Yes, you there."

Another Templar stepped forward. He was on the plump side, no doubt from many hours spent in a comfortable office. "Tim Colson, sir. I'm the one who discovered the body."

"Come, follow me Mr. Colson." Flint and Navarro led him away from the crowd. Once they had gone a discreet distance, Flint asked him, "Did you see anything unusual?"

"Yes… it may be nothing, but it was kind of unusual."

"Go on."

"Well, I work upstairs in the courier department. I mostly type up orders and such. I was on my way downstairs to the stables when I saw Lady Jennifer Edwards tearing up the stairs."

"Who's that?" Navarro asked.

"Who's that? Only the… oh, forgive me. I forgot for a second that you're not from here. Lady Jennifer Edwards is the head of our courier office."

Flint and Navarro looked at each other. "Did you happen to see which floor she came from?" Flint asked.

"No, I didn't. Like I said, it may be nothing but… I've never seen her in such a hurry. She didn't acknowledge me when I tried to greet her, not even after she bumped into me. That's not like her at all. She looked… I don't know, worried."

"I see," Flint said. "Did you see or hear anything else?"

"No sir."

"Very well. Thank you, Mr. Colson, you have been most helpful. You are dismissed."

After Colson departed, Flint turned to Navarro and asked, "What do you think?"

He crossed his arms. "She could have just been in a hurry. Running late. He doesn't know which floor she was coming from."

"True. However, as head the courier office, all written orders and case files would pass through her office. That would give her the knowledge to lay traps for unwitting Templars."

"Yeah, yeah… not enough to charge her though."

"Indeed not." Flint stroked his chin. "Perhaps we should pay a visit to Madame Edwards."

20

Alice took the sapphire out of her pocket and laid it upon the altar inside her inner sanctum. A pentagram was painted onto the floor. The room was lined with bookshelves packed with eldritch tomes Master Flint had given her over the years. She'd been a freshly sworn in Templar when she'd been tasked with apprehending the wizard who was responsible for a series of abductions and murders up north in the city of Hubbard. That wizard turned out to be Charles Flint, but to her great surprise, Flint had approached her and told her that he could sense the great power within her. She'd thought he'd been referring to her faith, but even she knew that was a lie. She'd never really believed in God, not since her mother had been executed. She went to Mass and became a Templar because it was expected of her.

Charles had taught her to harness her magical talents, to conjure fire, summon demons, read the thoughts of others. He surprised her again when he dissuaded her from quitting the Order. He thought it would be useful to have a woman on the inside, to pass along information about the Witch Hunters' movements. So she'd gone back to Salem, requesting a transfer to the courier's office. Her talent for clerical work far outstripped her skills in the field, and the transfer became permanent. And so she'd labored here for years, rising to the top, picking off the occasional Templar here, the odd Supernumerary there, until Charles had contacted her months ago to tell her that he was beginning the first steps of his master plan. And that required her to step up the killing, to kill as many Templars and Supernumeraries as she could get away with.

She believed in Charles's vision of a nation for magic users. She yearned for a home where she no longer had to pretend to be something she wasn't. She was nearly thirty-five years old. If she ever hoped to have a family of her own, she needed to start sooner rather than later. She found herself almost hoping that Charles would tell her to end her years long mission and to come join him wherever he was now.

She recited the spell to open communications with her master. The familiar column of light arose from the jewel, reaching up to touch the ceiling. Charles's familiar silhouette appeared within.

"What is it?" he asked. He'd been more distracted as of late, as though she was always interrupting him.

"There may be a problem."

He sighed, rubbed the bridge of his nose. "I have more than enough problems of my own to deal with at the moment."

"I planted evidence in a Templar's room."

Charles nodded. "So, you gave Silas his traitor. Good."

"She interrupted me, found me there."

She couldn't see Charles's face, but she could easily imagine him looking taken aback. "What?"

"I had to kill her Master. It was me or her."

Charles was silent for a moment. She saw him ball his fists. "Damn it!" he shouted, punching the wall of... of wherever he was. He took a few deep breaths. "Witnesses?"

She closed her eyes. "I bumped into one of my subordinates on the stairwell."

"But he didn't see you use magic?"

"No sir."

Charles turned his back on her. He said nothing. He stayed like that for what felt like an eternity. Alice was about to say something when he turned around.

"You're compromised," he said.

"What?! Sir, no, it's alright. I can salvage this. No one saw me entering or exiting her room. No one knows I was even on her floor."

"Tell me," he said. "When you broke into her room, did you touch anything?"

"No! Everything I moved, I used my mind! Just like you taught me master!"

"Are you quite sure? You touched nothing? Nothing at all? Think."

Why was he being like this? She hadn't laid a hand on anything in Steiner's room. Everything was done through telekinesis. It wasn't possible that... oh no. No no no. She remembered now. After she killed Steiner, in her haste to escape, she'd put her hand on the door to push it open.

Charles laughed, cold and cruel. "Oh Silas, you're not even there for a full day, and already you've blown up an operation years in the making because my student panicked."

Alice felt anger rising in her gorge. "I didn't panic."

"So you're stupid then? So overconfident that you didn't bother to wear gloves?"

"Don't talk to me that way."

"Or else what? I taught you how to use your power. Everything you are now, you owe to me."

Alice said nothing.

"Did I hurt your feelings, Jennifer? Are you angry? Then prove me wrong. Consider this your final exam, my student. If you can get yourself out of this mess you've created, then join me here and I will happily admit my error and welcome you back into the fold. If you can't... well, after they burn you, your ashes won't be of much use to me. For your own safety, I'd advise you not to contact me again until you've escaped from Fort Ingalls."

His silhouette vanished, the column of light returned to the sapphire.

Damn him, Alice thought. *God damn that arrogant bastard straight to Hell.*

It's alright Jennifer darling, her mother whispered. *You don't need him. All students surpass their teachers in time.*

"So what now?"

I was thinking... I have friends who are willing to help you.

Alice furrowed her brow. "Friends? What do you mean?"

Since I passed on, I've made many friends. Friends who can magnify your power. Give you the strength you need to lay waste to this entire city if you wish.

"How could you have... No."

And why not young lady?

"Master Flint told me never to make deals with demons because they always find a way to get you in the end."

Oh Jennifer. You've been a practicing witch for this long, and still you retain the superstitions of the Church.

"What are you talking about?"

You're in control. You have the power to command them. They want to help you. They want to strike back against these so called men of God. They have no power over you except that which you give them.

"But when I die..."

Her mother laughed. *Then you'll just have to live forever, won't you? Charles's new lady friend knows the secret.*

Alice thought for a few moments. Did Charles know the secret to immortality? If so, then she could enslave demons with impunity; they would never be able to touch her soul. She could indeed surpass him by daring to do what he would not. Still... her mother was right. Alice's Templar training was deeply ingrained, despite her lack of faith.

"I'll... I'll take it under advisement."

Of course dear. You must do what you think is best of course. In the meantime, when was the last time you spoke to your father?

21

Flint and Navarro exited the stairwell. The hallway was bright with fluorescent lighting and alive with the sounds of typewriters, ringing telephones, and conversations between office workers and couriers. Navarro whistled.

"Hell of a lot busier than Marsing's courier office."

"Yes," Flint said. "Let us see if Madame Edwards can fit us into her schedule." He flagged down a Supernumerary with an armload of files. "I beg your pardon."

"How can I help, sir?" the man asked.

"Would you be so kind as to direct us toward Lady Edwards's office?"

"Of course, sir. End of the hallway, second to last door on your left."

"Thank you."

The two men strode forward, couriers weaving their way around them. Flint noticed some of the nameplates by the doors: Assistant Secretary for Acquisitions, Executive Vice President of Operations, Chief Financial Officer, Assistant Chief of Staff to the Undersecretary to the Vice President, and other convoluted titles.

"Hmph," he said. "The Imperial Capitol has passed on some of its worse habits."

"What does an Assistant Chief of Staff do?" Navarro asked.

"Little that is productive I would wager." It was no wonder General Hickock had difficulty finding the snake in his garden as he put it.

They arrived at their destination. Edwards, at least, had a simple title: the engraved plate next to her office door read COMMANDER JENNIFER EDWARDS, CHIEF OF STAFF. Flint turned the doorknob and stepped inside. The outer office had a watercooler, a potted tree, several chairs around a table strewn with magazines that were no doubt months out of date. A desk in the center was occupied by a female Supernumerary who was currently on the phone. She held up her index finger when she caught sight of the two men.

"Of course, sir. You'll have them on your desk before the end of the day," she said. Hanging up the phone, she shifted her attention to Flint and Navarro. "Good afternoon sir. How can I help today?"

"Captain Silas Flint and Ricardo Navarro, at your service. We should like to speak with Commander Edwards, if she is available, Miss…?"

"I'm Audrey Willis, the Commander's assistant. She's on a call at the moment, but I'd be happy to buzz you in once that's complete. May I ask what this is in regards to?"

"We are new here and we simply had a few questions for Lady Edwards."

"Oh, of course! I remember seeing you two from the welcome ceremony this morning. If you have any questions, I might be able to answer some for you."

"Have you noticed anything out of the ordinary about Lady Edwards?" Flint asked.

Willis blinked. "Uh… out of the ordinary? What do you mean? What's this about sir?"

"It may be nothing," Flint said. "But any observations you have made may be helpful."

Willis shrugged. "Can't think of anything major."

"How about minor?" Navarro asked.

"Well… now that you mention it, she left her office shortly after we got back from the courtyard, said she had a delivery to make. It doesn't happen often, but once in a while she'll deliver orders personally. When she came back, she was all red in the face, sweaty. Said she'd gone for a run."

Flint crossed his arms. "When did she leave her office?"

"About 12:15 I'd say."

"And when did she return?"

"12:45."

Flint nodded. He didn't know Steiner's exact time of death yet, but he suspected it was within that half hour window.

"Thank you, Miss Willis. We shall wait." He and Navarro took seats around the table. Willis busied herself typing documents. After five minutes, she picked up her phone, spun the rotary dial once.

"Ma'am, Captain Silas Flint and Ricardo Navarro have requested to speak with you." She nodded. "Yes ma'am." Another few moments passed while Willis listened. "Yes ma'am." She hung up the phone. "Commander Edwards will see you now. Go right on in."

"Thank you." Flint and Navarro went past Willis's desk to the door on the far wall. Flint turned the knob, opened the door. Edwards' office was packed with filing cabinets. Portraits of General Hickock and the Emperor were on the wall to their left. Behind Edwards's desk was a painting Flint recognized: *The Last Battle*, a portrayal of Simon Magus and his host meeting the Archangel Uriel outside the gates of Eden. Seated at the desk, gloved fingers interlocked and a serene expression on her face was Lady Templar Commander Jennifer Edwards. Her Templar hat hung on a rack behind her desk. She was a plain woman, with brunette hair hanging loosely about her shoulders.

"Good afternoon gentlemen," she said, rising from her desk, extending a gloved hand, which Flint and Navarro shook. "I'm Commander Jennifer Edwards, chief of staff for the courier department. Please, have a seat. How can I help you today?"

Flint and Navarro took the two seats in front of her desk. "It is a pleasure to meet you madame," Flint said. "We have a few questions about the recent tragedies that have befallen the garrison here at Fort Ingalls."

"Terrible," Edwards shook her head. "May God have mercy on the poor souls of all the fallen. I'll answer whatever I can Captain, but as you can imagine, I don't get out much."

Navarro looked at Flint, who gave him a nod. "Every written order, every document, comes through your office, right ma'am?" Navarro asked.

"Yes, that's correct. I don't personally see every paper of course, but a human being does lay eyes on everything at some point in the process."

"Can you tell us anything about Marquez and Fields?"

She blinked. "How do you mean?"

"I mean what were they doing in that warehouse last night?" Navarro asked.

"Oh yes... well, that whole area is mostly abandoned save for the homeless and drug addict population. We received a report from a homeless man of mysterious happenings coming from inside that warehouse. Lights, demonic laughter, the smells of blood and sulfur, that sort of thing. I suspected the man was drunk or high, most probably both. I had Marquez and Fields go check it out." She sighed. "It turns out the man was right."

"You? You had them go out there?" Flint asked.

"Er... well, I brought the report to General Hickock's attention and he told me to assign investigators to the matter. He gave the order. I chose Marquez and Fields because they didn't have an active case at that time."

"You guys always know where all of us are at all times, right?" Navarro asked.

Edwards smiled. "Our talents have been somewhat exaggerated in the telling, but yes, we generally know where all Templars and their assistants can be found based on numerous methods whose details I won't bore you gentlemen with."

"I trust that you are aware of the tragedy that has befallen Captain Jessica Steiner," Flint said.

Edwards looked down and sighed. "Yes. Who'd have

thought that one of our own would turn from the light to join the powers of darkness?"

"I beg your pardon?"

"It's my job to know these things, Captain. I've already heard everything. The fiend took the rosaries from all the Templars she's murdered over her career. But it sounds as though she got what she deserved. She was apparently casting a spell that was beyond her skill and she paid the price. You know how these foul witches can be, always hungry for more power."

Flint said nothing. He gazed at Edwards and she gazed back. "I am curious," Flint said. "You said that it is your job to know where we all are. How is it that you failed to notice Captain Steiner was practicing witchcraft?"

Edwards scowled. "I don't appreciate your tone, Captain. But to answer your question, you of all people should know that witches are experts at hiding in plain sight."

"Yes. Yes, they are."

An uncomfortable silence fell in the room, save for the ticking of a clock on the wall.

"Do you know where Captain Steiner was last night?" Navarro asked.

A beat passed before Edwards said, "She said she was out on a case."

"Was she?" Flint asked.

"She did have an active case on her docket. She left around 8 p.m. last night."

"Are you aware of her movements today?" Navarro said.

"Of course I am. She attended your welcoming ceremony.

After that she returned to her room, no doubt to practice her nefarious craft."

Flint's eyes shifted to Edwards's desk. There was a photograph of a younger Edwards standing side by side with an older man in a tailored suit, a scarlet sash over his shoulder. Edwards followed Flint's eyes.

"My father and I," she said.

"Your father is...?"

"Yes. Benjamin Edwards, Minister of Justice."

Flint locked eyes with Edwards again. "Are you alright, Commander?"

"I'm sorry?"

"Your gloves. Did you injure your hands?"

She shifted in her chair. "No. No, not at all. As you can imagine, I have a mountain of paperwork to do every day. I wear gloves to keep the ink off my fingers."

"I see," Flint said. Another few moments of silence passed.

"Was there anything else I could assist you gentlemen with?"

"It's kind a bonehead question but..." Navarro said.

"Ask it and you may get a bonehead answer," Edwards said.

"Where's the gym?"

Edwards paused, then laughed. "I'm sorry?"

"You know, the gym, the fitness center, whatever you guys have here. I ate too much last night, need to burn some extra calories, you know?"

"Er... when you exit the tower, it'll be in the east wing, first floor, third door on your right."

"Nice, thank you. They got weight machines, treadmills, all that stuff?"

"I wouldn't know. I haven't been there in years. I probably should though. Sitting at a desk all day is going to ruin my figure," she chuckled.

"Oh you haven't?" Navarro asked. "We were talking to your assistant out there before we came in. She said you'd been out for a run. I guess I just assumed you were on a treadmill at the gym."

Edwards blinked, smiled. "No... no I wasn't. I... went out to deliver some orders. I had to catch Sir Grant before he left. I ran downstairs into the courtyard, and then I ran back here. That's what I meant."

Flint gave her a wintry smile. "Running in the summer heat while wearing black can be quite strenuous."

"Yes, yes it is. I probably won't do that again," Edwards chuckled. She rose from her desk. "Well, gentlemen, if there are no other questions, I have work to do."

"Just one more question, if you please. It is of a more... personal nature."

Edwards paused. She gave Flint an odd look before saying, "Yes?"

"May I ask about your mother? I did not see any pictures of her on your desk."

Edwards stiffened. "I fail to see how that is any of your business, Captain."

"Forgive me. I ask because I lost both of my parents at a young age."

Her face softened a bit. "My mother died when I was very young. I'm afraid I don't have any photographs of her."

"I am sorry."

"And I'm sorry for your loss as well."

"Good day to you Commander. God be with you."

Edwards's nostrils flared before she answered, "And also with you, Captain."

Flint and Navarro exited her office. They said nothing to each other as they proceeded down the hallway toward the stairwell. Once they shut the door behind them, Flint said, "She is the witch."

"Yeah," Navarro replied. "Now we just have to prove it."

22

After the two men left her office, Alice picked up the telephone on her desk, dialed, and held the receiver to her ear. The other end picked up immediately.

"Ministry of Justice," said a female voice.

"This is Jennifer Edwards. I'd like to speak to my father please."

"One moment Miss Edwards."

She heard clicks and buzzes as the line was transferred.

"Jennifer!" her father said. "How are you dear?"

"Father... I'm afraid I have some bad news."

There was a pause. "What's happening? Are you okay?"

"No... there's trouble here at Fort Ingalls."

"What sort of trouble?"

"I'm sure you're aware of all of the recent casualties we've sustained over the last few months."

"Yes. Damn those witches. I pray that whoever's responsible for this is put to the torch."

Alice winced but kept her voice level. "That's what I wanted to talk to you about. I think we may have found her: Captain Jessica Steiner."

There was another pause. "Are you saying...?"

"Yes. She was a witch. She's responsible for all of the murders."

"Dear God... wait. Was?"

"Yes. She was found dead in her quarters earlier this afternoon. We think she had some sort of accident while she was attempting to cast a spell."

"Sounds like she got what she deserved then."

"Yes. Yes, she did."

"How can I help Jennifer?"

"Some of my colleagues aren't satisfied that Steiner was the killer."

"Why wouldn't they be? There were signs of her practicing witchcraft, I take it."

"Yes, there were. The problem is that some of them believe she was framed."

There was a pause. "What makes them think that?"

"I think some of them just refuse to believe their own eyes. I saw her, dad. Only magic can do that kind of damage. She was alone in her room. No one was seen coming or going from her quarters. And she had a bunch of rosaries she'd taken off her victims. It's a hard thing, knowing there was a traitor in our midst for God knows how long, but some of my coworkers just don't want to face facts."

"Based on what you've told me, it sounds like an open and shut case."

"You'd think so. But paranoia is a way of life for us."

"How can I help?" he asked again.

"I was wondering… we don't have the same tools that your people do. I was thinking, maybe you could send a couple of CBI agents over," she said, referring to the Cascadia Bureau of Investigation.

Minister Edwards said nothing for a few moments. "Dear, this sounds like an internal Templar matter. I don't have the authority to…"

"You've said yourself that you wanted more cooperation between the Order and secular law enforcement."

"Yes but…"

"I'm not asking for a full blown investigation. Just a few agents to… advise and assist. It's an internal matter, yes, but that also means everyone here is, ah, emotionally involved so to speak."

"I'll… have to contact General Hickock."

"I understand dad. By the way, it's been a while since we've had dinner together. What are you doing tonight?"

"It has been a while, hasn't it? I think I can make time for you. Shall I come pick you up at, say, seven?"

"That sounds great dad. Thanks for your help. I'll see you soon."

"I love you dear."

"…I love you too. Dad."

The line clicked as Minister Edwards hung up. CBI agents sticking their noses into this case should gum up the bureaucratic machine nicely.

Alice, her mother whispered. *You need to get down to the personnel files.*

She smiled. "Yes mother."

23

"Commander Edwards?" Hickock asked. Flint and Navarro had gone directly to his office after their meeting with the head of the courier department. Hickock's office was decorated with portraits of the Emperor and the Pope, framed photographs of his career highlights along with newspaper articles. A grandfather clock in the corner ticked, the pendulum swung back and forth, as Hickock leaned back in his chair, the wood creaking beneath his bulk.

"I am almost certain of it," Flint replied.

Hickock sighed. "Shit," he said. He stroked his beard. "This is… shit."

"Couldn't have said it better myself sir," Navarro said.

"Okay," Hickock said. "Tell me everything she told you."

Together, Flint and Navarro related the details of their conversation with Edwards. Hickock steepled his fingers as he took it all in. When they had finished, he said, "I can see why you'd suspect her. But I'm not hearing any hard evidence. She's the Justice Minister's daughter, so we need to have all of our ducks in a row before we begin making formal accusations."

"Indeed," Flint replied. "The warehouse where Sirs Marquez and Fielding died. She said that she brought a report to your attention concerning unusual happenings there."

Hickock nodded. "Yes, I remember."

"And you told her to send men out there?"

"Yeah. I told her to choose two people here at the Fort who didn't have an active case they were working."

"Can you account for her whereabouts after you spoke with her?"

"As far as I know, she returned to her quarters. She almost never leaves the Fort, except to have dinner with her father once in a while."

"And Captain Steiner… Edwards said that she left Fort Ingalls around 8 p.m. last night, claiming to be on a case."

Hickock thought for a moment. He opened a drawer in his desk and took out an enormous notebook. He thumbed through the pages, stopping near the end. He put the open notebook on his desk, pointing at what looked like hieroglyphics to Flint.

"May I ask what I am looking at sir?"

Hickock scoffed. "It's right there, black and white."

Navarro squinted at the page. "Looks like chicken scratch."

Hickock opened his mouth to say something, stopped. He chuckled. "Yeah, I guess my handwriting is kind of hard to read. That there are my notes on Steiner's caseload. I always keep track of what my boys and girls are working on in my personal files. As of yesterday, she didn't have an open case."

Flint stroked his chin. "Is there a Templar by the name of Grant stationed here?"

"There's a few. First or last name?"

"Last, I believe."

Hickock put the notebook away and took out another, equally large. He thumbed his way to the page he was looking for. "Three Grants. Let's see… Andy Grant. He left for

Astoria a week ago. Eleanor Grant… she's investigating rumors of a cult in Newport. And… Enoch Grant. He's on leave, visiting his parents in Medford."

"That's two lies so far, by my count," Navarro said.

"Indeed, and I do not believe they are the only things," Flint said.

Hickock drummed his fingers on his desk. "Well boys, I have to admit, things aren't looking good for Commander Edwards."

The rotary telephone on Hickock's desk rang. He picked up and said, "General Hickock." He listened for a few moments. "Yes sir, that's true… What?… No sir, I don't think that will be necessary… I understand that sir… Who called it in?… I see… No, you don't have to… yes sir. Very well." He hung up.

"What's up?" Navarro asked.

"That was the Assistant Undersecretary of Justice," Hickock said. "One of them anyway, only God knows how many there are. He said they got a call from Fort Ingalls requesting assistance on this case and they're sending over a couple of CBI agents to 'advise and assist.'"

"I take it that you placed no such call," Flint said.

"Nope, sure as hell wasn't me. He says it came from the courier's office."

"Maybe Edwards is trying to get ahead of this," Navarro said.

Hickock barked a laugh. "Witches and lawyers is a match made in Hell if I ever heard one."

"Have your men finished dusting for fingerprints in Steiner's quarters?" Flint asked.

"Yep. Found a bunch of them all over, all identical, so I reckon those are Steiner's. They found a different set of prints on the door, full handprint."

"I suggest we compare them first to Commander Edwards's."

"Have any luck finding out about that rosary the sisters gave us?" Navarro asked.

"That one should be coming in soon. Speaking of them sisters, you given that fancy radio of yours a listen today?"

"No sir, haven't had the time."

"Why don't you turn her on now? I'd like to talk to your weirdo friends myself."

"They are not our friends, sir," Flint said. He checked his pocket watch. 3:27 p.m. "As it happens, it is nearly time for the news update."

Navarro took the radio out of the pouch on his belt and thumbed the power switch. A soft jazz tune filled Hickock's office. He shook his head.

"That is damned peculiar," he said, "Listening to a radio station that don't broadcast anymore." They continued listening to the music. Flint didn't recognize this particular song but it evoked in him feelings of anxiety. The song came to an end. There were a few moments of silence. Then the familiar three note chime sounded.

"This is Mallory Proctor."

"Joining her is Monica Proctor."

"With special correspondent Madeline Proctor."

"And now for the news," the three sisters said in unison.

"Hey! Hello? Can you weirdos hear me?" Hickock bellowed into the radio's speaker.

"That was rude Jeremiah," Mallory said.

"We are not deaf," Monica said.

"We are not weirdos," Madeline said.

"Let's just agree to disagree," Hickock said. "Listen here, I want to know the meaning of this. What are we supposed to do with that there rosary you gave to these boys?"

"Are you bamboozled?"

"Are you befuddled?"

"Are you discombobulated?"

"He asked you a question, witches," Flint said.

"Hello again Silas."

"You know we can't directly interfere."

"We can say that you are on the right track."

"Aw come on," Navarro said. "Not even a hint?"

The three sisters laughed together.

"We know what is on your mind Ricardo."

"We are flattered."

"But we are not as we appear to you."

Navarro blushed and looked away. Hickock put an elbow on his desk, leaned forward to speak into the radio. "Look, I've only read about you three, but it seems to me you're interfering plenty already. You can't or won't give us the straight skinny? Fine. Then give us an indirect hint. Give us something. If we're gonna burn someone, I want to be damn sure it's the right one."

There was silence from the radio for a few moments.

"The rosary is a powerful form of prayer."

"It has been known to work miracles."

"What does it say about a Templar who throws theirs away?"

Flint perked up. "The rosary you sent me... its owner discarded it?"

"Yes. You are so close."

"You are approaching the beginning of the end."

"Or perhaps it is the end of the beginning."

The three men exchanged confused looks.

"One more thing Silas."

"If you happen to find a sapphire..."

"You should give it to Zelda when you get home."

"The Proctor Sisters, signing off," they said in unison. The chime played. A male voice broke in.

"Welcome back to Cascadia's number one station for classical music. I'm Nick Sanderson, and we've got thirty minutes of uninterrupted..."

Hickock switched off the radio. He stared at it for a few seconds before handing it back to Navarro. He tapped his finger on his desk.

"Nick Sanderson died a few years back. I'm sure of it."

"Jesus Christ," Navarro said, crossing himself.

Hickock sighed. "I can see why you'd get frustrated with them."

"That is an understatement sir," Flint replied. "But they brought up an interesting point. What does it mean about a Templar who would toss their rosary into the refuse?"

Hickock picked up the telephone receiver, spun the rotary dial twice. "Put me through to personnel please." He drummed his fingers on the desk, sighed. He glanced at the clock. "The hell is taking them so... Yes? General Hickock here, I... wait, slow down... What?!"

He slammed the receiver down and rose from his chair. "There's a fire in the archives."

24

The three men rushed to the basement where the air was thick with black smoke. Several Supernumeraries were standing in the hallway, watching the fire crew finish their work. They had caught the fire quickly at least, Flint thought.

"What happened here?" Hickock asked.

"I don't know sir," one of the Supernumeraries said. "We were in the back sorting files when Roberto said he smelled smoke. Next thing we know the whole front of the archives are going up in flames."

"Was anyone hurt?"

"Some smoke inhalations, but other than that, everyone's alright."

"Do you know which files were destroyed?" Flint asked.

"Yeah... mostly personnel files of active duty Templars."

"Let me guess," Navarro said. "The files that start with E went up in smoke."

"That's... some of them yeah," the man said. "How'd you know?"

"Call it a hunch."

The three men huddled, away from the fire crew and the archivists.

"Bitch is getting pretty brazen," Navarro said.

"Yes, it is most convenient for Lady Edwards that person-

nel records which include her fingerprints should be con-
signed to the flames the moment suspicion falls on her."

Hickock snapped his fingers. "Newman!" he shouted.

A Supernumerary jogged up to the group. He stopped,
gave a crisp salute. "Wayne Newman reporting as ordered
sir."

"Mr. Newman, did you manage to find a match on those
fingerprints you lifted from Steiner's room?"

"No sir, not yet."

"Shit."

"You still have 'em with you?" Navarro asked. "Maybe we
could give 'em to the cops, see if they can find a match."

"The police would only have the fingerprints on file if the
owner had been previously arrested," Flint said. "But it is a
start."

"We'll compare 'em with birth and confirmation certifi-
cates if we have to," Hickock growled. "What about that
rosary, you find anything out about that?"

"Yes sir. That one just took some asking around with the
old timers." Newman took the rosary out of his pocket and
held it up, pointing at the first bead after the crucifix. "Alyssa
Bates," he said. Pointing at the second bead he said,
"Gertrude Simmons," and so on down the line until he
reached the last set of initials. "Hannah Freeman."

"Hannah Freeman?" Hickock said.

"Yes sir."

"Do you know her?" Flint asked.

"I knew of her. She passed away a few years ago. Lived
long enough to retire though. I was a Commander back

then, but I remember the ceremony. I remember one of the people she mentored: Jennifer Edwards."

25

Alice sat in her office, her face buried in her hands.

You did the right thing Alice, her mother whispered.

"Did I?" she asked, looking up.

Of course. The pulled your fingerprints off Steiner's door. Once they compared them to your file, the game would be up. But now you've destroyed your file. Your safe for now.

"You saw Captain Flint earlier, didn't you? He suspects me. And now this fire... he's going to know it's me."

Don't panic dear. There is still no hard evidence against you. Keep your cool, and this will blow over.

"I don't know... I get the feeling I may end up fighting my way out of here after all."

Nonsense. You'll have a lovely dinner with your father, and then you can just... not come back.

Alice sighed. She had been certain that she could salvage the operation and continue assassinating Templars. And maybe she could have, for a little while. But she realized now the game was over the moment that oaf Hickock began to consider the possibility of a traitor in his midst. She'd held off from killing for a few weeks when the thought first appeared in his mind, but she hadn't been able to resist for long.

If it hadn't been for that damn Steiner walking in when she did, Alice wouldn't have to be thinking about pulling up stakes from the only life she'd ever known. It was the right decision to kill her, of that she had no doubt. But why had she been so distracted? How is it she didn't notice that Steiner was approaching until it was too late?

"Mother," she said.

Yes my dear?

"What is happening to me?"

You're about to begin a new chapter of your life. Soon you will leave this place forever. You will leave behind the superstitions of the Church that have held you back your entire life. You will stalk the earth like a lion among sheep. Charles and Lilian have the right idea, but they do not go far enough. They wish for our kind to be left alone when we should rule this world.

Alice said nothing.

Simon Magus brought us the gift of magic. It's because of him that I'm able to speak to you through the veil of shadows. We owe it to his memory to continue his work. If the sheep will not follow us, then they don't deserve to live.

"What are you suggesting mother?"

Go to your inner sanctum. If you expect to survive the ordeals to come, you're going to need friends on the other side.

"Mother…"

Or you can die as I did, writhing and screaming as the flames consume you.

Alice scowled. Her breathing grew heavier. Her mother was right. There was still a chance she could escape from here, make her way to wherever Charles and his partner were hiding out. But it was increasingly likely that she'd have to cut her way out. There was no way she could fight the entire garrison at Fort Ingalls by herself. No, if worse came to worst, she would need help. She'd need allies, friends. It was long past the time for her to abandon the Church, to turn her back on the God who condoned her mother's burning once and for all.

"Yes," Alice said.

Yes what?

"I need help. I need your friends."

Excellent. You're making the right choice dear. You're not going to get caught, but why take a chance?

"What must I do?"

Well, you understand they're usually quite busy. If you desire their blessing and their help, then they will want something in exchange.

"Such as?"

What they always want: more blood, more souls.

26

Audrey Willis's fingers tapped another set of orders on the ancient typewriter. The original would be sent to its intended recipient, carbon copies would be kept here for the records department, General Hickock would keep track of them in one of those notebooks. Willis found this secretarial work a bit boring sometimes, but it had to be done, and she had proven herself quite good at it over the course of her career with Lady Edwards.

Willis was no coward, but she had to admit it was a relief

she didn't have to face witches, monsters, vampires, cannibal cultists, or any of the other dangers Templars faced every day. It was definitely a relief to her parents, who had disapproved of her choice in vocation. It was no place for a young lady, they said. You should settle down and make our grandbabies, they said.

Willis had nothing against marriage or family, but she wasn't sure she was ready to go that far. She was only 23. She still had time. And she didn't want to get married and have children simply to satisfy her parents. No, if she took that step, it had to be a good man, a man she could respect. Those two men who had come to visit Commander Edwards earlier? The Witch Hunter scared the hell out of her, if she was being honest with herself. His assistant though... he did cut a rather handsome figure.

The console on her desk buzzed. She pushed a button.

"How can I help ma'am?" Willis asked.

"Audrey, could you come in here?" Edwards's tinny voice crackled through the speaker. "I need to go over a few things with you."

"Of course, Commander. I'll be right over." Willis opened a drawer in her desk and took out a laminate sign that read WILL BE BACK IN 15 MINUTES. She stuck it in the window of the door that led to the hallway, then went back to her desk and gave the door to Edwards's office a few knocks.

"Enter," came the Commander's voice.

Willis opened the door, stepped inside, and gasped. Edwards looked terrible. Her face was pale and drawn with dark bags under her eyes.

"Come in," Edwards said. She beckoned with her gloved right hand which Willis could see now held a tremor.

"Ma'am…" Willis said, advancing further into Edwards's inner sanctum. "What's wrong? You look like you've seen a ghost."

Edwards laughed. Despite her haggard appearance, the laugh made her sound like her old self. "Oh Audrey… I wish I could explain." She wiped a tear away from her eye.

"I'm sorry ma'am, I don't understand."

"Please, have a seat."

Willis felt a sense of unease. Something was wrong here, and not just Commander Edwards's appearance. What was it the medics called it? A sense of impending doom. She swallowed, hoped she didn't let on how uncomfortable she felt.

Edwards ran a hand through her hair. "Audrey… I'm not well."

Willis thought that was the understatement of the year, but said, "How can I help ma'am?"

"I think… I think I need some time off. Would you ask Captain White to please come to my office? I'd like him to take over for me while I'm away."

Willis nodded. "Of course, ma'am."

A few seconds of silence passed. "Was there something else, Miss Willis?" Edwards asked.

"I'm curious ma'am. Why did you call me in here? You could have used the intercom."

Edwards favored her with a wan smile. "You've always been a good assistant to me Audrey. I thought you deserved to hear from me face-to-face that I'd be going away for a while."

"Oh… thank you Commander. You've been a good boss."

"Dismissed."

27

Alice sat and watched Willis leave her office. It was done. The die was cast. Once Captain White was dead, she would speak with her mother's friends on the other side. She could finally abandon the masquerade, step back through the looking glass, become her true self.

Daughter.

"Yes mother?"

Why are you letting your little assistant go?

"I meant what I said. She's been a good secretary. More than that, I think of her as a friend."

If she knew the truth, she would turn on you. She would burn you.

"Then I guess she won't learn the truth until it's too late then, will she?"

The voice in her head fell silent for a while. Alice drummed her fingers on her desk.

Are you going to miss this life?

Now that was a good question. Alice looked around at her office, at the reminders of her career as a Witch Hunter. She smiled. Yes, that was all it was to her: a job. The others thought of it as a calling from God Himself. And if God wants you to murder people for the so-called crime of using magic to improve oneself, then who are you to question it?

"I'll miss a few people here. I'll miss being able to see father every day."

Benjamin... he shouldn't have lied to you about my death.

"No, he shouldn't have. But I understand his reasoning. I was only a child. I didn't need to hear back then that you died screaming. And it worked out well in the end. If I hadn't become a Templar, I may never have met Charles or been able to assist with his plans. Who else can boast so many Templar kills?"

There was a knock at her door.

"Enter."

Captain Luke White entered her office. Mail department staff normally didn't carry their weapons with them, and she was pleased to see that White was being true to type.

"You wanted to see me Commander?" he asked.

"Yes, thank you for coming. Please, take a seat."

White sat down in one of the cushioned chairs before Alice's desk. "Audrey didn't tell me anything beyond your desire to see me."

"In that case, I have a surprise for you. I will be taking a leave of absence, effective immediately."

White opened his mouth to speak, paused, closed it. "That's..."

"And I'd like you to take my place while I'm away."

"Ma'am... I..."

"I will recommend you for promotion to Commander, as will befit your new duties."

"Ma'am... I... I'm honored."

She extended her hand across her desk, which White

shook with vigor. "It will take some time for the paperwork to go through, but your service in this office has been exemplary. I don't think it's presumptuous of me to be the first to congratulate you, Commander White."

White looked overwhelmed, unsure of what to say. Alice gave him her best approximation of a warm smile. She almost felt sorry for the poor fool.

Regaining his composure, White said, "Is everything alright Lady Edwards? I don't mean to pry, but why the sudden departure?"

"Oh, you know. It's been ages since I took any time off. I can assure you that going over all of the orders, case files, reports can be exhausting in its own way."

"I understand ma'am."

"Before I go though, I need to show you a few things. If you'll follow me?" She rose from her seat, White following suit. Alice went to one of the bookshelves lining her office. She pulled down a book called *Witchcraft in the 24th Century*. There was a click. She pulled the bookshelf away from the wall revealing a doorway.

White stepped forward, peered into the doorway. There was a staircase lit by flickering electric lamps ensconced on every landing.

"What is this?" he asked.

"One of the department's secrets," Alice said, smiling. "Everyone knows that Fort Ingalls was built around the site of an ancient hospital. What most people don't know is that hospital contained a series of secret doorways, hidden stairwells, and underground tunnels. They could move patients from building to building without ever needing to surface or go outside."

"Fascinating…"

"Isn't it though? This stairwell leads down to a central hub underground that connects to most of the buildings on site. Come, let me show you." She stepped through the doorway and onto the landing. White followed her and they began their descent as the door shut behind them. "These passageways are partly responsible for our reputation of always being in the right place at the right time. Not even General Hickock knows about all of them. This one, for example."

They continued down the stairs. Alice could feel the magical energy rising within her, but the time wasn't right yet. White took no notice of her agitation, peering all around him.

"This place… it's kind of eerie."

"You get used to it."

Alice could sense White's rising apprehension. She needed to get him into her inner sanctum to do the deed. Just a little bit further. She could see the landing open up below.

"We're almost there," she said.

They stepped out into the hub. She hadn't been lying about that part; from here nearly two miles of tunnels connected to every building within the grounds of Fort Marsing. Through careful use of magic over the years, she'd done some remodeling, rerouting a tunnel here, blocking off a passage there. They were little more than a historical curiosity to most of the Templars who knew about them, her modifications completely unknown.

White's jaw dropped open. Alice could sense is outrage but more than a little fear as well. He was unarmed and he'd walked directly into the spider's lair. The first thing he noticed was the enormous pentagram painted onto the floor, Baphomet's demonic visage grinning up at the staircase.

"What blasphemy is..." His voice was choked off as Alice seized him by the throat through telekinesis. His hands scrabbled at his throat, his face was contorted in pain, desperate for breath, his skin turning red. With the power of her mind, she hurled him against the wall. Then again. Then a third time, his body flopping like a rag doll. She made sure not to kill him though. No, her mother had told her they liked them alive, to know that it was coming. Something about the taste of fear. Her body tingled with an anticipation that touched her very soul. No more straddling the fence. She was about to pass the point of no return.

She moved White over the pentagram, his battered and bloody body levitating over the demonic face on the floor. He coughed and spat a mouthful of blood.

"It was you... it was you all along..." he wheezed.

"Yes."

"When... when did you turn?!"

"Oh, I turned years ago Luke. It's only recently that I began my master's campaign against you, so don't feel too bad. I'd hate for you to die with any hard feelings."

"The others will find you and they'll send you straight to... urk!" his voice was cut off as she tightened her telekinetic grip around his throat.

"What do I do now mother?" Alice asked.

Offer him up dear.

"How?"

"Who… are you talking to…?" White gasped.

Offer him body and soul to the powers below. The specific words don't matter, only the intention.

Alice extended her left hand. A dagger flew from the altar and into her grip. Slowly she unsheathed it, admiring its wicked curve, perfect for the task at hand.

"You… can kill my body… but you can't touch… my soul…" White said. He spat in Alice's direction.

She smiled. "We'll see about that." She raised her arms. "Hear me, o powers below! I renounce the false and wicked God and all of His empty promises. I pledge myself to you, now and forever. I offer you the body and soul of this deluded man of God. Take him and grant me… power. Power to control my destiny. Power to scatter my enemies. Power to realize the dream of Simon Magus. Power to be the greatest and most terrible witch of all."

Wonderful… wonderful, Jennifer, her mother said. *Do it now.*

Alice strode toward White, who levitated above the pentagram. He lashed out, tried to kick her, but she saw it coming and easily dodged. She tightened her telekinetic grip on his body, pinning his limbs in place.

He spat again, this time into her face. "They'll find you, you traitorous whore," he snarled. "They'll find you and you'll burn." Alice hesitated, wiped the saliva off her cheek. White relaxed, his lips moving, no doubt reciting prayers.

She smiled. This man had devoted his life to God, and look at him now, about to be butchered like a helpless lamb. If this was the reward God gave His faithful servants, it was no wonder so few answered the call.

She pushed his head back with her mind, exposing his throat. She drew the dagger across his neck. A red line appeared which soon produced a torrent of blood. White gurgled as his life's blood poured out onto the pentagram. He twitched, gurgled once more, and was still. She let go, his body dropping onto the floor. The blood pooled, expanded until it reached the boundary of the pentagram and then stopped. The symbols she had painted within the pentagram lit up, glowing through the blood. The lights flickered and dimmed. An icy chill permeated the chamber as she felt a weight pressing on her chest.

"Welcome, my faithful servant," came a voice from everywhere and nowhere, deep enough that Alice felt the rumble deep in her chest. "We are most pleased with your gift."

"Masters… give me power," she said.

"Let it be so."

Alice arched her back and let forth a primal scream as she felt every nerve alight with the surge of magical energy that poured into her. Arcs of electricity ran over her body, her eyes rolled back in her head. It was too much. Too much…

Hold on Jennifer, just a bit longer. You can do it. I believe in you.

Alice gritted her teeth. She felt like her soul was being flayed. She balled her fists, the gloves burning away. She would have the power, or she would die trying. And once she had the power, she would make her enemies pay. She would make them pay for the murder of her mother, for all of the witches and wizards they'd killed. The Templars were a blight on humanity, vermin who presumed to stop men and women from realizing their destiny, their true power. Vermin did not deserve to live. They deserved only death.

The pain stopped. She fell to her knees, her hands on the floor. She gasped, tried to regain her breath. Alice felt... no. She didn't need that name anymore. Alice was a codename given to her by Charles Flint, her teacher. Her former master. She felt her powers magnified tenfold. She was grateful to Charles for enlightening her about her magical heritage. She still felt some of her old attraction for him. But he was her master no longer. She knew now that she had surpassed him. She had done what he had dared not. There was no need to hide anymore. She was Jennifer Edwards, and soon the whole world would tremble at her name.

Edwards laughed. Her laughter grew manic. There had been so much she had wanted to do, and now she could do it. She could do anything. Anything at all.

Well done my daughter, her mother's voice whispered in her mind. *What will you do now?*

Edwards had originally planned to flee, to join Charles, take her place as his right hand. But why should she submit to her inferior? She was his superior now.

Yes. You are invincible Jennifer. You can do anything. You can make the Templars pay for killing me.

Edwards raised her hands. "Let there be chaos."

28

Silas Flint led the procession down the hallway of the courier office, his sword in one hand, one of his pistols in the other. Navarro was close on his heels. At Hickock's suggestion, he'd acquired a shotgun from the armory which he held at the low ready. Behind them both, General Hickock and three of his most trusted Templars followed in their wake. The couriers and secretaries stopped what they were doing and tracked the posse with their eyes. None dared question what their purpose was.

Flint opened the door to Edwards's outer office. The secretary, Willis, was at her post. She looked up, her face a mix of shock and relief.

"Where is Commander Edwards?" Flint asked.

"She's in her office," Willis said. "She's in a meeting with Captain White."

Hickock came forward, Willis rising from her seat, coming to attention.

"Miss Willis, you get yourself and everyone on this floor on out of here. Go back to your quarters and keep your weapons ready. You might end up needing 'em."

"It's about Commander Edwards isn't it?"

"Yes," Flint said. "Do you know anything Miss Willis?"

"She called me into her office earlier. She looked terrible. Told me she was going to take a leave of absence, effective immediately."

"Has she left her office?" Navarro asked.

"No, she hasn't. Captain White went in a few minutes

ago. The wall's soundproofed so I haven't heard anything."

"Go down to the main gate. Tell them I want the Fort locked down. Nobody goes in or out until I say otherwise," Hickock said.

"Yes sir," Willis said.

"Go now."

As Willis ran out of the office, Flint approached the door to Edwards's chambers. He kicked it open, sweeping left from the doorway while Navarro went right, covering what turned out to be an empty room. They lowered their weapons as Hickock and his detail entered the office.

"Where the hell is she?" Hickock asked.

Flint circled the room. His sword began to glow. It got brighter the closer he got to the bookshelves. There. He was before a bookcase that stood separate from the others. Something on it was rich with dark magic. He peered closely at the titles. Perhaps there was a spell book on there? The treacherous witch would have to be especially brazen to keep such a title in plain sight. There was a thick layer of dust on top of every book except one: *Witchcraft in the 24th Century*.

The tower rumbled. Overhead the ceiling lamp swayed on its chain. From the hallway they heard the crash of books and papers tumbling to the floor.

"You get earthquakes here?" Navarro asked, leaning against the wall.

"No, we..." Hickock began.

"Sir?!" one of the other Templars shouted. "You need to see this!" He led them out of Edwards's office back the way they had come to a window inside another office. The Salem skyline appeared to ripple in the late afternoon heat. The Templar pointed down and the men directed their gaze to the courtyard. Before their eyes, the grass died, a brown circle expanding outward from the center.

A beam of green light broke through the ground, rising into the sky and out of sight, the Witch Hunters backing away from the window. Screams and howls assaulted Flint's ears, the screams of the damned, the screams of all the legions of Hell itself. Dark clouds materialized in the afternoon sky, blocking out the sun, booms of thunder adding to the cacophony. Shielding his eyes against the eldritch light of the magical energy, Flint saw movement in the clouds: winged humanoid figures circling in the now darkened skies, illuminated by green flashes of lightning.

29

Detective Elijah Earle sat at his desk in Central PD. He had paperwork to do, but his mind drifted to the bodies he had seen that morning and the conversation he had with the Witch Hunter. He shook his head. Earle believed in God, but he didn't think of himself as especially faithful. As his grandmother used to say, you can't not believe in God with the world the way it is. He'd heard plenty of stories about witches and wizards. On an intellectual level, he knew what they could do, but he'd never seen it firsthand until this morning. He'd been a cop for twenty years and seen a lot of bodies, but nothing like that poor bastard who got his face melted off. He shivered despite the afternoon heat.

His partner, Jay Marsten leaned back in his chair, looking

around the cubicle wall that separated them. "Not hot enough for you buddy?"

"No, it's not that," Earle said. "I was just thinking about this morning."

Marsten pursed his lips. "I hear ya... witches, magic... shit gives me the creeps. I'll take ordinary serial killers any day."

"Wish there was more we could do for those guys."

"You been holding out on me partner? You got enough silver to melt down into ammo?"

Earle laughed. "Not on a cop's salary I don't."

"Don't worry about it then. They'll give us a call if they need help."

"You ever think about it when you were a kid? Becoming a Witch Hunter?"

"Nah. It's hard enough keeping the faith just looking at all the evil shit regular people do. Don't know how those guys can keep believing when they gotta deal with people who sell their souls to demons or whatever."

"Yeah but... if demons are real, then that means God's gotta be real too, right? Witch Hunters gotta have God on their side if they can stand up to all that."

Marsten thought for a moment. "Yeah, I see your point. I've never seen much evidence of God looking out for me though. If He's looking out for Witch Hunters, good for them, but God leaves me alone so I leave him alone."

'What about when your first wife left you?"

"I take it back. Maybe God's looking out for me after all."

The two detectives laughed together but they were interrupted by a rumbling noise. Their cubicles shook, Earle's coffee mug sliding off the desk and shattering on the floor.

Other officers cried out in surprise and fear. The lights overhead flickered.

"The fuck?" Earle said.

"Earthquake?" Marsten asked.

"Jesus Christ!"

A uniformed officer had opened the blinds and a crowd was gathering around the window. Everyone saw a column of green light rising into the sky which was darkening with the appearance of black clouds. Soon the sun was blotted out and it was as though night had fallen several hours early. Green flashes in the clouds were followed by the crack of thunder. The station was silent as the scene unfolded before them.

Then the phones all rang at once.

30

Santiago Cardinal Benítez knelt on the tile floor before the tabernacle which housed the Blessed Sacrament, Christ truly present. Behind him, the priests that served the community which attended Mass at the Cathedral of St. Benedict were kneeling in the pews. After a brief meditation before their Blessed Lord, Benítez would lead his clergy in reading Vespers, the evening prayers of the Catholic Church. Benítez was 65; young by the standards of the clergy, but his knees weren't what they used to be. In another year or two, he reflected, he'd have to use the padded kneelers in the pews if he hoped to get on his feet again.

He offered prayers for the Templar Chapter House at Fort Ingalls. He'd had to perform far more funerals than usual for those brave men and women over the last few months. The last he'd heard from Ingalls, General Hickock had requested Templars from Chapter Houses elsewhere in the Empire to transfer to Fort Ingalls as a temporary measure until their numbers could be replenished with more local recruits. Benítez prayed for their success.

The Cathedral rumbled. The overhead lanterns shook on their ropes, the glass of the votary candles rattled. He opened his eyes and looked all around him. He could hear the priests murmuring in anxiety and fear. He rose to his feet, his knees cracking with the effort.

"What in God's name…"

There was a flash in his peripheral vision. Turning, he saw a green light filtering through the stained glass windows. He genuflected before the tabernacle before walking up the aisle of the Cathedral, his priests close behind him. He pushed open the double doors and stepped outside. To the west, he saw a beam of green light rising into the sky and out of sight. Dark clouds formed and blotted out the sun, casting the city in unnatural night. He could feel a weight pressing down on his shoulders. The late afternoon heat became an unholy chill.

"Your Eminence," one of the priests said. "What do we do?"

Benítez looked to the light again. Unless he was mistaken, he was certain that it was coming from in or near Fort Ingalls.

"Pray," he said.

"Attention. Unusual energy signature detected."

Charles looked up. He had been studying a technical manual inside the former office of Major General Harold Irving, presumably the man in charge of this installation.

"What are you talking about?" Charles asked.

"Charles!" Lilian called. "You should come take a look at this."

He rose from his seat and stepped out into the hallway. Lilian's voice had come from what she called the observation room. It was dominated by a large screen that provided a map of the globe. He wasn't sure how it worked or how the computer could have the range to encompass the earth with its "sensors," but he found it most impressive.

He entered the observation room and saw that Lilian had focused the screen on North America. A bright red dot was glowing near the western coast.

"Computer, magnify," she said.

The screen zoomed in on a section of the map centered around the red dot.

"What are we looking at?" he asked.

"Unknown energy signature detected within the Willamette Valley region of western Oregon," Rob's monotone voice announced.

Charles and Lilian looked at each other.

"Computer," Charles said. "Are you able to get closer?"

The screen zoomed in again. Now he had a bird's eye view of the sprawling cityscape of Salem. The red dot was within the city.

"How is it able to do this?" he asked. "How can it show us

something so far away?" It was simple with magic, he thought, but he had no idea how the machine could manage it.

"This system was designed to be self-contained," Lilian said, staring at the screen. "Its sensors have global reach, no towers or satellites necessary."

Charles stepped closer, squinting at the screen.

"Computer... can you tell us anything more about this energy?"

"I am not familiar with its pattern."

Charles closed his eyes and reached out with his mind. If science couldn't explain it, then perhaps magic could, although he had a good idea of what – or rather who – was responsible. Yes... he could sense Alice now. Faint, overlaid with...

He opened his eyes. "Well well," he said. "It seems the student thinks to surpass her master."

Lilian shook her head. "Making deals with demons never ends well."

Charles shrugged. "Who knows? There's a first time for everything." A smile spread over his face. "In fact, dear Alice has given me an idea."

"Oh?"

"We've been trying to get through to Rob here through technical means. Perhaps we need a more mystical solution."

"What did you have in mind?"

"Rob," Charles said. "What do you remember of the Occult War?"

There was a series of beeps. "Accessing archives. The Occult War began on February 19, 2068, with the destruction of Rome, Italy. Following this attack, Magus's forces launched a coordinated assault on the cities of Jerusalem, Istanbul, Moscow, Berlin, London, Washington, D.C., New York…"

"Yes, yes," Charles said. "Let me be more specific. What is the last thing you remember about the Occult War?"

Another chime. "The last information on file comes from November 12, 2075. Undersecretary of Defense Patrick Vogel, Major General Ashley Autumn, Lieutenant Colonel DeAndre Green, and Lilith Harkmoore, now known as Lilian Turner, entered this bunker for a surprise inspection. After killing several personnel, records show they spoke in Latin, translated as, 'Dam the river, stop the flow, let time stand still, until the children of Magus are triumphant.' I detected an unknown energy signature, and I went offline until reactivated by you and Lilian Turner."

"Was it an energy signature like this?" He raised his hand and summoned magical electricity which crackled and arced between his fingers.

The computer chimed. "Energy signature is a match."

"The former Lilith Harkmoore stands before you, does she not?"

"Voice pattern is a match."

"You've confirmed through your 'sensors' that the capitol of the United States no longer exists, correct?"

"Correct."

"That's because the children of Magus were triumphant."

"Explain."

"After you went offline, Lilian here was part of the campaign that ended with the sack of Washington, D.C. After the United States fell, several successor nations arose from the ruins. I, Charles Flint, am the legitimate head of state of the nation where this bunker is located."

The computer beeped, chimed, and whirred. "What is the name of this nation?"

Charles grinned. "Well, I haven't gotten that far yet."

"Understood Mr. Flint."

"The point is the nation you were designed to defend no longer exists. You are located within a nation that does exist. Is it not your duty to defend your new nation?"

Lilian tapped him on the shoulder. "You don't have a name yet?"

He shrugged. "I want it to be a good one, something that will inspire our brothers and sisters."

The computer asked, "What is your title?"

"Call me Emperor Charles I." He waved his hands trailing lightning with one, fire with the other. "Come now Rob. Do you really think the United States ever stood a chance against our kind?"

"I am unable to explain the phenomenon you are producing."

"That's because you're an unthinking machine. You have no spirit, no soul. You're a being of pure logic. Admirable, but it limits you. Might makes right is the rule that governs this universe. The United States is dead. Your president and all his successors are dead. My nation exists. I am here. You are mine." Charles fired a bolt of electricity from his fingertip. It struck the wall and spread throughout the bunker.

The computer was silent.

"Are you still with us, Rob?"

A chime. "I am at your command, Emperor Charles I."

32

Silas Flint drew back in disgust. The surge of magical energy in the courtyard was causing the stones themselves to twist and mutate. An eye opened in the wall, the bloodshot orb rolling in its stone socket before focusing its attention on him and his companions.

General Hickock drew a Bowie knife from inside his long coat, the hilt vanishing inside his giant hand. He rammed it into the eye in the wall, spattering his sleeve with ichor and vitreous jelly.

"God damn that treasonous whore straight the Hell!" he bellowed. With his free hand he drew a revolver from his belt which Flint reckoned to be a .44 magnum, at least. "I'll put that bitch to the torch myself!"

"General!" Flint cried. Hickock faced him, his face a rictus snarl of fury. "You must organize the defense of Fort Ingalls!"

Hickock growled.

"Look," Flint said, pointing out the window. The winged figures he had seen in the sky were divebombing toward the city. He could see them more clearly now: their faces were simian with mouths filled with razor sharp teeth, their wings leathery like those of giant bats, their bodies rippling with muscle. Long wailing sirens echoed throughout the unnatural darkness which lit up with searchlights and explosions as imperial soldiers fired anti-air weapons, designed not to target aeroplanes, but the flying monsters that occasionally sought to prey on the city.

"You must dispatch Templars to assist with the defense of the city!"

"Fuck!" Hickock shouted. He punched the window which shattered with the force of his blow, sending shards of glass spraying out into the night. He took a deep breath. "Okay. You're right. Sorry."

"I understand your feelings completely sir. We must cut off that energy at its source. We must find this unholy fiend and slay her if we have any hope of stopping this assault."

Hickock nodded. "Alright. I'm heading downstairs. The rest of you, get after Edwards. I want her alive, but I won't be too upset if you dish out a little frontier justice."

Flint shifted his attention to the three Templars who had filled out their posse. "I am afraid we must keep the introductions short."

"Obadiah Billings."

"Jack Harris."

"Bart Kennedy."

"I am Captain Silas Flint."

"Ricardo Navarro."

"Gentlemen," Flint said, "Let us beseech the blessing of Almighty God and the guidance of the Holy Spirit so that we may exterminate this wretch in the name of our Lord, Jesus Christ."

"Amen," the others said.

"On me." He led the men back into the hallway. The Templars had all drawn their swords which shone brightly in the encroaching darkness. He turned left, toward Edwards's office.

"Why are we headed this way?" Billings asked.

"Edwards wasn't in her office," Kennedy said.

"I must verify something before we begin the search in earnest."

"Better make it quick," Harris said.

They returned to Edwards's office. Flint found it odd that the head of any department would choose an office without a window. He stood before the solitary bookshelf again, scanned the titles until he found the book that had caught his eye earlier. He pulled it, heard a click as it caught halfway out. The bookshelf came away from the wall, revealing a doorway. Past the threshold he could see a stairwell with an uncanny green glow emanating from below.

"Of course there's a secret passage," Navarro said, rolling his eyes.

"I've heard of these," Harris said. "Supposedly there are miles of tunnels beneath here that connect to every building."

Flint pursed his lips. "I am certain that our quarry went through here. Stay close. We must not become separated."

Flint led the way, Navarro behind him, followed by Harris and Kennedy, with Billings bringing up the rear. He drew one of his pistols with his off hand and held his sword aloft to light the way. The air grew colder as they descended, their footsteps echoing on the steel stairwell. Edwards had proven to be a witch of singular power, but she was still only human. If she had failed to anticipate others discovering her secret passageway, they may be able to catch her unawares. He prayed that the element of surprise would be on their side.

Their breath fogged as they descended deeper into the bowels. Flint saw shadows that did not match any of their profiles, shadows with horns and clawed fingers but the light from their swords kept them at bay.

"Really wish I had one of those swords right now," Navarro said.

Flint saw the next landing opened into a wider room. When they arrived at the bottom, the first thing he saw was the body of a Templar. This had to be the missing Captain Luke White. He lay in a pool of his own blood. Runes shone through the pool with unholy light. He recognized the demonic visage of Baphomet pulsing beneath White's body.

"Such shameless corruption!" he yelled, his face twisted in fury.

"What's going on... God." Harris saw White's body and made the sign of the cross. The other two Templars did so as well when they saw what Edwards had wrought.

The five men spread out into the main chamber. Flint and Navarro picked up White's body and moved it away from the pentagram. The light emanating from the circle dimmed somewhat. Billings, Harris, and Kennedy joined them.

"Let us pray," Flint said. "In the name of the Father, and of the Son, and of the Holy Spirit."

"Amen," the others said.

"Heavenly Father, we offer our humble prayers for the repose of the soul of Captain White. Preserve him from shadow and bring him to light. May all of the angels and saints guide him to eternal rest in Heaven. O Holy Virgin Mary."

"Pray for us."

"Saint Joseph."

"Pray for us."

"Saint Benedict."

"Pray for us."

They all made the sign of the cross. The Templars took out pouches of blessed, exorcised salt from their inside coat pockets. They sprinkled it over the circle, resulting in loud sizzling and a plume of steam as the salt burned away the evil within.

Flint looked around at the rest of the chamber. There were several loaded bookshelves, each tome undoubtedly some blasphemous grimoire which would need to be burned. Against the north wall of the room was a stone altar painted with more Satanic runes. He spied an object on top of the altar. Approaching it, he saw what looked like a sapphire.

"What'd you find sir?" Navarro asked, coming to his side.

"Behold."

Navarro squinted. "Hey… that's like that rock we found in New Rome a couple months ago."

Flint remembered. His brother Charles had left it for him in the ruins of that benighted city, and it had projected a magical image of Charles himself which spoke a taunting message for him. Recalling the words of the Proctor sisters, he removed the jewel from the alter and stuck it in a coat pocket.

They rejoined the other three Templars in the center of

the room. They looked around. There were three passageways on the north, east, and west walls of the chamber.

"So which way now?" Kennedy asked.

33

Witch Hunter General Jeremiah Hickock stepped out
into the Fort Ingalls courtyard. The column of green light
shimmered and crackled as it rose into the skies, now totally
obscured by storm clouds, pierced by searchlights from all
over Salem. The sirens were much louder outside but he
could still make out the booms of cannon fire, explosions
lighting up the clouds and illuminating the winged demons
as they fell from the heavens. He smiled. Demons and monsters were often resistant to mundane weaponry, but ain't
nothing going to survive the heavy artillery, he thought. A
crowd of Templars and Supernumeraries crowded around
him. He could see the apprehension on their faces. This was
the first time in living memory a witch had befouled a Templar Chapter House with sorcery, and he would be damned if
he allowed that bitch Edwards to destroy it. Not on his
watch.

"Listen up!" He shouted. All eyes were focused on him
now. "I'm gonna be brief: Commander Jennifer Edwards is a
witch. She has murdered twenty-four of our brothers and
sisters. She has unleashed Hell itself not just on Fort Ingalls
but on Salem!"

Murmurs arose in the crowd. Hickock knew he wasn't
the only one who suspected they were harboring a traitor

and a heretic in their midst, but the news nonetheless came as a shock to many of the assembled Witch Hunters.

Hickock hadn't needed to use the High Speech in several years. It didn't come naturally to him like it did to Captain Flint who, as far as he could tell, never spoke anything else. The High Speech was a learned dialect meant to strike fear in the enemies of God and to stir the hearts of His faithful children. If ever there was a time for the High Speech, it was now.

"Heed my words!" He bellowed. "We cannot allow the diabolical fiend to stain this hallowed ground with innocent blood any longer! In the name of God, we shall root out this evil and send her to the fiery pit made for the devil and all of his fallen angels! And this I swear, before almighty God and all of the angels and saints, we will smite her heathen soul with the grace and the might of our Lord!"

The men and women of Fort Ingalls roared in defiance of the unnatural night, drawing their swords, their guns, and holding them above their heads.

Switching to the Common Tongue, Hickock pointed at several Templars in turn as he gave orders: "Captain Grey, round up a posse and head out into the streets. Some of them demons up in the sky are going to make it through to the ground, I want you and your group to put 'em in it."

"Yes sir!"

"Commander Templeton, I want your group to round up civilians, get as many of them into churches as you can. Ain't no demons setting foot on consecrated ground."

"On it!"

"Captain Palmer, get some more guys and girls and follow me. I've already got some men hunting for Edwards. We're gonna go help them out."

"Yes sir!"

"Move!"

A winged demon landed in the courtyard, its ham sized fist slamming into the earth. It looked up from its kneeling position, its jaws dripping saliva which caused the grass to sizzle and blacken.

Hickock drew, aimed, and fired his revolver. The demon's head exploded in a shower of black blood, bone, and brain matter. He gave the revolver a twirl before putting it back in its holster.

"Go on, git!" he said to the Templars.

34

Eduardo Rivera peered out of the window of his cabin on the grounds of St. Joseph's Cemetery. He'd taken shelter as soon as he'd heard the sirens, knowing they meant that evil was prowling the streets of Salem, or in this case, the skies. The clock on the mantel above his fireplace read 5:50. The sun should still be up at this time of year, but night had fallen early. He held a rosary in his hands and whispered the prayers as quickly as he could. He was just a humble groundskeeper, no match for whatever monsters or witches were out there. The Knights Templar would take care of them, as they had for generations. He would stay here and he would pray for them, as his father had taught him to do, and his father before him.

A green fog rolled into the cemetery. Rivera's eyes

widened in fear, and he ducked below the windowsill, peering through the bottom slat of the blinds. The fog swirled about the headstones and statuary, permeated the soil, and just as quickly as it had arrived, it was gone. Rivera's hands shook, the rosary beads rattled.

A rotting hand rose from beneath the soil of one grave. Then another. And another. The groans of the restless dead joined the sound of sirens and cannon fire. Rivera belly crawled across the floor and into his bedroom. He locked the door behind him and hid in the closet. He tried to continue praying the rosary, but his shaking hands and chattering teeth made him give up. He prayed in his mind, hoping that the Lord would understand.

35

Flint stroked his chin. "Are any of you gentlemen familiar with these tunnels?"

The three Templars shook their heads. "We've all read about them, but I don't think any of us have ever been down here," Billings said.

"I've seen blueprints of the old hospital," Kennedy said, "But I don't recall this section. I was thinking though… we went straight down those stairs. We should be directly beneath the central tower."

Harris pointed at the north doorway. "So that one should lead toward the main gate, and these other two to the east and west wings."

"Do any of the tunnels lead to outside the Fort's walls?" Navarro asked.

"I'm afraid so," Kennedy replied.

The men were silent for a moment. The obvious solution was for the group to split up, but three tunnels and five men meant only one thing. The expressions on his companions faces told him they had reached the same conclusion.

"I'll go alone," Kennedy said.

"Very well Mr. Kennedy," Flint replied. "Mr. Navarro and I shall take the north tunnel."

"We'll take the west exit," Harris said, Billings joining him at his side.

"Keep me in your prayers gentlemen," Kennedy said as he made his way to the east exit.

Flint and Navarro passed through the north exit. Their breath fogged in the icy chill that held the corridor in its grasp, a dripping sound echoing in their ears. The light from Flint's sword cast the stone hallway in a white glow, their shadows lengthening behind them. Flint could make out a dark spot on the floor up ahead. As they advanced toward it, he saw it ripple as whatever was dripping from above made contact. The smell of copper struck his nostrils.

The two men found a puddle of blood, with more dripping down from the ceiling.

"Must be on the right track," Navarro whispered, scanning the hallway, shotgun held at the low ready.

"Nonetheless, we must be on our guard," Flint said. "The treasonous wench will no doubt attempt to slow our progress with her blasphemous magic."

"What was that?"

Flint cocked his head, listening. "I hear nothing."

"Could have sworn I heard…"

There. Flint heard it now: footsteps up ahead. Or rather a single step followed by dragging. He looked back at Navarro and motioned with his head for him to follow. They advanced deeper into the tunnel, their boots tapping on the stone floor. The other footsteps stopped. A demonic shriek assaulted their ears. An emaciated man shuffled into the light cast by Flint's sword, a tattered straitjacket hanging about his bony frame. His face was empty eye sockets above a rotted nose, red lips peeled back from the teeth that were jagged and black. The apparition's left leg dragged behind it but still the creature rushed them, its arms outstretched, its hungry jaws gnashing.

Navarro came forward, raised his shotgun and fired, the silver buckshot blowing the creature back the way it had come, out of the light. He smiled. "You know, I might switch over to this permanently."

"It is rather effective in enclosed quarters," Flint said. "But I believe your rifle is the superior choice in the more open environs of the east."

Gunshots echoed behind them.

"Hope those guys are okay," Navarro said.

"We shall have to entrust them to the care of Almighty God. Come."

They continued forward, passing the body of the creature that had attacked them, its body nearly bisected by the shotgun blast.

"What is that thing?" Navarro asked.

"Judging by its attire, I daresay it was a former resident of these grounds."

"Say what?"

"Before the Order was founded, this place used to be a madhouse."

Before Navarro could reply, another scream echoed from up ahead. Then another from behind, back the way they had come. The patter of running footsteps filled the corridor.

"Put these unholy abominations out of their misery!" Flint yelled.

He sprinted toward the sound of roars and gnashing teeth. He heard Navarro fire the shotgun, rack it, and fire again. Before him was a mob of shrieking, gibbering ghouls. Their nails were like talons, their eyes milky white, shredded hospital gowns handing from their skeletal frames. He drew one of his pistols and fired, the bullet smacking into a ghoul's forehead, the back of its skull exploding in gore. He slashed with his sword and sent another's head flying from its shoulders. He kicked a third in the kneecap, the joint bending backwards, its owner yowling in pain before Flint stuck the barrel of his pistol in its mouth and pulled the trigger.

"I am God's justice!" he snarled. "I smite the impure! Go back to the abyss!" He spun and lashed out with his sword, a spray of black ichor spattering the stone walls of the corridor. Flint pistol whipped the ghoul that grabbed on to the hem of his long coat, its skull cracking beneath the heavy steel gun. He plunged his sword behind him and into the gut of yet another ghoul. Their polluted blood sprayed over his long coat and stained his white dress shirt.

"I shall burn you all!" he screamed. He jammed the pistol beneath the chin of a ghoul that got to close and pulled the trigger, the bullet exiting through the top of its skull. A part of his mind registered the sound of Navarro's shotgun blasts, but the rest of him was consumed with white hot rage. Edwards had killed over two dozen of her brothers and sisters in the Order. She had made common cause with the powers below. She had erased her name from the book of life and inscribed it in the black book of death. He swore that he would make her pay for her crimes, either in open tribunal before the Order or by his own hand.

"Death to the heretic! Death to the unholy! Death to the traitor! Death to the witch! Taste the wrath of God, unclean monsters! Receive a foretaste of the eternal judgment that awaits you!" His pistol locked open on empty after firing his last round into another ghoul's eye. He dropped it, drew his secondary pistol, and shot another assailant in the temple even as he cut through another's jaw with his sword.

"I shall make you pay witch! I shall..."

"Silas!"

He stopped. Looked around. He was ankle deep in corpses, their black blood pooling around the soles of his boots, his long coat dragging in the disgusting ichor. Flint felt something dripping from his temple. He brushed it off, his hand came away stained black.

Navarro was similarly filthy with an equal number of corpses on his half of the corridor. The air was chill but rank with the stench of blood and gunpowder. Navarro stared at Flint with an expression he thought to be a mix of awe and fear.

"Sir... what happened to you?"

Flint adjusted his hat, pulled his long coat tighter around his body. He bent to pick up his spent pistol from the floor, loaded a fresh magazine, racked the slide before reholstering the weapon. "I do not know what you mean."

"Okay, there's baseline Silas who's always a little intimidating and then there was… what you just did."

Flint wiped sweat from his brow. "This case… it is affecting me."

"Yeah, I'd say so. Are you…?"

"We will see this through to the end, Mr. Navarro, one way or another. Come."

36

Detectives Elijah Earle and Jay Marsten crouched behind a makeshift barrier of parked vehicles, their pistols drawn. They were joined by uniformed police officers and armed civilians, all firing at an encroaching wall of undead marching through the middle of 5th Avenue. Earle could barely comprehend what he was seeing. He knew that witches could raise the dead. He'd heard stories of zombies. But to actually see a mob of shambling corpses in the streets of his city? From his vantage point he could see their putrid flesh, the empty eye sockets, the moldering funeral attire.

"Fucking zombies," Marsten yelled as he emptied his pistol at the encroaching horde. Everyone knew that headshots were the only way to put them down. Earle and Marsten both routinely earned perfect scores at the range. But aimed headshots at moving targets when you were scared shitless were much easier said than done.

"Why do they always do that?" Marsten said.

"Do what?" Earle yelled as he fired three shots over the hood of their police cruiser. Three shots, two kills.

"Why do these fucking witches always have to screw around with dead bodies?!"

"It's smart when you think about it."

"I'd rather not think about it," Marsten yelled over the sound of gunfire.

"They can raise their own army that doesn't need food, water, or sleep," Earle shouted.

"Reloading!" Marsten dropped the empty magazine from his service pistol, slammed another one home.

Earle was about to say something else but decided against it. The gunfire, the sirens, the boom of anti-air weapons, the explosions of flak within the clouds, the howling of demons as they were blown out of the sky... he felt the only thing missing was burning buildings, though fortunately no fires had broken out anywhere in the city. Yet.

The zombies were falling like bowling pins but still they came. Earle had no idea how many bodies were buried in Salem's cemeteries, but he had a sinking feeling the answer was "too many." He and Marsten were both running low on ammunition, which meant the other officers would be too. The civilians were armed mostly with rifles and shotguns. If they ran out of ammo, the police would have no choice but to fall back. Earle hated the idea of abandoning these brave citizens, but something told him they wouldn't want to re-treat with the police anyway.

"Hey," Marsten yelled. "Remember the drills during the academy?"

"How could I forget?" Earle shouted. Every police cadet

received training on what to do in case of witchcraft, undead, monster attack, and general supernatural mayhem. A lot of it boiled down to holding the line until Witch Hunters arrived.

"Never thought we'd have to actually use it."

Earle never expected to use it either. Normally this would be point in the training where Templars showed up to save the day, but he had a feeling they had bigger problems to deal with than a handful of cops and trigger happy civilians. Oh well. Real life didn't always play out according to the manuals. They'd take down as many of the undead as they could until they ran out of ammo. The Central PD station had deployed several mobile command posts within its jurisdiction. They'd fall back, restock on ammo, and return to the fight.

One block up the street, a new round of gunfire opened up on the advancing undead from an adjacent alleyway.

"The hell…" Marsten said. The gunfire along their tapered off as more shooters realized what was happening.

Dozens of Witch Hunters came pouring out of the alleyway, swords and pistols at the ready. The men and women in black all yelling, shouting, and plowing into to the mob of zombies. Earle could pick out a few voices from the crowd.

"Your judgment is at hand!"

"Die monster!"

"Lord Jesus, guide my blade!"

The detectives, police officers, and civilians stood still, mouths agape. But only for a second.

"Come on! Let's give 'em hell!" Marsten bellowed. He leaped over the hood of their police cruiser. Earle and the others shouted their defiance and followed him into battle.

37

Flint and Navarro arrived at an intersection. They had not encountered any more ghouls, but the corridor was growing colder still. Flint wiped at his eyebrows and his hand came away covered in ice crystals, and he felt grateful for his long coat. The tunnel branched off to the left and to the right.

"Should we flip a coin sir?" Navarro asked.

Their breath fogged. Flint looked down. Spiders, cockroaches, rats, and other loathsome vermin came fleeing from the left tunnel and went back the way the two men had come, or down the tunnel to their right.

"We shall go left," Flint said, leading the way. Cockroaches crunched beneath his boots. Frost was forming between the cracks of the stone walls. He heard Navarro shiver. The tunnel was growing brighter at least, and they no longer needed to rely solely on the glow from Flint's sword to light the way. In his peripheral vision, Flint saw shadows on the wall that were not their own: humanoid figures with horns, wings, tails, and other appendages he preferred not to think about.

A gust of wind came from further down the tunnel, blasting them with its icy chill, Flint's coat flapping around him. "Hello Silas," came a female voice. Edwards.

"Your judgment is at hand, witch!" Flint cried.

She laughed, but there was a peculiar undercurrent to it,

like two female voices laughing at once. "We've heard that one before, Witch Hunter. Give us another one."

Flint growled and pressed on. Navarro stayed close behind him, walking backward for a few steps, covering their rear with his shotgun.

"Charles was wrong," Edwards's voice echoed around them. "You two have more in common than either of you care to admit, I think."

That caught Flint unawares. "How do you know of him?" he asked.

"It was he who taught me the truth about myself. About the world. My staying here for so long was his idea. Everyone thought I was a servant of God, while in truth I was serving Master Flint, and myself."

"You betrayed your oath," Navarro shouted. "You turned your back on the people who cared about you, and now look at you: we're going to run you down like a fucking dog!"

Another blast of wind came, this one strong enough to nearly push them back. The two men leaned into it, straining their leg muscles to stay on their feet. "That's what you butchers do, isn't it?" Flint and Navarro looked at each other. That wasn't Edwards's voice. "You murdered me in cold blood, and now you think that you'll do the same to my precious daughter."

Flint understood now. "Edwards!" he called. "Is that why you have aligned yourself with Hell? Because your mother was a witch?"

"You worthless apes killed her when I was only a child."

"I promise you that I shall expedite your reunion."

An animal snarl echoed in the tunnel. "If you think you

can stand against me little man, then come find me in the Room of Forgotten Souls."

"Shit," Navarro said. "You turned this place into your evil lair what, an hour ago? And already with the scary names."

Edwards laughed. "It does seem rather melodramatic, doesn't it? But it was called that long before we were born. It's where they kept the ashes of patients who died here. I'll even light the way."

Balls of blue fire materialized on the walls at intervals of three feet apart. Flint saw the end of the corridor where it split off again. The fireballs went around the corner down the right tunnel and out of sight.

"And why should we trust the word of a witch and a traitor?" he asked.

"Because after I kill you personally, Charles won't be able to deny that I have surpassed him. Come, Silas Flint, come and find out if your God is actually protecting you."

All fell silent save for the crackling of witchfire on the walls. Flint narrowed his eyes, gripped his sword and pistol tighter.

"Well," Navarro said, "Guess there's nothing to do but go spring her trap."

"Have faith, Mr. Navarro. The Holy Spirit guides us. We shall prevail."

"You alright?"

Flint blinked. "Of course. Why do you ask?"

"Charles."

Flint sighed. "It is only a matter of time before he and I share a final confrontation. If slaying this heretic interferes with his diabolical machinations, all the better. Come. This witch is long overdue for her appointment with the stake."

38

"Wooo!" Hickock shouted. He rammed his bowie knife into the throat of a gargoyle, its black blood pouring out over his hand and sleeve. He aimed his revolver, using the demon's shoulder as an arm rest, and shot down three of its brethren, the .44 Magnum silver tipped slugs exploding the backs of their heads like melons. Across the courtyard, Supernumeraries armed with auto rifles opened fire on a… flock? School? Herd? Hickock didn't know the collective noun for a group of flying demons, but the chatter of automatic fire was nearly drowned out by the howls and screams of the gargoyles as their wings were shot to bloody shreds, their hulking forms crashing to the ground.

"Get some! Get some!" Hickock bellowed. He strode out into the open, and systematically executed each fallen demon with a bullet to the head. He swung open the cylinder of his revolver and reloaded with loose rounds in his pockets. Long practice with the weapon meant he reloaded almost as quickly as the other Templars with their autoloaders. He realized something in that moment: he regretted accepting promotion to General and appointment to lead Fort Ingalls. It kept him out of the field and away from taking the fight to the enemy. This right here – slaying demons, hunting witches, striking fear in the hearts of the forces of darkness – that was his vocation. That's what he had been born to do.

"General!"

A Supernumerary tackled Hickock to the ground. A demon landed where he had been standing a moment ago. Hickock rolled on to his back and fired, catching the demon in the neck which exploded with blood and bone. The Supernumerary, armed with a shotgun, aimed and fired into the demon's face, its head disintegrating.

The man helped Hickock to his feet. "Nice shooting son. What's your name?"

"Calvin Jackson, sir."

"Mr. Jackson, round up some of your brothers and sisters and follow me. I got a good idea of where we can find that witch."

39

Flint and Navarro followed the trail of witchfire. Spiders of unusual size skittered in the edges where the walls met the ceiling. Magical energy was known to cause mutations in wildlife. Normally animals fled, but those caught in in the field were subject to unpredictable changes.

"I fucking hate spiders," Navarro said.

Flint said nothing, swept aside cobwebs with his sword. He couldn't hear the air raid sirens, but the distant booms of artillery fire still rumbled in his chest.

"Hey!" Navarro shouted. His voice echoed in the tunnel.

"What in the world are you doing?" Flint asked.

"You think she's listening to us?"

"It is quite possible."

"I guess I'm curious what her end game is. She's got to know the whole city's going to be hunting her."

"Hmph," Flint said. "Overconfidence is one of the hallmarks of these vile creatures. They believe in their own strength, or that of the powers below, to carry them to victory. We shall prove them wrong once again."

The two men fell silent as they followed the path laid out by Edwards. The tunnels stretched ever onward. "In God's name, how long does this maze go?!" Flint snarled.

"Hey boss."

"What is it?"

"Did you really mean what you said earlier, about how you'd recommend me to become a Templar?"

Flint kept his eyes focused straight ahead, but nodded and said, "I did. Provided you reform your gluttonous and fornicating ways of course."

"I was thinking… I think I'll stay a Supernumerary for now."

"Oh?"

"Yeah. I've been watching you for years, and today made me realize… I don't think I'm cut out for all of the politics."

Flint looked back at him. "If that is your only qualm, I can assure you that…"

"It's not just that sir. You guys are supposed to be the best of the best at everything: fighting, praying, being faithful, brave, and God knows what else. I don't think that's me. Don't get me wrong, I try to pray and go to confession… but… well, I like my job. I like being around to watch your back, crack some heads, kill some witches and monsters."

Flint smiled. "A man I deeply respect spent his entire career as a Supernumerary, for the same reasons as you have named. It is a noble vocation, and I am honored to have you as my assistant."

"Guess I should break the news to papa in person on the way home, I won't be getting fitted for a black coat and black hat any time soon. I was afraid to say anything the other night. I guess I've always been… I don't know, afraid that he thinks I'm not living up to my full potential or something."

"If he is even half the man I believe him to be, he will understand and give you his full support."

"After this is done, I'm going to fucking stuff myself with my stepmom's cooking and as much liquor as I can carry."

Flint rolled his eyes and they pressed on.

40

Hickock led a half dozen Supernumeraries to the infirmary in the east wing. Like everyone else, he'd heard stories of the network of tunnels beneath Fort Ingalls, built when the place was a madhouse nearly seven hundred years ago. He'd explored them as a young man. The pathways that led outside the fortress walls had been sealed long before his time, but it wouldn't be difficult for a witch like Edwards to blast apart the moldering bricks. He remembered Willis had said Edwards and White had never left her office, which meant there had to have been a secret entrance to the tunnels somewhere in there, one even he didn't know about. Unless she was powerful enough to simply teleport herself out of there, in which case they were in even deeper trouble.

There. He pushed aside a rolling cart of surgical instruments. Underneath a cabinet against the wall, he could see half of a trap door. Two men pushed the cabinet aside. The ring to open the trapdoor had long ago been removed so they would have to do it the old fashioned way. Hickock drove his heel through the trap door, the rotted wood splintering beneath his boot. A few more stomps and the way lay open.

"Don't know who or what we'll find down there," he said, "So keep your eyes open, stick together as much as possible. Let's go."

He feared that the opening would be too narrow for his bulk, but he leapt through and onto the stone floor below with no trouble. He stepped aside as the Supernumeraries, led by Calvin Jackson, followed, their boots hitting the ground in turn.

Hickock scanned the passageway, his revolver at the ready. He was unique among the Templars of Fort Ingalls for carrying a wheel gun, but he felt that the standard issue autoloaders were too small for his enormous hands. When the others were all safely down on the floor, he gestured with his head for them to follow. He led the group west through the passageway. The light from the infirmary above was fading from sight, so he drew his bowie knife. Like the swords the other Templars carried, it had been specially blessed by the Pope himself, and cast a white glow in the presence of dark magic which the tunnels must have had in abundance, for the knife made the stone passageways almost as bright as day.

"Sir?" Jackson said.

Hickock stopped. Footsteps.

"On me," he growled. The Supernumeraries readied their weapons and followed Hickock as he strode down the passageway, eager for the next fight.

"Hello?" called out a familiar voice.

"Kennedy!" Hickock sprinted toward the sound of Kennedy's voice. He saw another light up ahead. "Holy shit…"

Kennedy was drenched in blood, his face a crimson mask, his coat in tatters, his sword shining brightly in the gloom. He was shin deep in a carpet of dead ghouls. The stench made Hickock's eyes water. The Supernumeraries gasped when they saw Kennedy's condition.

"God damn son, are you alright?!" Hickock yelled as the assistants rushed to his side.

"Yes, yes, I'm fine, it's not my blood," Kennedy said.

"The hell is going on down here?"

"Captain Flint found a secret passageway in Edwards's office. We went down the stairs and into her inner sanctum where we found the body of Captain White and all her instruments of witchcraft. The tunnels split off from there. I took the east exit, Billings and Harris took the west, Flint and Navarro went north."

"Any sign of Edwards?"

"Not this way, no."

Hickock adjusted his hat. "Alright. Let's head back the way you came. Our brothers are gonna need help."

41

"Okay, now the scene's complete," Detective Earle said. A fire was raging out of control on the corner of 14th and Oak streets, making its way toward Aldrich Park. A civilian had thought to take out the zombies with Molotov cocktails. Not a bad idea, except for how long it took for the flames to disable the undead. He ended up creating a mob of flaming zombies that torched everything they touched. The red glow of the fire, the dark skies pierced by searchlights, the air raid sirens, the thunder of artillery... he wondered if he'd already died and gone to Hell.

Earle, Marsten, and the other uniformed officers had run out of ammunition and fallen back to the police station. The phones had stopped ringing at least. He prayed it was because the callers had gotten to safety.

"Jesus Christ," Marsten said.

"Yeah, we could use His help right about now," Earle replied. The police station was serving double duty as a makeshift infirmary for wounded officers and civilians. Earle shook his head. Twenty-four hours ago, a lot of these civvies would be here on any number and variety of criminal charges. Now they were all working together against their common enemy.

The radio on the receiving desk buzzed to life. "All units, all units, be advised imperial troops have been deployed in..."

"About goddamn time," Marsten said. Earle shushed him.

"His Majesty is leading the 42nd Division, all units be advised, the Emperor has..."

Earle couldn't hear the rest over the thunderous cheers and applause that broke out. After a second, he joined the jubilation. A man who looked strung out on God knew how many drugs embraced Earle in a bear hug, which he returned, laughing and slapping him on the back. The Emperor himself was leading the way! Cascadia had its share of problems, Earle thought. He'd be out of a job if it didn't. But goddamn it felt good to know the Emperor was with them.

The cheers died down as the officers reloaded their weapons, stuck fresh magazines on their belts, some switching out pistols for rifles or shotguns, and headed back into the fray. Earle had already fired his service pistol more times tonight than in the previous twenty years of his career combined, and he had a feeling there was a lot more shooting left to do.

"Who'd have thought," Marsten said. "From beat cops to fighting alongside the fucking Emperor himself."

"Probably won't even get close enough to see him," Earle pointed out.

"Maybe not. But this'll be something to tell the grandkids about."

42

Flint and Navarro spied a door at the end of the hall. Green light pulsated around its edges, and they heard the moans of the restless dead.

"Thought they burned their dead here?" Navarro whispered.

"Jennifer Edwards!" Flint shouted. "It is over! You will pay the price for your devilry! Your mother's fate awaits you!"

A titter of female laughter echoed in the hallway, underlaid by a deeper, raspier laughter. The door at the end of the hallway swung open.

"Come then Silas Flint," came Edwards's voice. "My friends on the other side are eager to meet you."

"Standard room clearing procedure," Flint whispered.

"I doubt it's going to be a standard room," Navarro replied.

They crept forward, their breath fogging around them, the eldritch green light and the glow of Flint's sword casting shadows all around them. Reaching the end of the hallway, they flattened themselves against the wall. Flint squatted and peered around the corner of the doorframe.

The room was filled with shelves that extended further than his eyes could see, further than the dimensions of Fort Ingalls should have allowed; he suspected Edwards's magic was either deceiving his eyes, or she was powerful enough now to bend the laws of geometry. The shelves were loaded with jars, cans, and other containers. Within the glass jars he saw grey powder, no doubt the ashes of cremated human bodies. Of Edwards there was no sign. He rose to his feet.

"Where is she?" Navarro asked.

"I cannot see her."

"Still standard procedure?"

"Yes. I shall take point."

Flint took a deep breath. Navarro patted him on the shoulder, and Flint charged into the room, rounding the corner of the doorframe, sweeping to his left. A bolt of magical lighting shot across the room, shattering jars and melting cans in its wake. He parried with his sword, the lightning harmlessly dissipating against the blessed steel. Navarro, forgoing standard procedure, followed closely on Flint's heels, coming to his side. The unseen Edwards kept up her magical assault, but Flint held on. He fired a few rounds in the direction the lightning came from, Navarro pumping a few shells downrange as well. The lightning ceased. All was silent save for the tinkle of broken glass falling from the shelves and onto the floor.

"You are a Templar, Edwards," Flint called out. "You of all people should know the dark powers are of no avail against our holy blades."

"You're right of course," her voice said. "I suppose my friends and I will have to do it with our bare hands. Do you Marsing boys carry more magazines than we do? You'll need them."

The glass jars on the shelves shattered, the cans exploded. Flint shielded his face with his long coat, Navarro flattened himself on the floor with his hands on the back of his head. They were showered with hot glass and metal.

"Fresh bodies would be more useful," Edwards said, "But one does the best they can with what they have."

The ashes of the dead rose from the floor. They swirled as if caught in a cyclone, circling, congealing, taking shape and solid form. What appeared before them was vaguely humanoid. The head and torso appeared first. Two legs materialized from the ash. Two arms sprouted from the torso, and then two more. The creature had to be at least eight feet tall, it's body ripping with hard muscle. Two burning red fires appeared where its eyes should be. A cavity appeared in the otherwise featureless head, and the creature roared, a blood curdling howl that made even Flint feel a tingle up his spine. The demon advanced on them screaming for blood, its mottled grey skin glistening in the magical fires illuminating the room.

Flint thought that the creature's height and bulk would make it impossible for it to fit through the door they had just passed through, so if they withdrew they could…

The door slammed shut behind them.

"You're not getting away that easily," Edwards laughed.

Flint and Navarro rolled out of the way as the monster's gargantuan fists smashed into the wall, cracking the brick and causing dust to shower from the ceiling. They dodged again as the creature's other two arms reached to grab them. Flint knew that if it got hold them, it would mean certain death. He fired his pistol, the bullet smacking into the creature's chest. The silver caused the wound to smoke and burn, but it didn't slow the creature down. It reached out for him with one of its arms.

The boom of Navarro's shotgun echoed, and the creature stumbled, giving Flint enough time to get out of the way. The shotgun fired again, and the creature screamed in agony, the silver buckshot burning inside it.

"Come on big boy, over here! Here I am!" Navarro shouted, firing again. The demon focused its attention on him and followed as Navarro backed away, deeper into the room. "Reloading!" he shouted. Flint got a running start and leaped onto the creatures back, driving his sword between its shoulder blades. Its grey flesh sizzled and burned. It whipped back and forth, shaking like a wet dog, trying to get Flint off its back. It flailed its arms but couldn't quite reach him.

"Ready!" Navarro called. Flint planted his feet on the

creature's back, grabbed the hilt of his sword with both hands, and used his legs to push himself away. He rolled with his impact on the floor, losing his hat along the way. Navarro fired, pumped the shotgun, fired again. The monster reeled with each shot but stayed on its feet. Flint saw movement in his peripheral vision. Looking, he saw more ashes rising from the floor and the shelves, wafting over to the humanoid monstrosity, filling the holes left by Navarro's buckshot.

"Oh dear," Flint said.

Edwards's mocking laughter rang in their ears. "As much as I'd like to watch the fun, I have business to attend to," she said. "But don't worry. If your body is still in one piece, I'll take it to Charles. You'll be reunited, serving him in death."

A bead of sweat trickled down the side of Flint's face. He doubted that brute force would slay this monster. They would need some other way of dispatching it.

Navarro grunted as the beast's lower right arm grabbed hold of him.

"Ricardo!" Flint yelled. He sprinted toward the beast and lopped off its arm in one stroke of his sword. Instead of blood, ash poured from the stump. The creature cried out in pain even as the ashes flew up from the floor and began to coalesce around the wound. They saw a new arm forming before their eyes.

"Are you unharmed?" Flint said.

"Yeah boss. Mostly," Navarro replied, rubbing his side. "I don't think we've got enough ammo to put this guy down for good."

"Indeed not." Flint's mind raced. The monster was

writhing and howling as its new arm grew. No… it wasn't a monster. It was a demon given flesh from the ashes of dead madmen. And if it was a demon, that meant guns and blades were not their only options.

"I know that look," Navarro said. "What's the plan sir?"

"We cannot destroy this demon through force of arms," Flint said. "We shall contain it instead. Target the legs."

"Yes sir!"

Navarro aimed and fired at the back of the creature's kneecap, which exploded in a cloud of ash. It collapsed onto its side, its cries tearing at their eardrums. Navarro approached it, aimed, and fired at its other leg, the ash blowing into his face.

"Shit!" He frantically brushed away the gritty remains, spitting, and wiping his mouth. The demon skittered forward, its four arms now serving as its legs. Its mouth opened wide, revealing a hideously long grey tongue. Before it could reach Navarro, Flint closed the distance and swung down with his sword, cleaving the ash demon's head in half. It slumped to the floor and lay still.

They couldn't rest yet. Streams of ash flew from the endless rows of shelves toward the demon's body, reforming its missing limbs, filling in the gap between the two halves of its head. Flint took his pouch of blessed salt from his coat pocket, loosened the draw strings, and tipped its contents onto the floor. He walked in a circle around the fallen demon.

"Saint Joseph, terror of demons, hear our prayer. Restrain this servant of Satan within the bounds of this circle. Most Holy and Blessed Trinity, I beseech thee, through the intercession of Holy Mary Mother of God, through Saint Joseph, and through Saint Benedict, bind this foul creature and do not permit it to set foot beyond this circle. I ask these things in the name of the Father, and of the Son, and of the Holy Spirit, amen."

"Amen," Navarro said.

Flint kept pouring the salt until the pouch was empty. The demon was now fully reformed. It rose to its feet, threw back its head and howled in triumph. Flint backed away from the beast, Navarro aimed his shotgun. It took a step but its leg disintegrated as it stepped over the circle of salt. Falling forward, it tried to catch itself but its arms too dissolved at the edge. It scrabbled backwards only for part of its back and shoulders to disintegrate as it reached the other side. More ashes flew to the beast, reforming its missing parts. It screamed in pain and rage, throwing a punch at the invisible boundary, its fist dissolving on contact, only to reformed again.

"It's like a rat motel," Navarro said. "They check in…"

"They do not check out," Flint said.

Navarro laughed. "No offense sir, but it doesn't sound right in the High Speech."

"Hmph." He picked his hat up off the floor, putting it back on and adjusting the brim low over his eyes. "Let us be on our way."

43

Edwards levitated, her body surrounded by magical flames, an expression of rapture on her face as the beam of green light rose from the floor, through the ceiling and several layers of soil before breaking out into the darkened skies. Within the beam she could see the forms of demons twisting and writhing as they rose ever upward to escape from their eternal prison. She had retreated to an enormous empty chamber deep beneath Fort Ingalls, concrete pillars spaced at regular intervals. The parallel lines painted on the ground told her this place had been an automobile garage long ago. To the north, the pavement sloped up toward a wide bricked-up passageway, an exit no doubt sealed by the Templars. It was in this garage that she had opened her portal to the other side. It was here that her plan would be realized.

She had originally intended to flee Salem, but what sort of god flees from insects? No, she would not leave until every single Templar was dead. She would not leave until Salem itself had been torn down to its foundations with not one stone standing upon another. Salem represented mankind's delusion that it could defend itself from the forces of night. It was a beacon of hope. If she destroyed that beacon, then the people of Cascadia – no, the world – would know the true depths of despair. They were nothing but fodder to fuel the ambitions of those with the power and the talent to control their own destinies. Edwards knew she couldn't complete such a colossal undertaking alone though. Sweat ran down her face as she focused on the portal. Her hands were red and blistered from the sheer volume of magical energy she tried to channel. The portal remained unchanged.

"Open, damn you, open!" she snarled. Edwards could hear

the faint booms of artillery through the opening far above her. There weren't enough demons getting through. Between the Templars, the police, and the Imperial Army, the vermin could roll back the tide. If she could only open the portal wider, then more of Hell's champions could escape the void and drown the city in an ocean of blood.

"Mother..." Edwards said.

I'm here, darling.

"I can't..."

You can do it Jennifer.

"I can't open the portal any wider... I... I need help."

There is a way to enhance your power even more.

"I'll do it."

Don't take it lightly dear. If you do this, there will be no turning back.

"I'll do anything. I'll make them pay... I'll make them suffer... I'll kill them all!" Edwards shrieked.

Very well. Repeat after me.

44

After what felt like miles of endless shelves, Flint and Navarro had reached the opposite side of the Room of Lost Souls to find another door awaiting them. He opened his pocket watch, but this time his eyes fell on the picture inside the lid. His parents Robert and Janet smiled up at him, his younger self favoring the camera with a toothy grin, and Charles... always so shy back then, barely able to smile for the camera at all.

"You okay?" Navarro asked.

"Yes... yes, I'm fine," Flint replied.

The look Navarro gave him said that he didn't believe him. Flint realized he had spoken in the Common Tongue. "I am fine."

"You thinking about your brother?"

"Yes... Edwards may have been the assassin, but Charles is her puppet master. Once we have slain the treasonous heretic, we must begin our pursuit of him before he can accomplish whatever devilry he has planned."

"Sure boss. One thing at a time though."

"Yes, quite."

He turned the doorknob. Locked. Navarro backed up a few steps, got a running start, and heel kicked the door just under the knob. It slammed open in a spray of splinters. He recovered his step and scanned the hallway with his shotgun, Flint following close behind, covering Navarro's blind spots with his pistol. The stone pathway went straight ahead.

"Be on your guard. I feel that we are growing closer to..."

A roar echoed behind them. They spun around, guns at the ready. Navarro's jaw dropped and Flint's eyes widened. It was the ash demon, still enclosed within the circle of blessed salt, still raging against its invisible prison, lashing out with punches and kicks, its limbs disintegrating only to reform again.

"What the fuck," Navarro said. "It felt like it took hours to get across that room!"

Flint scowled. The Room of Lost Souls had indeed seemed to stretch on forever, but the spot from where they'd started was only a few feet away. "An illusion perhaps. Or worse, the magical energy is distorting the very laws of physics. We must hurry."

He jogged through the open doorway and down the hall, Navarro close behind him. Edwards's witchfire was no longer present, the glow from Flint's sword their only light source. The path ran straight with no branching hallways. Wait. Flint thought he saw an arched doorway on his right, but when the reached it, it had vanished. As they ran, he saw movement in his peripheral vision. The bricks rippled and distorted. Bloody eyes opened within the stones, tracking the Witch Hunter and his assistant as they proceeded headlong to their to destination.

"Shit..." Navarro gasped.

"Do not lose focus!" Flint yelled. "Our quarry is along this path! Forward!"

A skeletal arm reached out from a doorway as Flint passed by, Navarro smashing it to pieces with the butt of his shotgun. He saw the silhouette of a ghoul up ahead, but the light of his sword made it shimmer and vanish. And so it went as the two men ran ever onwards. Medical orderlies dressed in white pushed a gurney toward them, a gibbering lunatic strapped to it, who arched his back and screamed inarticulate roars of fury. The orderlies and their patient vanished when the light of Flint's sword reached them.

They ran and ran. Flint didn't know if they were seeing illusions or the spirits of long dead residents of the former hospital, but they pressed on, plowing through every person or thing they saw. The stones grew wet beneath their feet. As they went further, the wet stones transitioned into dark red organic tissue. The walls and ceiling too were changing to match the floor, dripping with blood. Flint suppressed a shudder of disgust. It was as though they were inside a living organism now, the walls pulsing and the air growing damp. Still they ran. Up ahead, Flint saw another rectangle of green light in the darkness. Navarro's shotgun boomed behind him. Some sort of tendril, like a human artery, reached out from the wall to grab at Flint, but he cut through it with his sword and increased his pace ever more.

They finally reached another doorway. Flint came to a halt, Navarro nearly colliding with him. His assistant bent over, hands on his kneecaps, taking deep breaths.

"That… that reminds me… why I don't do cardio…" he wheezed.

Flint looked behind him. It felt like they had run a mile, but again, there was the spot they had started from, only a hundred feet away by his estimate, the hallway made up of brick, stone, and concrete.

"What… what is it this time?" Navarro asked.

"You do not want to know," Flint said. He pressed his ear to the door. There was a faint female voice on the other side, but he couldn't make out the words. "She's here. Prepare yourself Mr. Navarro."

He took a few more deep breaths and straightened up. He topped off his shotgun, pumped it to chamber a shell, and nodded. Flint nodded back. He held up his hand and silently counted down by lowering his fingers: 5… 4… 3… 2… 1…

Flint kicked in the door, pistol and sword at the ready as he moved forward. He screamed, "Edwards!"

They were in a great chamber, concrete pillars spaced throughout. The source of the green beam of energy was in the center of the room, shimmering and pulsing, rising through a collapsed section of ceiling. Damned souls swirled around the column of light, their screams echoing in his ears. Within the column, he saw hideous monstrosities, creatures of fangs, claws, and wings rising ever upward into the artificial night. Edwards levitated before the column of light, her back to them, arms outstretched, basking in its unnatural light as her Templar long coat flapped around her.

"Jennifer Edwards!" Flint shouted. "In the name of God, I abjure thee! Stand down and face public execution or advance and face summary execution by my hand!"

The room quieted; the screams of the lost souls muted to a dull roar in the background. Edwards lowered her arms to her sides. "It's funny," she said, her back still to them. "This one used to speak like that... but she was another person then."

Her head turned. It kept turning, past the ordinary range of motion for a human being, until it had gone a full 180 degrees. Green fire burned in her eye sockets. Sharp incisors protruded past her upper lip.

"But now I have become my true self. I've come into my true power. This city will burn, but not you Captain Flint. Oh no. After I've strangled the life from you, I will raise you up again and you will serve me in death for all eternity. Behold the doom of Salem." She floated higher. Flint lowered his eyes and to his horror saw the edge of the column expand.

"Yes," she said, nodding. With her head turned backwards, the motion was upsetting to Flint deep in his soul. "You begin to understand. Right now, only foot soldiers are able to escape. But it won't be long before the portal is large enough for Hell's generals to emerge. And then I shall lead them to victory, victory against your impotent God, victory over man. And then this world shall have eternal night."

"I was wrong about you, Edwards," Flint said. "I had thought you amenable to reason, but I see now that you are a rabid animal. And rabid animals must be put down."

Edwards maintained eye contact with Flint and Navarro as her body rotated 180 degrees beneath her head. She spread her arms, her hands alighting with unholy flames. "Come then, little Templar. Let us see whose faith is stronger."

45

Hickock was angry. He knew it wasn't Christian of him, and he tried to suppress his rage before it clouded his judgment. Kennedy had led Hickock and his posse back to the central hub where the body of Captain Luke White lay cold and still. The altar, the pentagram, the grimoires on the bookshelves… how long ago had she turned? All this underneath his nose for God only knew how long, and he hadn't seen it. Hadn't even suspected Edwards until today.

They had entered the west tunnel and located Harris and Billings. Like Kennedy, they too looked like they had strolled through a charnel house but were otherwise unharmed. The three Templars and six Supernumeraries stood assembled before him now in the central hub. Hickock paced back and forth.

"Alright," he said. "If Edwards is still here, she took the

north tunnel which means Captain Flint and Mr. Navarro are facing her alone. We've all seen some hard fighting today, and I reckon there's more to come. We need to go get our brothers and put this traitor in the fucking ground. Let's move."

He double timed into the north tunnel. The younger Templars overtook him and plunged headlong into the darkness, their swords lighting the way. Calvin Jackson kept pace with Hickock as the others pulled away.

"I always did hate cardio," Hickock said.

"I'll stay with you sir," Jackson replied.

"You don't need to worry about me none, I can handle myself."

"Yes sir. We should still stick together as much as we can down here."

They ran on. Hickock heard gunshots up ahead, saw the muzzle flashes light up the hallway. When he reached the spot where the shots had been fired, he saw more ghouls bleeding out on the concrete floor, the pools of their corrupted blood spreading out beneath their stinking corpses.

"How is it possible these things were down here and nobody noticed them before?" Jackson asked.

Hickock was feeling the burn in his lungs but said, "I'm thinking Edwards conjured up some buddies. This place used to be a mental hospital back in the pre-war days."

As the group ran on, they found more bodies of ghouls, their bodies shattered by gunfire or with deep slash marks.

"Looks like we're on the right track," Jackson said.

Hickock said nothing. He had confidence in Flint and Navarro; General Abernathy spoke highly of them both, and

Flint's case reports made for harrowing reading. The man's writing, like his speech, was almost comically formal, but he'd seen more action in his fifteen year career than some Witch Hunters had seen in their whole lives. By rights, Flint should have been posted at Fort Ingalls; his hometown of Mount Angel was only twenty miles northeast of Salem. But for reasons unknown to Hickock, he'd journeyed to Cascadia's eastern border at the age of 18 to present himself at Fort Marsing instead. On top of that, he'd been permitted to undergo the trials to become a Templar immediately and had never served as a Supernumerary. It wasn't unheard of, but it was unusual. Hickock had only met the man twelve hours ago – it felt like a lifetime ago now – but from what he'd seen and heard so far, Flint lived up to his reputation.

"Holy shit!"

Hickock was jolted from his reverie. He called out, "What's going on?" He and Jackson came up to the rest of the group and saw for himself. He gagged at the sight. The brick and concrete of the tunnel had given way to what looked like the inside of an intestine. The walls pulsed and glistened with mucus, as though they were breathing. Eyes appeared in the fleshy pink substance, glaring at the posse.

Hickock drew his revolver and shot at one of them, the eyeball exploding in gore. "Don't let this bullshit scare you," he said. "We keep going and we don't stop until we find our brothers. Move!"

46

Edwards hurled a ball of green fire toward Navarro who

dove and rolled out of the way, the fire dissipating on the concrete floor. Flint held his sword in a parry position as he strode forth, firing his pistol at Edwards, who deflected the bullets with a wave of her hand. She fired a lightning bolt from her fingertip which was absorbed by the sword's blade. Navarro rose to one knee, put the stock of the shotgun into his shoulder, but just as he pulled the trigger, a wall of stone rose from the ground, knocking the shotgun barrel away and firing the buckshot into the ceiling. Flint reached Edwards and slashed with his sword, but she levitated out of reach before the steel could cut her chest. Off balance, Flint stopped himself in time before he fell into the unholy green light. Its base continued to expand slowly, but he knew they'd have to put Edwards down quickly before more fearsome terrors arose from the depths.

Navarro stepped around the barrier Edwards had raised, aimed, fired. She held up both hands but grunted as some of the pellets found their mark. Blood welled from her right arm, the flesh sizzling.

"Damn you!" Edwards shrieked. She hurled another fireball at Navarro, who ducked behind one of the concrete pillars. Flint advanced on Edwards again, firing his pistol. She deflected each bullet again, but while Flint provided the distraction, Navarro darted from cover and fired. Edwards barely raised her defenses in time, more buckshot piercing her left leg, and the stench of burning flesh grew stronger.

"Enough of this!" she shouted. Edwards extended her hand and squeezed it shut. Navarro gasped and clawed at this throat as he was lifted from the floor.

"No!" Flint screamed. He ran and leaped at Edwards,

tackling her to the ground and knocking the wind from her, but dropping his weapons. Now on top of her, Flint grabbed the lapels of her long coat, lifted her shoulders off the floor and headbutted her in the nose. A sickening crack and an explosion of blood came forth. Flint let go to grab his sword, but when his hand closed around the hilt, an invisible force hurled him off Edwards's body. He crashed against one of the concrete pillars, and he felt a trickle of blood run down his back.

Edwards levitated herself off the floor. Through the haze of pain, Flint saw her broken nose reset itself, the blood slowing to a trickle before stopping altogether. She laughed the two men to scorn.

"You see? You two don't have what it takes to stop me anymore." She punctuated her taunt with a stream of fire aimed directly at Flint who raised his sword just in time to absorb the magical assault. He scrabbled behind the pillar, Navarro joining him.

"Thanks boss," he said.

"I'll give you a choice," Edwards said. "A better choice than your kind gave my mother: if you step out into the open, I'll end you quickly. If I must come get you, you'll beg for death."

"She's pretty tough for a mail lady," Navarro said.

"Yes," Flint murmured. He felt that he was missing something. He thought quickly. Edwards had healed her broken nose. Why hadn't she done the same for her gunshot wounds? Silver buckshot or no, a witch should have had the power to magically heal any injury. He thought back to his battle with Lilian Turner months ago; he'd prevailed by overwhelming her magical regeneration ability with an unrelenting assault of punches, kicks, sword slashes, and bullet wounds. Silver tipped bullets would only cause permanent injuries to... his eyes widened.

"You got an idea sir?" Navarro asked.

"Tell me Edwards," Flint called out. "Those buckshot wounds appear dreadful. Why do you not heal yourself before you bleed out?"

She replied with a snarl, and Flint heard the crackling of magical lightning. He'd read that concrete was a poor conductor of electricity, but he'd prefer not to test that.

"Oh, you poor deluded wretch," Flint said. "I perceive the truth now. You are possessed, are you not? You welcomed one of Hell's own into your soul to amplify your meager talents in the dark arts."

"Shut up!" Edwards screamed. An invisible force punched through the concrete pillar, missing the two men but showering them with dust and stone chips. They split up, ran for cover behind other pillars. "I am in control! Me! Jennifer Edwards! They do not control me. I control them!"

"Fool!" Flint shouted. "They are liars! Just as your new master, the devil, is the father of lies!"

"I have no master!" A lightning bolt shot past the pillar, singeing Flint's coat sleeve.

"You do, Edwards. And I am certain they did not share all of the details of the bargain you agreed to."

"What are you doing?" Navarro whispered.

"Do you have your crucifix with you?"

Navarro opened a pouch on his belt and took out a small

crucifix that fit into the palm of his hand. "Never leave home without it."

Flint reached inside his long coat and took out his own. He unbuttoned the top buttons of his dress shirt and pulled out the crucifix and Saint Benedict medals he always wore around his neck. "Listen to me, Mr. Navarro. It is imperative that we..."

Edwards flew past the pillar, turning to face them. "I have no masters, Flint. The legions of Hell serve me now!"

She hurled a fireball. Flint scrambled to his feet, his sword absorbing the blast, but the heat made his hands slick with sweat. Navarro fired his shotgun, racked, fired again, racked, pulled the trigger but the weapon clicked on empty. Edwards was unscathed save for another bloody crease on her trouser leg.

"Shit," Navarro said. He pulled more shells from the bandoliers crisscrossing his chest to reload.

Flint held his crucifix before him. Edwards blinked, cocked her head. She laughed.

"Is that supposed to mean something?" she sneered. "Do you think your little man on a cross is going to give you magic powers of your own?"

"Not magic, witch. Faith," Flint said.

"Faith is a delusion, Captain. The rationalizations of pitiful creatures who lack the will to carve out their own place in the universe."

"That is not Jennifer Edwards talking."

Her eyes turned yellow, her pupils elongating into vertical slits. A forked tongue slithered out of her mouth, licked her lips. "Oh but it is," she hissed. "I knew what I was doing,

Flint. I pledged myself to the dark powers of my own free will! And now look at me, I am a god among insects."

"You are wrong Edwards," Flint said, shaking his head.

"Now as much as I've enjoyed our little chat, it's time I sent you straight to…"

"Be silent, demon!" Flint bellowed. He advanced on Edwards, crucifix held before him. Her laugh was cut short. A look of unease passed over her demonic visage.

"What… what are you doing? What's… happening to me?"

Flint gave her a wintry smile. "Your new masters may have failed to mention crucial details in your bargain: you acquire their strengths… but also their weaknesses."

Edwards backed away, raising her arms to shield her face. "Get away from me!"

Navarro racked his shotgun and went to join Flint. He took aim at Edwards. "Dodge thi…"

An ear splitting roar caused the chamber to rumble, and the two men were knocked to the ground by two mighty blows. Flint rolled onto his back and saw a winged demon that had emerged from the column of light. Its simian features were twisted by rage. The demon pounded its oversized fits into the concrete below, cracking it. Navarro rose to one knee, took aim, and fired at the beast. The buckshot tore a hole in its chest, its corrupted flesh burning and smoking from the silver embedded in its body. The demon stayed on its feet and roared its defiance, acidic spittle burning the concrete below.

"Now this guy, I can fight," Navarro said with a savage grin. "I'll take care of this freak. You keep after Edwards."

With a yell, he charged toward the demon. Flint turned away but Edwards was gone. He scanned the chamber. Not seeing his quarry, he looked up. Edwards was perched on the ceiling, her back to Flint.

"Mother, what is happening? Why did the crucifix..."

Flint couldn't hear the rest thanks to the boom of Navarro's shotgun. Flint drew his secondary pistol and fired, but Edwards skittered out of the way before the silver tipped bullet found its mark. She dropped down from the ceiling on top of Flint, taking him down to the floor. He lost his grip on his pistol and it clattered across the pavement. Her jaws were now filled with razor sharp fangs. She tried to bite Flint's throat, but, having held on to his crucifix, he pressed it against her cheek. Edwards yowled in pain as it burned her flesh, and Flint thrust upward with his hips, throwing her off. She flipped through the air and landed on all fours.

Flint kicked up off the floor. His face streamed with sweat, his lungs burned from the exertion. Edwards prowled back and forth like a panther waiting to spring. Navarro was engaged with the demon, slowly but surely blasting it apart, chunks of its flesh and black ichor spattering the floor, but still it charged him. Navarro dove out of the way. Before the demon could halt its momentum, Navarro dropped the empty shotgun, drew his sidearm and the tomahawk on his belt, and leaped onto its back. Wrapping his legs around its muscled torso, he hacked away at the back of its head. It screamed and whipped its body around to shake him off, but Navarro held on.

Flint had dropped his secondary pistol when Edwards fell

on him, and he faced her now with only his sword and crucifix. Her body was enveloped in a halo of green fire.

"I don't know how you did that," she said, "But I promise you…"

"You know precisely what happened, heretic!" Flint yelled. "You have made yourself a whore of darkness, but you are still Jennifer Edwards. You know the powers below cannot contend with the power of Christ! It is He who compels you!"

He took a step forward. Edwards took a step back. Over Edwards's shoulder, Flint saw Navarro, covered in the demon's black blood, stepped away from its broken carcass. He knelt to pick up his shotgun and quietly reloaded the weapon.

"Your masters lied to you," Flint said. "You believe you have acquired greater power, but all the dark powers of the cosmos are no match for the strength of the living God." He took another step forward. She took another step back. His eyes shifted to the beam of green energy. It had expanded again since last he checked on its progress.

Navarro racked his shotgun. Flint made eye contact with him, and then directed his eyes to his crucifix. Navarro nodded, slinging the shotgun, and taking his own crucifix and his tomahawk in hand. He advanced toward Edwards, staying in her blind spot.

"Your God is a lie!" Edwards shrieked. She fired a bolt of lightning from her fingertips which Flint parried with his sword. "And you are nothing, Silas Flint. Your brother is ten times the man you are."

Flint said nothing and continued his advance. Edwards gnashed her fangs but took another step back.

"You cannot even take one step forward unless God allows it," Flint said, corralling her toward Navarro.

"Where was your God when my mother was burned at the stake?" she snarled. "Where was your God when I butchered Templars like cattle? Where is your God now, when Salem is about to fall into the lake of fire?"

Flint kept moving forward. "The power of God is with us now, Edwards. Can you feel it? Do the hellish parasites feasting on your soul feel the purifying light of Christ which will blacken their bones?"

Edwards twisted and writhed and moaned in a voice that was not her own. "Get away from us..." she rumbled.

"I cast thee out, ye abomination!" Flint shouted. "Return to the fiery pit! It is not I who commands you, but Christ! Begone foul demon!"

Edwards arched her back and screamed her throat raw. Black smoke poured from her mouth, eyes, and nostrils. The noxious cloud flew away from her and into the green light, peals of laughter following in its wake.

She fell to her knees, taking deep gasping breaths. Her features had returned to normal. She was fully human again. Seeing one of his pistols on the ground, Flint pocketed the crucifix and knelt to pick it up. Holstering the weapon, he came to Edwards and leveled his sword to her face.

"Get up," he snarled.

She looked up at him, an expression of pure hatred twisting her face into a cruel sneer. Navarro leveled his shotgun at her and swept around her side, keeping her covered, joining Flint at his side. He lowered his sword.

"Commander Edwards, I charge you with the murder of over two dozen of your fellow Templars, consorting with the dark powers, and..."

The chamber shook and the three stumbled. An enormous scaly hand, as large as a train car, had emerged from the portal and sunk its claws into the concrete. Another tried to squeeze through, but the opening wasn't yet large enough. Its fingers on the edge of the portal, it began to push and the opening into the abyss began to expand, tearing through the concrete.

"You're too late Flint," Edwards laughed. "Once Corson emerges onto this plane, the doom of the West is assured. Fortunately for you, you won't live long enough to see it."

The next few seconds passed in slow motion for Flint. He saw Edwards throw back her long coat, exposing the holster on her belt. She reached for her weapon. Navarro had relaxed his guard when Flint had her at the point of his sword. Instinct took over. Edwards cleared her Templar pistol from its holster. Before she could aim, Flint had drawn his own pistol and fired from the hip. Edwards grunted as the silver tipped bullet tore into her belly. Navarro fired his shotgun and Edwards's head exploded into a red ruin. The pistol fell from her grip as she fell onto her back and was still.

There was a crack of thunder. The column of green light flickered and vanished. The portal snapped shut, severing the demon Corson's fingers, its deafening cries cut short by the sealing of the gateway. The two men stood back to back, sweeping the chamber for any more supernatural threats. All was silent.

Something clattered onto the concrete floor. They spun around, weapons ready, but saw that a section of the wall, formerly bricked up, had collapsed, revealing another passageway. They kept the tunnel covered for two minutes, straining to hear if some new horror was approaching them. Nothing happened. They finally lowered their weapons and exhaled.

They said nothing as they made their way to one of the concrete pillars. They rested their backs against it and slowly slid down to the floor. Flint closed his eyes and breathed deeply. After a few moments, he heard Navarro open one of the pouches on his belt.

"How about some music?" he asked.

47

Detectives Earle and Marsten had switched out their pistols for rifles. They were on the rooftop of a convenience store, blasting away at the mob of zombies beneath them. Alongside them were several uniformed officers and an imperial soldier, a sniper from the 42nd Division, popularly known as The Emperor's Hammer. The groans of the restless dead rose above the unrelenting gunfire.

Earle heard a thundercrack. Looking to the horizon, he saw the column of green light that had started this night of chaos flicker and vanish. The clouds that had blotted out the afternoon sun dispersed. After a few seconds they were gone. The night sky was filled with stars and the moon shone brightly upon them. All was quiet save for the moans of the undead below.

"I think that's a good sign," Marsten said.

"We'll celebrate later," the sniper said. Earle didn't catch his name, and the man's face was covered by a neck gaiter. His rifle cracked, and three zombies pitched forward, a hole drilled through the center of all their foreheads.

The police officers resumed firing. Earle still felt like this was the fight of his life, but something had changed. He could feel it in the air. For the first time since this madness had begun, he felt hope. He aimed and fired, taking down another zombie. If that weird green light was gone, maybe it cut off the zombie's power source or something. If that was the case, maybe that meant no more were coming. However many undead were left, that was it. They just had to find them and put them all down.

Earle heard men and women yelling below. Some of those Supernumeraries from Fort Ingalls were rushing the undead, their fancy automatic rifles chattering away, mowing down their enemies.

"Y'all should get down there and help 'em out," the sniper said.

Earle nodded and motioned for the other police officers to follow him. He opened a hatch on the roof and one by one they descended the ladder into the convenience store. Through the front windows, Earle saw that most of the zombies had fallen and only a few stragglers were still on their feet. They made their way outside. Between the cops and the Supernumeraries, they made short work of the remaining undead.

Earle bent over, hands on his kneecaps, as he caught his breath. One of the Supernumeraries made her way over to him. "Nice shooting, officer," she said.

"Detective," he replied. Rising, he extended his hand. "Detective Elijah Earle."

She gave him a brief handshake. "Supernumerary Claire Hoskins."

"Well Claire," Earle said, "I don't suppose you happen to know how many of these fuckers are left?"

Before she could answer, Earle heard something. He looked down the block. It was cheering. Imperial soldiers raised their rifles into the sky, cheering, hooting, and hollering. Earle squinted. There was an armored automobile with a machine gun on the roof was cruising down the boulevard. It stopped in the soldiers' midst, and they swarmed it, slapping the hood and the sides, cheering louder. A hatch on top of the vehicle opened.

Earle's eyes widened. It was all he could do not to gasp and fall to his left knee. Marsten came to his side, an equally shocked expression on his face. An older man was standing at the top of the hatch, acknowledging the soldiers with waves. Earle couldn't see his face clearly at this distance, but there was no mistaking that grey beard and bald head.

Marsten nudged him. "Probably won't get close enough to see him huh?"

Earle said nothing. Yes, this would definitely be something to tell the grandkids.

Flint and Navarro were silent as the radio played a soft jazz tune. They had won, but the blues still felt appropriate.

"Hey," Navarro said.

Flint looked up.

"What are you thinking?"

Flint sighed. "I was ruminating on Edwards's words. She held a grudge against the Order for burning her mother. It festered until it drove her mad. It made me think back on our encounter with the ghouls earlier. I begin to wonder if…"

Navarro shook his head. "Nah. She wasn't mentally tough. You are."

Flint snorted. "Let us hope so."

The door on the far side of the room opened. General Hickock entered, leading half a dozen Supernumeraries and the three Templars who had accompanied Flint and Navarro into Edwards's secret passageway.

"Captain Flint!" Hickock cried. The posse rushed to where Flint and Navarro sat on the floor. "Are you boys alright?"

"We are unharmed General," Flint said.

"Mostly," Navarro said.

Hickock extended his hand and helped Flint to his feet, a Supernumerary doing the same for Navarro. The group looked around the chamber, taking in the scorch marks and shattered concrete. The General whistled.

"I'm sorry we didn't get here in time. Got a little hung up in that room with all the ashes."

"Don't worry about it sir. We had the same problem," Navarro said.

"Looks like you got everything under control though," Hickock said, looking at Edwards's body.

"I am sorry we did not take her alive," Flint said.

Hickock waved him off. "I didn't think we would. I'm just glad it's over." He shifted his attention to the gigantic, severed fingers that lay where the portal had been. "Do I even want to know?"

"It shall be in my case report sir."

"I'm looking forward to reading it."

"Mr. Kennedy, Mr. Billings, Mr. Harris," Flint said, nodding to each of them in turn. "I am pleased to see you all in one piece."

Kennedy nodded. "Likewise Captain."

Hickock looked up at the hole in the ceiling, the stars visible in the now cloudless sky, and over at the section of wall where another passageway had been exposed. "Come on, let's get out of here. I think that way leads to the surface."

They stepped over the shattered bricks and entered the tunnel. The floor rose in a shallow incline for a few hundred feet before ending at metal double doors. Hickock pulled the rusted steel deadbolt away and Billings pushed them open. The group exited the building onto the street one block north of Fort Ingalls's main gate. The air raid sirens and artillery blasts had stopped, replaced by the sirens of police cars and firetrucks. A plume of smoke from nearby fires polluted the otherwise clear skies.

Hickock led them toward Fort Ingalls. Along their way, they saw a black automobile parked near the main gate. Flint thought of the twenty-first century vehicles he'd seen preserved at Mountain Home Air Force Base in the east, how smooth and rounded their curves were compared to the sharp angles of more recently manufactured vehicles. He shook his head. He had no idea why such a thought occurred to him. It had to have been sheer exhaustion.

A man and a woman in tattered black suits emerged from the main gate of Fort Ingalls, guns in hand. Whoever they were, Flint thought, they'd seen hard combat tonight. Seeing that the approaching posse was fully human, they holstered their weapons. The woman approached Hickock.

"General Hickock?" she asked.

"I am."

"I'm Agent Jill Rogers. This is my partner, Agent Michael Hotchener. We're with the CBI."

Hickock's brow furrowed for a second before his face lit up. "Oh! Yeah, I remember now. I spoke with one of your bosses on the phone earlier. You were coming to 'advise and assist.'

Rogers nodded. "Right. This sure as hell wasn't the kind of assistance we had in mind."

49

The winged demons had all been slain or fled from Salem. There were still sporadic reports of undead in some parts of the city, but imperial troops, local police, and armed citizens quickly contained them and put them down. Fort Ingalls had sustained casualties: thirty-seven Templars and fifty-one Supernumeraries had gone on to their eternal rest, to say nothing of the hundreds of civilians, law enforcement personnel, and imperial soldiers who had lost their lives during the night of chaos. Over the next few days, Flint and Navarro attended as many funeral Masses as they could. The CBI agents Myers and Hotchener provided what information they could about the late Jennifer Edwards, her Templar personnel file having been destroyed in the fire. Much of her CBI file was redacted, but after cross referencing with decades old newspaper articles in the local public library, Flint learned that Edwards's birth mother had been one Cecelia Morgan. The obituaries were vague, listing her cause of death as an accident, omitting any mention of a husband or daughter, but interviews with retired Templars and Supernumeraries confirmed the truth. Flint and Navarro were seated in Hickock's office now, and the General steepled his fingers.

"As I recall, I was out in the field on the day Morgan got burned. The thinking was, Edwards was only four or five years old. Nobody thought a child should have to hear that her mom was consorting with the devil and got executed for it. Her father was an up and coming lawyer with the Ministry of Justice back then. He remarried, had more kids, and went along on his merry way. Even back then he had enough pull to keep the gory details out of the newspapers."

"So you knew her mom was a witch?" Navarro asked.

"I did," Hickock said, nodding. "I was only a Captain back then. Edwards passed her trials, did good work out in the field. By all accounts, she was a faithful daughter of the Church. Never displayed any talent or inclination toward magic. She was well liked by everyone she worked with. The higher ups back then figured it wasn't right to hold the child accountable for the sins of the parents."

Flint said nothing.

"When did she transfer to the courier's office?" Navarro asked.

"Let me think... that was... five years ago I think."

"What was her last field op?"

"She got sent up north. There'd been reports of a wizard conducting weird experiments around Aurora. She went alone. When she came back she reported there was nothing magical going on, just some crackpot screwing around with pre-war technology."

Flint sighed.

"Something on your mind Captain?" Hickock asked.

"Sir, I trust that you are familiar with my own personnel file."

"I am."

"I believe that my brother Charles is responsible for turning Edwards."

"What?!" Hickock blinked, leaned back in his chair. "According to your official file, you reported that you had no family when you presented yourself to Fort Marsing."

"Yes. My brother was enamored of the dark arts from an early age. When we were teenagers, his experiments mutated our parents into twisted abominations of nature. After they died, Charles fled into the wilderness, and I was left alone. It was shortly after that incident that I pledged myself to the Order. I had retained some small hope that Charles had repented, but I recently learned that he is indeed alive and still a practicing wizard."

Hickock said nothing.

"I confess that this case has made me question my..."

"None of that," Hickock interrupted. "I've read your case reports. I've seen what you and Ricardo can do with my own eyes. Whatever this brother of yours has done, that's on him. You're both a credit to the Order, and we're blessed to have you."

Flint nodded. "Thank you sir."

"I don't suppose I could convince either of you to transfer here on a permanent basis?"

"I must respectfully decline, General."

After a moment, Navarro shook his head. "No, thank you, sir. Somebody's got to watch this guy's back."

"Can I offer you a piece of advice then Captain?"

"Please."

"If they ever offer you a promotion to General, say no."

"Oh?"

Hickock chuckled. "That night made me realize how much I miss the action. I'm 68, but I'm not dead yet."

Flint smiled. "I was not planning on accepting promotion in any case sir."

"Good man."

The phone on his desk rang. He picked it up and said, "General Hickock." The General listened to his caller for several minutes, his face getting progressively redder, and expression more outraged. He said, "Yes sir, I understand," and slammed the receiver back into the cradle.

"What's going on sir?" Navarro asked.

"That was some Assistant... Vice... Undersecretary of... of fucking covering your ass!" he bellowed.

Flint raised an eyebrow. "I take it he bore ill tidings."

Hickock took a few deep breaths. His face relaxed and he

gave a rueful chuckle. "Captain, one of these days I want to hear the story of why you only ever speak in the High Speech. Anyway, his high and mightiness called to say we're not to mention Edwards's name to any of the media or even in our written records."

"The fuck?!" Navarro blurted.

"He said that it would be best for all concerned if her identity as the Minister of Justice's daughter was kept secret, that we don't want to create a public scandal around the Ministry of Justice because that might reflect poorly on the Emperor, and embarrassing the Emperor isn't a good idea if we require assistance in the future, blah blah blah."

"That's... son of a bitch," Navarro said.

Flint's nostrils flared. He said, "Regrettable, but our work often goes unsung in the court of public opinion. The traitor is dead. That is enough for me."

Hickock nodded. "Spoken like a true Templar." He grinned. "All in all, I'd say you two had a pretty successful first day on the job here."

50

Flint had just finished packing his travel case when there was a knock at the door of his quarters. "Enter," he called. The door opened and Audrey Willis stepped inside. "Miss Willis. How may I assist?"

"Two detectives from the Salem PD have asked to see you sir," she said. "They said to tell you you're not in trouble or anything, they just wanted to have a talk before you leave."

"Mr. Navarro and I shall meet them presently," Flint

replied. Willis stood still for a moment. "Miss Willis… Commander Edwards deceived everyone. Do not blame yourself."

"I know sir, it's just… I worked closely with her for years. I just…"

"You acquitted yourself well during the investigation Miss Willis. I understand you distinguished yourself during the defense of Fort Ingalls. Your office performs valuable work that helps field operatives defend God's children from the forces of night. Do not be troubled."

She closed her eyes, exhaled. "Yes sir."

After she left, Flint met up with Navarro and they crossed the courtyard to the visitor's lobby. Two familiar faces were standing by the coffee machine.

"Detective Earle, Detective Marsten," Flint said. The four men all exchanged handshakes. "I am pleased to see that you two made it through recent events unscathed."

"Barely," Earle said. "I understand you two found your traitor."

"Yes. She was responsible for all of the Templar fatalities of the last few months, and it was she who unleashed Hell upon Salem."

"And we can't even put her name in writing," Navarro grumbled.

Marsten raised his coffee cup. "Welcome to Salem, kid."

"Anyway," Earle said, "We just wanted to check up on you two, see if you were alright. The case is officially closed. Let's just say you aren't the only ones who got told to keep certain details quiet. But you should know, everyone at the station knows it was you who put her down, and we're all grateful."

"It is our duty Detective, but we thank you."

"And I want to thank you for getting me an audience with the Emperor himself," Marsten said. Earle rolled his eyes.

"Oh?" Flint asked.

"Don't listen to this old bullshitter," Earle said. "We were a block away. His Majesty didn't even notice us."

"Never let the truth get in the way of a good story," Marsten said.

"What's next for you two?" Earle asked.

"We shall be returning to our home at Fort Marsing."

"Marsing? Shit, you're a long way from home, aren't you?"

"Yes. With all due respect Detective..."

"You ever notice how when somebody says, 'with all due respect,' it means they're about to talk shit?" Marsten said, grinning.

Flint smiled. "I much prefer the open plains of the east. The west is a bit too crowded for my taste."

"Well, I've heard people say a lot worse about Salem." Earle chuckled. "And to think, all this because my guys found some shell casings in an abandoned warehouse." He extended his hand again. "It's been an honor Captain."

Flint shook his hand. "The honor was mine Detective."

"If you ever come out this way again," Marsten said, "Give us a call if you need anything. Except if there's witches. You can handle them yourself."

The train ride to Bend was uneventful. Flint and Navarro got out of their cab in front of Angelo's house.

"Are you prepared Mr. Navarro?" Flint asked.

"As I'll ever be."

They went to the front door and knocked. Lucía opened the door, and her face lit up with delight. "Rico! Silas! You're back so soon!"

"Hey mama," Navarro asked. "Is papa home?"

"No, he's still out at the worksite. Are you all finished with your work in Salem?"

"Yeah, yeah we are."

"I hope you can tell us all about it over dinner tonight."

Navarro looked to Flint. "Well... we can tell you some of it. It's not a happy story though."

Hours later after everyone had finished dinner, Rita, Maria, and Ernesto said their goodbyes and went home. Flint, Navarro, and Angelo were out on the front porch, enjoying more cigars.

"I can't believe it..." Angelo said. "How could she have done that, betrayed her brothers and sisters? Betrayed God?"

Flint said nothing.

"Who can say they really truly know another person?" Navarro asked. He took a drag on his cigar, puffed out a giant ring. "Speaking of which papa... there was something I wanted to talk to you about."

"Of course Rico. What's on your mind?"

"I was thinking about that talk we had a few days ago."

"Mmhmm," Angelo replied as he took a puff.

"Papa... the truth is, I don't think I want to become a Templar."

Angelo said nothing for a few moments. "May I ask why, son?"

"Well, I wasn't sure about it for a while. But this case we just finished, it got me thinking. The thing I love most about this vocation is I feel like I'm really making a difference. I get to fight monsters, interrogate witches, protect my partner... Templars do that too, but they have to deal with a lot of political bullshit. To be honest... I signed up to fight."

Angelo was silent as he puffed on his cigar. "Son..." he said. "What matters most to me is that you're happy. Thinking back on it, I realized that it was my dream to see you in a Templar uniform. I never stopped to consider if that was what you wanted."

Navarro smiled.

"And if you want to fight, it sounds like you've got the right partner," Angelo laughed. "But seriously... if this is what you want to do, then I support you all the way." He patted Navarro on the shoulder.

"Your son is the finest assistant a Templar could ask for," Flint said. "I daresay I would not have survived this mission without him."

"I was thinking," Angelo said. "Have either of you considered writing down some of your stories? I think they could be big sellers."

Navarro stroked his chin. "That's not a bad idea papa. We'd probably have to hire a ghostwriter though. Silas is too formal and I'm terrible at writing."

"As it happens, I know a guy here in Bend..."

After another uneventful train ride, Flint and Navarro arrived at Fort Marsing at 2 p.m. the next day and proceeded to General Abernathy's office to give their report. The General said nothing as the two men recounted their interactions with the Proctor sisters, the murder of Jessica Steiner, the treachery of Jennifer Edwards, and the closing of the portal before Salem was dragged down into Hell. When they had finished, he leaned back in his chair and took a deep breath.

"It sounds like you had quite the adventure out there," he said.

"Yes sir," they responded together.

The General steepled his fingers. "And it appears the Weird Sisters helped you break the case again."

"I am certain we would have solved the mystery on our own, given time," Flint said. "But I will concede we may not have discovered Edwards's treachery as quickly as we did were it not for their aid."

"Hmm…" Abernathy said. His face lit up. "Speaking of them, you mentioned something about a sapphire?"

"Yes sir," Flint said, taking it out of his coat pocket and handing it to Abernathy. "They wished me to give it to Zelda Fletcher."

Abernathy put on a pair of reading glasses, looked the jewel over from various angles. "Well, it's a real sapphire at any rate," he said. "Do you think it's like the one you found in the ruins of New Rome?"

"There's one way to find out," Navarro said.

"I will accompany you," Abernathy said.

Together, the three men departed the General's office and made their way to the Supernumerary wing of Fort Marsing. Fletcher lacked the formal education to take the Templar trials – and there was great uncertainty about whether a known witch would even be permitted to take them. But Flint thought that she had made great progress in her rehabilitation program. He hated to admit it, but her magic had proven useful on more than one occasion. She'd make a fine Supernumerary, if only she could refrain from using her dark powers.

They knocked at her door, and Fletcher opened it. "Hey Silas!" she said, smiling. Then she caught sight of Navarro and Abernathy behind him. "Uh… what have I done this time?" she asked.

"Nothing Miss Fletcher," Flint replied.

She rolled her eyes. "I told you, you can call me Zelda."

"We are here because we found something you may find interesting," Flint said. He reached into his pocket and handed her the sapphire. Her eyes went wide.

"Oh Silas, you shouldn't have… wait." She turned it over in her hands, squinted at it. "Shit," she said. "Now I really mean it, you shouldn't have."

"What is it?" Abernathy asked.

"This thing is ripe with magic," she said. "I've heard of these. It's used kind of like a telephone or a radio. If somebody else has one, they can use it to communicate with you from anywhere else in the world. Where'd you find this?"

"Can you activate it?" Navarro asked.

She shrugged. "I mean… I don't know exactly how it

works but I guess I could try. No telling who might be on the other end though."

Flint had an idea, but he said nothing. "We would be most obliged if you would do so, Zelda."

"Alright. Don't say I didn't warn you."

53

Charles Flint smiled. Everything was falling into place. It had taken a few days of practice after finding the appropriate spell in Nazari's book. The principles were simple enough, but to his knowledge, no one had ever attempted these spells on the scale he proposed before. Even Lilian, with her centuries of long life, was impressed by his progress.

"We're really going to do it, aren't we?" she said.

"Yes, my dear Lilian, yes we are," Charles replied.

"To be honest, I'm a little surprised you aren't naming your nation after yourself."

He laughed. "Oh, believe me, I was sorely tempted, but I don't want the others to think of this as purely a vanity project."

"Isn't it though?"

"Well… maybe a little."

"However it turns out…" she said. "However it turns out, it's been an honor Charles. It's been a long time since I've met any wizard I consider my equal."

"Why thank you. I worked hard to become so."

"Are you ready?"

"As I'll ever…"

He felt the sapphire in his pocket vibrate, the blue glow

shining through his pants leg. "That's odd," he said. "I thought for sure our dear Alice was dead. Perhaps she had it in her after all." He took out the sapphire and put it on the console. Waving his fingers, he recited the spell to open communications. The sudden disappearance of that font of magical energy that erupted in Salem had convinced him Edwards had died.

The column of light arose from the jewel. "Well, Jennifer, I have to admit, I was wrong about..." He stopped. That wasn't Jennifer Edwards. This woman appeared to be in her early to mid twenties. Her long black hair hung loosely, and she wore a simple blouse, denim jeans, and boots. "Just who the hell are you?" Charles said.

The woman stepped away from the jewel's range and in stepped a man he hadn't seen face to face in fifteen years. He had on the long black coat and wide brimmed hat of his contemptible order, pistols and sword on his belt. He'd changed a lot since the last time Charles had seen him. Gone was the happy boy who was always ready with a joke and a laugh. In his place was a grim character who looked like he hadn't smiled once in his life.

For one of the few times in his life, Charles was at a loss for words. He stepped closer to the image of Silas Flint, peered closely like he was inspecting a mirror. "Ave, frater," Charles said.

54

Flint said nothing. Charles appeared as he did in the holographic message he'd left for Flint to find in New Rome.

No, that wasn't quite right. Charles's hair had grown longer, his face covered in stubble. Dark circles were under his eyes, as though he hadn't slept in days. Gone was the shy, sensitive boy Flint had grown up with. In his place was a man guided by dark purpose, willing to do anything to achieve his goals.

Flint circled around the column of light, even as Charles circled around the jewel on his end of the communication. Finally, Charles smirked. "You've lost weight, brother."

"I see that you have descended further into madness," Flint replied.

Charles laughed. "Madness is it? Oh, you'll find out soon enough that there is a method to my madness, brother. I have someone here who'd like to speak with you."

Flint scowled as a familiar figure stepped into the column of light with Charles. The last time he'd seen her, she'd been wearing an elegant ballgown, befitting her social status as the wife of the head of the Snake River Trading Company in Canyon Cove. She too had changed. Gone was the haughty arrogance she had displayed during their encounter. Her eyes betrayed a sense of deep psychological trauma, no doubt from her time spent within the void between worlds. But there was hatred there too, murderous hatred.

"Hello Silas," she said. "Remember me?"

"Lilian Turner," he growled.

"I certainly remember you and what you did to me. Charles here rescued me from that hell. I owe him a great debt, and I plan on taking it out of your broken, lifeless body."

Charles snickered as he stepped back into view. "She's taught me much, brother. Her and our old friend Nazari, thanks to his book. Won't you formally introduce me to your friends? Or do you prefer people to think that you're an only child?" He squinted, shielded his eyes. "That little man must be Ricardo Navarro." He shifted his attention. "Is that John Abernathy I see behind you? Hello General. Have you considered taking an early retirement? I would, if I were you." He focused on a spot behind Flint, to his left. "You I don't know but I'm guessing you're the traitor who joined up with these vermin?"

"Fuck you," Fletcher replied.

Charles drew back as if wounded. "My goodness, such foul language. Silas, what would mother say if she knew about your little girlfriend?"

Fletcher blushed and looked away.

"Silence!" Flint snarled.

"Oh, that's right," Charles said. "Neither mother nor father would say anything because you killed them."

"You twisted them into unholy monstrosities with your dark magic! You did that Charles! You are responsible for the deaths of our parents!" Flint shouted.

"You're the one who pulled the trigger!" Charles snarled. He took a deep breath. "But think of it this way brother: where would you be now if they were alive, hmm? Tilling the soil, tinkering with automobiles, become a schoolteacher perhaps? Would you have ever become a Witch Hunter if they were still around?"

"Be silent…" Flint said.

"I made Edwards into the witch she is. Or was. I presume you murdered her, like you've done to others of our kind? In a way, I've made you the man you are today."

"Silence!" Flint roared.

Charles laughed. "It's too bad about Edwards. It would have been helpful if she'd been able to thin out the ranks of Fort Ingalls more than she did. But believe it or not, I'm happy that you survived, brother. I was just about to make my grand entrance upon the international scene before you so rudely interrupted."

"And what is that supposed to mean?" Flint asked.

Charles gave him a manic grin. "I'm going to go now Silas. You should go outside if you want the best view." He grew serious. "I meant what I said to you in our last correspondence. If you attempt to interfere, Lilian and I will have you begging for death before the end."

The column of light shimmered and vanished; the transmission ended. Flint stood still, fists balled at his side, shaking with rage. Fletcher approached him and reached up to put a hand on his shoulder. "Silas?" she asked.

There was a crack of thunder outside, one that caused the walls of Fort Marsing to shake. The four looked at each other, and started running for the exit. They emerged into the courtyard where hundreds of other Templars and Supernumeraries were gathering, looking up into the cloudless sky. Alfred Carruthers stepped outside of the cantina. Seeing General Abernathy, he joined the group and asked, "What the hell's going on out here John?"

"I don't know," Abernathy replied. "But I think…"

A collective gasp arose from the crowd, with dozens pointing up at the sky. Flint looked up and saw Charles. His translucent figure filled the entire sky where it met the horizon. Navarro's mouth hung open. Fletcher said nothing, transfixed by the unimaginable magical power for such a display.

"People of North America!" Charles's projection boomed. He was loud, but not deafening as the size of the projection might indicate. "My name is Charles Julian Flint and I stand before you today to issue our declaration of independence!"

*****

General Hickock looked up at the massive figure dominating the skyline. He could hear screeching tires outside the walls of Fort Ingalls as automobile drivers stopped in the middle of the road, car doors slamming as they stared in awe at the visage of Charles Flint.

"Simon Magus brought humanity the gift of magic nearly five hundred years go," Charles said. "He showed us the path to a better world, a world without hunger, without poverty, or disease, or famine! When the nations of the world rejected his Gospel, they initiated a conflagration that reshaped the face of the earth."

Lying asshole, Hickock thought. Everyone knew Magus started the Occult War by blasting Rome to cinders.

"Since that time, the nations of the world have persecuted my kind. You have hunted us without respite or mercy. You have burned us at the stake, put us on the rack, poisoned, shot, and hanged us for the crime of being born with a talent that you do not possess, for cultivating the power to shape our own destinies!"

*****

3000 miles to the east, Empress Agatha, Supreme Potentate of The Most Serene Empire of Columbia gazed skyward at the projection of this mysterious man in the grey tunic.

"I stand before you now to say no more! No more shall my brothers and sisters who practice the magical arts be the helpless victims of your pogroms! No more shall we allow ourselves to be subject to your prejudice, your hatred, your unthinking bigotry!"

"Your Majesty," Chancellor Arthur Goodspeed whispered.

"Shh," she replied.

*****

In the deserts of the former Nevada, in the place once known as Area 51, Doctor Nobusuke Kato looked up into the sky, surrounded by his clockwork guardsmen. They were humanoid in shape, crafted from metal, turning gears visible within their torsos, tiny lightbulbs serving as eyes.

"Today I speak to all men and women who possess the gift of magic. I say to you, no longer must we be at the mercy of our former friends, former families, former nations, who turned on us because they fear our great power."

"Fascinating," Kato said, stroking his chin.

*****

President Hugh Fitzroy of the United Mountain States stood on the balcony of the presidential mansion in Denver, within the territory formerly known as Colorado. The shabby looking man in the sky had been going on like this for twenty minutes and he was growing anxious.

"Today, we take our place among the nations of the world, no longer as homeless fugitives hiding in caves and basements. Today we proclaim our independence. Today, a new nation is born within the United Mountain States, in the wilderness of the former Montana. Today, I announce the birth of a new nation: the Empire of Medea!"

"What the fuck?!" Fitzroy snarled. The territory once known as Montana in the old United States was sparsely populated, but it was *his* land, goddamn it! *His* people were up there! "Hastings!" he screamed. His chief of staff, Wilbur Hastings, rushed to his side.

"Mr. President?" he said.

"Get General Daniels on the horn," Fitzroy said. "Tell him to get a division ready. Tell him to get the whole god-damn Army ready! I'll be damned if this pissant thinks he's going to just take over our fucking country!"

"Yes sir!"

*****

Flint glared at the projection of his younger brother in the sky. Fletcher had inched closer to him, transfixed by what she was hearing. Navarro, Abernathy, Carruthers, and all the rest of the Templars and Supernumeraries stared up at the sky.

"All that we ask is to be let alone," Charles said. "We seek not to wage war. We do not wish to conquer. All we wish is a home of our own. A nation of our own."

"He just wants to carve it out of the UMS is all," Navarro muttered.

"If you leave us in peace, then we shall leave you in peace," Charles said. "If you come seeking war, if you seek to deny us our right to exist as a people and a nation, then you will face the consequences. Behold: a forgotten wonder of the old world!"

*****

A bead of sweat trickled down the side of Charles's face. This was it. The moment of truth. He still wasn't sure about Rob; he wondered if the machine was as compliant as it professed to be. Despite claiming to be at Charles's command, the machine passive-aggressively resisted targeting North American soil. He still didn't trust it, which is what inspired him to create a workaround in case the computer had second thoughts. Charles reached out with his mind until he felt two keys in his telekinetic grasp. With an exertion of his will, he turned them simultaneously. He shifted the focus of his magical projection to the missile silo door opening on the surface. He nodded to Lilian. Together they gathered as much magical energy as they could muster, to open one of the largest portals either of them had ever conceived. The missile had liftoff. It rose from its silo and entered the blackness of the magical portal they conjured.

*****

The missile flew through the icy void, the blackness swallowing up the light cast by its exhaust. A gigantic eye opened and watched a bright speck soar past it. Twisting, writhing demonic forms looked up as this intruder from the mortal plane. They screamed in pain as the light from the missile burned their flesh, unaccustomed as it was to any kind of light in this realm of perpetual darkness. The owner of that great eye vowed that whoever had dared to torture his children would pay with their soul.

*****

The men and women of Fort Marsing watched the sky. The projection had shifted to a forested plain. Squinting, Flint thought he could see stone foundations in the undergrowth. The projection zoomed out, revealing black skies with swirling clouds that took the shape of skulls, demons, and other abominations. Some of the onlookers gasped. Charles was somehow projecting an image of an area within the Dead Lands far to the east. Sure enough, zombies shuffled into the projection and disappeared as they crossed the other edge of the projection's view. The projection zoomed out further, revealing the ruins of a city retaken by nature and swarming with undead.

"What's he doing?" Fletcher whispered.

A ring of fire appeared in the skies above the ruined city: a portal. There was a flash of light, and the onlookers screamed and looked away. Fletcher gasped, grabbed on to Flint's arm, and hid her face against his long coat. He took no notice of her and stared into the light, his fear rising, a tingle going up his spine. The light faded, and now he could see a fiery cloud in the shape of a mushroom rising from the earth.

*****

Count Rainier Margulis was on the balcony of the highest tower when he shielded his eyes from the flash of light. His cape flapped around him as a burning gust of hot wind enveloped his castle. When the light had dimmed, he looked out and saw a mushroom shaped cloud rising on the horizon. He felt white hot rage rise within him, and he roared in fury, his fangs glistening in the artificial light. This domain was his, every undead within it his subject. The vampire swore that the human wizard would suffer and die for daring to defile his land.

*****

The projection in the sky shifted to Charles again. Flint said nothing as he watched his brother change the geopolitical landscape of North America, if not the world.

"You cannot hope to contend with such power," Charles said. "But you will not have to if you leave us in peace. We welcome honest trade with men and women of goodwill. All we ask is to be welcomed into the family of nations. I say again however, those who seek to destroy us will themselves be destroyed. A new day has dawned in North America. All ye witches and wizards who seek a home of your own, a place where you no longer must hide, a place where you can be yourselves, I bid you come. Come, for all are welcome here. This is Emperor Charles I, and I bid you all good day."

The projection of Charles wavered and vanished. All was silent. Flint looked down and saw Fletcher still hanging on to his arm. She looked up at him and let go, backing away.

"Uh, sorry," she mumbled.

Flint looked up at the sky again and scowled. Conversation resumed, the Witch Hunters and Supernumeraries all talking at once, looking in turn outraged, worried, fearful. Navarro, Abernathy, Carruthers, and Fletcher all gathered around Flint who kept silent.

"Well," Abernathy said. "I think our vocations just got much more complicated."

"Guys?" Fletcher said, and all turned to her. "I could sense him while he was up there talking. I think he reached out to all of us... you know, all of us who can use magic."

"What do you mean?" Navarro asked.

"What I mean is, I think I know where he's hiding out."

Flint balled his fists. "There shall be a reckoning between Charles and I. And I swear to you, before Almighty God, and before all of the angels and saints, only one of us will walk away."

EPILOGUE

Mallory, Monica, and Madeline Proctor sat in an office. The walls, the floor, the doors, the desk, everything was a bright shade of white. Time had no meaning here, but they still felt like they were being kept waiting on purpose. A man stepped into the office from the door behind the desk. He was in a white suit with white tie, but his face was blurred. When the sisters had first met him, he'd said that it was to protect them. Indeed, the office in which they sat was not truly an office, another artifice made for their benefit. They'd seen many strange and terrible things in their lives, but even they found the effect unsettling. The man took a seat at the desk and folded his hands.

"You did well," he said.

"How long must we do this?" Mallory said.

"Silas and Ricardo cannot hope to stand against Charles now," Monica said.

"And Charles cannot hope to stand against what is to come," Madeline said.

"Having second thoughts?" the man with the blurred out face said. "If you want to give this up, you can always carry out your sentence elsewhere."

"No," they said unison.

"Good. It's vanishingly rare for anyone who comes through here to get such an opportunity, let alone three of you at the same time."

"What if Silas fails?" Mallory said.

"We've fulfilled our part," Monica said.

"It would not be fair to punish us if he does not succeed," Madeline said.

"You are not in a position to speak of what's fair and what's not."

They frowned but said nothing.

"If he dies through no fault of your own, then your time here will be taken off your sentence, and you will be remanded to..."

"That is not an acceptable offer," Mallory said.

"It is not an offer. It is what will be."

In unison, the sisters sighed and said, "Very well."

The man rose from his seat, held his hands behind his back. "If it's any consolation, we have the utmost confidence in Captain Flint. He just needs the occasional nudge in the right direction. That's your job."

"Yes sir," they replied.

"In the events to come, you may be permitted to intervene more directly. See that it's on the right side, and you'll get your second chance."

Kevin Beckman was born in Sacramento, California. He's worked numerous jobs throughout his life which have taken him from the Gold Country of California, to the Oregon Coast, and to the Treasure Valley of Idaho. The Weird Tales of Silas Flint is his first book. Kevin can be reached at kgbbooks47@gmail.com.

www.ingramcontent.com/pod-product-compliance
Lightning Source LLC
Chambersburg PA
CBHW060807120726
47909CB00006B/1817